An
ELEGANT
Solution

Books by Paul Robertson

According to Their Deeds

Dark in the City of Light

An Elegant Solution

The Heir

Road to Nowhere

An ELEGANT *Solution*

PAUL ROBERTSON

BETHANYHOUSE

a division of Baker Publishing Group

Minneapolis, Minnesota

Published by Bethany House Publishers
11400 Hampshire Avenue South
Bloomington, Minnesota 55438
www.bethanyhouse.com

Bethany House Publishers is a division of
Baker Publishing Group, Grand Rapids, Michigan

Printed in the United States of America

Library of Congress Cataloging-in-Publication Data

Robertson, Paul.

An elegant solution / Paul Robertson.

pages cm

Summary: "In a quiet 1720 Swiss university town, math prodigy Leonhard Euler is thrust into a dangerous web of jealousy, intrigue, and murder, and he will need both his genius and his faith to survive"—Provided by publisher.

ISBN 978-0-7642-0570-5 (pbk.)

1. Mathematicians—Fiction. 2. University towns—Fiction. 3. Jealousy—Fiction. 4. Murder—Fiction. 5. Basel (Switzerland)—History—28th century—Fiction. I. Title.

PS3618.O3173E44 2013

813'.6—dc23 2013026767

This is a work of fiction. Names, characters, incidents, and dialogue are products of the author's imagination and are not to be construed as real. Any resemblance to actual events or persons, living or dead, is entirely coincidental.

Cover design by Lookout Design, Inc.

Author represented by The Steve Laube Agency

13 14 15 16 17 18 19 7 6 5 4 3 2 1

It has been among my greatest Pleasures to teach the ancient Subjects of Mathematics and Natural Philosophy to a new Generation of Scholars, and in so doing, continue the unbroken Enterprise of giving to the Future the immense Treasure that has been received from the Past.

So, Martin, Bryan, Sarah, Owen, Justin, Chris, Elizabeth, Matt, Nate, Shana, Ben, Hannah, Zach, David, Katherine, Carina, Jesse and all the others; and Ellen, Greg and Jeff; and all my own teachers; and Lisa: this book is dedicated to you.

I believe that, if there was no other proof, that because of Mathematics, I would still believe in God. I'll let Leonhard tell you why.

. . . eternal, immortal, invisible . . .

1

The Ash Gate

Of dust is man made, and to dust man returns. So I sat, watching for the dust of men returning.

I was on a hillside above Basel. My Master Johann had me on an errand to watch for the return of his sons from Italy. It was late on a spring day; the sky was exactly blue, cut at the edge of the world by sharp white mountains. The fields were perfect green, engraved by the Rhine. And finally, around the side of my hill was an airy indistinctness. Dust.

That was my signal, but I waited to be sure: that it was dust raised by the coach from Bern. Once I saw the coach, drawn by four horses, I ran down the hill toward the city; I loved to run. I was first by minutes to the gate at the city Wall. The coach wouldn't stop there. It was bound for an inn and stable inside.

I waited there anyway. The gate was the Ash Gate and was only passed with burning. Ashes were the symbol of renunciation; the passage of any gate was renouncing one side to enter the other. Ashes to ashes and dust to dust, the coach came into view.

The road passed over the moat on a causeway and through an arch beneath a high, narrow stronghold. The coachman had his horses at a fast pace. I knew the man; he'd been driving the route for centuries. He waved to me. Then his coach, like an arrow on the straight road, shot over the bridge and pierced the gate. I followed through it.

⁂

Immediately inside, the Ash Street was hedged with houses, in unyielding and uninterrupted lines. Always in Basel the doors would be closed and the windows curtained. That afternoon the street was empty and the coach hardly slowed. I was just as quick and kept with it. The street soon ended in another moat and Wall and gate. This was the inner Wall and the old city, and a short distance inside was the coach's destination and destiny. I reached the tavern as it did.

There was a large public market square here, one of the few open spaces in Basel where its people would be found outside their homes. The inn waited on one side, and across from it stood the blunt face of an ancient church, the largest in Basel, even bulkier than the cathedral. The tavern was the Boot and Thorn; its opposite was called the Barefoot Church.

⁂

The coach halted. Knipper, the coachman, dropped nimbly from his box to the cobblestones as a lout from the inn was already scrambling upward toward the luggage. From the Beginning, Knipper had driven that coach. He brought Erasmus to Basel and Oecolampadius and the Reformation; he brought Holbein and Paracelsus and the Renaissance. Knipper took Charlemagne through to Rome, Caesar conquering the Gauls crossed the Alps with Knipper, and Hannibal crossed the other way with his elephants in the luggage rack; and Knipper's horses, I knew, were named by Adam.

"I know who you're for!" he bellowed to me. He was a boisterous and cantankerous man, quick to answer, agile, and a dead shot with his pistols. A coach driver had to be all those. "They're in there safe and sound!" His hair was short and all white, though it would shine like silver in the sun, and he had no beard.

"Their father's wanting them," I said.

"As I value my life, I won't keep *that* man waiting," Knipper answered in a suddenly low voice, and then back louder, "So let's get them out!" He gave the handle a twist and the door a wrench, and opened it onto a black cave. From that shadow the passengers emerged.

The first was a tiny old woman who descended the step with her bonnet bobbing like a pecking bird; the next was a wide man who swayed on his small feet like a swinging sack of wool. I let them both pass.

Then a shoe buckle, and shoe, and stockinged leg, were planted on the step, and a three-cornered hat and white wig bowed low beneath the low door, and I knew I had my man. The whole accordion unfolded.

"Daniel!" I said. I hadn't seen him in the two years since he'd fled. He was dressed beyond sere Basel's tastes in a wine silk coat and ruffled collar. Italy and aging had done their work on him.

"Leonhard!" he answered, and I knew from his smile that his cheerfulness was unchanged. He shook my hand vigorously. "Well met!" He'd hardly put himself on solid ground when another hat and another wig followed. But his brother Nicolaus was a very different fish.

Brothers contrast as bells do: near the same and discordant

the more alike they are. Daniel and Nicolaus both had their father's large, brooding eyes in their mother's long and narrow face. Daniel achieved this well, fixing the world with the stare of a philosophic hawk; in Nicolaus the effect was perplexing, something like a furious sheep. At the age of thirty, Nicolaus had the gentle rounding of affluence, more than the still sticklike Daniel and taller. Daniel was just twenty-five, seven years my senior.

In temperament, the common inheritance from their father was their eternal curiosity and from their mother, a piercing perception. But two other traits from their parents were odd crossed. Daniel thrived on conversation, having his mother's love of talking and his father's care at hearing. Nicolaus had the reverse: his father's dislike of speaking and his mother's disdain for listening. The parents had been compatible. The brothers, a torture to each other. They still had a strong fraternal fondness, though: a common enemy had made them allies.

"Blasted long ride," Nicolaus said.

But Daniel was shaking my hand eagerly. "How have you weathered these two years?"

"Very well," I answered.

"And the Brute?" he asked, and I knew his aversion to his father was also unchanged. Master Johann was the most opposite among mankind of an unthinking animal, and Daniel among mankind most knew that.

"As well as ever."

"I feared as much! But he won't live forever, will he? He'll have to die sometime."

"We all will," Nicolaus said. "But who'll carry the baggage?"

"That's the lot of the living, to carry what's left behind by the dead," Daniel said.

Yet Nicolaus, who was lean with words, would use one

sentence to say more than one thing. He'd meant the luggage from the coach. "The boy's hired to bring it to the house," I said, "and the driver, too." Knipper himself was already unloading the first bags, and Willi, the hulking tavern lout, was bringing out a cart. "We're to go on right away."

"We're to go right away? Then I'll stop right away. Join me in the Boot and Thorn for a cup, Leonhard."

"Not I."

The innkeeper had come out to watch us, and he and the coachman had whispered words. That man was earth and fire to Knipper's wind and fire, and I'd seen many sparks between them. Then Knipper took the first bags into his hands.

"Perhaps in the church for a kneel, then?" Daniel said to me. "That's what you'd rather."

"I'd rather get you to the Master's house."

"And be at it," Nicolaus growled.

The first street toward Master Johann's house from the Square was the Contention Alley, and it was well named for what it was leading us to. I had a quick sight of Knipper turning the corner ahead of us, while the brothers were looking back at Willi tugging heavy trunks onto the cart. Then we were off, and the march to Master Johann's house was short and sharp.

In the minute of walking, I asked Daniel about Italy. It was really to hear about himself, and my ears were quickly filled. Daniel had been my close friend in the first lonely years I was in Basel away from my own parents. He and his brothers had been brothers to me, and Daniel the most. I'd grieved when he left. I'd grieved for why he'd had to leave. I'd worried he would never return.

Nicolaus was silent, of course. He hadn't lived in Basel in the years I'd been here, but for the last two that Daniel had been away, Nicolaus had lived in Bern and been a frequent visitor to his father's house. When I did get him to talk, he was worth listening to, and had been kind to me in his own way.

ᘐᘑ

Two quick streets brought us to the second of Basel's open spaces. The bare Munster Square was much different from the market square of Bare Feet. The brick Munster, Basel's cathedral, was more daunting than the old white church, taller, and sharper. The plaza was less square than rectangular and too holy for the sellers and moneychangers. Its houses were larger and fewer, and the largest and fewest was my Master's. Daniel must have had painful memories to see it. But as we came into that square, and in sight of that house, I knew Nicolaus, and even Daniel, felt that delight, universal to men, of homecoming. I knew it well from the occasions I saw my own father's house.

I considered the house of Master Johann to have been at least as much as it should. It was close by the University, three dun stories high and seven dark blue shuttered windows across, with a high pitched roof snarled by the gabled windows of two more stories within it.

The doors of Basel were not entries but sentries. Even the grand entranceways of the town hall and the churches were kept closed to intimidate. My Master's door was imposing, cut wide but a bit short. He entered it as a perfect fit. His sons, who were taller, bowed to pass. I commonly entered through the back alley and kitchen door where I could hold my head high.

It was always blindingly dim inside that door. The hall was dark wood plank floor, darker paneled walls, and darkest beamed ceiling, which all sponged the air clean of light. We stood in the saturating murk, the sons and I, and their homecoming delight was de-lit. As for me, I found it comforting. There was other sight than by light.

"Blasted dark in here," Nicolaus said. Yet some ray of our presence had penetrated beyond the hall and above us there was motion. Starting in some far off corner but descending the stairs rapidly, the faint rattle became a jangle, then a clatter, and a glow came bobbing around the corner of the steps; and then appeared to us like a spinning clockwork the lady of the house, the Mistress Dorothea. Her black dress and white apron and bonnet blurred in the dusk and from her constant motion. Her candle, in hand at the length of one long arm, was an errant planet far from its sun. The other arm unfurled. "My babies!" she said. They braced themselves and were embraced. Nicolaus deftly took the flaming candle as it orbited by and the arms wrapped themselves around.

There would be no escape until she released them, and she did not. They were showered instead by thunderstorms of words in all the languages of motherhood. They bore the soaking willingly and inevitably. No one could be offended by Mistress Dorothea, though one would be overwhelmed. She finally reached "Come, come, come," in her flow and her arms still around the two captives, and with irresistible force, impelled them toward the sitting parlor adjacent to the front hall. I stayed behind rather than intrude on their intimate moment, and I was not alone.

The light was gone from the steps but a shadow remained: a boy, or young man, standing where the stairs turned their corner. He had wide open eyes and a mouth closed as if it would never speak, and straight fair hair, and he was still not quite grown to the height of his brothers. This was Little

Johann, the third brother of the three, fifteen years old and named for his father.

"They're both well," I said to him. "Daniel even looks Italian in his silk coat."

He did speak. "Did he tell you how long he'll stay?"

"I didn't ask."

"He hasn't told us yet. There're letters for him. From Paris and Russia."

"Russia?"

"I saw them on Poppa's desk."

"Is Master Johann coming down?"

"When everyone's had to wait long enough."

I still hesitated. There was no reason for me to remain, but I had a curiosity to watch the Master greet his sons. For all the time I spent in that house, I'd rarely sight him. I pictured him ponderously descending, pompous, portentous and proud. Just then, behind me, the front door opened.

To compare what I'd just envisioned with what I now beheld: If my Master was a fresh, firm pumpkin, this was its collapsed, dried-out rind, similar in appearance but with all the energy drained. We comprehended Cousin Gottlieb.

Gottlieb had grown up in Master Johann's household and was nearly another brother, even having travelled with the family to Holland when Master Johann had held a position there twenty years before. Now at thirty-eight he had his own household. He was actually named Nicolaus for his paternal grandfather, as are many of his relatives, but had forever been called Gottlieb to avoid confusion.

Gottlieb was an arid man. I bowed politely: I would not usually engage him in conversation for fear of desiccation. Mistress Dorothea drenched a listener and Cousin Gottlieb dried him out, yet I've been fond of him as I am of all the family. It's an odd taste, but well founded, for they're all worth knowing.

"They dared come back, did they?" Gottlieb in his sharp, rasping voice.

"They're in there," Little Johann answered.

"I'd like to know why. And Uncle Johann?"

"I hear him coming."

I had as well, and I knew it was time to be gone. There was more of the family in Basel, far more, but these were my Master's closest. Gottlieb was the prime cause for Daniel's departure two years before, though the composite cause was Master Johann himself. The tinder in that parlor was stacked high awaiting the fatherly torch. Rather than walk boldly out the front door, I took the corridor to the kitchen and the back.

In the kitchen was a remarkable sight. It was Knipper, the coach driver.

In normal times I'd nod and wave to Knipper and keep my distance. He was explosive. But here he looked dangerous as a wet kitten. "Oh, you," he said, seeing me, and mournfully. "You'll help me, won't you?"

"Sure I will," I said.

"It's that." I'd certainly seen *that* as quick as I'd seen him. *That* was a black trunk, big as a man, weighing down the stone floor. "That goose Willi brought it from the coach and it's not theirs. I should have stayed to be sure he only had the right ones. This one's not meant for here."

"Should we carry it back?" I asked.

"It's too heavy." Coach drivers were made of old oak roots; I'd never seen one wilted like this. He didn't look able to carry a feather. "But I can't leave it and have the Master or his sons see I've made fool with the luggage." The dilemma had poor Knipper pickled. "Run back to the inn and fetch that knave and send him here and his cart."

"I'll go," I said, and it was even better reason to miss Master Johann's grand entrance. I could ask the next morning if there'd been warm greetings or hot words. Knipper nearly thanked me to death, he was so relieved.

I left Knipper there, with Master Johann's family, and quick tracked back to the inn. The innkeeper pointed me to the stables without a word when I told him what Knipper was wanting Willi for. The tavern-boy was there, hammering some horseshoes into shape, and I rousted him. I asked if he wanted my help, but he didn't. He was ox strong. That was as well, as by that time the firewood in my Master's house was aflame, or already ashes. Ashes to ashes. I was ready to be home, glad to have seen Daniel and Nicolaus, and hungry for supper.

⁂

It was only a few steps from the Boot and Thorn, and the Barefoot Square, to my own home. I lived with my mother's mother. She had a tidy house very near Saint Leonhard's church, where she was revered. Her husband was pastor there until his death. My father was also, until he left for the village of Riehen soon after my birth. It was hoped that I would follow them to the pulpit, and I would never have regretted if I had. But for good or ill, I've had an even deeper love. So I was here in Grandmother's care. Riehen was only five miles from Basel, but too far to travel daily, so for these last five years this house has become my home. I have left my father's house to walk among men, placed by him in my grandmother's and Master Johann's care.

At supper, after I told Grandmother my day and all the doings at my Master's house, she gave me a warning. "A family should be for peace, Leonhard. There's trouble enough outside the door. Keep a watch on yourself for all you have to do with them."

"They've always been this way," I said.

"Every kettle only holds its own measure and no more. Someday they'll reach that and overflow."

And then late, as I laid my head on my pillow, thinking about the day and my Master's family, I could hear an overflowing. Not a kettle, but a river. Not the Rhine, but something else, something rising and disturbed. I heard it murmuring, and felt its pull, and was pulled by it to sleep.

That had been Thursday. The next morning, Friday, I was out early to fetch water. There were three fountains equally near and I chose the one in the Barefoot Square so I might see Knipper before he was off to Freiburg. The coach was in front of the inn and the passengers were impatient beside it and the horses restless in their harnesses, but the whole was Knipper-less. I was careful to fill the buckets only to their measure and not overflow them; and there was still no driver. I set the buckets on the paving stones, not too close to the horses' edgy hooves, and asked. I had an earful back. "Where is he? I'd like to know where is he! I'm told to be up at dawn and the driver's still sleeping!"

I was sure he'd soon be by. Knipper kept a schedule as ancient and immutable as the planets: Thursday from Bern to Basel, Friday Basel to Freiburg, and Saturday Freiburg to Strasbourg. Monday, Tuesday, and Wednesday he turned his horses back. Inns in the four cities owned his coach and paid him to drive it and deliver his passengers to their front doors. He linked Basel to the French, German, and Swiss lands that surround it. Basel was properly a part of Switzerland, but to its own people it has been a land separate to itself.

The keeper of the Boot and Thorn was Old Gustavus, and he would be closest of anybody to knowing anything of Knipper. He was standing at the door smoldering. He came out to look close at the coach to see, I thought, that it really had no Knipper. Of course I was as curious as all the rest, but it was time for me to be on to more chores and I turned away from the inn. Right at my elbow I found Daniel.

"What's the rumpus?" he said.

"Knipper's been lost."

"Knipper? Oh, the driver? Then where is he?"

"Lost means not knowing where he is."

"Well, it's you I want anyway, and you're found."

"I'll be to your kitchen in an hour," I said.

Daniel had put his hand on my shoulder in pity. "You still labor for him, Leonhard? It's brutes that labor, and not you for the Brute."

"But I do and I'm glad to. What are you wanting with me? And did you have peaceable words with him last night?"

"Words, not peace. Supper was tolerable though. But you were lost before I could talk to you, and I want your help with an idea I've been hatching."

"If it's your idea, then it's cracked."

"There'll be cracking." Daniel's other hand took hold of my other shoulder, and we were face to face between his arms. "It's why I came back to Basel," he said, and there was a hard passion behind his soft smile. "It's to do with Uncle Jacob."

Uncle Jacob: that was a scorpion's egg he was hatching. I'd heard very little about my Master's oldest brother, and he was very firmly not discussed in my Master's house. "What about him?"

"He's dead."

I knew that. "I've seen his epitaph."

"But why is he dead?"

I had thought much about mortality and so answered, "For his sins." I didn't mean it uniquely to old Jacob, as he died before I was born and I never met him, but I had always been firm on this point. And Daniel would benefit from a reminder. "And for a fever, too, most likely, and with every hope for resurrection. Your father is the youngest of ten children, and he's nearly sixty. You should expect to have dead uncles. And you know Master Johann is touchy on Jacob."

"Because he has reason to be, and that's why I'm back in Basel, Leonhard. I'm going to look into Uncle Jacob, and the more Brutus doesn't like it, the more I will."

"I won't be part of it."

"Sure you will. I need your help."

"I won't have time this morning."

"Tonight?"

"Tomorrow night," I said. "After my lesson."

"That'll do. If you can still talk or think after that bruising you go through." He nodded toward the Boot. "I'll be at the inn tomorrow night." And today's night, I was sure, and many another. I took my leave and my buckets.

⁂

Away from the Barefoot Square, I came into the Wages Street. Paving stones and packed soils carried Basel's traffic, its wheels and shoes; houses, churches, and structures constrained it. I would often stand at a corner or in a doorway and watch the motion. I would see the good citizens and their horses and carts. I watched University scholars with books under their arms. I saw grand merchants and councilors, the Day Watch and the Night Watch. And I would also see Reformers in vast robes contending for their faith. In the open squares I saw Romans with swords and barbarians with pikes, and marching through the gates I saw knights in chain mail with Crusader crosses on their shoulders. In narrow alleys I saw long corteges, cart after cart on misty mornings, filled by the plague's harvest. In the church cloisters I saw monks chanting and druids moaning, and Irish friars storytelling, returning the faith of the Roman city to the city of Goths and Vandals. And in archways I would see angels, and in stairways, saints, and in shadows, shadows. It had always been that I would see invisible things.

Then I was to the Hay Street and my grandmother's house. Even on the most clouded days the sun always shone on her door. There had always been an anchor that held her firm, and none of the ages in the street outside would ever shake her.

So I brought in my water and took in as much of her calm as I could hold, and readied myself for the rest of the day.

Next in the mornings, Monday through Friday, after my chores at home I would present myself at Master Johann's back door. Mistress Dorothea would scoop me into the kitchen. The Mistress was the wife of a very great man besides being the sister of the present Chief Magistrate and the daughter of a previous, but she was no idlewoman; no one in Basel, no matter how great, didn't work. A wealthy family would hire labor, though, and this Mistress did. She had a girl, a seamstress's daughter, who helped her with washing and cooking. I did the heavy work. I would stoke the fire and empty the grate and chop wood and fetch water, and most days there would be a floorboard to hammer back or a pot to undent; I've been apprentice carpenter and tinker and smith and cooper. It was mostly the same that I did for my grandmother, but for a grander house and household. I would never see Master Johann these mornings. I would see the others of the family, and it was in years past that in these hours I met the sons and made my friendship with Daniel.

The seamstress's daughter was fourteen years old, a good laundress and passable cook, but she was flawed: she chattered continually. Worse, she and the Mistress together were deafening. The clatter and slap of dishes and ironing and kneading and all else would be bearable; the gossip and pure inanity that congested the air were not, but I bore them anyway. The ridicule I endured from my friends was as hard: working with women made me a laughingstock with them.

And I wasn't paid a copper for any of it! Every morning but Saturday and Sunday I did this. I stopped my ears against Babel, I submitted to the common labor lot of man, passed from Adam to Noah to Greece to Rome to my Mistress's kitchen, and I toiled. Yet, yet, like Jacob's for Rachel, my labor seemed fleeting, for my wages were worth so much more than anything I could have been paid in money. Though Daniel scoffed, he knew well what great value I received for my chopping.

That Friday morning I saw no more of Daniel or any of Nicolaus. Little Johann was waiting alone for me in the kitchen, kneading a ball of dough. I didn't think he talked to anyone else. He'd never liked work, though he did his share. Breadmaking was an odd hobby for him. "You should have seen us last night," he said.

"I shouldn't have. Who was glad for the homecoming? I know the Mistress was."

"Poppa said he was, even despite Daniel's ungrateful pernicious heart. Daniel said he was glad, too, to see every familiar stone in the city and even the one where Poppa's heart should be, and Nicolaus told the two they weren't father and son but plain squabbler children, and Gottlieb said he would like very much to know why Daniel had come back at all."

"Did Daniel say why he had?"

"He said it was because he'd missed Gottlieb so dearly. Then I went to my room."

"Does it vex the Mistress?"

"She frets and worries, and she doesn't believe they mean what they say."

"Do they, Johann?" I asked. In truth, he'd know better than they did.

"Not all."

"And you?"

He was pounding and shoving his dough. "I'm angry that they're all angry. I want Daniel to go back to Italy."

"He said supper was tolerable."

"No one talked but Mama. If the rest just stay quiet I don't mind them." I felt badly for him and for his ball of flour. Then the Mistress and her maid joined us and no other talk was possible. When I left her kitchen, the streets were silent as midnight in comparison.

My labor ended for the morning, it was time for solemn seriousness. I ran back home. For me, the path between my grandmother's house and my Master's was well worn. I ate my quick lunch of bread and cheese and went to my room for my stark transformation.

I removed myself from the rough brown garments I preferred and pulled on white shirt and black breeches, then white stockings and black waistcoat, then black and buckle shoes and black justacorps coat.

I had an extra head in my room. A white wood ball on a short stand, it considered life from the top of my dresser. It did this without sight or hearing, which surely improved its ruminations. It wore a white wig and black hat. Each day would I borrow these, transferring them between heads, from the one on my dresser to the one on my shoulders. If any of that wooden block's thoughts transferred also, I was the better for them. The hat wasn't tricorne, which was for men of gravity, but had a wide brim turned up on each side.

All in black and white I was a changed man. I stepped more

steadily. I didn't run, or not much. I seemed thoughtful. But despite my best effort, in essence, I would remain myself. Yet observers noticed only appearance, not essence, and so for the next few hours I appeared a peer to my peers.

Later in the afternoon I made my de-conversion. I moved my wig from one block of wood back to the other and hung and folded my blacks and whites. A world where everything was only one or the other would be preferable in many ways, but we lived in a world of browns.

Finally at dinner I told my grandmother that I would be at the tavern Saturday evening. "It's Daniel. He wants my help."

"Help to make trouble?"

"Yes," I said. "But I don't know what, so I'll go to find out."

"A wise man runs from strife. I have a worry, Leonhard, of what will happen with all that family back in the city."

"Blessed are the peacemakers," I said. "I have a hope, Grandmother, for what could happen."

I'd refused Daniel for that Friday evening because I had work to do, work that had to be finished before Saturday afternoon. I planted myself in my room, rooted to my chair, and soon sprouted leaves all over my desk: large leaves of white paper, which the birds of the field roosted in. One particular bird, a goose feather in my hand, was making its nest of inky black scribbles.

Saturdays for me began very early. I'd be out for water and breakfasted by sunrise. I had kept this schedule even in the summer when the sun was also an early riser. I'd quickly finish all my other chores. Grandmother was as strict a taskmistress for me as she was for herself, and only when she was satisfied might I go on to the list of tasks from my other masters that must not be incomplete come Monday. Some weeks I was thorough enough with my time that the list was empty; but if not, I'd fly through it. If I'd been industrious and swift, it was still well before noon. I wouldn't take time for lunch, and a full stomach would muddle me anyway. Instead, I'd settle at my desk and clear my brain to prepare. Saturday was my Sabbath of hardest labor, my rest from idle life.

First, and crucial, I would take down a book.

Leibniz and Newton waited at opposite ends of my shelf, and Descartes in the center, and Fermat and Pascal, MacLaurin and Taylor, de Moivre and L'Hopital, Hooke and Boyle, and many others between. I would have planned this choice through the week and reached the decision in the last waking minutes of the Friday night before, in the dark of my bed.

Then, with that book on my desk, I would take out my folio of notes and thoughts from years of Saturdays past. I would set paper and ink and quill beside them all. And finally I would read.

I would pour myself into it and I would pour it in to me. I'd think on every word and every equation, of what it means, and what it means more, and what it finally means, and what it means past that, and why, and why, and why. I only read with a pen in my hand. I'd write to myself but I could never write enough. And always I would push on.

If there had been a shadow on all this, that this was devotion stolen from my devotion to God, it was always beyond me to stop. What else could I do? The hours passed and the book's pages turned slowly while my own piles of paper grew. I lost my senses, and the world I sensed with them. I lived in an invisible world of logic and theorem more evident to me than ink and paper, more rigid and immutable than the desk and hard chair I'd been sitting on, purer than air, more part of me than my own hands, and unmatched in perfection among all other created things.

But then my cock would crow.

I've taught myself to hear the clock in Saint Leonhard toll three. When it did, I'd blink and firmly close my book: If I didn't immediately I might not until the bell tolls that three again, which would be far into Sunday morning! But I was never dismayed, because even this pure time would have been only a preamble.

Then I'd dress myself in my student finery, buckles to wig, and on this day when no other student in Basel cared much how they look, I cared most. Grandmother would inspect and correct me, and I'd tuck my folio under my arm and set out. I have done this every Saturday for five years, and always with trepidation and anticipation together.

This Saturday, at the very instant of three thirty, I pulled the bell on the grand doorway in the Munster Square. It was opened by silent Mistress Dorothea, who saw me all other times in peasant brown at her back door with so many words. Now I was to receive the wages I'd earned by my labors of the week. She solemnly ushered me into the dark hall and escorted me up the stairs to a hallway that was smaller but the same dark, and knocked on a door, so firmly closed that it seemed a wall of stone.

I still remembered the first time, when I was thirteen and trembling in my shoes, that she knocked and how nearly I fled at the stony voice that in answer commanded, "Come in." Now it thrilled me, though I still took stock one last time whether I was completely ready. The Mistress opened the door.

The room was as dark as the whole house, but a single bright candle burned on the table, which with its two chairs was the only furniture. In one chair was Master Johann, and the other chair was empty. It was for me. For two hours I would sit alone under his instruction, and he was the greatest Mathematician in the world.

༄

My Master was a man of substance, not to be trifled with, celebrated across the continent, distinguished in every manner, Basel's first citizen, impressive and remarkable. His eyes, reflected in his sons, were heavy and brooding and pierced like spears. He did not speak often and his mouth and jaw were hard in his wide face. He wore an old wig in our meetings and his forehead was very high. He was short and broad compared to others, especially his sons. His hands were somewhat thick with short fingers yet he had a beautiful script, the equal of any scribe. This physical skill was surprising for a man whose abilities and efforts were mostly centered inside his head. And in his opinion, the whole world was centered about his head. He has lacked any vestige of modesty, sympathy, generosity, leniency or, sadly, paternity.

Master Johann was the Professor of Mathematics at the University in Basel. He'd had his Chair for twenty years. He was the second man to hold that Chair. Before him was the Chair's founder, his brother Jacob.

༄

During the two hours that he taught me, I was like Little Johann's ball of dough: pounded and stretched and rolled, and finally brought out thoroughly baked, in need of cooling. My head was full and my stomach empty and I then would stumble, top-heavy, home. I had so much to think about. The papers in my folio, to be read slowly and thoroughly, would give me hours more of thought. They were like a river to be poured down a rabbit hole.

I'd be ravenous when I arrived home, and I wouldn't even change out of my black and white. My strict grandmother allowed herself one weekly moment of sympathy: she'd have a table full for me and I'd wolf it and tell her what I'd learned. For my sake she had made herself interested in Mathematics. My final challenge of the very challenging day was to distill two dense gold hours with Master Johann into twenty simple crystal minutes with Grandmother. If I could do that, then I had mastered my lesson.

2

The Boot and Thorn

In my first year in Basel, I was given a book. I was only thirteen, still apprehensive of my new life, an uprooted sapling fighting to grow new roots in hard soil. Master Johann was a rocky cliff that I grasped, and my roothold in his house was wholly tenuous. I was ignored or mocked in my classes. Then, what a pleasure it was to be befriended! For Daniel, who was a twenty-year-old man of note, took note of me; first with cordial greetings, next with amicable conversations, and then with the full shine of his winsome character. Finally, on a morning three months after my arrival in Basel, he'd sought me out as I was sweeping his mother's kitchen and tossed a leather volume into my hands.

"You say you like books?" he said. "This one's new, just from the printer. See if the ink's dry yet!"

I didn't know it then, but I'd been given a challenge and not just a book; it was only later that I learned that particular gleam in Daniel's eye. On that morning I only saw the pages of Latin and symbols and equations, and my heart leaped.

"Thank you!" The ink was plenty dry and I was caught like a fish. A page describing the Mathematics of Likelihood was open before me, and I read the lines and paragraphs without hope of being able to close it. The words were astonishing.

"Hold, hold!" Daniel had laughed. "That's terrible stuff, there. You'll need help to understand it."

"I'll take any help," I said, and meant it, but it seemed plain to me. The Latin was lucid and straight, though wordy, and in just that one page I knew the thesis. "Who wrote it?"

"It was Cousin Gottlieb who made the manuscript and bundled it off to the printer. But he's only the scribe. The author's someone else. Have you heard of Uncle Jacob?"

I pulled away from the text and found the title page. The title was *Ars Conjectandi*, the Art of Conjecturing. The author was Professor of Basel, member of the Societies of Paris and Berlin, and of my Master Johann's family but not my Master. It was Jacob. And below the title was the explanation, *Opus Posthumum*, published after his death.

"I don't know Jacob."

"Gottlieb took his notes and made a book of them, and that was ten times the labor of a stonecutter carving Cupid from a boulder."

"But who was he? Tell me about Jacob!"

"Father's brother, father's teacher, father's Master. But don't tell me you can read it!"

"I can," I'd said eagerly. "Oh, thank you, Master Daniel! Is it mine?"

"It's yours," he said. "And if you can read it so well, then I'll have you explain it to me!"

Even making his joke, he was still treating me as an equal.

I was in awe of him then! This was a young man who'd spent a year in Heidelberg and had returned to Basel to finish his doctorate in medicine, and was the son of my revered Master Johann. And I hoped to use his good favor to gain an extra step in my climb of Master Johann's steep ladder.

That next Saturday, five years ago, I approached my Master's house with confidence and Uncle Jacob's book both tucked under my arm. I was taken upstairs and through the door. I still felt very much on trial, having to be perfect in my preparation and understanding each week just to earn my next week's session. So I sat in my chair and set my papers on the table, and then with pride and desperate hope, I placed my offering, the *Ars Conjectandi*, on the table for him to notice. My young heart skipped as I waited for my Master's hard face and the severe gaze to soften.

He took one glance. He recognized the title. Then he transfixed me with the most hostile stare I'd ever experienced. I hadn't known that such animosity existed, and I was its target! He held me on his sword point for an eternity. Then he proceeded with my lesson, never mentioning the book.

As soon as I could, I slipped the volume into my lap, out of his sight. He ignored the motion. I endured the two hours in agony. I walked home through streets of fire. I ate no dinner but only ran to my room and sobbed my heart out, and vowed never to pester Master Johann with my miserable existence again.

I didn't keep that vow. I did return, and repaired over months the damage done in that one moment. I believed Daniel should have warned me, but he may not have thought to, or that I would be bold to show off my possession. And since then, I have wondered what became of that boulder of notes from which Gottlieb carved his *Conjectandi* Cupid. I never have asked Master Johann, of course. Besides stirring his anger at their mention, I was never sure he knew himself where they were.

Years later, when he was in Italy, Daniel sent me a copy of his own book, *Exercitationes*, Mathematical Exercises. His note with it said, "More leather for your excellent shelf, Leonhard, and more bait to anger the Bear, if you didn't learn your lesson before." But I had learned my lesson, and Master Johann never saw that in my hand; and I'd had my first introduction to Uncle Jacob; and most important of all, both the meticulous *Conjectandi* and the elegant *Exercitationes* were gems.

So I went forth Saturday night to meet with Daniel, setting my foot on the dark evening streets of Basel. As always the windows were shuttered. Just pins of light pricked out. There was little to fear with the Night Watch always close. I walked with one of them, he swinging his lantern and his jaw, and I listening for those moments to tales and tall tales of battle and adventure. In the Barefoot Square, the windows of the church were unshuttered and bright. The inn was lit with darker light. Through its weary door I left the overworld.

Enter the Boot and Thorn! *Steifel und Stachel*, Tavern primeval, vast beamed of ancient trees, smoked by the unquenchable flame, dark unyielding to light. Inside the door was a passage with no seen end, twisting into distance. Doors and stairs lived in it, and dragons. On its walls were pictures painted before there was light or color, and rails and moulds carved by gnomes. The air was soot and hay and mead. A gray cat with white eyes was named Charon and was Cerberus. I paid for my passage with a bow and crossed the hallway Styx.

On the right was a fissure, and through it the Common Room. A gaping, howling hearth lit the room, and oil lamps burned with more smoke than flame. Driven up through each table was an iron spike with a candle fixed on it. These were the best illumination in the room. As the evening would pass and each candle breathed its last, and the lamp glasses would blacken and strangle their glow, only the conflagration in the ruddy fireplace would enlighten.

The pillars that held the ceiling were not cut by human hands. They, and the ceiling they supported, were really a primordial forest of trunks and branches that grew themselves into that room with its soil floor. Shelves, eye-high, belt-high, high as good thoughts and high as foul plots ran the circuit of the walls. Tankards packed them. They were wood and clay, little gargoyles who watched in benign grotesquerie over the transacted business.

The tables were immovably heavy. They might have been filled or near empty and it would have appeared the same. The presence of men in the room was heard and sensed, not seen, and to enter the room was to be made part of it, to be made subterranean, to be lit by fire and breathe earthen air.

As I stood in the entrance, my vision was blunt but my ears were sharp, and I quickly knew where Daniel was. He would have preceded me, likely by hours. Only when I came close did I see that his brother Nicolaus was there, also.

A Master from Oxford, a Chair of Mathematics on a visit once to Master Johann, told me that in England there were coffee rooms for gentlemen in taverns, separate from the commons. Here was no division. Black and white mingled with brown. I wouldn't know which I was meant for if I had to choose. The Room, like temptation, was common to all men. I hadn't been noticed and I paused while Daniel spoke.

"There's no word," he was saying to his brother. "Not a breath of a whisper. I was sure there'd be a letter waiting." He had a cup of dice in his hand and tossed them to the table.

"Who else could have won the prize? There's not a one who could have beat me."

Nicolaus answered him, "It's a hundred who could."

"I'll go to Paris myself and see. I'll have them show me a better piece than what I sent them. I know I won the competition."

"Then where's the letter?"

"I'll go to Paris and get it." I could see his peeved frustration in the dark as well as I could hear it. He pulled the dice back into his cup. His words interested me, but the dice in his hand did more. The subject of Master Jacob's *Ars Conjectandi* was Likelihood or Chance, what had more recently been named Probability. The *Conjectandi* presented the rolling of dice as a type of equation, but not one that gave a result. Instead the Mathematics gave possibilities of results. It was an odd prophecy, to say with certainty what might happen, but not what would happen. I had wondered at the role of Providence in guiding affairs: Did God know how the die would land?

"Daniel," I said.

"Leonhard!" There was no chance to that. His greeting was certain and exactly as I'd known it would be. He pushed a bench toward me. "Still breathing? Not smothered by your hours in the Holy of Holies?"

"I'm breathing. It's the air in here that would smother a man."

"Then breathe it deep and listen to me." Now, Daniel had his winning smile and friendly ways. All the ire he'd had a moment before was gone. "I've come back to Basel with a goal." The hearth glare fell full on him. It made his grin fiery. "You have a part in it."

"Tell me, then. I want to know what it is that I want nothing to do with," I said.

"Your part's easy enough. It's about Uncle Jacob."

"That's poking bears, Daniel."

"That's reason enough itself."

"I won't help you, not for that. You know it's a rule that he isn't discussed in the Master's house."

"I just want to know how Jacob died, that's all. There's nothing wrong with that, is there?"

"If you want to know, just ask."

"I am asking."

"Ask someone who knows!" I said. "Your mother."

"She'd tell Brutus that I asked."

"Ask your cousins. You have plenty."

"It'll all get back." He leaned into my shadow. "There are nets laid and webs spun, and I don't want a whisper of anything to reach those ears."

The answer to this seemed evident. "Ask your Uncle Faulkner." This man was the Chief Magistrate of Basel, and Mistress Dorothea's brother. "He's part of no one's net."

"But I can't hold him to confidence, either. No, you're the only one I can ask."

"And I'm the only one who can't answer. I don't know how your uncle Jacob died."

"But you can find the answer. I know you can, Leonhard." He'd always been this way. Daniel had made friends in every street in Basel, as he pried open the closed doors and searched their shadows. Whoever knew him was fond of him, and whoever knew him well distrusted him, as well.

"There's something amiss," I said.

"There is," he said, "and I want to know what it is."

"Amiss with you. It's your own uncle, and your own family, and I'm the one you're sending into a lion's den."

"I can't let the lion know what I want. It has to be you." He laughed. "You've nothing to fear, old friend! Just throw a few little words, an innocent question. Then listen very close."

Nicolaus had been silent the whole time, and he'd been listening very close. "And are you a part with this?" I asked him.

"I'm no part."

"He's part and parcel," Daniel said. "It's his plan anyway."

"It isn't," Nicolaus said.

"It is, all of it. Nicolaus is the cunning one, you know. I said *Uncle Jacob*? and Nicolaus said *Leonhard!* and I said *Oh, that's our man!* " And Nicolaus said nothing.

"I know Jacob's epitaph because I've seen it, and I've heard a few other bits. He was Chair of Mathematics here and he died twenty years ago. And you know all that."

"I know it," Daniel said.

"And I know his Mathematics," I said, "because of his book that you gave to me."

"You only know what dearest cousin Gottlieb put in the book. That's all any of us know."

"Except Gottlieb himself," Nicolaus said.

"There must be more," I said.

But that was not Daniel's interest of the moment. "There's only one thing I want to know," he said, "and that's how Jacob died."

"That's all?"

"Nothing more. Was it in his bed, or in the river, or in between?"

In Basel, to die in the river was an evil thing. There was a history to it, of burning and drowning, and Daniel had made a poor joke. "And why do you want to know? Why did you come back to Basel?" I asked him.

"You answer my question, Leonhard," he said, and he shook his cup. That rattle was the only sound in that room that cut through all the other sound. He tossed the dice and put his hand over the numbers, hiding them. "And I'll answer yours."

Daniel had always been a mule. The more he was pulled on, the less he'd move. I'd only get more perplexity from him and I'd had enough. Besides, as we had talked there in that Underworld, its Lord arrived.

This was Old Gustavus. He was an innkeeper and a blacksmith and looked both with heavy arms from pounding and a heavy brow from scowling and a black beard like a burned forest. He was old but not aged; he'd hardened like mortar. He came in with a barrel on his shoulder and set it at the counter and then nearly extinguished the lamps with his stare. He fixed on Daniel and drew heavily near.

"Good evening, Master," he said. "An honor for you to visit here." He spoke cavernously, when he spoke. Most often a nod of his head and glint of his eye would get done what he wanted. "Is there anything you require?"

"A Chair at the University," Daniel answered. He had no fear of the man. He'd bought him over many times with the money he'd spent in that room. "Mathematics would do well, though I'd take nearly any of them." He laughed and didn't wait for any answer. "But I'd settle for less. What do you have in the stable tonight?"

"Horses, Master."

"I thought you would. I might want one for the month."

"There'd be one."

"Send Willi around with it. I'll look it in the mouth."

Gustavus' dark darkened. "Willi's gone with the coach to Freiburg, Master. I'll send Fritz."

"With the coach?" Now Daniel was curious. "What would Knipper want with him on the coach?"

"Willi drove it, Master. There was no Knipper."

"He never came?" I asked. I was not afraid of Gustavus, either; not much.

"No." No *Master* for me. I was in brown.

"Where'd he get to?" Nicolaus asked, and it was odd he'd spent the words.

"No place I know" was the answer. "I'll send Fritz around with the horse, Master."

"No need," Daniel said. "I'm sure it's fine. I'll want it Monday. About noon."

"Where are you riding?" I asked. Then, as a joke, "Russia?"

"Russia?" Daniel was authentically amused. "Not in an afternoon. It would be a fast horse for that."

"Paris, then?" I asked, still with my joke, and that brought less amusement.

"Not Paris, either." He turned. "That's all," he said to Gustavus, and that was all. Daniel was ready to leave, to return to the living streets, so I was pleased to return with him. We left the eternal dark for the simple black of earthly night, and I turned our conversation toward Italy. This was my interest. I'd always been so curious about the peninsula and all the world beyond Basel and I even coaxed a few words from Nicolaus on it. He knew the land well; before he took the Chair of Law in Bern, he'd been Chair of Mathematics in Padua, the same Chair Daniel now had. Even Gottlieb had held the Galileo Chair of Astronomy there years before. I wanted to go myself to Venice and Rome and Padua. Someday I'd Knipper south. We talked awhile before they left toward their home and beds, and I watched them leave. But I stayed in the Barefoot Square.

❧

It has always been the poor whose feet were bare. Their Square was named for the church on it, and their church was plain and very large and worth more to them than shoes. It was built in old times by barefoot friars who knew poverty. I went in. It was lit by a few candles and they brightened more than all the fires in the Boot and Thorn.

The ceiling was higher inside than the roof outside, so far above the stones of the floor that the air inside the church was pulled thin by it. It was plain timber, not like the decorated toppings that crown wealthier churches. Two central walls hung from the ceiling a short distance, then split into peaked arches. Long pillars gripped the arches, held up by their tight hold. The pillars reached down to the stone floor and pulled upward on it, so the whole church was supported and lifted by its highest steeple. The floor grasped the crypt and the crypt was bedded in the rock and soil of the earth, which meant that Basel, and the whole planet, was held up by the church and the church by the heavens. If the chains to heaven were cut, the planet would plummet. The heavens would also be freed from the earth then, and would rebound away like a tree branch pulled down and released. But the chains were too, too strong. They would never break. I sometimes feared, though, that the church might break loose from its foundation and be wrenched into the sky. If it did, I hoped to be in it.

It was important of Basel that it was caught like this, held taut between earth and heaven like a knot between ropes. It was part of each but was not either. One day the city might be pulled fully to one side, and what a sundering that would be.

That night it did not. I sat some minutes on the back bench in a corner, a place where I listened and watched. That night in the Barefoot Church I saw winged Michael in holy flame, and slue-foot Lucifer in brimstone, the two of them in dispute, and between them a slab of cold stone. I knew it must be the body of Moses they were contending over, but I couldn't see clearly.

Finally I went back out to the Square. The church was many centuries old, and built on centuries more of foundations. But the Boot and Thorn was very old, also. These two have faced each other across the Square, contending over it. So far neither had prevailed.

⁂

Sunday morning was fine and clear as glass. I rose early; I couldn't help it. I walked in thought through Sabbath empty streets to the Munster square. Master Johann's house was blank and not my destination. I was going to the Cathedral itself. Erasmus was buried in the left aisle and Oecolampadius in the center, but I wanted a different grave and passed by to the cloisters.

I knew just where to go. The shaded red stone columns divided the dim walk from the bright grass square. On the white plaster walls, carved stone epitaphs divided the shaded lives of remembered men from those bright living who remember. Soon I stood at a black oval surrounded by a garland wreath of marble, and capped by a globe and two shields.

One shield was of three seven-leaved branches, which was the symbol for Master Johann's family. The other shield was a lion. The engraving was in Latin. At the top of the oval it named Uncle Jacob. It said of him that he was *Mathematicus Incomparabilis*. It listed that he was Professor of Mathematics at Basel's University for eighteen years; member of the royal academy of Paris; and had held many other honors. The Roman ranks of M's, C's, L's, X's, V's, and I's marched through the years of his life, from his *Natus,* through his *Augusti Aetatis*, to his *Extinctus* twenty years ago.

Beneath the large oval was a smaller medallion, a circle. In the circle was an Archimedean spiral of five revolutions. Around it was the inscription *Resurgo Eadem Mutata*, I Arise Again the Same Though Changed. It was a thoughtful statement, and I thought on it, as I had before. It had always bothered me that the spiral it circles, the Archimedean *spira mundanus*, did not match the thought. It was an obscure point, but Mathematicians held strong opinions on spirals and their meanings.

Finally I left the cloister, not back to the Square, but to the back of the Munster, to the river. This was where I would finish my walk through memories and meanings of lives, lives current, lives recent, and lives before.

In the age before Basel, if that age ever was, there was still the Rhine. The bank would have been a high grassy hill steep down to the water. In ancient, ancient times, one Basel was built of rough stone that Roman hands never put there. I'd seen these stones. They were found beneath and pulled from the crypt of the Munster when it was repaired many years ago.

Two thousand years ago the Romans built on the hillside and named their city Basileus, which meant Kingship. A thousand years ago, the Germans ended Rome and took her cities. The people who lived inside the walls today were those German conquerors of Roman conquerors. Of what I knew of conquest, the blood of the ancients and the Romans both still flowed in Basel's veins.

Those stones of that first Basel were its only epitaph, but not the only memory of it. Basel's people walked in their streets on the dust of earlier cities, and all the cities were only different ages of the one Basel, and the city had always been within its own walls and not part of the world around.

Now the Munster stood on the hill, and a paved court behind the cathedral was high above the water. The old bank was buried beneath its sheer walls.

I stood and looked out at the water. The river was high. It hadn't rained more than other Aprils but the Rhine drained many lands; we saw it pass, but knew not whence it came or where it was going. Somewhere above Basel there'd been rain. The city had high walls and very little from outside ever passed them, but the river always had. I supposed that Uncle Jacob had died closer to his bed than the river.

⁂

Later, dressed proper, I took my grandmother's hand and promenaded her solemnly to the Saint Leonhard's Church. Every Sunday I'd sit and stand with her for the hymns and readings, and hear the sermon, which was always of great interest to me. I was reminded of watching my own father in his pulpit. A few times each year I would take my grandmother to Riehen, for her to visit my mother, her daughter, and we would sit under my father's Sunday teaching. But those times were rare.

⁂

It had only been one day before that I'd been immersed in the ocean of Mathematics; now I floated in the air of Theology.

Both were unseen and undefinable. What were the rules of Mathematics? What were those of God? They both existed with or without our knowing, they were universal truths, and our lives were ruled by them absolutely. Could I say that two fish are three? Could I steal a fish and say it was right? Was it two different laws that I would be violating, or were they both one? All the princes and armies in Europe couldn't change a point of either.

And both laws divided between right and wrong. Stealing was wrong, and a Mathematic error was wrong. The wages of sin were death, but the wages of incorrectly adding were less severe. But still, for each there was right and wrong, yes and no, good and . . . not good. And just as Mathematics was sure and a man could build a house firmly on it calculations, so he could also build his life's house even more firmly on God's law.

And I had a feeling now, something that had been with me since I last passed the Ash Gate, that the contention between right and wrong was nearer to the surface than it had been before. I'd never known for what king the Roman city was named. But the kingship of Basel, through all its ages, had always been contested.

⁂

Afterward, at two in the afternoon, we returned to the dining table and *dined*. It was the only meal of the week that could be described that way, where we were dressed well and sat with pewter plates and a platter with as much food as we wanted. Every other meal was eaten plainly, in thanks and humbleness. On Sunday, we accepted that God was bountiful.

Then, through the afternoon, I read to Grandmother; that Sunday from Job. Who could wrestle with Leviathan? And who has beheld Behemoth, with limbs like bars of iron? The Lord warned Job of them both, and not only Job. I have thought that Leviathan and Behemoth walk Basel's streets. They came sometime long ago, even when the streets were slight paths between straw and wood huts, and the streets only hardened since then.

The Sabbath was the day of rest. We both went to bed early. We had done no work on this one day of the week. That was hard for me, but it was proper.

⁂

The circle of the week returned me to Monday, to beneath Master Johann's roof and Mistress Dorothea's tongue. "Leonhard!" She was, as always, in her perpetual constant motion. As I entered the kitchen door she was seated but never still. A chicken waited on her table. "A dog's put a hole in the fence and it needs mending." The girl who helps her in the kitchen was somewhere else that morning. I didn't know where, and I would certainly not ask. If I did, I'd be told where, and why, and why not the next day, and because of who, and on. But without the girl, I alone remained for the Mistress's bombardment. "My sister-in-law's fever is back. And don't put the wood in the settle. She worked too hard before she could become well. She has too many feathers." This was about the chicken she was plucking.

I stood for a moment with my load of wood. "A fever?"

"It wants washing first, get a brush. She's always digging and chewing." This was about the wood settle, and then the dog. "My brother says to let them run." This was likely about the fever, but might also have been about the dog, or even the chicken. "I'll have him warn the Council." What Mistress Dorothea would have her brother warn the Town Council of, unmanaged dogs or contagious fevers, I didn't yet know, but surely not chickens. The threat, though, like everything else concerning her, was not idle. Magistrate Faulkner's warnings to the City Council of Basel carried great weight.

The wood I was carrying was also a great weight. I set it on the floor beside the fireplace and started on the settle, brushing the bark and splinters into the fire and then scrubbing harder. "Are there other fevers in the city?"

"I know of some," she answered, and I knew that I would soon also know. I finished the settle and filled it with wood, and heard the list of my Mistress's acquaintances who had any complaint against their health. It was short enough but very detailed.

"Your own family's been blessed with good health," I said, remembering the story. "Your father lived long, didn't he?"

"Seventy-two years, and hale but the last four."

"And you returned to Basel from Holland to care for him."

"I never wished for Holland," she answered. "Flat as the sea, and nearly the sea. That was a hard move, with a baby and the armies."

"You moved with armies?" I asked, taking bellows to the fire. It, and she, really needed little stoking.

"Move with armies? What would that be? We moved from them."

And I moved from the armies, also. "And it took you long?"

"Two months. We were stopped in Strasbourg for half that, waiting for the road to be clear."

"Clear of the armies," I said. That would be what she was speaking of. Louis of France's armies were fighting in that area at that time, as they had been in most areas at most times. And the baby would have been Nicolaus.

"Ten years in Groningen," she said, "and then Master Johann accused of being a heretic Cartesian! It was scurrilously we were treated. But the Master didn't want to leave his Chair. He was never Cartesian." I knew Master Johann was the most orthodox of Reformed men, if not the most heartfelt. But I didn't believe Cartesian ideas should be dismissed; that philosophy, and Monsieur Descartes himself, had been a study of mine.

"He was Chair of Mathematics there," I said.

"A petty Chair next to Basel," she said, "but still nothing to throw off like ashes, and the Master's honorable above all and wouldn't let gossip drive him from his work. Then the Dean here sent for him to come for a Chair. It was my father who wrote to us of the invitation, and also old Master Nicolaus." This would have been Grandfather Nicolaus, Master Johann's father. Both families were wealthy and both magisterial and none of the Deans of the four colleges of the University would have ignored their requests.

"Any University in Europe would have pleaded for Master Johann."

"They did, they did. When we left Groningen, the Provost of Utrecht pursued us a hundred miles to lure the Master there! But Basel was grandest and kin was dearest and so he did come, even if it was for the Greek Language Chair. And so I could be here for Father's declining years. It was the Lord's mercy to us all, and I was at his bedside with him and his two precious grandchildren. They were his joy and his light, those two, and he was theirs." We'd come back to the first question of her father's health.

Thoughts of chance were still on my mind. "He would still have had to win the draw, though, to get the Chair. It would still have only been one out of three?"

Mistress Dorothea had already cocked her head and given me a shrewd glance. "The fence is waiting. Mend it, Leonhard, before the dogs make the hole worse, and I'll be grateful to you."

⁂

It would be time soon to dress black and white, but first while I was in brown I ran to the Barefoot Square, and the Boot and Thorn. Daniel had said he'd be collecting his horse.

Day in the Common Room was like day in heavy forest. Light found its way to the tables and walls like rain in the forest would, only after touching many distant surfaces first. The fire was low, just smolderers, because it hadn't yet died from the night past and it must return to life for the night coming. Daytime was the fire's purgatory and a half life for night dwellers. Charon the cat slept with one eye.

I sat for a while with two men I knew, a stonecutter and

a bookprinter, eating noon lunch in the twilight. They were arguing over which had the greatest permanence.

"What tears it?" the mason said. "What burns it?" He was an old man, and strong, with gray hair streaked dark and white, and the veins in his hands stood out. "Words written in stone, they never fade."

"But what's said with them?" the printer answered. "You cut one word while I press a thousand." The printer was younger but his hair was white with thin black patches like marks, and his skin was brown and leathery.

"Which of those thousand last? Paper. Here, then gone."

"I'll print a thousand more when they are."

"And my one still lasts. There's a hundred men buried in the Munster yard, and all that's remembered of them is what I chiseled."

"There's a thousand men whose graves are lost, but they're remembered for their books that I've printed.

"If there was anything to remember about me," I said, "I'd want it said with both."

"There was a man," the printer said, "dead more than a decade, but I printed his book and he was remembered again."

"But I cut his epitaph and he was never forgotten."

"I print the words he said."

"I print the words said about him."

"I publish his soul."

"I chisel his life."

"Lithicus," I said to the stonecutter, "I know of that man. Was it my Master Johann's brother Jacob?"

"That one, yes."

"Did you know him?"

"I knew him."

"And Lieber," I said to the bookbinder, "I have that book, also. The *Ars Conjectandi*. Did you read any of it?"

"That Latin? I don't know any of it."

"You carve Latin," I said to Lithicus. "Do you remember the words you cut?"

"I don't know that Latin, either," he said, and he and Lieber shook their heads together, that anyone would.

When Daniel did come in, I was still thinking of languages only spoken now by men in black robes. He sat and toyed with his cup of dice and I thought of the Latin his uncle had written about the arts of chance. And I told him what his mother had told me.

"Greek?" Daniel said. "He'd take the Greek Chair? He couldn't crawl in that language."

"I think he could crawl," I said of Master Johann, "and walk and run."

"But he wouldn't sit. He'd never take a Chair of Greek. Leave Mathematics at Groningen for Greek at Basel? It's not believable."

"Your Grandfather Faulkner wanted his family close."

"I remember that," Daniel said warmly. "He was kind and a gentle old man. I'll long remember that."

"That's what brought your father back to Basel."

"Half a Chair, and half a family wouldn't add to a whole."

"His own father was here."

"That's a subtraction, not an addition."

"Do you remember your Grandfather Nicolaus?"

"Not any. He died the year after we were back. Brutus had fled Basel to Holland to be away from him."

"Why?"

"I was never told."

"Will you tell your own children why you fled from your father in Basel?" I asked.

"No!" He laughed again. "Because they'll have fled Basel themselves to be away from me." As he said it, Gustavus came into the room and on his back was a log for the fire; a true log near the size of a man, four feet long and from low in the tree. "And Leonhard," Daniel said, "I'll tell you this from my own wisdom: When any of us flee from Basel, we only come back if we have a strong reason. I don't believe Brutus only came back because Grandpoppa Faulkner wanted him to, and not for hope of a Chair in Greek, either." With a thump that would have broken any other stone but not that hearth, Gustavus threw the wood onto the embers. "There was only one thing that would bring him to Basel, and that was the Chair of Mathematics."

"But your Uncle Jacob had that Chair."

"And he died." The log ignited. That fireplace was a fire-womb; a flame would spring from anything thrown in it.

"But before, or after, or when?" I asked.

"You tell me!" Daniel answered. "That's the task I've given you!"

"I never liked the task, and I like it less as I see it more."

"What have you seen of it?"

"There's seeing other than by sight."

"More of that?" he said. "Still seeing what's unseen, are you, Leonhard? Then see what I want to know, and you'll be done with it. Brutus came here for the Chair of Mathematics and nothing less."

"And is that why you've come back?" I asked.

"I've come back to learn the truth about Uncle Jacob. Now, who has Greek today? Desiderius still?"

"He does."

"And who was it before? I don't remember."

"I don't know. Desiderius had just taken the Chair when I came five years ago," I said.

"Ask him who was before, and how that man took the Chair. Or more, what was it that happened twenty years ago? Greek must have been empty at the time."

"You could ask him," I said.

"I'm watched every minute."

Gustavus was watching. "Your horse is ready, Master." I'd seen him approach and wait while we spoke, but Daniel hadn't and he was startled.

"Have Willi bring it out front to the Square," he answered, and then to me, "He was promised Greek. And the drawing, that wasn't a hindrance. He'd have the one chance in three, but he knew he'd be chosen in that. Yet Greek. No, he knew Mathematics would come open." He slapped my back, very pleased. "You've made a good start, Leonhard. How long was Jacob alive after we came, or was he at all? How'd he die? Get that for me, Leonhard. Get that! I'm pleased. This is coming even better than I'd thought!"

But Gustavus wasn't pleased and hadn't moved. "It will be Fritz. Willi is away with the coach."

"Yes, yes," Daniel said. "I remember. Fritz, then. Whoever you have. Mare or stallion?"

"Stallion, Master. Spirited as you've preferred."

"Come on and let's see him, Leonhard. Want a ride? Come with me. They'll have another in the stable. Did you say you wanted to see Paris? Or Russia? Those are an odd pair for you to have asked of. Have you heard something?"

"I only listen to my Master's lectures, and I have one this afternoon, so I can't ride with you."

"What do you have left to hear? You should be giving lectures. Who is it you're hearing?"

"Master Huldrych."

"Aged Huldrych! Still here? How is he?"

"More so," I said, and we were in the Barefoot Square

with the ironshod horse, black as anything and eyeing Daniel thoughtfully. Daniel gave him the same look back.

"So Huldrych's still alive," Daniel said, and then to his black horse, "and the ride's to begin. And Leonhard won't come to moderate us. We'll be wild and free." The horse was satisfied.

3

The Death Dance

I returned to my room to become a student. On my dresser, beside my wig, I kept two artifacts and one marvel. Two wooden bowls, man-made, were the artifacts, but the marvel was purely God's creation. It was a conch shell that my father had given me. I didn't know from what far seashore it came. Sometime I would stare at it and become lost imagining how it came to be, and I would run my finger along the ridge of its top; this was the most marvelous part of it, because it formed a spiral more perfect than any which could be drawn by hand. How could it have been made? I believed that it proved that Mathematics was deep in all Creation. I even wondered, between Mathematics and the physical world, which was deeper. But Master Huldrych disagreed.

Master Huldrych held Basel's Chair of Physics. Twenty years ago he held it, when it was the Chair of Natural

Philosophy, and forty years ago he held it. Perhaps sixty years ago; no records had been kept.

He was a genial and cautious man in his narrow house on the Death Dance Street. The street floor was a single room where his lectures were held. The room above was a laboratory where various scales, quadrants, sextants and octants, lenses, and less recognizable objects were engaged in a lengthy experiment which concerned the accumulation of dust. On the highest floor, the Master himself lived in an advanced state of bachelorhood. I had been in this room on a few occasions, as the class occasionally had to select one of its members to arouse the Master from his deliberations when the lecture was to start. The basement of the house opened to the river bank. It flooded at any opportunity and was thus kept clean and empty.

Other floods had scoured the houses of Basel from time to time. Nearly three hundred years ago the Black Death came to the Rhine and passed the city walls. There'd been no count or memory of how many died or how many lived. Instead, the wall of the cemetery of the Preacher's Church was painted with the city's Death Dance. Many cities had these Dances of Death; the Black Death swept many, many cities. Basel's was famous, though, for its size and artistry. It was a mural a hundred feet long on the cemetery wall, made in the plague years, just opposite the house where Master Huldrych now lived. Perhaps he lived in it then, as well.

I'd seen engravings of other Dances from other cities and they all had the same form of a line of many panels, and in each panel a man or woman danced, with a partner. Every dancer's station in life was easily recognized from their dress despite centuries' difference. There were kings and priests and farmers, bakers, knights; children and aged; monks and nuns; paupers, and scholars and students and knaves. But the partner was always the same. It was a sprightly cadaver, Death, grinning, spouting worms and decay, and enjoying the gavotte much more than the reluctant living. In every scene he mocked his mate, twirling the farmer's plow or brandishing the knight's sword or wearing lopsided the king's crown.

These dances were drawn and carved in observation of the Black Death's sweep and carelessness. Even now there were churches in Germany standing empty and alone in old wide fields. Their villages dead and worn away, the stones of God's house were the only remainder.

Though drawn in that time centuries ago, the Dances' meaning was just as painful now. Everyone would die. The dance showed that no one, no one, would escape, whatever their station, rank, or achievement. Life was only a dance with death.

That Monday afternoon I took my place in Master Huldrych's lecture room along with the dozen other students who paid the Master for his lectures. We were all in black and white for lectures, and we jested and teased and ignored the moral lesson available to us so close by.

In my first years I was often the object of the jeering, being younger than the others. Now I was the same age as them and I still received a generous share of their torment, but I didn't mind. I also received a share of their purses for tutoring them in their Latin and Greek. I wasn't asked to tutor other subjects: I had gained a reputation of becoming too enthusiastic and lengthy in my sessions.

Finally, as the church bells began their noon lecture, Master Huldrych appeared to begin his. We sat on a bench built around the walls of the room and the Master stood at a podium. He was expert in the Physics current in his youth but not the Physics current in his old age. He still referred to the subject as Natural Philosophy. He was one of the few masters at the University who still lectured in Latin. I wasn't sure that he knew that he did. His great energy had dwindled though his curiosity was unflagging. He questioned any visiting scholar on the newest discoveries and ideas, but nothing new would ever seep into his lectures.

He was aware that the atmosphere was a gas, and that it exerted pressure on surfaces. He had himself collected gases in containers and observed that the volume and pressure in the container were somehow related. But the basic principle eluded him that this relation was a simple Mathematic inverse proportion, though Mr. Boyle stated that sixty years ago. He had described to us the experiments and proposals he'd entered into the Paris Competition, though he had not competed for many years. He had never won the competition. He may not even have entered, but only remembered that he had.

His lecture that morning was on the theory of waves, and I was in misery! I was fascinated by waves. From the square behind the Munster I would watch them on the Rhine. And this was my theory, as ridiculous as Master Huldrych found it: that sound was a wave.

I believed this because I was convinced that waves could move through volumes, not just across surfaces. How could a bird in flight be heard? What was the sound? Huldrych said it couldn't be a wave, because no surface connected the bird and the ear, and plain observation showed that waves occurred on surfaces. I believed instead that sound showed that an invisible wave might occur in a gas. There were so many invisible things!

The air itself was invisible. It had been a century since Monsieur Pascal stated he believed that we were not surrounded by a vacuum, but by a type of matter like water, that filled our world like an ocean. At the time, Monsier Descartes derided him by saying the true vacuum was between Monsieur Pascal's ears; but later, Mr. Boyle in England was able to evacuate the air from a bell pressed firmly against a tabletop. This true vacuum had many strange properties, including the phenomenon that no sound could penetrate it: a small, jangling bell inside the vacuum couldn't be heard outside. So, air was necessary for sound.

Daniel agreed with me; we had exchanged letters on this subject while he was in Italy. The difficulty was in the Mathematics. What were the equations that described these waves? I believed I had a solution, but there were so many difficulties. Oh, how I loved difficulties! How I loved these invisibilities! And how difficult it was to listen to Master Huldrych lecture on his simple, visible waves of water.

The lecture ended. The students exited respectfully but I lingered, and when the others were gone, Master Huldrych noticed I'd remained. "Leonhard?" he asked, and peered carefully to see that it was. There was a mass to him, a bulginess, that was both height and girth; he was like a ruin of a castle. His wide robe contributed to his indefinition.

"Master," I answered. "How long have you lectured at the University?"

"How long? Very long. Very, very long."

"Has anyone been longer?"

"Oh, no. No one." He shook his head in wonder at the very thought. "How could they?"

"Even Master Balthazar? He's had his Chair of Law for a long time."

"He has. He has. I remember when he came." He smiled at me. "So I must have been here before, mustn't I! All of the other Masters, I remember them all coming."

"The Master of Greek?"

"Desiderius? That was only five years ago."

"The Master before, I meant. I don't remember who he was."

"Master Jankovsky. He had been Chair fifteen years, but he was young when he was elected. That was very unfortunate, what happened to him. It would have been expected he'd have lived longer. I have. Or it would have been expected that I wouldn't."

"Twenty years ago, then," I said.

"And Master Stuber before Jankovsky. He was old. He was very old."

"Master Johann has been here for twenty years."

"I remember that day very well. Johann and Jankovsky were elected the same day."

"The same day?"

Master Huldrych nodded slowly and his thoughts seemed focused on something long ago. "When Master Jacob died." He turned his head upward, as if he were looking toward heaven. Or perhaps just toward the ceiling. "Much has changed!" he said. "I think it's best to not talk about that year."

⁂

The Death Dance paintings had faded over their many years, as had Master Huldrych, though they were still clear; but one scene seemed far more live and real than the others. It was the Lawyer. Every scene had written above it Death's pronouncement and the Living's appeal. I knew the Lawyer's words well: *God gives all laws, as are found in books; no man may change them: hate lies, love truth*. But it wasn't the Lawyer watching me from the wall. It was Nicolaus standing in front and matching the mural's stance.

"Old Huldrych," he said.

"Old but durable," I answered. "He'll outlast us all."

"His Chair's worth having."

"Once it's empty, and it isn't."

"He's mortal," Nicolaus said again; and flanked by hundreds of feet of Death Dance, he was irrefutable.

"So was your uncle. Do you remember him?"

"No."

"Was he alive when you came to Basel, or had he already died? You were ten years old. If you tell me, I can tell Daniel, and you won't report any of us to Master Johann."

Nicolaus only asked my question back. "What have you learned of my Uncle Jacob?"

"I know his Mathematics," I said. "He was Master Johann's teacher." Though Nicolaus had the Chair of Law in Bern, he was more a Mathematician than many who taught Mathematics.

"How do you know?"

"I've read the *Ars Conjectandi* and I've had my Master's lessons. I can see what he learned from his brother."

"I know the lion by his paw." Nicolaus said it oddly. It was a saying in their family, with a meaning of recognizing one thing from another. "I don't know that he was alive when we came. We had stopped a month in Strasbourg on our way."

"A month?"

"There were armies on the Rhine, and battles. We had to wait. And no news from Basel. But Gottlieb went on. He'd been living with us." Then he said nothing else.

It was odd how the conversation mirrored his mother's, how the journeys had been symmetric. I asked, "What does Daniel want, do you think?"

"He bears watching."

"He means to cause trouble, I guess."

"He has reason."

I was unsure if this meant he had a reason, or if he could

reason. It was Nicolaus's manner of speech, always leaving me unsure.

"Did you come to Basel to watch him?"

"I have reason, too. I am only the lion's paw." He smiled at me. "What reason do you have, Leonhard?"

"I don't know. . . ."

He nodded to me and even tipped his hat, and our talk was over.

Late in the afternoon, just as the shadows of western houses were at the feet of eastern houses, I passed through the Barefoot Square on an errand. There had been many walls around Basel, of sod and wood and stone, but the oldest standing was the Old Wall, the inner wall built six hundred years ago. The New Wall was a century or two younger and enclosed three times the area. The Barefoot Square, between the church and the inn, had the inside of the Old Wall as one of its sides, and the Coal Gate as an entry; a man entering from Coal Street had the Boot and Thorn on his left and the Barefoot Church on his right. I called it the Half-Shod Gate.

The Wall and its gates, though deep inside the city now, were still maintained. On the key of the gate's arch was a shield carved with a Bishop's crook, which was Basel's emblem, though there'd been no bishop since the Reformation. But the shield had cracked, sometime recently. I saw scaffolding up the side of the wall at the gate, and a workman repairing the shield. It was Lithicus. He saw me watching from below and set down his hammer. "Would you make this of paper?" he said.

"No. Nor any of the Wall."

"Nor the houses, nor the church."

"I'll ask you a question," I said. "I've looked at Master

Jacob's epitaph stone often, and I wonder if you remember its spiral."

"Spiral? I remember it!" His countenance was instantly angry. "I remember it too well!"

"What do you remember?"

"That it's a spiral and you won't tell me it's not." And he was fearful, too.

"Oh, it is," I said.

"Some say not, and they say what isn't is."

"What do they say is?"

"Stretched bendings that no one could carve."

"Who says—" I began to ask, but exactly then I was knocked from my feet by a black stallion. I'd always been an inattentive fellow when I walked the streets, and I'd had practice enough picking myself up from collisions. A hand took hold of mine and pulled. It was Daniel, and his other hand still held the stallion's rein.

"Keep an eye out," he said, laughing.

"Or you keep an eye on me," I said, and laughed with him. "And you had a good ride?"

"Wild and free," he said. "And the innkeeper's waiting for his horse, so I'll take it to him." In the doorway of the Boot and Thorn, Gustavus had his eye on Daniel, and I thought it was Daniel he was waiting for, and it was Daniel that he led into the inn.

~

Later, I was cast ashore into my grandmother's kitchen, to a supper of fish and dark bread. I felt troubled, as I had Sunday morning before, and I asked my grandmother's counsel. "Who is king in Basel?"

"You know that the town's Council and its Mayor are all Basel has of a king, and the Magistrates are its judges."

"I know those," I said. "But who is king?" I was as unsure of the question as of the answer.

"Whose laws are followed is king," she answered. "Whose laws do you see followed, Leonhard?"

There was a great deal to consider about laws. There were the city's laws that lawyers read and the Magistrates judged on, and people obeyed these laws mostly, so the Council was a king. Also, there were laws of gravity that everyone obeyed, so the earth was our king; and laws of civility and custom that weren't written but ruled us. There was an elegance that each law had its giver and its reason, wise or poor. And there were deeper laws of good and evil in which we chose our own Master. "*God gives all laws, as are found in books; no man may change them: hate lies and love truth,*" I said. "Grandmother, do you remember when Master Johann's brother Master Jacob died?"

"I remember the man well."

"Was it before or after Master Johann came back from Holland? I think it must have been close either way."

"I don't know. Jacob was alive and Johann was away, then Jacob was dead and Johann was here. It wasn't told beyond that."

"I think Knipper would remember that ride," I said.

"Ask him when he comes with the coach tomorrow."

"He didn't go," I said. "Gustavus had to send Willi with the coach. But I'd have to find him, and Gustavus couldn't. Or maybe when Willi comes back, he can tell me if Knipper was still in Mistress Dorothea's kitchen when he went for the trunk."

Tuesday began with water: a steady rain falling and I fallen upon, fetching from the fountain rain that had fallen in the weeks before. A barrel beneath my bedroom window caught rainwater from the roof, but it wasn't full yet.

Just as the people of Basel carried the blood of the ancients, the veins of the city were as ancient. In the inner city, the old city, the streets must have been laid sometime, some year. One evidence of this was the fountains. They were fed by pipes or tunnels beneath the streets. Every person in Basel used the fountains but no one knew when they were set, or how, or by whom.

There was a stream, the Birsig Flow, that entered the city from the southwest. Before it came into the city, it split in three parts. One fed the moat and another passed between houses inside the city, then disappeared. That was a foul course of water and no one would drink from it. But the third split dove beneath the wall into an ancient tunnel. It must once have been unfettered on its journey to the Rhine, but very long ago it was covered over by the streets and houses of Basel. Now even its path was unknown. I believed it fed the fountain in the Barefoot Square. That one always had a sharp taste.

I sheltered for a moment from the rain inside the door of the Boot and Thorn, and caught Old Gustavus as he passed, like the stream, toward some hidden place. "Master Daniel's made himself well at home here," I said. "He likes what he finds in the Common Room."

"He finds what's Common to all men."

And with that wet answer, I took my buckets and carried home water through the rain.

The heavens were not yet emptied when I sailed forth to Master Johann's house. I cleaned my boots and took them off inside the kitchen door. By the faintness of the sound waves, I calculated that Mistress Dorothea was about two floors away. I knew my jobs without being told, though. There was dry wood aplenty in the shed, but I still had to keep the fire high enough to swallow wet logs.

I wasn't alone anyway. Little Johann was at the table with his dough, and I knew when he needed a listening ear. "What's it like now?" I asked. "They've been here a few days and settled in."

"Just as bad."

"How are they with you?"

"Daniel's either hot or cold, and Nicolaus is lukewarm."

"How are you to them?"

"Not better. I don't care."

"I think you care, Johann," I said. "You're brothers."

"I won't do anything for them. They won't for me."

I took a guess on what he was wanting to be asked. "Have you told Daniel about the letters you saw on your father's desk?"

"I can't! I'd be hated by Poppa if I did."

"I could tell him."

"I don't care if he ever gets them. Poppa's burned them anyway."

"Burned them? I doubt he has. And they're from Paris and Russia. I think he'd want them. I'll tell Daniel, and no one will know you saw them. He can ask for them himself."

"Poppa doesn't want him to have them. What if Daniel asks for them? There'll be a fight."

That was true. "I'll think on it," I said. "And I won't let you be hated for it."

"I know you won't, Leonhard."

So I'd made a promise and Johann's dough was given rest. Mistress Dorothea arrived and was quickly praising her son, and worrying for him, and pressing him with questions, kneading him with her words.

❧

On Tuesday I was lectured to on Greek, in Greek. I would go to Saint Alban's street where Saint Alban's church stands within Saint Alban's cloister, and just beyond was Saint Alban's Gate beside the Rhine. This was the city's easternmost gate, the closest of the gates to Greece. Standing on the wall beside the gate, I sometimes watched the river flowing in from closer eastern lands: from Wurttemberg, and Zurich, and the Bodensee where the Rhine is born. I'd never seen those places. Beyond them were Austria and Russia and Greece. And farther beyond were the Indies and China, and finally Basel again. Disciples of Natural Philosophy knew that the planet was round, and that a straight path was finally a circle. A day circles the planet and returns as a different day. I wondered what Basel would be like to return to.

The gate wasn't immediately beside the river. There was a space, with the gate and Saint Alban's street on one side, and the river on the other. In the space was the paper factory. This far corner of the city was Switzerland's greatest center for the manufacture of paper; it produced much of the country's supply. I liked to watch the workers shred and pound the rags and feed them into the stamps. These powerful presses were the reason the factory was here at the river: they were driven by water wheels and had been for nearly three centuries. The canal for the wheels was even older, dug long earlier by monks for Saint Alban's flour mills.

The pulp was soaked and crushed in another press into sheets that were then dried, first between layers of felt, and then by hanging. Paper for writing was bathed in lime and dried again. I learned this especially when I tried to use the cheap un-limed stuff for writing and it drank ink from the pen like a thirsty horse at a trough, and made my equations into veined black spots and wriggles. The paper looked like the muddy road the horse trampled on its way to the trough!

All the paper I had in my room was from these mills, and I had so much paper! I'd known many geese, and if someday I could visit the place the ink was made, I'd have a good knowledge of my precious tools: paper, pen, and ink. I knew less about the ink except that it was made from ashes. I'd looked closely at it as it dried on the page, trying to see the flecks, but it was pure black. It seemed a worthy use of ash. A man would write, and what he'd written outlasted him: It was his ashes.

But the paper was dearest to me because it was what I started with. It was the promise and the potential and it was so pretty, just white.

Saint Alban's street wasn't only for paper. In the large houses facing the factory were the printers. What a greatness they were! Lieber had apprenticed in Frankfurt but was of a very old Basel family with generations of ink in his veins, and I thought his books to be the highest quality. He only printed books, not broadsides and flyers. But I wouldn't have cared even if they were printed on burlap; it was the words written. I wrote because I read, and I needed to think when I read, and I needed to write when I thought. What others have written, though, was far more excellent.

And among the printers were the booksellers! I needed complete discipline to not peer into *those* shops. It was a very dangerous street for me.

But I had to go to Saint Alban's Street on Tuesdays, despite the peril. Among the papers and books and words was the home of Master Desiderius, who held the University's Chair of Greek.

Desiderius was a man not yet forty, and he held a special place in my admiration: He was the greatest read man I knew. Where my reading had covered an acre, his had covered a continent. Even the densest Mathematics I had on my shelves he had also read. I might have understood more of what I'd read than he did, but he had read more of what I understood than I had. And Mathematics, of course, was just a particle of his reading. He had read the Ancients and the Classics and the Moderns, he had read Philosophy and Theology, Anatomy and Botany, History and Logic, Rhetoric and Dialectic; he had read Virgil to make the mind tremble, and Homer to make the heart race, and Provencal romances to make the cheek blush. He was a very quiet man with a peaceful wife and studious children. They all read. He would read to each child in a different language depending on their age: first in German, then in Latin, then Greek, Italian, English, and I suppose in obscure Hebrew and Persian and Chinese! When they did speak, the family was hushed Babel.

His lecture room was small, for only a dozen students at most. His larger lectures were given at the University building in the Old Lecture Hall and were attended by the larger mass of beginning students who all were required to take Greek, and from whom I earned my pocket money tutoring. Those who came to his house were we who craved the language. The dozen seats were seldom full.

The Master himself entered and greeted us and we immersed ourselves in Homer, Hesiod, Aeschylus, and Aristotle. Every classic writer was fair game in our hunt, all save one. Plato was considered too vast and deep to even consider except on his own, and he was given his own special days.

The double thickness of Greek was the speaking and what was spoken. It seemed impossible to me to ride the wine dark Aegean with Odysseus, or visit bloody dark

Thebes with Sophocles, in awkward thudding German. Even Latin was hollow. No, it must be Greek for the Greeks! And on other days, when Master Vanitas wasn't looking, we discussed the New Testament. Vanitas held the Chair of Theology. He was a dismal man, very unlike Desiderius, and I'd sat under only one semester of his lectures, and though I respected his thoughtfulness, I would take my Theology in a sunlit church on a Sunday instead of under Vanitas' clouds. But within the billowing cloak of a Greek lecture, there was ample room for almost anything, and I was especially glad that the Fathers wrote in the language that Desiderius taught.

When the lecture concluded, I stayed behind. Master Desiderius was not to be bothered with a wig, so his red and brown curls were like autumn leaves among his students' snowy white headdresses.

"Master Desiderius," I said. Unlike with Master Huldrych, I often stayed behind in this class. "May I borrow a book?" This was my usual reason.

"Only if you'll read it, Leonhard." This was his usual answer, and it was humorous. He knew I wouldn't be able to walk home without my nose between the pages. "What book do you want?"

"Any."

"Come and we'll choose one."

Few words stirred a deeper joy in me.

⁂

Minutes later, many minutes, I stood at his door, my feet toward the street, my heart still among the shelves of his library, my fingers firm on Boccaccio, and my eyes on the Master's face.

"And next, after that one," he was saying, "I have a Faustbook for you. It's a new telling, and when you read it I'll lend you Paracelsus with it. And there's also a new Homer. It's an Englishman named Pope. Do you read English?"

"No," I said, and I must have sounded less than enthusiastic.

"It would be a good text to learn it. There's more than just Greek and Latin, Leonhard."

"Yes, sir. There's French that I hardly know, and Italian even less." I held up the book in my hand. "And I think my brain is more than full already!"

"Then make some room. You could empty some of your numbers and Mathematics."

"Oh, no, sir!"

"No, no, I wouldn't, that, either. You have a gift for them, Leonhard, and I think there's a purpose in that."

"I hope there is," I said. "Anyway, I think they're stuck."

"I've plenty wedged too tight myself. And there's more to put in! With every lecture I give I find more I need to learn."

"You've many more years of lecturing still."

"I've already had five here and five in Strasbourg."

Surely I'd known before he'd come from Strasbourg. "Why did you come here?"

"I was elected to the Chair."

"How were you, though?" I asked. "Had you been asked? Did they know you'd come if it was offered?"

"Master Vanitas wrote me to say his committee would nominate me if I was willing. They prefer to have candidates from other universities as well as from Basel. I agreed that I was. And then, of the three candidates, it was my name drawn."

"Had you known Master Vanitas, then?"

"By reputation and by correspondence. And I'd known Master Jankovsky."

"Oh! Master Huldrych mentioned him. He said it was unfortunate what had happened to him."

Master Desiderius looked away, as if something unpleasant had been thrust before him. "But that was five years ago. And I was in Strasbourg."

That seemed a better subject. "What is the University in Strasbourg like?"

"It was once significant."

"Basel is significant."

"Very much. Strasbourg was worth leaving. When the city surrendered its independence and became part of France, many things declined." He glanced about the room. "Such as books and printing. There are more books here in Basel! I remember asking the coachman to tell me about the city."

"The coachman? Knipper?"

"Yes, it was. He brought me the letter from Master Vanitas, and I rode back with him on his return to give my nomination lecture."

"Did Master Johann ever have the Chair of Greek?"

"Johann?" This surprised him. "But he has Mathematics! Why would he have Greek?"

"I was told he was considered for it, long ago. But then Mathematics came open."

"He has never had the Greek Chair. His name is not on the list." He seemed very surprised at the possibility, and even alarmed. So I asked about the Faustbook then, and perhaps I drove the memory of Master Johann from the Master's thoughts.

It seemed worth finding Daniel to tell him a few things I'd learned, and as it was Tuesday afternoon, Willi would be back from Freiburg and Strasbourg, and that would also be worth attending. So I opened my eyes for Daniel and wandered toward the north, facing Saint John Gate. And when Daniel was in Basel he was hard to hide.

I went walking the Rhine Leap, the street which ran from the Munster Square at one end to Saint Martin's Church and the Rhine Bridge at the other. The University Building itself faced the river beside the bridge, in front of Saint Martin's. Centered between these pillars, Cousin Gottlieb lived in a house of the same quality as Master Johann's and only somewhat less quantity. Daniel was there to be found, occupied with glaring at it. I tugged his sleeve.

"What?" Daniel said. "Who? Oh, is it you, Leonhard?"

"It is," I laughed. "Are you calling on Gottlieb?"

He said blackly, "I'll call on him, and see how he likes it."

"No you won't. Come with me. I see what you're doing, you're sulking."

"Well, I am." He brightened. He'd hold a grudge forever, but not tightly. "I was only strolling and I forgot where I was. It's not fair for his house to stand in my path."

"Ignore him," I said.

"That I won't. Not ever." He said it with a smile. Lest I think he wasn't part serious, though, he said, "It's only logical that I wouldn't."

⁂

Two years before, when I was sixteen and beginning to understand the ways of the University, the Chair of Logic came open. It was an interesting Chair, tasked to lecture on Dialectic, Rhetoric, Logic, and Geometry. It had for many years been held by Master Grimm, whose lessons had so solidified over his tenure that I doubted they varied even by a word from one year to another. Of course, logic didn't change.

But then he left. It may have been that he went to visit a

sister in Leipzig. His absence became prolonged, and finally, undeniable. An Inquiry was held, which was a serious undertaking, and a request for information was sent to the Court in Leipzig. In the end his Chair had been declared vacant and an Election was held to fill it.

A University Election in Basel was the city's most complex and obscure ritual.

The design was this: Three committees of professors and high University officials would be formed, with six in each committee. Each committee would then nominate a candidate to the empty Chair, and a stone, or lot, for each candidate was then placed in an iron box, to which only the Provost had a key. Each candidate then gave a lecture on the Chair's subject; Anatomy, Physics, Law, Theology, or whatever. The lecture was only final proof of the candidate's expertise. It had no bearing on the Election itself, except that a very poor lecture might disqualify a candidate. The lectures might take place in just the few days after the nominations, or over a longer period if a candidate wasn't in Basel and must be notified, and travel to the city. Finally, after the lectures, the box would be opened and the Provost would blindly choose one lot from the three.

It would seem a reasonable and elegant procedure. Three qualified men, and one chosen at random. No bribes, no secretive bargains, no personal prejudices or nepotism could influence the selection of the Chair. Even if the winner wasn't the most qualified man, he'd be one of the three-most.

In practice, factions did prevail within the committees, with each party advancing its own favorite. So, the random choice was meant to stymie those improper influences.

However, it was not certain that it did.

Three candidates were nominated that year for the Logic Election. Daniel was one, chosen by professors enamored of his charming ways. The thought of an invigorated, lively Chair of Logic was beguiling. I, of course, as lowly a student as I was, was all for his Election. It seemed so grand a picture, to have him pacing the streets in his black robe, his students tripping to keep up with him. But it wasn't to be.

The two other candidates were an odd Polish gentleman from Cracow, as it has been customary to nominate at least one candidate from outside the city, and Cousin Gottlieb. Gottlieb was nominated by Master Johann. The committees' deliberations were in secret, so it would never be known what was discussed. Gottlieb was a respectable and dry lecturer in Law, and generally avoided. I attended his lectures and considered them perfect specimens, competent and parched, as Gottlieb himself was. Actually, his real competence was Mathematics. Though his only book was his uncle's *Ars Conjectandi*, he'd managed correspondence with most of Europe's great Mathematicians: Hermann, de Moivre, Montmort, and Leibniz himself. He finished his Doctorate in Mathematics under his uncle Master Johann before he took his Chair in Padua. But Gottlieb returned to Basel years ago, before I started at the University, and he made a poor comparison to his cousin Daniel.

When the lot was chosen, though, it was his.

I remembered very well the next few days. My Master's house was like an armory of swords and maces, all at hand and often used. Then Daniel decided that a Basel with Cousin Gottlieb was worth less than an exile without Cousin Gottlieb. In only two weeks, Daniel announced his own Election to the Chair of Mathematics in Padua that had been vacated by his brother Nicolaus, and he was gone.

❧

And now he was back, glowering at Gottlieb's house. "It was by chance," I said.

"Chance, you say?"

"The chance of the draw."

"That is your conjecture, your *Conjectandi*. He wrote his book about chance, didn't he? But I don't believe in chance. Not when there's a Chair at stake. Chance wouldn't be given a chance."

"The final choice for a Chair is meant to come from God's hand," I said.

"Sometimes His choice is predestined."

"Then that makes it even more sure."

"Predestined, but not by God. There were letters, Leonhard, there were whispers, there were glances, and it wasn't the first Election that there were."

"But the Provost's blind hand chose the stone, Daniel. How could a whisper put one indistinguishable square in his fingers over another? It couldn't even be done if he was trying to choose a specific one."

"There's seeing other than by sight."

I shook my head at him. "Look, Daniel, I've learned more about Jacob."

"Oh? Jacob?" He was uninterested. "Are you still on him?" He started walking with me, toward the river.

"It isn't three days since you put me on him!"

"Well, don't give it mind. Not anymore."

"Daniel," I said. "Is that your plan? That's the only one thing you could say to make me want to give it my mind."

"I hardly even know what you're saying. A plan? There's no plan. Old Jacob, let him rest in peace."

"And keeping it all from your father's ears?"

"Let him rest in peace, too."

"He's not dead, Daniel."

"No, not at the moment. He's still in his chair. But Italy's fine, Leonhard! You should go sometime. It's a fanciful place, all ruins and art and idiots. Not a whit of hard work. The streets are full of strolling and time-wasting and sweet life."

"But your Chair in Padua . . ."

He frowned at that. "Blast it! What's Padua? A Chair in Basel only comes once in years, a worthwhile one." We'd reached the Rhine Bridge. He wasn't crossing it, and I was, so he turned to resume whatever wandering had brought him out. "And it comes open by chance, the same chance that it's filled by, and the same chance that keeps all the University ordered to Brutus' liking."

"Those are evil words, Daniel."

"Then pay them no mind, Leonhard." He clenched his fist, then let it loose. "Let them be the breeze, here, then gone, then forgotten."

We parted and I went on my way, across the river.

❧

There were two Basels, and the Rhine was the reason. The beginning of the city was on the west bank and it survived through its different ages well enough. But it was only one city of many on a very long river. Five hundred years ago Prince-Bishop Heinrich, who ruled the city, decided the city would be greatly strengthened and made distinct if it built a bridge.

There were no other bridges across the Rhine. Trade would be increased if Basel became the single road from east to west. Tolls would enrich the city. River trade would be controlled, as well, as boats could only pass the bridge at Basel's pleasure.

The Rhine was hundreds of feet wide, yet the city had already leapt the water and a straggling of houses perched on the far bank. The bridge was built and the two became one Basel; or actually, the one Basel became two. The settlement on the right bank has grown to be one fourth of the city, of proper streets and houses and churches, but the river still was wide, and it cut as deep; and Small Basel on the east, and Large Basel on the west, remained each suspicious of the other. The Town Hall was in Large Basel, and the Munster, and the larger houses and the market; and the University, all prospering from the trade the bridge brought. Across the bridge in Small Basel were none of those. Both Basels were ruled by the same laws and Council, yet even after five hundred years the bridge still isolated them as separate people.

Even the bridge itself was two bridges. Large Basel and Small Basel each built and have kept their own half-bridge, and each crossed just their half of the Rhine and met in the river middle. The Small Basel bridge was on five stone piers. The east half-river was shallow and slow. The Large Basel bridge was on seven wood pilings, crossing a deeper and faster west river half.

In the center where the two Basels' bridges joined was a small, spired room built into the rail. This was the Yoke Chapel, where the two sides were yoked together. It was used for prayer and executions. For centuries criminals were thrown into the river from the chapel to be drowned. The method wasn't reliable, though. Too many could swim, even weighted. More trustworthy methods were now used. Still, though, in Basel, it was an insult to say of a man that he died in the river.

Another insult the bridge delivered was the River Gate. Where the bridge crossed the Rhine, Large Basel had a tower as strong as any other, but Small Basel had only a guardhouse. This meant that an enemy who broke into Small Basel could still be kept out of the Large city, which lessened the need to defend the homes and churches of the Small city. The gate could also defend the Large from the Small itself, if there was ever strife between the two. There has been strife. At times in its past, Large Basel has charged a toll at the gate for any citizen of Small Basel entering, but no toll for any citizen of Large Basel returning.

So the bridge divided as much as it connected. But it still realized its first purpose. That afternoon, on my way to the North German Road where Willi and his coach would soon be returning, I did what could only be done in Basel and not for all the hundreds of miles to the sea: I crossed the Rhine by foot. I came to Small Basel, and to my eyes the streets on that side of the river, though fewer, looked just like the streets on the other. I ran through them, not because I was hurrying, but because I hadn't had enough running. I even ran some extra streets because the direct path wasn't long enough.

There were two gates in the Small Basel Walls. The Riehen Gate pointed northeast to my home village. Sadly, that wasn't my destination. I ran to the Saint Blaise Gate.

Blaise faced north toward Baden and all of Germany. The road from it led up the Rhine's right bank to Freiburg, a day's ride north. I went through the gate and walked a short distance beyond. I wanted to climb onto the coach as it passed and ride in with Willi, and have a minute with him before he reached the inn. The road bent out of sight some ways ahead; above the bend, in the air, after a wait, was dust. Of dust men were made, and by carriage did they arrive.

The horses and their burden came into view and I saw that I would not ride with Willi. The seat beside him in the driver's box was already filled. The place was taken by a uniformed gendarme. An extra passenger might ride with the driver on his box seat if the coach is very full, but a gendarme would be the last one to suffer this discomfort. Then I saw that it wasn't Willi anyway, but a yellow-haired slovenly equal from some northern stable.

I stood and watched instead of waving or running beside, yet the driver pulled his reins and slowed the horses and stopped. The man leaned down. "Where's there an inn, the Boot and Thorn?"

"I'll take you," I said.

"Boy," the gendarme said to me. "Not that inn. We're for the Town Hall."

"The inn, and that's all I'm for," the driver said petulantly. From the look of them, it wasn't the first disagreement the two had had.

"The Hall's on the way to the inn," I said. "Come on." I didn't want to squeeze into the box and be a part of their dispute. Instead I set out on a good pace running ahead and the driver whipped the horses after me. The animals could have taken the coach to the inn themselves. I was some winded as we finally reached the bridge and River Gate. But just up the hill was the end.

As the Munster commanded its Square, and the Barefoot Church attended its Square, Basel's Town Hall ruled its Square, the Market Square. The Town Hall of Basel was red with towers, windows, gold and clocks, pillared balconies and paintings and statues, and sharp-peaked roofs.

"But where to the inn?" the driver said when he was stopped beside me. "I'm not stopping and waiting. I didn't want this ride and I'll be done with it."

"It's just up there by that church," I said. The tower of the Bare Feet was easily seen over the houses. But before they could argue more, the argument was ended. The door of the coach had opened from inside. A leg was planted on the step, not stockinged but black leather booted. A polished ebony black walking stick was planted beside it. Then followed a glossy black tricorne and a very long and tightly curled wig and a glistening and very black silk frock coat.

Then, a face, black with anger. The man was out, and stood, and blasted Basel with his stare.

The gendarme stiffened into silence and the driver slouched into subservience.

"This is Basel?" the man questioned, as if it was so much less than he'd thought it would be that it might not really be at all, in a German that was slippery and French-bent. Onlookers had begun to collect, but distantly. I was the only native close at hand.

"Yes, sir."

"Do you know where your town hall is?"

It was difficult to not notice it. "Yes, sir. It's this building here."

"Oh, really." He peered at it. "Find a magistrate and bring him to me. And be quick." He looked up to the partners in the box. "Sergeant, bring it down."

I looked to the gendarme, who seemed more likely to answer a question. "Where are you from, sir?"

"Strasbourg." That was the far end of the coach's route, beyond Freiburg.

"Where's Willi? The driver from here?"

"He is arrested in prison. Bring the magistrate, boy."

Magistrates would not be *fetched*, not easily; and Willi imprisoned was worth staying to ask more questions. But I'd become ambassador of Basel to this Strasbourg invasion, and I tried to think what to do. A magistrate was the greatest of a city's citizens. A magistrate was a judge; the Chief Magistrate advised the town council. In most cities no one was his equal, and in Basel even a Professor of the University or a Dean of the Cathedral was only the peer of a standard magistrate; the University Provost alone stood on the same peak as Chief Magistrate Faulkner. "I don't know if there's a magistrate to be brought," I said.

He looked at me as if I was quite stupid, and for his purpose I was. "I said to be quick."

I ran to the main door of the Town Hall. Whoever might be inside would be more help than me. The first I saw was a captain of the Day Watch, one that I knew. "Simeon!" I said. "There's a man out there. He's from Strasbourg and he wants a magistrate."

"A magistrate?" The captain was even more skeptical than I. He was gray-bearded and a fountain of good sense; he'd led a life of seasoned authority. "And who is this man?"

"Well, he looks to be about a magistrate himself."

Together we returned to the court, where a very large crowd was stepping forward from the market stalls. They had a scene to gawk at, as marvelous as an acting troupe's play, or a fire. The coach was still stopped direct in front of the town hall. The driver was just climbing back to his box, with little of the dexterity that Knipper would have shown. The gendarme was at rigid attention. The personage of Strasbourg was now obviously a magistrate: He had put on a black judgment robe. At his feet was a large trunk, freshly lowered from the luggage rack. I knew the trunk. I'd seen it before in Master Johann's house on the kitchen floor.

The Strasbourger's annoyance was increasing, from an already high level. He saw us and decided that Simeon was sufficient authority. "Open it," he said to his gendarme.

The man stooped to the trunk and unlatched the clasp. As he did, he grimaced; he expected something unpleasant. In one motion he lifted the lid and rolled the trunk forward to spill it out. It did spill, and what it spilled was Knipper.

Poor Knipper! He was mottled purple and blue, and tangled, dumped on the paving stones. I fell back from him, and everyone did, as the black robe and hostile frown of the visitor gave a visible shape to the sudden fear we all felt. Then the crowd began to step forward again toward the stranger, hostile in return. But the man was unflinching and his stare judged and condemned the whole Market Square of unspoken crime. "I am Caiaphas, Magistrate of Strasbourg," he spoke, scarring the air with his prophet voice, "and I charge you, Basel, with sending this murdered corpse to my city."

The mob was both cowed and enraged by that stare and that proclamation, and Simeon knew a riot coming when he saw one. "Back away," he shouted. A few more of the Day Watch had been in the crowd and they stepped forward to show themselves to the people. There was muttering and dark looks, but Simeon's command had had effect. He said to me, quietly, "Go for Magistrate Faulkner, Leonhard, be quick and tell him what you've seen."

I took a last look at Knipper. Even dead, he seemed so uncomfortable tumbled on hard ground. It was a bad end for him. And Basel, made of stone and brick, had a tear made in what it was, the soft fabric of living inside its hard parts.

I spoke to Magistrate Faulkner. His house was large, outside the tight spaces of the old city, with a garden and trees. He came to the door after I spoke to the maid who answered my knock, and he listened carefully to my tale. Magistrate Faulkner was an austere and severe man, very humble despite his high station, generous as his sister Mistress Dorothea but far quieter, and he could hurl thunderbolts if one was at hand. He'd been Councilor, Mayor, and most fearfully, an Inquisitor; but that was long before I'd known him. He asked me whether the Day Watch had the crowd in check, and then dismissed me. He has his own servants and messengers.

Then I walked slowly home; I didn't want to return to the tragic stage in the Market Square. I wanted to mourn Knipper. As I was walking, Faulkner on his horse galloped past me, his magistrate's robe flying from his shoulders as black as Caiaphas'.

My grandmother set a somber table and we ate without the conversation we usually have of the day's happenings. Instead, we both thought on death. Everyone in Basel knew death, and not because the Death Dance reminded them. They'd seen it. No family did not have at least an aged parent they'd buried, and most had a child, a mother, a brother. Babies were born to great uncertainty, except that they would die, and many made a quick job of it. Illness like fire swept the city time to time, and fire like illness would take a dozen lives in a moment. Basel lived on as each of its parts died, always being torn and always slowly mended.

I visited the Boot and Thorn that evening, with all Basel, every craftsman, tradesman, scholar, knave, lord, and priest: every dancer. Calamity was always profitable for Old Gustavus. Daniel was in the center and Nicolaus at the edge. I found an inch of bench and listened.

"What killed Knipper?" was the question I heard first.

A Day Watch, just off duty, let everything he knew boil out his mouth. "He's taken to the Watch barracks. He's purple mess. Five days in a trunk, and he's no Lazarus. Rough riding on the top of a coach. But that wasn't what killed him; it's his head's half flat. A good heavy battering that was."

"But who would have?" Knipper was no one's friend but no one's enemy. There wouldn't be love or hate for the man who leveled that blow, only disapproval for evilly disturbing Basel, and veiled admiration for whoever could crack such a tough nut.

Then a fishmonger who was cousin to a baker who was husband to a sister of a town clerk's housekeeper had stronger news. "A Grand Inquiry's set. The Council will hear it in two days. Noon on Thursday." This was disbelieved, very strongly.

"So quickly?" and "The Council?" The questions were the essence of the commons' incredulity. Two days was swift even for Basel, but even more that the Town Council itself would hold the Inquiry for a low coach driver. Then a sergeant of the Night Watch arrived to say it was so and he had one answer to both questions.

"Caiaphas."

"He's here." Fritz the stable lout said it from the fire where he sat as an oracle. "He wouldn't take an invitation from Faulkner. He'll stay at the Inn while the coach goes to Bern, then he'll ride it back north on Friday morning."

"The Inquiry's not for Knipper," Daniel said, interpreting the oracle's riddles. "It's Caiaphas who demands it."

"Why does he?" and "Why did he come?" and other questions became a broad wave of discontent against the Magistrate of Strasbourg. There were some in the room who'd seen him in the Market Square and they fed the resentment with their descriptions of his harsh words and evil stare. The speculation ran wilder, the offense deeper. Then the rare sound of Nicolaus' voice asked through the smoke and sounds, "Who is Inquisitor?" And that caused silence.

I knew little about Inquisitors: Their selection and actions were shrouded. The Inquiry into the disappearance of Master Grimm of the Logic Chair was the only appointment in my five years in Basel. That man, a lawyer named Reichen, had since died.

I knew more concerning the power of the Inquisitor. Inquisition was an ancient right of the Town Council. They would place all their authority onto the person of the Inquisitor. He would have the prerogative to search, imprison, and torture summarily and was only limited by his short tenure. Reichen was given three days, then four more, later, once the reply from Leipzig was received. He reported to the Council in secret and no one but the Council and his clerk ever knew what he found. That was unusual. An Inquisition would normally be concluded in a public meeting of the Council.

"Who's Inquisitor? Well, what lawyers are there?" Daniel answered. "It will be one of them, but a low one. It's an Inquiry for a coach driver, that's all."

"It's an Inquiry for a magistrate," Nicolaus said. "That's who demanded it. Those were his first words to Uncle Faulkner. And I remember this Caiaphas. I've seen him before."

⁂

At home I told Grandmother what I'd heard. "What is the man Caiaphas like?" was her only question.

"He's like crows," I said, "and like wolves," and I went upstairs to my room and books.

4

The Oscillating Hourglass

Late enough in the evening that Grandmother was already in bed, and the only light was my desk candle shining, and the only sound was the scratching of my quill and rustling of my papers, a lantern came into my street and then a fist to my door. I thought it might be the Night Watch. The church bell finished eleven tolls as I opened the door to see a dim lantern held out and a dimmer Cousin Gottlieb behind it.

"Leonhard. I want you."

"To come?"

"Yes," he said, impatient. "To come."

It had become a chill evening but I didn't stop to find a coat. I only took my brown hat from the peg, and the key, and I left and locked the house.

"Where do you want me?" I asked.

"To the inn," he answered, and I followed and waited to hear why. The houses were more closed than when I'd walked home from the Boot and Thorn earlier, and it was back to there that we went. In the Barefoot Square, near enough the tavern door to be in its fiery glow, Cousin Gottlieb stopped and asked, "Did you bring paper?"

"No."

"That's a poor start. You'll need it."

"What would I write?" I asked.

"I'm questioning the innkeeper. You'll write it down."

"That's why you brought me?"

"Why else do you think?"

I'd thought nothing else, but not that, either. "I'll remember what you say and I'll write it when I get home. I've a good memory. Will that do?"

"It'll have to do. Now, where's the man?"

He might have been anywhere under that roof. I looked into the Common Room for him first. It was emptier and quieter than before and I heard familiar voices, but not his. "Not in there. Maybe in the kitchen or the stable or a cellar." Charon the cat listened.

"Find him, then. Why else do you think I brought you?"

I was wondering that somewhat more. But I went hunting and found him first shot and brought Cousin Gottlieb into the kitchen. The Common Room was lit by fire; the kitchen was consecrated to it. The hearth was the biggest in Basel, stretching the whole wall and all ancient stone. Four fires had space in it. All the pots and cauldrons were blackest, and the ironmongery of spits and braces and hooks that held them in the flames was blacker. Everything had been heated in such innumerable fires then cooled to bone by hours as immeasurable as the kettles that nothing was left but essence and hardness. And of everything Gustavus was the hardest, standing in the center pillar-like, Hephaestus in the pits of Olympia.

Cousin Gottlieb took a chair. Kitchen maids as tough and heated as the stews they were stirring ignored us. They were chopping meat and their cleavers flashed and the table shook with every blow. Cousin Gottlieb ignored them.

"What do you want, Master?" Gustavus asked in his voice of coals.

"I am Inquisitor," he answered like dust, and then I knew why he wanted his questions recorded. The council had chosen him to manage the Inquiry. I felt very sorry for him; and I felt sorry for Basel.

"What are your questions?" Gustavus bowed his head in respect. He knew the Inquisitor's power. And Gottlieb knew it, too.

"Who was Knipper?"

"He was a man." His answer wasn't frivolous but profound.

"What was his life?"

"To drive his coach."

"Why did he die?"

"Because his life ended."

Cousin Gottlieb preferred proper beginnings. He found these answers satisfying. "Was he family to you?"

"He was no kin."

"Was he to anyone?"

"Only he would know."

"Then we won't. And you employed him?"

"We were partners."

"And the other inns, as well?"

"The four inns. We had an arrangement."

"What are the four inns?"

"The Broken Shield in Strasbourg. The Fiery Arrow in Freiburg. The Roaring Lion in Bern. This."

"Who'll drive the coach now?"

"Someone else."

"Do you grieve that he's dead?" I doubted Gottlieb was asking after the innkeeper's well-being.

"No." And for the first time, Gustavus answered more than he was asked. "He was ill-tempered. I'll be glad for a less troublesome driver."

"Did you see him the evening when he came in from Bern?"

"I saw him."

"What did you see of him?"

"That he'd come."

"And who killed him, then? Was it Willi?"

"Ask him."

"He's in jail in Strasbourg. It was someone here in the inn who killed Knipper. This is where he was seen, and where the trunk was, and where he was put in the trunk. Whose trunk was it?"

"I don't know. I haven't seen the trunk."

"It's at the Watch barracks. Did it belong to one of the passengers?"

"Ask them."

"They're not here. Who carried the trunks to the rooms?"

"Willi did."

"And who carried them back to the coach in the morning?"

"Willi did."

"Was the trunk ever opened?"

"I don't know."

"To put him in it, it was," Gottlieb said. "Did it come on the coach? Was it from Basel instead? Was it anywhere besides the inn? Was Knipper anywhere besides the inn? Tell me everything you know!"

"I haven't seen the trunk. I know nothing of it."

"Would you, if you did see it?"

"I don't know."

"I haven't seen it, either, yet." Gottlieb fell silent and his silence lasted more than a minute. I waited patiently, and Gustavus, not patient or impatient, just stood. The cooks never stopped. The cleavers, lifted high, fell to the table and cut by their own weight. I didn't know what beast it had been, four-legged surely, and the women seemed to have no end to their hewing. "Who were the passengers in the coach when it left?"

"There were two, a man and a woman. The same that came."

"Where were they bound?"

"I didn't ask."

"Why do you know so little?"

"Because I'm no fool."

"It's knowing little that makes a man a fool."

"No, Master. Fools aren't made, they're born. And only a fool wants to know more than what's needed."

"There's more that I need to know. Go to the Barracks and look at the trunk, then tell me what you know of it. And learn something of it, and Knipper, and the passengers, and what passes under your roof, innkeeper. It begs imagining that you know so little."

There was no anger in what he said, or even suspicion. It was just a statement. Gustavus nodded. "Yes, Master."

"Magistrate Caiaphas is here?"

"He is staying here."

"Why has he come?"

"For his own reasons."

"Why for Knipper, and not for anything else for all these years? All the years Knipper drove, he never brought Caiaphas. It was Knipper not driving that brought him. There are reasons, his own, you say. I'd like to know them. Do you know them?"

Gustavus only said, "They are his."

"It would be worth an Inquiry to learn them," Gottlieb

answered. "Tell him I'll see to him tomorrow, and to have his reasons ready. Tell him the questions will be harder than last time we met. You know they will be, keeper, so tell him. And the boy who drove the coach from Strasbourg?"

"He'll be in Knipper's room, Master. His name is Abel."

"I'll see to him now."

I'd never seen Knipper's garret at the Boot and Thorn. In it, I still didn't see it. I saw a bed of planks with a straw pallet, and a floor of planks, and a shadow everywhere else, and a candle on a stump table. On the bed was Abel, sitting, not as hulking as Willi, but strong like any stable hand with yellow hair like straw and a block jaw and angry blue eyes like bruises, and he wasn't glad to be wakened. But Gottlieb had no regard for the man's sleep.

"I have questions," he said.

"I won't know your questions," Abel said. Caiaphas's speech had been jagged like broken ice, and Abel's was jagged like gravel.

"You'll know them. Are you from Strasbourg?"

"I know that and I am."

"Did you know Knipper?"

"I knew him."

"What's the inn in Strasbourg?"

"The Broken Shield."

"Who keeps it?"

"Dundrach's the keeper."

"Were you there when the coach came in? Did you unload it?"

"I unload the luggage and carry it."

"You took down the trunk?"

"I did, and was all I did, and set it by the coach wheel."

"Who opened it?"

"It was opened and Knipper was in it. It's no matter who opened it."

"Who opened it?"

"I didn't."

"Did Dundrach?"

"No."

"Whose trunk was it? Which passenger?"

"None of them opened it. It was none of theirs." Abel's shoulders were hunched and his head tilted like he was expecting a blow, but I saw that he might be ready to give one, as well. If he were to strike Gottlieb, as Inquisitor, it wouldn't go well for him. Gottlieb himself showed no anger, though not patience, either. But he leaned forward, closer toward Abel, held him in an unblinking gaze, and said, "Did Caiaphas open it?"

"What if he did?"

"Why him? Why was it a magistrate who opened an unclaimed trunk? It should have been the innkeeper."

"I'm not saying he did."

"You've been told not to. By whom?"

"I didn't say anything!"

"Dundrach? Or Caiaphas himself then. What did he tell you?"

"Old Vulture? Nothing. Nothing to me."

"Why was the driver from Basel arrested?"

"For bringing a corpse into the city."

"Who ordered that arrest?"

"Old Vulture, and ask him why."

In the bare candlelight, Gottlieb seemed less and drier than ever; but dead wood was harder than green. He stared at the sullen lout for minutes, longer than he'd been silent with Gustavus. Abel seemed to sense there was danger to himself.

"Vulture," Gottlieb said. "Magistrate Caiaphas, you mean."

"Yes, that's him."

"You'll be away in the morning, to Bern."

"I'm to Bern, then back, then to Strasbourg, and I'll never be here again, if they whip me I'll still never be here again."

"You'll have whipping. The Masters you have are easily displeased. You won't have Caiaphas on your trip to Bern, though. He'll stay for the Inquiry."

"Ask him your questions. I won't answer any."

"Tomorrow I'll ask him."

❧

We traced our path backward to the kitchen, which was empty of life now but for its fires. Gottlieb stopped there to think. "Is Daniel still here?"

"I heard his voice when we came in."

"I want him next."

I followed up the corridor to the Common Room. Daniel's voice cut through the room, as it always did. A near hour had passed from Gottlieb's knock on my door. It was already late enough that the candles were yawning. The fire was intense but withdrawn into its hearth. I felt Cousin Gottlieb was uneasy beneath the weight of the beams.

Dice were rolled from a cup onto a table, and that sound turned my eyes toward Daniel, still there, and Nicolaus, and I saw them for the second time that evening. They hadn't moved but most other of the men had left. Daniel looked up to see Gottlieb, and me with him, and smiled his most mischievous smile; he'd been waiting.

"Leonhard," he said. "What's this I see? Are you being tainted? Beware, beware!"

Gottlieb answered for me. "You'll beware."

"If you don't corrupt me," I answered Daniel myself, "nobody can."

"That's a challenge, then. But what's the purpose of this? I'm placid and smug, and I've no use for an interruption."

"You'll make use," Gottlieb said. "I'll want answers from you."

"You? You! Brutus has made you his Inquisitor, and you'll use the weight of that to bother me? Isn't there a better use for Olympian authority?"

"The Council appointed me."

"At his wink and nod. So, cousin, what will you pretend you need to know from me?"

"It's an odd chance that the driver dies after he drives you."

"Inference and induction, and that's not Logic. Shouldn't you know that?" There was an energy in Daniel's voice that meant more than just wheedling and sparring. "Beside, you'd have reason to murder the driver who brought me home. I wouldn't."

"I would have done it then before he brought you, not after; and after he had I'd have every reason to keep him alive to take you back away."

I had heard plenty of Gottlieb's speech, in the lecture hall and in the parlor, and I heard a note I hadn't before. But Daniel knew it, and he approved.

"That's clever, cousin. I like an answer with wit. There was a time when you were known more for it."

"There aren't many who know it."

Daniel nodded to that. "It's a street of dunces we walk." He leaned back and put space between them. "But it's time, Cousin. What are you after?"

Gottlieb leaned forward and closed the space. "Why did you come back to Basel?"

"It's my family here." He answered it quickly, with a shrug, "That's why you left. I want to know why you came back."

"And that's what Brutus wants," Daniel said. "To know why I've returned, and he'll use the Inquisition to find out."

"That's not an answer to my question."

"It's an answer to mine. If I don't answer yours, will you torture me?" He laughed. "Brutus wouldn't let that."

"You fully deserve it."

"We shouldn't any of us get what we deserve, should we? What would you get, Cousin? Not a Chair, I think." It was very difficult to tell how these words were spoken; but it seemed something like a horse race, with the riders each straining to pull ahead of the other. With this last word, though, the race ended.

Gottlieb only said, "Who murdered the coachman Knipper?"

"Is that how you'll do your inquisition?" Daniel said, and now with contempt. "What's the logic in asking bald questions? If I knew, wouldn't I have said already? That doesn't need an Inquisitor."

"Unless you knew and wouldn't say."

"Then I'd have a reason to not say it, and I wouldn't answer you. Two premises, opposite, that both lead to the same end, and so it might be either." He rolled his dice. "That's logic. Are you learning from him, Leonhard? Is that why you're here?"

"I'm just to hold the red hot irons for him," I said.

"He'd do it," Daniel said to me. "He would but for Brutus telling him not to."

"You'd rather have torture than be humble and answer me," Gottlieb said. "And you still haven't. Do you know who killed him?"

"Sure I do."

The dribble of light from the open doorway was stopped as Gustavus entered. He took a place behind the counter and nodded to the woman there to be finished. She seemed glad to be. Though the room was near empty, there were still hundreds of eyes on us: all the tankards on all the shelves, high and low, and all were staring directly at us. If we'd moved, their gaze would have followed.

"Who killed him, then?" Gottlieb said.

"Huldrych."

"Daniel!" I said. "Don't mock."

"Why not? If that old artifact is cleared out of the Physics Chair, someone better could have it. I say it was Huldrych that did Knipper in."

"You'd accuse him to have him executed?"

"You think I'd kill to get a Chair?" Daniel said. "Maybe I would. I wouldn't be the first in the family to do it."

"What do you mean?"

"Or the second, either. What bargain did you make for yours?"

"I wouldn't bargain," Gottlieb said.

"You didn't win it by chance."

"Prove that I didn't."

"Deny that you didn't." Daniel leaned into the sudden silence. "Deny it? You don't."

But Gottlieb only said, "I never bargained."

"What happened to the missing Logic Chair? What was his name? Grimm. And now you have his Chair. That was the last Inquiry, wasn't it, Cousin?"

"Which Chair are you trying for now, Cousin?" Gottlieb replied.

"Perhaps Logic again."

"It's taken."

"The lord giveth," Daniel said, "and the lord taketh away."

"Don't use scripture for malice," I said, "or the Lord's name."

"Not that Lord," he said, glancing up. It was hard to imagine heaven in any direction from that room. "I mean the one here who has a real say over the Chairs."

Gottlieb was done with Daniel's bitter stream. "Was the trunk on the coach from Bern?"

"I don't count luggage."

"Where did it come from?"

"I don't ask it questions, either!"

"Did you see it anywhere?"

"I haven't seen it at all."

"What did you see of Knipper?"

"I was too taken with nostalgia at the sight of my dear home to notice coach drivers."

"Why is there an Inquisitor?" They were Nicolaus's first words I'd heard that evening, and they were an ox to throw a cart out of its ruts. Gottlieb and Daniel both shot their heads around to look at him.

"Because the Magistrate of Strasbourg demands it," Daniel said. "And because Brutus finds it useful."

"No," Nicolaus said. "Why is there an Inquisitor?"

I understood his meaning. "Because the world has unanswered questions," I said.

"And why's that?"

"So that we'll answer them."

"Are you an Inquisitor, Leonhard?" Nicolaus asked.

"That kind, I'll always be," I said.

"Choose fit questions, then." Whatever Nicolaus's purpose had been, he was done with it. Daniel waved away those airy thoughts with his own advice to Gottlieb.

"I'll tell you where to look, if you're genuine in solving this," he said. "There's one man who has any answers."

"Who's that?"

"You know."

"You think your father is the murderer?" Gottlieb said.

"You think he crushed a skull with his books and papers? Knipper was never in the house, and your father never left it. None of us did. It's our family who're the only ones I know couldn't have killed him."

"But there's no one outside our family that's scheming enough," Daniel said. "I'll wager you, Cousin, that I solve this before you do."

"You'll neither be first." Nicolaus stood, and looked at me. I stood to follow his lead. "Or even first to bed." And that ended their joust. But Daniel held back in the hall, and Gustavus was there with him as we left, and Nicolaus stayed also, keeping watch on his brother.

I would often be awake late reading, and it never tired me. But standing in the Barefoot Square, at only about midnight, I was yawning and nodding. "I'll want you tomorrow," Cousin Gottlieb said.

"When will you?"

"Come to my door at noon. Have what you've heard written by then for me."

"Yes, sir," I said. "I'll have it all."

"Just the first. The innkeeper and the driver. Not the last."

I stumbled home. Night in Basel was the dwelling of soft sounds and faint smells, and gentle brushings in the dark, all unseen. I unlocked my own door and saw a light in the kitchen. My grandmother was at the table in her nightdress.

"I'm back," I said.

"I saw your bedroom open and empty."

"Cousin Gottlieb came for me. He's Inquisitor and he has me for his clerk."

This was a stark statement of news that was important to

both our home and our city. Grandmother breathed a sigh. "Then you'll be part of the Inquiry."

"I'll only be secretary. I have to write what I heard tonight."

"What did you hear, Leonhard?"

"I've heard about Knipper and his driving, and I've seen his room in the Boot and Thorn, and I've heard that the last anyone saw of him was at the inn that evening unloading the coach."

"That was after he came to Master Johann's kitchen?"

"No, Grandmother. The last he was seen at the inn was before that."

"You saw him, Leonhard. You told me you had. And you told me also that a black trunk was on the floor there, which is the trunk he was brought back in."

"I told you truthfully," I said.

"Tell Master Gottlieb."

"Then Master Johann's family would be accused."

"Master Gottlieb is part of that family. He'll use wisdom in it."

"It wasn't any of them."

"It's Master Gottlieb's task to find who did."

"It won't be him or Daniel who's first to solve it," I said. "Nicolaus told them that. And that's not Master Gottlieb's true task. His questions were for something else. I don't know what."

And then I went upstairs and started writing as Gottlieb had told me to do. I had a good memory, though I was very tired of the day.

I'd wanted to wake early on Wednesday but my bed was very comfortable. It was nearly sunrise before I pulled myself from my covers. I endured my grandmother's disapprobation and hurried to get her water, and I made sure to get it from the Barefoot Square. The coach was there in the morning light, but no light shone on glowering Abel already in the box, and Fritz from the inn was pushing luggage onto the rack. None of the bags and trunks was larger than a hound.

Nothing withstood Abel's whip and the thunder of those hooves; yet he'd have to return. Less than nothing could withstand the immutable rhythm of those roads from Basel south and north. Knipper was everlasting but finally died. Yet even death wouldn't stop the ancient law that the coach would leave for Bern on Wednesday and then come back, and that the coach would leave for Freiburg and Strasbourg on Friday and then come back. The coach was a pendulum, hung from history and swung unending through its path. Even the Magistrates of two cities only planned their Inquiry within pendulum swings.

Like Basel, Strasbourg was also a University city. Yet as Master Desiderius said, its University was much less prestigious. Not always, though: The school was planted with Martin Luther himself as one of its founders when he took refuge there. The city also joined the Reformation and became one of its centers, like Basel. It had the first printing presses in France, sent by Gutenberg. And it had its own great reformer, Martin Bucer, as great a man as Basel's Oecolampadius. It was a rival to Basel and a mirror.

But forty years ago the city, having for centuries been a free city, as Basel still was, was annexed by Louis the Fourteenth, and Strassburg became Strasbourg. The Protestants weren't persecuted and exiled as the Huguenots had been, but the Cathedral was given back to the Pope and now the city was known as Catholic. The University was carefully un-reformed and lost what luster it still had. It was certainly an advance for Desiderius when he left Strasbourg for Basel. And though the annexation was military and by force, it was the great

Reformed University, unlikely as it seemed then, that pushed and convinced the city into giving up its independence. Certainly in Basel, only the University would have the prestige and force to bring about such a transition.

Though Wars of Religion had ended, the Wars of Philosophy now raged, less violent and more literate. Strasbourg was Cartesian, while Basel was not. Strasbourg was also a Rhine city, but not on the Rhine. It was a mile from the bank on a small tributary river. And if a man in Strasbourg wished to cross the Rhine by carriage, with his horses' hooves on a dry road, he would need to come the eighty miles to Basel.

For the greatest difference was that Strasbourg had no Rhine bridge.

I was still thinking of pendulums as I came to Mistress Dorothea's kitchen. I watched her broom swing, and a hanging pot sway, and a clock hand swirl, and a ripple in the washbowl swim, and the sunlight through the window walk; all of them in motion repeating. I thought about how words went out and echoes came back, how word went out and consequence came back. How ideas went out and change came back, how something unknown could go out, and a death come back.

Wondering how anyone could stay unmoving in that storm, I came to the front sitting room to take wood to its fireplace. I found Daniel there musing; and his reverie was also oscillatory. He was standing and in his hands was a small table. He gripped it firmly, and the table flew up, and around, and down, like a bird wheeling and circling. Some odd mechanism was on the table but not falling off as the table flew. He saw me and cried, "Leonhard! You'll drown!"

"In what?" I said and dropped my wood on the hearth.

"In the waves and wind!" He leaned to one side and to the

other and his table rode high and low, a ship in a storm. "It's a rare tempest about you here and you're walking on water."

"Peace, then, Daniel," I said, "and be still. What sea are you in?"

"A sea of deception. Look what I have." He set the table to safe harbor on the calm floor. It was an hourglass tied to it, with twine from the table legs knotted to the glass's odd base. "See the sand? It's about to run out. Now look." From another, un-wavetossed table, he held another hourglass. "Identical. They both have kept the same time, one through the storm and one landlocked." The last grains of sand did run through each at the same moment. I looked at the intricate base twined to the table. It was gimbaled and pivoted, and as I watched he tilted the table one way and another; the glass stayed upright. "See it? An hourglass that measures time evenly, even as a ship pitches. I had a blower in Padua make the glass for me, and a tinker make the frame to my design."

It was an anti-pendulum, still while all else was moving. "Why did you make it?"

He was very intent on it. "For the Paris Competition." He made an effort, for a moment, to seem as if it was trivial. But then he saw my grin, and no veil could have covered the bright light in his eyes and his own broad smile. "The problem this year," he said, with passion, "is to tell how fast a ship moves against the water." I knew this fervor in him. The only time that he was completely sincere and truthful was when he was in its grip, and it only sprung from his fascination with machines and their Mathematics: Daniel rendered childlike! "The captain throws out a log on a rope and measures how many knots on the rope the ship passes in a minute. But how can they measure the time? A time glass only keeps steady time if the ship is steady."

"Until now," I said.

"Yes, until now! Now a captain can have a glass that keeps steady in an unsteady world. Last winter I sent the plans to the Paris Academy. And a working model!"

"What was their response?"

He collapsed. Childish joy was brittle. "No response. I haven't heard from them. The judging is complete, though. I'll hear one way or another, and I know which way it will be."

"Where would they have sent their letter?"

"Here."

"Have you received any mail here?"

"Not a scrap."

"None was waiting, either?"

"Not any." Then the old Daniel returned, bright, shrewd, confiding. "And he wouldn't, I know it. Not even him."

"Your father, you mean?"

"Even he wouldn't hold mail from me. It would come out soon enough, then he'd be in a real scandal."

"Could there be any reason he would?" I asked.

"His strongest reasons are jealousy and spite. He couldn't stand that I've won! He'd be in delirium."

"But you say he'd never hold mail from you. And the winner of the Paris Competition is no secret. How will you hear who won? It would be in newspapers. There'd be more letters, too, from Societies."

"I know it'll come," he said. "I want to hold that letter in my hand!"

"What will you do with it?"

He went cold, as cold as ice. "I'll wave it under his nose, till he faints from the smell of it."

An hour later, back at home and done with all the morning, I pictured the hourglass. To a man on the deck of a ship, it would seem it was the glass that was whirling and twisting; and to the glass, the man would be. And which would be right? Was there any true level to measure against? Or was every man the only measure of his own life? Everything would be shaken, and then maybe it would be plain what was fast and what was loose. I could hear a storm about me, with wind and rain, and saw its clouds and felt its cold and penetrating wet, even if the streets of Basel were sun-filled and pleasant. I wasn't sure what was an anchor.

My grandmother gave me a warning as I left the house in proper black and white. "You aren't too wise, Leonhard, as you might think, and you might be too clever."

"I know that," I said. "I don't think I'm wise at all, and everyone's more clever."

⁂

As appointed, I awaited and met Cousin Gottlieb at his own front door at the hour of twelve. I'd been unable the previous night to present myself appropriately as the Inquisitor's Assistant. Now, even properly black and white and with paper and ink, I still did not meet Cousin Gottlieb's expectations.

He frowned at me from his door. "Is that all you have?" he asked. I knew what he meant.

"It is my only."

He returned to his closet and then returned to me, and in his hand was an item I viewed with both awe and anxiety.

"Put this on," he said.

I put my hand on my own hat. As it had always been, it was plain black with a wide round brim, turned up on either side, and projecting from my head front and back, as was proper for a student. I took it off. From Cousin Gottlieb's hand, I received, and donned, a slightly worn but still unimpeachable tricorne. It sat on my wig emanating maturity, respectability, wisdom, and significance. I could feel it. My fellow students would laugh if they saw me, but nervously. There were consequences for mocking a gentleman.

"I will examine the trunk first," Gottlieb said, though he was still examining me, weighing whether I could hold up my hat. My head had never had such a weight, and I hoped my brain was dense enough for the task. "It is at the Watch Barracks."

So, to the Watch Barracks we went. This military hub of the city was on Martinsgasse, directly behind the Town Hall. It was once nearly a small castle, but years of peace had softened its castellation to mere heaviness. Narrow windows had been widened, wide towers lowered. The last real threat, two decades past, had been from France. Since then sharp edges had rusted and dulled some, but were still at hand and could be re-sharpened at need. The world wasn't yet peaceful.

It was Simeon who took us past a mess hall, a sleeping hall, an armory of muskets and axes, a cell with thick bars, and a line of rusted suits of plate armor on stands and tired of standing, to a storeroom lit by high, tiny windows only a flying mouse could have got through. But there was enough light through them to see the black trunk, dull, heavy, and empty of both life and death, in the center of the floor.

I'd seen the trunk twice before, in Master Johann's kitchen and in the Market Square, and both had been with Knipper woeful. Now it was without him, dusty, old, and black, and maybe as his coffin better than the box he'd had for burial. I tried to remember it on Mistress Dorothea's stone floor; I thought it had been dusty there, also. Dust to dust. Gottlieb seemed turned to dust himself, staring at it. He took in a deep breath and it was a long time before he let it out.

"Open it," he finally said. I knelt to do that, putting my black breech knee onto the plank floor, and the same dust. I had a tremor of nervousness as I put my hand to the latch, and I must have looked the same as the gendarme when he'd opened it. But it was empty. I lifted the lid and laid it back to the floor, and stayed bowing and close while Gottlieb inspected from above. Its open throat had little to say. There was no sign on the wood, either the strong frame or the smooth planed sides, of its last contents. But it wasn't purely plain. "Is there a marking in it? In the back corner, on the left. At the bottom." I'd already noticed there was. I looked closer. An emblem was branded into the wood.

"It is a spiral," I said.

Gottlieb was displeased. "What type?" he said bluntly and as though he knew what the answer would be.

"Logarithmic."

"That complicates greatly."

I considered Logarithmic spirals superior to Archimedean, and I knew Gottlieb also must, so it must have been not the spiral itself that irritated him, but its implication. I put my finger on it and something rubbed off, not quite hard, and crumbly. I rolled a crumb of it over my thumb. Gottlieb was no longer watching me. He hadn't been, much, since he'd seen the trunk. But at this point he was not at all.

A boot had stepped into the room and onto his thoughts; the gendarme of Strasbourg had arrived.

"I've been sent for you" were his first words. "Come immediately."

Gottlieb only looked up at him from the trunk. Perhaps he truly had to pause and think what he would say, but certainly the hesitation was an affront to the soldier. Finally he said, "You were sent by your Magistrate Caiaphas?"

"Yes, of course!"

"What is your name?" Gottlieb had clasped his hands together behind his back, but made no other move.

"I am Foucault."

Gottlieb nodded. "I have questions for Caiaphas. Take me to him."

This presented Gendarme Foucault with a difficulty: To obey his own Master, he needed also to obey Gottlieb. When he finally managed a reply, it was simply, "You must come at once."

But Gottlieb had him off balance. "Who opened this trunk in Strasbourg?"

"Magistrate Caiaphas did," he said, before he thought to refuse.

"Caiaphas himself! Even the driver was afraid to admit that. Why did he open it? And why doesn't he want that known?"

This was far beyond Foucault's ability. He was a picture of confusion. "You must come!" he said at last. "At once!"

"Yes, take me to him," Gottlieb said, and I only had time to close the trunk and run after them.

⁂

Many places in Basel were suitable for a Magistrate: the Town Hall; the wealthy homes of the great merchants, the grand Councilors, and the Deans and leading Chairs of the University; even the highest churches had very adequate guest quarters. Of course, no place in Basel was sumptuous. Instead, they were honorable and worthy. But the Boot and Thorn was not any of these. Caiaphas had chosen to be a protestant against Reformed Basel by exiling his person to a private room in an inn. At least Gustavus had done him the honor of not requiring him to share it with other travelers.

As we had been the night before, we were taken to somewhere within the pile of the inn that surely couldn't have existed in real geometry. In and up and in more, all the time turning corners, I felt we must be in the middle of the Barefoot Square if all the distances and angles had been measured. But we were at a door in a narrow hall that had no other doors.

Foucault knocked on that door. "Your guard, Lord Caiaphas. I have brought the man."

I thought the barracks where we were apprehended must have been Gethsemane. Foucault might have been better named Malchus. I determined myself not to deny that I knew Gottlieb.

"Then bring him in," Caiaphas said.

Foucault opened the door as if it had been to an imperial chamber. He bowed and stood aside for Gottlieb to enter. The room was no better than any inn had in German or French lands. It was small with bare floor and walls; this had one window. Outside the window was a courtyard which must have been internal to the inn. I'd never seen it.

The only furnishings in the room were a plain chair and barrel table, and the huge bed. The bed was the reason for the room, and on Gustavus's profitable nights it would hold three or four or five paying sleepers. It filled the space as law filled a courtroom. With Caiaphas present, in his wig and robe, the chamber became a tribunal.

"You are Gottlieb?" he asked.

"You are Caiaphas?" he was answered.

"You know that I am!"

"I do, and you know that I am, though it's been twenty years since I saw you. I want to know why you have come to Basel."

I anticipated the Magistrate bursting. He seemed to live in a state of anger. "I have come to require an Inquiry of you."

"I am the Inquiry," Gottlieb said. "You have some reason for wanting it, and it wants to know why. Why did you open the trunk?"

"Who told you that I did?" Caiaphas said, and Foucault answered by gasping.

Gottlieb pressed in. "Did you know what would be in it?"

"Your authority doesn't run here," he answered. "I am not answering questions."

"I have authority in all of Basel."

"You are not in Basel. When I am in this room it is Strasbourg."

I looked out the window again. The roofs had a different shape than those in Basel, and the houses were darker colors and lower. It might have been Strasbourg.

"Then I will withdraw," Gottlieb said. "The Inquisitor is required to stay within Basel." He stepped back across the threshold into his own city, and through the doorway faced the Magistrate in his. "A corpse was sent to Strasbourg and I have been instructed to learn why. To do so, I must know the reason you have come here."

Caiaphas stood, angered beyond his control. "My reasons have nothing to do with your Inquiry!"

"Basel, not you, appointed me. I am Inquisitor and I will ask my own questions. Why did you come? Why did you open the trunk? What is important enough to bring you here? I will have those answers." Then his voice changed, less sharp but more pointed. "Twenty years ago we faced each other and you had the better of it."

"Yet now you have what you wanted," Caiaphas said, suddenly less angry.

"That has nothing to do with you."

"What if it does?"

Gottlieb asked, slowly, "Is that why you've come?"

Caiaphas said, slowly, "It is one of my reasons."

"The Inquisitor can only serve his own city. Not anyone else."

"A servant doesn't choose his Master!"

"The Inquisitor has only one Master, which is the Town Council of Basel." He turned from the threshold border between cities and disappeared from our sight.

His repatriation had been too sudden, and I was still in the room. I realized I'd been abandoned, or I had abandoned my superior by not moving quickly with him, and I jumped to follow. But the border closed.

"Stop him," Caiaphas said, and the gendarme blocked my way. I turned back.

"Yes, sir?"

"What are you writing?"

"I'm Master Gottlieb's clerk," I said. "I'm instructed to write his inquiries."

"Where have I seen you before?"

"Yesterday evening, sir. You sent me to fetch a magistrate."

"That was *you*?"

I'd been in brown. Now I was in black and white. It was as if a stone had become bread; neither could be trusted afterward. "Yes, sir."

"What is your position?"

"I'm a student, sir."

"In what?"

"Mathematics."

The bread had become something else, I couldn't tell what.

"I see. What is your name?"

"Leonhard, sir."

I might have hoped that his questioning was only his habit and not for a reason. But my answer and my name were significant to him. "You are the one?"

"Sir?"

"You ordered the stablehand to put the trunk on the coach."

"Not me, sir—"

"I am now aware of you, Master Leonhard." He nodded to Gendarme Foucault. "Release him."

So I did go. But I didn't feel that I'd been released.

◈

I made my labyrinthine way to the light of the front door. Gottlieb was there in silhouette. "What took you?" he asked me.

I'd only been a few words behind him in leaving the room, and I'd hurried to catch up, so I didn't know how I could have more than seconds later reaching the Common Room. But it seemed that he'd been waiting a longer time. "Magistrate Caiaphas held me back."

"Oh, he did?"

We came out into the sun of the Barefoot Square. The face of the Barefoot Church was whiter than paper. "He asked what I was writing in my notes."

"And anything else?"

"What I was studying, and then who I was."

"Now he knows who you are."

"He had heard my name. What did you mean, that you'd met him twenty years ago?"

"On our return to Basel. We stopped in Strasbourg. How old are you, Leonhard?"

"Eighteen," I answered.

"I was eighteen then."

"You said he had the better of your meeting."

"Just as he's had the better of his meeting with you. That was how it started."

"And he never answered any questions of yours."

"He only wanted to see that I was who he thought, and I the same." Then, without a pause, he said, "Next we will question Master Huldrych."

"Daniel wasn't genuine when he accused Master Huldrych. He was only mocking."

"He might not have been."

◈

Master Huldrych did not have a housekeeper, and so his house was not kept. At other Masters' houses, the students knocked and waited to be admitted. Students quickly learned to enter the house of Physics on their own. That was not for Master Gottlieb, however; we knocked, and with all the authority of the City of Basel. Repeated knockings and minutes were required until the Chair opened the door.

He tried to make sense of what he saw. First of me. "It isn't class, is it? It isn't Monday. I know it isn't. Or Thursday. No." Then of Cousin Gottlieb. "Gottlieb? A meeting of the faculty? But I don't remember that one was scheduled. No." Then of my hat. "Another Black Death? But no, that was you, Gottlieb, when Jacob died." And then he nodded. "Another trunk, then?"

"No, no!" Cousin Gottlieb answered, suddenly very, very annoyed at Huldrych's wandering. "I am here to inquire."

"Oh? Inquire? About what?"

"Knipper."

"Oh! Oh? Oh. " He said each as its own full meaning. "Knipper?"

"Knipper."

"You're the Inquisitor, then, Gottlieb?"

"I am."

"That's an odd turn." Huldrych stepped aside to allow us in. "What questions?" We passed with him through the tiny entry and into his lecture room. I'd sat there many times, but now it was upside down as Cousin Gottlieb stood while Huldrych sat. At least I was taking notes as I always did there. The room had a small window to the front. Windows in Basel were not meant to be seen through, only to allow in light, and that to a people who preferred dimness. There was another small window in the back, which must have looked out onto the river. I'd never seen it unshuttered.

Gottlieb continued to stare for a moment, and longer. Then he calmly, and even gently, asked, "Why was Knipper in Jacob's trunk?"

"It's odd if he was," Huldrych said, not any surprised, though I was. "But was he?"

"I saw it. Why was Knipper in it?"

"He must have been, if you say he was. But why? That's harder to say." Huldrych looked slowly and mournfully to the floor. "And he can't say, can he? He's dead. I'd heard that. In the trunk? I don't know why he'd be there."

"How'd the trunk come to the Boot and Thorn?"

"To the Inn? It was there? Then it wouldn't be here, would it? It wouldn't. But I'm sure it is. I'll look at where it is, or where it isn't, *if* it isn't." He stood, as vague under his robe as the thoughts in his head. He moved, as ponderous as those thoughts. We went with him and he climbed the stairs to his laboratory.

I'd seen into this room a few times, looking for the Master when students were waiting for him, though I'd learned soon enough he was never in it. Only dust was. The many tables and their very many objects were coated with dust as a chicken with feathers, so that shapes were clear but softened and colors muffled. Master Huldrych looked about as if he'd never seen the room before.

"Who moved it?" Gottlieb asked and the dust rose just at the abruptness.

"I put it here," Huldrych answered. That seemed to be the same as saying it wouldn't move ever again.

"When, sir?" I asked. It wasn't my part to ask questions, but I was quite amazed at the thought of any motion in that space.

"When I first had it."

That was all I had the temerity to ask. But Gottlieb didn't scowl. He pushed me on. "Ask him more," he said to me, and I was thrust, in that moment, into the place of Inquisitor myself, and over my own Physics Master.

"When did you first have it?" I asked. But this was not the question I had been meant to ask.

"I know that already," Gottlieb said. "Ask a better question."

The day was Wednesday and in the morning, but I felt Saturday afternoon anxiety, as if Master Johann himself was testing me. I grasped for the better question, and Huldrych waited patiently for it. "Where did you put it in here, sir?"

"Well, just here, of course." And he pointed. Of course we all turned to see where, including Huldrych himself, and the motion of his arm and our quick spin raised a strange new cloud of the omnipresent dust; and I was reminded of the cloud that followed Knipper on his last drive into the city. Light from the window opaqued the haze and all we saw for the moment was a solid block of golden, glowing air. Then it faded to translucent, and to transparent, and we were staring at a glow and a wall and floor, lit by the same light that had filled the dust, released. It was the far wall from the door. The floor against it was occupied by blank space, between a table on one side and a cabinet on the other. The trunk could well have sat there, as the emptiness was just the size of it, but the space was so heavily coated with the ever-dust that nothing could have been there for a very long time. "It was there," Huldrych said. "I quite remember putting it."

"Was that long ago?"

"It must have been, I think."

I'd already put myself forward into Gottlieb's role. Now I tried an even bolder request. "May I go look?"

"Go?" Huldrych said. "Of course. Why shouldn't you?"

That no one ever before had seemed a possible reason, at least no one in at least a half inch, with time measured in dust. But I put my foot deliberately forward and then again, and walked as slowly across the floor as if it were slick, thin ice. Clouds rose against me, disturbed from their sleep, and I was blinded. I paused and moved again, and finally I came close to where the trunk wasn't. I stopped.

Years at least had passed since anything had held that place. I very slowly leaned down and in the dust I saw a line where the trunk's edge had been. And even very faintly, I could perhaps see the press of feet placed wide in the brown and gold dust, and more faintly yet a shade of gray dust in those places. I moved my own feet back to the door. "It was there," I said. "But it's been moved long ago."

"How long?" Gottlieb asked, of me, and Huldrych, and the dust. Huldrych answered.

"I don't remember anyone coming for it. Not after you did." Then he coughed. The dust was choking him.

"What was in it?" I asked.

"Just what's always been in it," Huldrych said, struggling to breathe. "You remember, don't you?" he asked Gottlieb. He coughed again, more violently. "It's the—"

"I know what was in it. I want to know when it was taken. You should have been watching it, Huldrych." That Master couldn't answer, besides that it seemed he didn't know the answer, because he was choking and gasping. I'd been fearful of the dust and held my sleeve over my mouth. Gottlieb had stepped back from the cloud.

I took Master Huldrych's hand and led him back from

the doorway. "But who'd want it?" he asked, finally, when he could.

Gottlieb shook his head. "That's all. We're finished." We would have left Huldrych there, regaining his breath, and the hallway gray and clouded, but he still seemed weakened. I stood with him a moment and Gottlieb waited.

In that moment the air cleared. "I'm right now, Leonhard," Huldrych said.

In the street, I didn't know where we would go and I waited to be told our destination. I still had plenty of paper and ink. "Who is next?"

Gottlieb only stared at the wall opposite and the many figures on it. "Next? I don't know who will be next." He was still contemplating the wall. "There is no coach driver in the Dance."

"There's a peddler."

"That's closest. He goes town to town and lives in none. And there," he pointed, "is an innkeeper, and there a laborer, and there an Academic, and there a gentleman. And there a Magistrate, or what they had of them in those times. The Black Death took them all."

"What did Master Huldrych mean about the Black Death?"

"Something he shouldn't have remembered. There is no one else for us to question," he said, in answer to my first question. He'd meant it completely: We were finished. I wondered myself, looking at the wall, which of the characters I might be.

"Master Gottlieb?" I said. "What was in the trunk? Where did it come from?"

He might have dismissed me and my audacity, and I could see that his gaze wasn't on anything near, especially on me.

But he did focus back and said, "It is no coincidence that it should appear just as my cousins have returned from Italy."

"But . . . why was Knipper put in it?"

"That must not be a coincidence, either." And that was a dismissal and his plain answer to me that he would not answer me. I wasn't finished trying.

"There weren't many replies to your questions. Did you learn anything from them?"

"Not from the questions. From the trunk. Now hand me your papers and go. The Inquiry is tomorrow and you'll appear with me."

"Is there anything I need to do?"

"It's already done." And I think he meant more than just the notes that I'd given him. But I still tried once more.

"Can you tell me, sir, why you returned back from Italy yourself?"

His answer surprised me, not least that he even answered, or answered plainly. He gave me a curious look that reminded me of the one wink he'd given Daniel the night before. "For a Chair in Basel, of course."

5

The Barefoot Church

In black and white I wandered the streets. Others did, also. In the Market Square, beneath the Town Hall's festal brick, the stalls were very crowded. Farmers sold their vegetables, grains, and rustic wares. Goliath was there, with a grindstone, sharpening customers' cutlery. Near him, David was selling wool and slings, keeping count of his business with smooth stones. Demetrius sold his silver, Paul his tents and Lydia her purples, though Basel had no imperials to want them. There was a commotion as someone upset some tables of moneychangers, but I walked on.

I came to the Barefoot Square. Lithicus was on his scaffold, chiseling, and I watched him awhile and thought of spirals. Then I stepped over a white threshold into the Barefoot Church and sat on my customary bench.

The Church of Bare Feet was the oldest church in Basel. It wasn't the first established, but it had been the most sturdy.

The Black Death had come to Basel nearly four centuries

ago. It had first come to Italy and spread like the ripples on a pond, always moving, always outward. In a year it reached to Basel. Once it did, nothing could stand against it. Death danced in Basel.

The citizens of the city were, of course, greatly confused, and terribly frightened. Soon an accusation was made: the Jews, who lived in Small Basel, were dying at a lesser rate. That was unfortunate for them. It was taken as proof of their guilt. They were assumed to be poisoning the wells and causing the epidemic.

On a day in January, with the sickness at its height, and despite many pleas on their behalf by the town leaders, the general population, incited by the trade and craft guilds, gathered the Jews together and rowed them to a wood barn on a small island in the Rhine. The barn was burned and the six hundred souls in it. The victims were left unburied, their cemetery destroyed and their synagogue turned into a church. Their 140 children were not included in the flames, and were raised as Christians. Basel was not alone in this, at least. Many cities in Europe reached the same conclusions. In Strasbourg, the next month, two thousand Jews were killed. Of the Christians in Basel, it was the Bare Foot Friars and their church that strove hardest to prevent the massacre. Their defiance of the popular will placed them in great danger themselves.

But they'd withstood the anger. They had a deep foundation in their faith.

Eight years later an earthquake shook Basel. All the accounts spoke of terrible devastation, and greater in Basel than any other city, though it was felt from London to Berlin to Rome. It was a great woe, and so soon after the plague. Houses were broken to rubble, the Walls were damaged, and every church in the city fell. All but one. The Barefoot Church had a deep foundation. Besides, it was held from above.

This Barefoot Church stood then, and stood now, like Daniel's hourglass. I walked back to the door to look out on the Barefoot Square, and it surely was pitching and rolling like a sea, and the people in the Square oblivious to their motion. I took a step out and felt the momentary dislocation, as stepping from a dock to a boat. Then all seemed still and normal. But I knew it wasn't; the Square was still spinning, and I was just spinning with it. If somehow the church was to be found one morning in a different part of the city, I would be sure that Basel had moved, not the church. As I stared at its solid, still, white walls, I felt again the movement beneath my feet.

I had a book in my pocket. I was surprised to find it there, and then I remembered: It was Boccaccio, the volume I'd borrowed from Master Desiderius, put there the last time I'd worn my coat. Boccaccio wrote in Italy in the time of the plague:

> How many valiant men, how many fair ladies, breakfasted with their kinfolk and the same night supped with their ancestors in the next world! The condition of the people was pitiable to behold. They sickened by the thousands daily, and died unattended and without help. Many died in the open street, others dying in their houses, made known by the stench of their rotting bodies. Consecrated churchyards did not suffice for the burial of the vast multitude of bodies, which were heaped by the hundreds in vast trenches, like goods in a ship's hold and covered with a little earth.

The plague has returned many times since the first terrible appearance. The last outbreak in Basel had been only thirty years ago, though there had been single deaths more recently. The latest great outbreak in Europe was Marseilles just five years ago. The news had been that a hundred thousand died.

More than war and siege, Black Death was the greatest fear of Europe's cities. The most severe laws applied to it to prevent its spread. Even the clothing and bed-clothing of a victim must be burned; there have been reports of how even a tatter of a sheet could start a contagion, and even years after its owner had died.

⁂

As I watched the Square, I imagined the city's frailty in the face of such illness. As I did, the paving stones before me began a slow circle inward toward their center. I stepped quickly back into the church. Their motion accelerated and I held tight to my unmoving foundation. The Square became a Charybdis. Everything in it was pulled down into the center. The buildings tore loose from their moorings and began their descent. Only the Barefoot Church, and the Boot and Thorn, and the Old Walls were grounded firm and held firm.

I shook off the vision. The Square returned to its old form; risen, changed and yet the same, though I still had the image of the wide spinning left in my mind. I kept it in my mind. A whirlpool was a Logarithmic spiral.

I put my foot on the paving stones and they held firm. I walked across the Square to the Old Wall and the Coal Gate and called up into the scaffolding. "Oh, Lithicus!" To dust I was returning: the whole paving under the gate was covered in fine, gray stone dust.

"You?" was answered. His face appeared white from the shadow like a cherub or monster of carved stone.

"I'll ask you about spirals," I said.

"Ask nothing about them," he said.

So I asked nothing. I dragged my boot through the dust on the ground, circling. "That's the spiral you made for Master Jacob," I said.

"That is the spiral."

I wiped the dust smooth and drew again, as I'd seen in the whirlpool. From the center and out, but growing and widening. "That's what they said they wanted."

"It's no difference from the other!" he said, "but that it's poor and wanton for a spiral."

"There's no complaint against you, Master Stonemason," I said, "and no fault in your craft. But this is a spiral, too, and the truth is, it's the better one."

"Then they'd have shown it to me before instead of after."

"They should have. Who was it that gave you your instructions?"

"Now, look, you! You've asked enough. You've asked enough! I've done nothing but what I was told, I was told nothing but what I had to do it! I'm no one to do anything else."

"Then there's no fault to you," I said. "They said a spiral, and you carved it. Only what you were told." I tipped my hat to him, and I think it was then that he saw it was three-pointed, and fully comprehended that I was in a scholar's gentleman costume.

"As you say, Master," he said, very sullenly.

"And Lithicus," I said. "Is it still the same stone in the arch you're repairing?

"No, Master. There's more to do. The cracks are deeper than they'd first looked."

I finally walked my last steps home. In my room, I could feel again the sliding and twisting of the house and streets. It was my books that were stable and gave me a reference to my own motion. But suppertime was nearing and I had to turn my back on them and undress my solemnity and return to plain brown. But in doing that, I felt again the whipsaw movement of not being anchored fast. I changed myself many times in a week from near-gentlemanly student to near-commoner. But it wouldn't always be. My ship would have to come to port someday, and there were many docks on just the Rhine. Nicolaus had been to Italy, and Daniel to Heidelberg, at my age.

There was a principle in Mathematics called Elegance. It described a statement or a proof that was exactly right: not only correct, but also complete, and yet simple, encompassing every necessity for its meaning but nothing else. It was seldom that life was elegant. Mine own seemed to have become complex, burdened with disconnections and incompletions and particularly, on my head, this hat.

I'd left my wig on my own head while I dressed and I was a strange sight, in plain wool brown with a pompous top; but now was the moment to put the wig off, and I'd hesitated for the reason of the hat. My old hat was still in Gottlieb's keeping for lack of any other place to have put it when I stood at his door, and my neglect at retrieving it. The tricorne was still crowning me and I wasn't sure it should crown my wood head, which had more common sense and fewer pretensions.

I decided the wood wouldn't mind and I put them all together. Now I was in the presence of a gentle-stump, and I was honored. As I studied it, respectfully of course, I knew I felt more comfortable and proper that the emblem of wisdom and respectability and maturity was on that head and not mine. Mine wasn't ready.

A true Mathematician must be a gentleman, so I would need to wear that hat. But someday.

That evening I ate supper with my grandmother. "Must you attend the Inquiry tomorrow morning?" she asked. Inquiries were respected and approved of in Basel, yet they made a thin fear like frost that chilled the city.

"Yes, Grandmother. I'm only a clerk. I won't be even noticed."

"What has Master Gottlieb learned?"

"I don't know. He knew much more before his questions than I knew even after them."

"You asked your own questions, also. Why are spirals important to you?"

"Because they're marvelous. They are to any Mathematician."

"That you ask a stonemason about them?"

"Master Jacob chose a spiral for his epitaph, and someone chose a spiral to mark the trunk. They were different spirals. But now I know they were meant to be the same."

"What does that mean of the trunk? That it belonged to Master Jacob?"

"I believe it did. I believe he'd chosen the Logarithmic spiral as his emblem."

"Then why was it a different spiral on his epitaph?"

"The stonemason didn't know there were different types of spirals and carved the wrong one. And I didn't want to ask him much about it, Grandmother. He seems very vexed and angry at the mention of it, and suspicious, even after twenty years."

Thursday morning dawned chill. Light was latecoming and when it came, from just the edge of the sky, the streets hid behind the houses' long shadows. Only the open square of Bare Feet welcomed radiance. I was there as usual to get water, and the face of the church, all white, was in silhouette of the sun rising behind it. But I saw an amazing light in it, as if it was glowing of its own. Then I saw across the Square that the Boot and Thorn, with the sun direct on it, was all dark. The church had its light. I didn't know how the inn was able to spurn the sun and the church embrace it. I went in the church, through its gleaming door.

Saint Leonhard's parish, which both my father and grandfather pastored, and of which my grandmother and I were part, was a church I closely loved. The Church of Bare Feet was different and I loved it just as well. There was something both less and more personal about it. It was the visible of Saint Leonhard's that was dear to me; the servants of the church and families who worshiped there. It was the invisible of the Bare Feet that drew me to its benches.

Beyond the brilliant front, the church inside was dim, but only so that the light through the windows could be immense and eternal, entering with vast strength and stepping down from heaven onto the receiving floor and laying hands on the willing walls. I'd seen it many mornings but never like it was this morning.

The light walked toward me slow and stately as a king. It touched the bench two ahead of me, and that plank seemed to shake from it. Outside, the sun was seeming to rise of its own in the sky, but it truly seemed that those steps down the aisle were the motive, and the sun was pulled through the window by them. They came to the row just ahead of me and I heard a sigh, or a gasp, and I stayed as still as I could and waited.

Somewhere in Bern Knipper's coach was standing in front of an inn or was already a storm driven toward Basel. In Basel's inn, brooding black across the Square, Caiaphas the magistrate like a barb was pierced into Basel's skin. In the Watch barracks, Knipper was undisturbed and beyond the disturbance he was the center of. I could see them all, those three: the coach, Caiaphas, and the corpse. The bench ahead was filled with gold whiteness and that purity was coming toward me. And there was something else I saw: my Master's house, and my Master's presence inside it, like a fixed stone that the waves of turmoil could only break against.

"Leonhard!" It was Daniel, just come in. "It's never hard to find you, even if no one else would be where you'd be. I need you, and quick."

I hesitated; the light was inches away.

"Now, quick, fast!" he said. "Come!"

"I'm coming," I said and I stood. Daniel needed me.

⁂

"What do you want?" I asked, running, and already halfway to his house. I still had buckets in my hands! He was already dressed in his finest.

"For you to hurry."

We were quick to the Munster Square and his front door, and most of the water I'd pulled spilled on the streets behind us. I left the buckets and what was left in them at the door, and we both bowed our way in. "I'd have been here in an hour."

"That's an hour too late." He took my arm in a tight grip, as if he was above a horrible drop, and I was a tree and his only hold. He pulled me into the dark entrance and to the stairs, more and more urgent.

"What is it?" I said. We scrambled up one floor. He didn't seem afraid, just determined and frenzied. We climbed a second floor. "What do you want of me?"

We came to the hallway I knew well, but only from Saturdays. This wasn't Saturday and the hall was decidedly different: it was not a place I should have been.

"Knock on that door," he said.

It was my door, but not mine when it wasn't Saturday.

"For what?"

"As if your life depended on it!"

"But who is in—" There was no finishing that question. Daniel beat on the door himself. The house shook with the pounding, enough to wake anyone in it.

"Just break it up," he said.

He beat again, enough to wake the next house.

"Just stop them," he said.

The echoes died. In the terrified silence I heard a chair scrape. There were footsteps. The handle rattled and the door opened with an angry jerk.

I was face to face with Master Johann.

And Magistrate Caiaphas was seated at the table behind him.

And Daniel was vanished.

It was a difficult moment. Master Johann was confused to see me as I was to be there at all.

"Master Johann," I said. I mustered enough confidence to seem that I knew my purpose.

"Yes? What is it?" He was still bewildered, which I knew would last at most very briefly more. But I thought for a moment that he was also distracted, and I realized I was, also, by the third presence.

"I was sent . . ." I didn't know which word would come next from my lips. I listened closely to hear it. "For Magistrate Caiaphas. I'm sorry—"

My apology was unnecessary, and even unheard. The name I'd uttered had been like a pistol shot. The Magistrate sprang to his feet and Master Johann turned to him in irritation. "Who knows you are here?"

"No one!" he said. "Who sent you?"

"Who sent you, Leonhard?" Master Johann repeated.

I didn't know who'd sent me. I only knew who'd brought

me, but that name wouldn't be any help. "The Inquisitor," I said. "I'm his clerk."

Caiaphas was shaken. "How did he know I was here?"

"I went to the Inn—"

"The innkeeper told you?"

I was more a spectator to my own words even than the other two. "I asked in the stable and a boy said he'd seen you."

"Tell the Inquisitor that Magistrate Caiaphas would not speak with you," Magistrate Caiaphas said to me. "Tell him that you asked at the Inn and were sent away."

"But Master Gottlieb—" I began, and was very glad to be interrupted.

"Tell him only that! Only that!"

I looked at Master Johann, who had stood back from the conversation. He frowned, then sighed. Then he nodded.

"Yes, sir," I said.

"And you must go," Johann said, and I thought he meant me, but he was speaking to Caiaphas.

"We have not finished."

"I have finished," Master Johann said. "Your Inquiry will be held as you demanded. I will not stop it."

"I want it stopped."

"It is too late. I will not stop it."

Caiaphas was shaking in anger. "The truth is perilous for you—"

"And for you, sir. You should not have demanded an Inquiry before learning more. I will manage it."

"Else, I will act!" Caiaphas said loudly. Then he seemed to notice again that I was there. "If I must act, I will," he said quietly. He looked at me. "Give that message to your Inquisitor," he said. "I will act."

He swept past me. I was pushed back, and I thought to

make my own retreat in his wake. But my Master caught me with his eyes.

"Leonhard."

"Yes, Master."

He had not forgotten I was there. "Master Gottlieb sent you."

"Master Johann, I—"

"You will be at the Inquiry today."

"I will, sir."

"Use wisdom."

It was unclear what he meant. The last thing at that moment I felt was wise. "Yes, sir."

"And this moment will not be discussed again."

That seemed only somewhat more clear. "And I'm sorry to have knocked so loudly—"

"Did you?" he said, and I didn't know how to answer. "I know the lion by his paw." Then he closed the door.

❧

"Masterful!" Daniel said. Exactly as the door closed, he was present again. "Pure mastery! Oh, I knew you were the man. That was wit, to throw in Cousin."

And I was still shaking and it was difficult to move my muscles even to turn to face him. "Daniel, I'm the one thrown. What lunatic scheme was this?"

"That's no matter, now it's over. Come along, get downstairs before the beast comes out of his lair."

"No matter?" I let him pull me to the stairs and down them. I was more concerned with breathing again. "How can you say that? Look, Daniel," I said as we reached the dark hall where just some crack of light was cutting through the door and air, "I'm near dead of fright and you're saying it's no matter. What were they doing in there that you're so desperate to stop?"

"I wasn't desperate to stop. Not ever."

"You weren't?! Yes you were! What were they talking about?"

"How would I know?" Daniel said. He was calm now, joking as his usual self. "I can't hear through walls, can I?"

"Then why did you want me to interrupt them?"

"I wouldn't have done, would I? There's no cause for either of them to know I even knew they were there."

"But you were. You wanted it stopped."

"It's no matter now, I said." He put his arm on my shoulder and put the most calming comfort into his voice and eyes. "Leonhard, there's nothing to even remember about it." He opened the door and the light of the Munster Square, slowly filling from the low rising sun, came billowing in. It was full morning now. "See, here're your buckets. Just get them filled and be on with your day. You'll be back for Mother's chores?"

"I will."

"Then hurry, you'll be late to it. And the Inquiry! It's no day to be late for anything."

He was right on that, and I didn't waste more time talking. I took my buckets. They were empty from the running and spilling, and I was feeling empty and spilled, too.

I came to the Barefoot Square. The sunlight had moved on. It wouldn't be shining into the church window as it had been. But then of a sudden I was caught in a white circle, so bright I had to turn my eyes from it. The sun was reflecting from a window, concentrated lens-like on just me.

***

When I returned a half hour later to my Master's house I saw only Mistress Dorothea, and she whipped me and her maid girl with work. But before I was done she paused, and I paused.

"That's enough. Be away, Leonhard, for your true day's work. There'll be hard tasks, to make chopping wood seem like play."

"I'm to go to Master Gottlieb next."

"Do as he bids. I'll be at the Inquiry myself." No function of the University would suffer a woman to attend, but the intricacies of Basel's laws and traditions allowed matriarchs of Mistress Dorothea's position to attend the public events of the Town Council. "I'll see if you shirk your duties."

She knew I wouldn't, though.

I left that house and kitchen for the streets. It was still mid-morning but the time would pass and noon would come. As I walked, the clocks rang through their hours; hours waiting in line since the beginning, entering, walking past, and exiting to where they would remain until the end. The designated hour was in place to take its turn and I had to be ready. In Basel, though, even time was changed.

The city had Basel Time. Stand outside the city until the sun is highest, and it was noon. Faint chimes from far off village clocks would confirm this. But enter any gate and walk to the Munster Square. The journey would seem to only take a few minutes, but the shadow of that same sun fell on the sundial at well after one o'clock. The Cathedral's dial was the Master of time in Basel and it bowed to no clock carried in from outside. If an outside clock disagreed, that one was wrong, even if it had been set by every church warden in Europe.

It might be that the city Walls have had some effect on time, and when a traveler passed through a gate, an hour of his life would be taken. Some people have wondered what happened to the hour lost at the gate. I'd found from experience that it's not lost, it was just kept for safekeeping, a ransom held against a visitor's good behavior. When the visitor left, the hour would be regained from hiding. A man born in Basel would find this reversed. He'd be given an hour when he left the city, but must surrender it to return.

Others claimed that there wasn't an hour lost or changed, just that the clock was kept to a different time. This was more than true, though. It *was* kept to a different time. Anyone in Basel knew that the city was not fully attached to the world around it. It had a different time and was a different place. The city was tied to some other foundation than the countryside, and the time was a telltale that it was a different world.

There was a battle fought two hundred years ago in the Swabian war, within sight of the city Walls, between the Swiss and the Emperor Maximilian. Men from Bern and Zurich and Solothurn were in danger of defeat when reinforcements from Lucerne arrived with trumpets and shouting, bursting from the forest and routing the mercenary Germans. The people of Basel just watched from their Walls. The war was outside their Walls and so it wasn't theirs. They hosted the armistice and treaty afterward to conclude the war, and took the opportunity to secede themselves from the Empire to join Switzerland. But they still kept all the gates, north and south, guarded. The city was really no more part of the Swiss than it was of the French or the Germans. The world was outside their gates, and so it wasn't theirs.

And the time that was outside their gates wasn't theirs, either. They had their own.

What else was different inside and outside? What was

greater than the Walls? Even Basel couldn't have one Mathematics inside its Walls, different than the Mathematics outside. No war, no clock, no machine, no plague, no death could change it. That alone made Mathematics beautiful and mysterious. There were other laws, laws of good and evil, laws beyond men, that again Basel couldn't change. What from outside Basel could Basel's Inquiry find the truth of?

I'd stood on the Wall of Small Basel, farthest northeast in the city, and listened to the Munster bell sound twelve, then faint moments later heard the clock in Riehen five miles away answer with eleven. In Riehen, I'd heard that church, just outside my parents' house and where my father is pastor, sound three, and then I've walked out into their garden to hear the Munster clock's dim four.

But I listened to distant clocks for another purpose than contemplating the separateness of Basel. Knowing the distance and the time between Basel and Riehen, I'd calculated the speed that sound moves through the air. Even sound had laws to obey.

But now the bells were tolling for Knipper. It was his time. He was neither in Basel nor outside it.

I stopped in the Barefoot Church to think a moment, and pray, but only briefly. And when I came out into the Square, Daniel was coming out of the Boot and Thorn opposite me. He almost turned away but then his compulsion to talk overcame and he came over. He was jittery and tense.

"Now Leonhard," he started, "for this Inquiry." He was the most changeable man, all different from his morning cockiness, different again from his morning urgency.

"What is it you want, Daniel? I won't interrupt anything else for you today."

"Why would I ever want you to? But look here, there is something I want of you. You've been with Cousin and all his questions, and I know you talked with Old Huldrych. Do you think he would really have had a part with Knipper? What was it that Gottlieb asked him?"

"For that, you'll have to ask Master Gottlieb yourself. You know that."

"I won't, and you know that. But you can tell me what his questions were. If there was anything he didn't want known, he wouldn't have let you know it yourself. So there's no reason that you shouldn't tell me."

"And no reason that I should, and so I won't." Then I thought perhaps I saw a pattern to Daniel's eagerness. "But I don't think Master Huldrych is guilty of anything, and I doubt Gottlieb thinks that, either. So he won't be thrown from his Chair into the river, if you're hoping that."

"Not in the river, at least."

"Daniel," I said, "You already have a Chair in Padua."

"No. I've given it up."

"You've resigned it?" I hadn't known. "But you said you might go back to it."

"I haven't even told Nicolaus yet. I'm done with Italy."

"But why?"

"I wrote a paper," he said, and grabbed my shoulders in sudden passion. "It is genius. You'd say it is. Anyone would! And the Dean tore it in pieces. The very sheets."

"Why, Daniel?" I was incredulous. "How could he?"

"He said I had strayed from Mathematics. My Chair was in that subject and I was to remain within it."

"What was the subject of the paper?"

"Hydraulics. The motion of fluids."

"What did you write?" For a moment, Italy receded. I was very interested in Hydraulics.

"The forces, the flows and rates, the pressures. All of it. It's what I've been doing in Italy. Oh, it was beautiful!"

"But that's all Mathematics."

"But the fool claims that Mathematics is a Logical Philosophy, and Hydraulics is a Natural Philosophy, and not to be bewildered into each other."

I was even more amazed. "Daniel. You had equations . . . pages of them . . . and he tore them?" It was beyond belief; I was nearly crying at the thought. "But you have copies?"

"It's easy enough to write them again." He shrugged off his grief, and also mine. "I've already done most of it. But for that I wouldn't stay. I resigned on the spot. And it was a relief."

"And you haven't told anyone?"

"None. You're the first. I don't want the Brute to hear it."

"Well, I won't tell him. And Daniel, there are other Universities."

"Leipzig? Konigsburg? I know you wouldn't say Groningen, not to me. But none of them are Basel."

"Then outside of German states. Paris. It's more than equal to Basel."

"In Theology. In Latin. Not in Mathematics. Not now."

"There must be somewhere else that's worthy of you."

He thought for a moment. "There's Russia. You said it yourself! That I might ride to Russia."

"I was joking."

"But don't you know, Leonhard? The Tsar is beginning a University."

"I didn't know."

"It's a grand endeavor. A new academy in Saint Petersburg, and the patron is Peter the Tsar himself."

"That would be excellent!" I said strongly. "Daniel! You'd be part of the beginning."

"I would be." But then he shrugged off the thought. "But

Russia . . . it's barbarian. I might be in America, for being so far."

"But Saint Petersburg! All that's said about it! It's a marvel."

"If they wrote me," he said, "I might think more. But I won't beg."

"Would they write?"

"The Chair of Physics in Padua, Romini, received a letter. And I've heard of others."

"You're well known, Daniel," I said. "And young. They would invite you."

"And when I win the Paris prize, then even more! But Russia." He shook his head. "No, I want Basel."

"But there are no Chairs open."

He almost answered me. The words were so close out of his mouth I should have heard something of them. But he caught them back. "Not yet," he said.

"Or anytime soon."

"If we need to act, we will."

I could only stare at him. "You've been talking with Magistrate Caiaphas."

"Him? You're mad, Leonhard. What would I want with him?"

"You didn't want your father to talk to him before you had."

"You've got business to attend!" he said in answer. "The Inquiry's only an hour off and you're key to it!"

"Daniel—"

"And Cousin is pure spite, so he's requiring me to be part of it, too. To the Chamber, and bring your hot irons."

And he was pure confusion. I gave him up and went on. He was right, that I had business to attend. I had to change to black and white.

◎

Thirty minutes later, the usual preparations of stocking and coat and buckle were accomplished. With all the pomp I could muster, I put on my wig and my wig put on its tricorne and grandly together we entered my kitchen. Grandmother was waiting and her two-edged sword was in her hand.

She was pleased with my straight back and honorability, but her sharp eyes searched me for pride. Of course, all that I had quickly withered. That was good. I knew it would be a hard fought day and I needed all my focus and no distractions.

"That will do," she said. "Do you know what's to be said at the Inquiry?"

"No one does. Gottlieb's been silent. I don't think he knows at all who killed Knipper."

"Is that what the Inquiry is for?" She knew it wasn't.

"No. But I'm not sure what it is for. Everyone believes that Magistrate Caiaphas has some reason."

"Truth will come out anyway. It won't be hidden forever."

"I hope it does come out."

"There's truth that you've hidden, Leonhard."

"When I know what the truth is it will come out. But I have to hide it now."

"Will harm come of that?"

"It may. Harm will certainly come if I don't hide it. Scandal and accusation would be attached to Master Johann's family."

"And if you are asked for the truth?"

"I would never lie, Grandmother."

6

The Holbein Chamber

The painter Holbein came to Basel two hundred years ago. It has been said that he saw deep and drew deep. His pictures were very real but filled with symbols and hidden powers; I'd looked at them for many hours and I believed he could see invisible things. His most profound work in Basel was ordered by the Town Council, which didn't realize its consequence: He was charged with the painting of their meeting chamber. His murals covered its walls.

In two centuries they have darkened and strengthened from great age. Dozens of scenes from classical and ancient ages brooded over the council. Saul was berated by Samuel, Croesus was burning on the stake, and Achilles was sulking in his tent. They were scenes of folly. Their purpose was to instruct the councilors on the importance of wise governance, and to remind them of the consequences otherwise. They accomplished this with a powerful elegance beyond words. There were invisible laws not made by man which governed man, and Holbein drew them into his pictures; they were still seen and unseen now. It was in this room and under these stares that the Council and citizens of Basel gathered to hold their Inquiry.

൭൭

The citizens entered first. Wealth and lineage were the criteria for their seats, and there were both men and a few women. They sat on three rising rows of benches which followed the room's back and sides. As noon approached, these filled. Curiosity was really the only reason to attend. The great citizens were as fascinated as anyone else.

At one end of the side benches, near the front, was a row set apart by a surrounding rail. This served different purposes: to seat the accused, or petitioners, or men called to answer to the Council. It seated four witnesses for the Inquiry. Daniel wore his defiant wine red coat, just as I'd seen him at sunrise. Beside him was Old Gustavus in brown coat and breeches and heavy boots; the only brown worn in that room. Master Huldrych was in his University gown which should have been black but was only dust. Nicolaus alone wore the black suit that every other gentleman wore. Of the few women present, Mistress Dorothea sat in the audience seat closest to her sons, with only the rail separating her from Nicolaus, and Little Johann sat in her shadow.

The center of the room was empty.

൭൭

Then the council entered. These were seven men cut of the same black and white cloth as the audience. They were all merchants, sons of the councilor merchants who'd ruled the city from before the Reformation. They sat behind the Council Table.

That table was as heavy as the deliberations that had taken place around it, as old and wise as the walls, and worn dark and smooth. Wars had been made; fortunes had been awarded or destroyed by the grant of a single trade tolerance; men had been condemned or released, allowed back into the streets or taken direct to the bridge and thrown to the river. The table had never been moved from its place across the front of the room. Behind it, built into the wall, were the Councilors' seven seats. The high-backed center was for the mayor. He wore a gold chain with a medallion of office, and velvet robe, and the heaviest wig. Great above the table was Holbein's largest mural, of captive Valerian, the Roman Emperor, stooped on the ground as Persian king Sapor used him as a footstool to mount his horse. This was to remind the Council that the consequences of their actions would be brought back onto them.

Another high chair was placed to the right of the table, against the wall, for a Magistrate, when he attended. He wouldn't sit on the council but beside it as judge, parallel, and advisor. This occasion was unusual, though. Three magisterial chairs were evenly spaced against the right wall, and above them was another mural, of the triumvirs Caesar, Pompey, and Crassus, with their right hands held in peace and their left hands hiding daggers.

Opposite these chairs, on the left of the council, was another chair. Gottlieb sat in this place, behind a desk table, and below another trio, of Bildad, Eliphaz, and Zophar. Aside from them was one last single chair, the most exposed and humbling of all in the council room.

Magistrate Faulkner entered. There were many hues of black in Basel: sober black, arrogant black, studious black, respectful black, intimidating black, imperious black. All of these would be seen in the streets every day. Magisterial black was particular among them all. His robe had a strange billowing weight that lifted with his movement and settled slowly. Blacker, but not as black, Caiaphas entered just behind him, and his robe seemed rigid like armor. The gendarme, Foucault, came in at his side, and took his position standing in the corner behind them.

He was in uniform and armed with a short sword, which was very unusual. The Sergeant of the Watch, in the other corner behind Gottlieb, usually held the only weapons in the council room. This was a noticeable concession by Basel to the prerogative of Strasbourg.

The empty chair between them, beneath the Roman Triumvirate, now received its occupant, and this was Master Johann. He entered in his academic gown, black with scarlet chevrons, and every other black was reduced to gray. Only Faulkner held his own. Master Johann wasn't a magistrate, though he had served as one temporarily in the past.

But he dominated. By position, Chair of Mathematics was high but not highest. Instead, he took his place as center of the ritual by a deeper and ineffable power. Everything about his attendance was extraordinary, that he sat between two Chief Magistrates, that he exhibited an authority over the Inquiry so openly, and that no one questioned his right. He was Master Johann of Basel.

He leaned first to his right, murmuring to Magistrate Faulkner, then to his left, with an undisguised familiarity, to Magistrate Caiaphas, with whom he had a longer whispering. Neither seemed pleased, and this might have been the first resumption of their interrupted meeting in the dark morning. Then Master Johann turned back to his right, caught the eye of the Mayor, and nodded. He, a visitor to the council, was giving it instruction to start the proceedings.

But perhaps I was the only one who saw the glance. I was

in the other chair, the chair behind Gottlieb, most exposed and alone, and from my angle I could see what most others in the room couldn't. And I was in black, also, tremulous, uncertain black: black coat and breeches and boots, with my tricorne complacent beneath my chair. At that moment I would have easily given up all pretense of a black and white future for the safety and un-remarkability of brown.

I sat beneath Icarus, and Daedalus wept at my side.

There were a few quiet words at the Council's table and I surveyed the room, especially the Holbein murals, which I'd always appreciated. On the side wall was King Rehoboam wagging his finger as he boasted to the Israelites, and beside that was Esau eating Jacob's stew. The edge between these was also the line of the witness box, where Daniel yawned in ease and boredom, and Nicolaus saw me watching him and smiled. Between them Old Gustavus was still as a cold hearth, and Master Huldrych very pale, and his hands were shaking. I'd never before seen him so agitated. The next mural, just outside that box, above Dorothea and Little Johann, was Oedipus and Jocasta.

Gottlieb stood from his chair. A heavy blanket fell on all sound except the clap of his heels on the wood floor. With fate and doom he took the podium. He spared no glance at anyone but the council and prepared to speak. The Mayor lifted his hand, palm up, which was the signal to begin.

"Humble before Mighty God," Gottlieb said, "I come to state truth." Every Inquisitor began their case with these words. "Those who deceive shall be exposed and set to the left. Those who are blameless shall be known and set to the right. Then may God have mercy and be just."

The mayor answered. His name was Burckhardt, and his

family had been cloth merchants for generations. "Master Inquisitor. We measure you to the standard that you measure others, and to twice their reward, whatever we judge it will be. Begin your Inquiry." And so, it began.

"You have charged me," Gottlieb said, "to inquire into the murder of Knipper the coachman. I have done as I was charged, and so I warn the Council that there is a danger to Basel." The audience and Council all took note of what he said.

It was then that I noticed for the first time that Master Desiderius was also an observer among the townspeople, beneath a mural of Ephialtes of Trachis bowing to Xerxes. Desiderius had always seemed to me more interested in past or distant than in present, yet he was very alert to the proceedings, and to the expressions and glances of all the actors.

Gottlieb pronounced, "I first summon Gustavus, who keeps the Boot and Thorn."

The man stood and came to the center of the room where he settled, feet apart, arms crossed, and beard bristling, just as he would in his own kitchen, and a whiff of his fires was with him. "I am Gustavus."

"Gustavus employed Knipper, he and fellow innkeepers in the four cities, and he knew Knipper as well as any man."

"I don't know who killed him," Gustavus said. It would have been a fearless man to challenge him. And Gottlieb had no fear, but also no need to challenge.

"Gustavus met Knipper and his coach, and no one saw Knipper after that," Gottlieb said. "On the next morning Knipper wasn't found to drive his coach. Gustavus sent the coach to Freiburg with the boy Willi driving it. The corpse of Knipper was packed in a trunk among the luggage. Is this all true?"

"I know nothing of it to be false," Gustavus said.

"And Willi put the trunk on the coach?"

"Ask him."

"Ask him." Gottlieb said more in long silence than words would have. "He can't be asked. You're finished. Sit down."

Gustavus returned as heavily as he'd come, and his boots sounded like axes against a tree. Huldrych was trembling, very visibly. Gustavus stood for a moment in front of the Physics Master watching him, then sat between the brothers Daniel and Nicolaus.

"Yes," Gottlieb said once more. "Willi must be asked, but he is in Strasbourg."

"He was arrested," Caiaphas said, like a rasp on the wood of the room. "He brought a corpse into the city, which is against our law."

"And you have brought a corpse into Basel," Gottlieb answered. "Which is against our law."

"I was returning it!"

"Returning. So you have proof that the coachman was a corpse when he left here." Before there could be an answer, Gottlieb said, "I summon next Masters Daniel and Nicolaus, who were passengers on Knipper's last drive."

Nicolaus was always averse to public attention. In Daniel's company, he was never the center of it. He was hardly noticed beside Daniel's jaunty brilliance. "Go ahead, Cousin," Daniel said. "Have at it."

"Have care," he was answered.

"Have it over with."

"These two were also last to see Knipper," Gottlieb said. "Their arrival in Basel was well anticipated."

"As is our departure, by some."

"The date of your arrival was known. The date of your departure is only imagined." That, for a moment, left Daniel without a reply.

"But why is this important?" Caiaphas said, interrupting again. "It isn't important."

"You're a poor judge of importance," Nicolaus said. As always when he chose to speak, it was unexpected, and far more in that heavy and formal room. "In particular your own."

That affront was a lightning bolt. It was as if the air had been pulled from everyone's lips, and a soundless vacuum had been created. That made the next words even greater.

"My sons' arrival in Basel was very important." Master Johann's voice was like the Rhine: broad, deep, unstoppable, and difficult to cross. No one could say anything beyond that statement, least the sons themselves.

"These two," Gottlieb said, "returned to Basel, well-known in advance. Upon their arrival the coachman was murdered, and the stable boy who could tell more of it has been withheld from us. For what reason did you return?"

"What reason?" Daniel said, and he may have been daunted. The question was pointed, the tip of the spear that Gottlieb was holding toward him. Or he may not have been daunted. "I hadn't seen my family in two years. Why wouldn't I have returned to my family and city?"

Nicolaus was silent.

"I think there was another reason," Gottlieb said.

"Think what you wish."

"I want to know the reason."

"It's not important!" Caiaphas said. "Go on to something else."

"And I want to know, as well, why the reason is important to you, sir," Gottlieb said to Caiaphas, "that you don't want it known." He waited a few moments. Daniel and Nicolaus waited, one patient and one not. Caiaphas didn't answer. Then Gottlieb said, evenly and plainly, "Then I summon Magistrate Caiaphas before this Inquiry to answer my questions."

"Me?!" Caiaphas did stand, but in his own authority and anger. "Me? I will never answer to you! What insolence!"

"I am Inquisitor," Gottlieb said, still very evenly. "For my term, I have every authority in Basel. And this is Basel."

"I will not answer to you." Caiaphas slowly sat back into his chair, and leaned farther back into it. "I will not answer to you. Foucault."

"Yes, sir?" The gendarme could hardly breathe, but he understood threat, and he knew to answer with threat. His hand was on his sword. The Sergeant-at-arms of the Day Watch answered with a hand on his pistol.

"You saw Knipper that last hour, just as Gustavus did." All attention was drawn from the Magistrate of Strasbourg to the one of Basel as Faulkner spoke, to Daniel. It was another profound assertion of right. Faulkner didn't ignore the conflict that had erupted in the Council chamber; he overrode it. "What did you see of the coach driver?"

"He opened the coach door," Daniel answered, and respectfully. "But I wasn't concerned with him after."

"Knipper was seen nowhere besides the inn?"

"All the testimony on this is agreed," Gottlieb said, leaving Caiaphas aside for the moment. But with his glance, he showed that the battle would soon be rejoined. Then suddenly, he turned to me. "Clerk, please refer to your notes. Tell us whether Knipper was seen anywhere else. Anywhere else besides the Inn. Was he? When? By whom?"

I was still unrecoverd from my fear of swords and pistols, and this question muddled me much more. I looked in my notes, which told me just what I'd written in them. I'd been asked a question and I could only answer truthfully. I coughed to clear my voice. "The testimony—"

But Master Huldrych had stood. Everyone could see now how tremulous he was, how anxious and fearful. His hands and arms were shaking. His face was white and drained and sagging. "Help him," Gottlieb said. Daniel and Nicolaus were closest and they took him at either side and replaced him into his chair and then moved to give room. The chamber leaned toward him, all quiet. Dorothea was behind him, loosening the collar of his shirt. And Old Gustavus having stepped out to face him, knelt, and stared into his eyes.

Huldrych stared back. He whispered, very quietly but I heard, "Is it? I'd thought it wasn't."

"It is," Gustavus answered. He'd heard also.

I heard because I was beside him. I can run quickly and I had. When I heard him sigh, I knew what he knew. I put my arm around his shoulder and laid my head on his robes, above his heart, holding him dearly. Old Gustavus said, to him and Gottlieb and the Council and magistrates and audience, and to me, "Black Death."

"This is what I feared," Gottlieb said, with anger, and staring at Caiaphas.

And I heard Huldrych's heart's last beat.

7

The Outer Wall

"They've buried him already," I told Grandmother. Lunch waited on our kitchen table but I wouldn't eat it. "It was to get him away, out of the Walls. They don't want it to spread. They carried him straight out from the Council Room."

"What did each one in the room do?" she asked.

"There was fear," I said. "Like smoke and it hid everything. The mayor called the Watch to take him out, and Gustavus went with them. Everyone was frightened, and Daniel most. And Master Johann only sat and watched. He was still there when I left. Mistress Dorothea hurried Little Johann out, but then she was back right away. Nicolaus wasn't scared, but he left quickly. I didn't see him go."

"And Caiaphas?"

"He just stood and walked out as if it was nothing, but kept his gendarme close with him."

"What did you do, Leonhard?"

"I cried."

"And now?"

I still was.

⁂

Later I went out of the city, looking for respite. Huldrych was old and to my discredit, I'd known impatience with him. But I'd been so fond of him, too. He'd been always patient with me, even when he'd doubted my ideas. I wasn't ready for him to die. I wished at least he'd lived until I was older.

I had my place on the hill, and my sky and warm low sun. All that was, was at peace. I waited, wanting peace for myself. But for all the calm that was around, none came to me. Instead, my own disquiet spread out from me, running down the hill and on wing to the sky, until I saw what was really surrounding me: a foaming, blowing turmoil, and nothing at rest. There was no hourglass pivoting to stay still. Nothing was still. Where could the storm reach? The far mountains were so distant that they should have been invisible.

⁂

The dust, when I saw it, floated thick above the trees that hid the road. I hadn't even thought of the coach returning. I held my hillside. Inside the Walls they'd be waiting for it. The Day Watch would have orders about it, though I didn't know what they would be. I didn't want to be any part of the coach and the crowds, so I walked around the Walls away from the Ash Gate, and to the Stone Gate. I wanted stone permanence, stone hardness.

Still, I came to the Barefoot Square only as the coach did, led by two officers of the Day Watch, and heard the tale the crowd was gossiping, that the coachman Abel had refused to come in to a plague city and the Watch had taken him under guard. Even as I stood with the gawkers I saw them escorting him into the inn. The coach was brought round to the front door and met by Gustavus and Fritz.

Fritz tossed down baggage from the rack as if it were rocks, then dropped like a stone himself to the ground. Gustavus caught the pieces as he opened the coach door. Abel gave no thought to the sweating, gasping horses or the tumbled, bruised passengers. He pushed ahead of his guards and into the inn and anyone could hear him bellowing for his supper. Gustavus said nothing. He unhitched the horses and handed them to Fritz, then he pulled the coach by his own hand to its place in the front of the stable tunnel.

Abel had entered Basel again under protest and by threat of harm. He'd known of the plague because black pennants were already flying above the gates, and I saw the notice hammered to the troubadour pole in the Square's center. It ordered that illness be reported, and that any sick person was to be brought to the Barefoot Church for the Physicians to see and they were empowered to put anyone out of the city who was deemed to have the contagion. I'd seen in the Council's Law Code what would be printed in later notices, if they were needed: how corpses were to be collected, how their death-bedding was to be burned, and on, even to the laws regarding estates that were forfeit because no heirs were surviving. All those laws had been kept through centuries and called out as necessary like funeral dress.

Lieber the bookmaker hurried past me with a bundle under his arm. "What are you printing today?" I asked him.

"More of those," he said, meaning the notice on the pole.

"But you're a book printer." He'd always left cheap broadsides to lesser printers.

"Plague laws," he said. Those required that every printer

produce these notices if the Council instructed. Much of common life was upended by the plague.

I left the Square. Not by a street, but through a doorway and into the Barefoot Church.

The falling sun in the west was on the face of the building. No direct light came in the high hall, just diffused glowing. My bench was still and I could feel that the church was still firmly held by heaven and wasn't moving. It couldn't be moved.

The Inn had its own foundation deep into the earth and couldn't be loosed from it. Between earth and heaven, the Barefoot Square was stretched taut and Basel rocked by waves as a boat tied to two different piers. Someday the tension would become too great and the Square would tear loose from one side or the other. Or the city would tear in two between them.

I stayed a very long time there.

I rose early Friday morning; it wasn't morning but still night. My grandmother never woke while I dressed and took my water buckets and went out. I heard a single declaration from the clock in Saint Leonhard's, so I only knew it was half past an hour, but not the hour. There was no moon. It must have been after three. There was no dawn. It must have been before five.

I heard muffled, quietly drawn wheels and hooves. The Barefoot Square was formless and void. I waited at the edge until I could see the coach at the door of the inn. The horses somehow knew to be soundless. Their breathing was little more audible than it was visible. But one of them smelled me and whinnied. Abel, hard lout he was, still could quiet a horse with a whisper, and I heard him do it.

Voices in the door were crashing bells to the silence of the Square, but they were only murmurs. I could hear sullen displeasure from the passengers pulled early from bed and herded to the open coach, and the coach door closed but not latched. The luggage was already on the roof. I walked closer, hidden only by darkness in the openness. The horses knew I was there. I came close enough and stopped. Then we were all waiting. It was far earlier in the morning than the coach was ever readied, which showed how far more urgent was its reason to leave.

Silence and dark made time slow. The long minutes went by, but they were only minutes. Finally there were two voices and I listened. One was like coals and one like sparks. I couldn't hear their words, only their heat.

Blacker than the night, making it light in contrast, black robes issued from the Boot and Thorn, and black boots and coat. Abel opened the coach door and the robe stood in front of it to climb in. The boots braced to help steady the high step.

"Magistrate Caiaphas," I said. His foot had already been lifted. He set it down and very slowly turned. Gustavus beside him had his eyes on me. Then Abel unveiled a lantern and its single beam struck me and everything else was perfect black.

"Master Leonhard. What are you doing here?" Caiaphas said. Immediately he'd known me. His voice and words would have scratched rock.

"I'm getting water." I held up my buckets.

"What do you want of me?"

"Only to wish you well," I said.

"That?" he said. "What, nothing more?"

"Not for myself, sir. Will Willi be allowed back?"

"I've no use for him. But you, in poor peasant clothes. Is there nothing you want from me?" The words were bent up at the end like a hook.

"No, sir."

"Soon you will."

"Only for now, sir, that you have a safe journey and God-speed."

"Speed from here!" he answered in his sudden screech. "I leave my curse on this city! Curse it to the desolation of plague, and speed on its journey there." He took hold of Gustavus's arm and entered into the coach. The door closed on him. Abel climbed to the box and held his lantern out and whipped the horses. They leapt from statues to gales, and sparks shot from the stones under their shoes. The coach pitched and almost fell. Then it flew across the Square fast and loud as cannon shot.

The words had struck hardest. I'd taken them full force. But they'd been blocked and captured and exhausted, kept from reaching the Square and the city, and that had been my intent. The Church of Bare Feet behind me had held me firm, I'd felt it.

So the day had started, I alone in the Square, and through the dark, Abel driving like a mad bull and the roads forsaken before him.

At home, my grandmother said nothing, and only watched me do my chores as she did hers.

With such little sleep, my arrival in Master Johann's kitchen was subdued and my appearance depressed. But I thought I'd had more rest than Mistress Dorothea. She had even less of her usual manner, and an odd stare at me, too.

She was only sitting at the table. She had a knife in her hand and potatoes in a bowl, but they were waiting. There was no motion.

"Good morning," I said.

"Oh, Leonhard. Yes, good morning."

My first job is always to tend to the fire and the wood settle, and I saw the hearth was cold. "Should I start the fire?"

"Yes. Thank you. I see that I haven't."

There was no kindling brought in. I went to the yard to bring some sticks and then set to igniting. The wood was dry and there were still a few embers. I had a flame quickly, and two split logs against it to catch, and when I turned back, Mistress Dorothea was still in her chair, still holding her knife, and still. So I went up to her and set my knee on the floor to lower myself to her height, and asked her, "Are you well, Mistress?"

"I'm not ill," she said.

"You're not well," I was bold to say.

"There's little well."

"There's plague in the city."

"I don't fear that, Leonhard."

"You don't? Everyone does."

"Master Johann says it's not to be feared, not yet. If it should be then we'll leave Basel."

"Is there something else, then?" I asked.

"The hub and the spokes," she said.

This was a proverb in Basel. It meant, a family was like a wheel. The children were the spokes and the mother was the center. She held them in place, and felt the ruts and stones that any of them struck. The father wasn't mentioned but I thought he was the axle, and all the weight he carried was also pressed onto her. So, she was admitting to me that it was her family that was not well. I waited and the kitchen was the most quiet I'd ever known it with its Mistress present. "If you see regret," she said, finally. "Or grief, Leonhard. If you see remorse or regret, I'd like to know that you have."

I nodded.

"And if it's penitence or repentance, even more I'd like to know. Anywhere you see it."

"I'll tell you. I think there's much I regret myself."

൭൭

But later, when Mistress Dorothea was upstairs, Little Johann came into the kitchen. "What did you mean?" he asked, kneading his dough. "What do you regret?"

I made light of it. "Where were you listening from?" He hadn't been in the kitchen when I'd said it.

"You said you had regrets."

"For my hat," I said, just jesting.

"Your hat?" He squeezed the dough and it bulged out between his fingers.

"Cousin Gottlieb took it and I regret I don't have it back. It was from my father."

At Gottlieb's name he pressed the dough all the harder. And I realized I did regret that I'd lost the hat.

൭൭

I walked from Mistress Dorothea's kitchen slowly, not toward home. There were odd creatures in the streets: wolves and vultures and half-beast minotaurs. But they left the people alone, for the moment, slinking in shadows and growling low. I walked out on the bridge to look at the Rhine. It was calm. But somewhere underneath something stirred and touched the surface and a ripple appeared, a perfect circle. It spread out, just the one circle on the smooth water, its radius growing, and finally fading.

That circle was like so many other circles. Usually I would be reminded of how sound travelled that way through the air, but that morning my thoughts were on other circles. Plague spread like a circle. Fear did. I saw a man crossing the bridge, pulling a bag-laden cart, and with a wife and children walking behind him. It was a sight that had instant meaning. He was fleeing the city. But so far, he was the only one I'd seen. He reached the far end of the bridge in Small Basel and turned toward the Blaise Gate.

So Basel had lost Huldrych besides Knipper, and now it was losing others. It was all loss, and I felt it.

The bell of the Munster clock rang ten, all melancholy and pleading, as if calling out. I found myself counting as it ended, not at first even remembering why. Then I knew. Just at thirty seconds, I heard a far off clock in Riehen, from my father's church, that bell ringing nine. It was an answer, louder than I'd ever heard in the middle of the city.

"There've been no other reports of plague," I told my grandmother at lunch. She knew that, of course. She never gossiped or rumored, and wouldn't abide anyone else telling tales. Yet she always knew important news.

"You said Master Huldrych spoke of Black Death?" she asked.

"When we came to his door, Gottlieb and I. He asked if there was another Black Death. And Gottlieb was angered by it. Grandmother? Would you know? When did Gottlieb first wear a tricorne hat?"

"He had it when he came from Holland."

"When he came back with Master Johann?"

"The first I saw him when he came back, he was wearing his tricorne."

"He was younger then than I am now!" That was hard to imagine. "Or at least as young."

"He was a serious youth."

"I'm not very serious," I said.

"You must try to be."

"Yes, Grandmother. Have there been any other deaths in Basel of plague?"

"If there have, it's not been announced. What happens inside a family's house isn't always known."

"But to not tell is against laws."

"Some are below the law, and some are above."

"Huldrych saw Gottlieb, and a tricorne worn for the first time, and he thought of plague. It persuades me that Jacob died of plague. Gottlieb didn't want that memory revived."

"Those of us who are old don't always remember well," she said. "The University will meet soon. They'll choose a new Chair to replace Master Huldrych."

"That takes months," I said. "It took three months to choose Desiderius for Greek."

"What will become of Master Huldrych's lectures?"

"Master Staehelin is the Lecturer for Physics. He'll take the lectures until the Chair is filled."

Plague was bad for all business in a city. Doors were closed and locked and the streets were even emptier. That afternoon the Boot and Thorn was empty. I only saw it walking past; I didn't go in. I was returning Boccaccio to Master Desiderius.

He wouldn't have minded my keeping it longer, but my return of one book often led him to press another into my hands. And he might have heard, in some language only he knew, of any other news of the events of the week.

One of his children answered his door, a boy about six years old. His name was Theseus and I hoped his father's hope in him would be achieved. *"Eínai o patéras sou edó?"* I said. I also hoped I had my Greek grammar correct. If I didn't, he would correct it.

"*Tha ton párei,*" he answered, and I waited. And soon, his *patéras* arrived.

"Leonhard," he said, as he saw me. "What? Done with it already? Of course you are. And a strange book to read, wasn't it?"

I handed him the Boccaccio. "Very strange, sir. I've not read any other book like it."

"The book itself, yes, but I meant the reading of it now. I pray we won't see anything he describes with our own eyes."

"There've been no other reports of plague," I said.

"I think there will be none." This was the second time that day I'd been assured of that.

"Master," I said. "You said you came to Basel from Strasbourg?"

"Yes. Five years ago."

"Then did you know of Magistrate Caiaphas?"

"To have lived in Strasbourg is to know of Magistrate Caiaphas."

"Did he know of you?"

"Yes. He knew me. He knew of me."

"Master Gottlieb knew him, and asked him why he came to Basel."

"It is best to not know that. Leonhard, your questions are difficult."

"I was greatly saddened by Master Huldrych's death," I said.

"And what does that have to do with Magistrate Caiaphas?"

"I don't know."

"The Inquiry is over, and also the time for questions. We'll move to other things."

Of course, I asked, "What is the result of the Inquiry?"

"The result is no result. The city was indulging Magistrate

Caiaphas with the Inquiry, and Magistrate Caiaphas is no longer here." Master Desiderius smiled at that, as likely most of Basel did. "And what, hasn't Gottlieb said anything to his own clerk?"

"I'm dismissed as clerk, and anyway he's dismissed as Inquisitor. But he said there was a result to be told, and he never told it."

"He'll tell the Council, and Magistrate Faulkner."

"And he said there was a danger to Basel," I said.

"He did, didn't he?" Master Desiderius said. "But we don't know what. Could it have been about the plague? No one knew that Huldrych was ill. Perhaps Gottlieb had a fear that someone might be? Did anyone say anything about plague?"

I chose my words carefully. "Gottlieb never said anything about plague. Not to me."

"I was hoping, Leonhard, that you might have known more."

"I wish I did, Master."

"Anyway," he said, "thank you for the return of the book. And I have another for you. It's even in German." It was odd that we didn't spend time choosing one together; it usually took us a long time. Instead he handed me a book that seemed very new, and slender.

"Oh, yes," I said. "I remember you said you had this for me."

The first page showed that it was new, printed that very year, in Frankfurt by a printer named Meynenden. But the title was something of a discomfort to me, as I knew it well. This book was a new telling of an old tale, a Faustbook.

Faustbooks had been common in Europe for centuries. The story was usually short: The book in my hand had only some forty pages. The history of this story was long, from the ages of alchemy. It was, of course, about the life of Dr. Faust of Heidelberg. He was learned, terribly learned, but wanting always more knowledge, more and more. He wanted knowledge of anything, but mostly of mysteries and secrets and powers. He was greeted by Mephistopheles, a fallen angel, who offered him a bargain: all knowledge, and life as long as he wanted; but when he tired of living, he must give up his soul. There were different endings but the sum of them was he did tire finally, that his knowledge was too great to endure, and he would rather surrender to damnation than keep living.

If there was no true Dr. Faust, there have been others who might have inspired the tale.

There was a man named Philippus Aureolus Theophrastus Bombastus of Hohenheim, who took the scholarly name Paracelsus, to mean he was the equal of the great chemist Celsus of ancient times. I thought it might have been Paracelsus who was the true Faustus. He held the Chair of Medicine in Basel at the same time that Holbein was painting the Council room. He was an alchemist, when that profession was only suspect, and not sinister. So, Basel was part of the soil that the story had grown from. Its roots may still have been in the soil.

I was interested to read this new version, though I'd never enjoyed the tale. "Thank you," I said.

"It's only imagination," he answered. "Such things don't really happen. But it's cautionary, too. A good caution to have." I think he was emphasizing that. "Think it through well, Leonhard. It isn't Mathematics but there's still hard truth in it to keep in your mind. It might even be that the questions you have of the Inquiry are answered in it."

"How could that be?" I asked.

He shook his head. "And I have a copy of Paracelsus for you, also. But not today; that is enough."

Dr. Faust was a scholar, and that was important to the story. If a man didn't have fame and wealth from birth, the University could be his path to those.

It was easy enough to find Basel's wealthy men. Their houses were displays, in the subdued Basel manner. The family names of the magistrates and the council were very regular from year to year and century to century. These families had their wealth from trade and guilds, and some from land. None of this was irregular, or unique to Basel. For every Faulkner or Burckhardt in Basel, there was a Zimmerman in Zurich, a Hofburg in Frankfurt, and a Weil in Bremen. It was the University that gave Basel another class of great men.

This special parallel city was made of students as commoners; student graduates who studied toward higher degrees as the skilled tradesmen; lecturers and associate professors as wealthy younger sons; administrators and Deans and Provost as greater patricians; and at the highest level, above officials, equal with magistrates and bishops, were the Professors, the holders of Chairs. These were meant to be great men and masters in their fields. Among them were Physics, Law, Medicine, Theology, Logic, Greek, Latin, Anatomy, Rhetoric, and others. In Basel the greatest was Mathematics.

And as the University was a parallel city, Europe's universities were a parallel continent, and they were its kingdoms and duchies. Heidelberg was a power, Paris was a kingdom, Bologna held its independence. In the realms of Mathematics, though, Basel was Hapsburgs and Bourbons and Romanovs all in one. In the parallel continent it was unparalleled, because Master Johann was its center.

The story of Faust could only be in a place where a man could become great through knowledge, a place such as Basel. In all the Faustbooks, the story always took place in a University.

❧

I walked Walls that Friday evening. That was common in Basel, though more often to watch the sun's mid-morning rise, not its setting. I walked the whole Wall of Large Basel. It was near three miles long and I didn't run any of it. I started at Saint Alban's Gate in the late afternoon. The first stretch was the two long sides of the angle that the Ash Gate pivots. That was almost a mile. There were guard towers every few hundred yards and ramps up from the streets at every gate and barbican.

The barbicans were wide and flat, just as high as the Wall itself, protruding from it in sharp triangles to give defenders a vantage over attackers at the Wall's base. Basel had never been taken, and rarely attacked. That could be proof that there was no need for the Wall, or proof that there was every need for it. It was an odd logic, and I wondered what Gottlieb would say about it.

As I reached the far corner past the Ash Gate and turned toward the Stone Gate, the sun was full in front of me just ready to touch the horizon. The path on the Wall was wide, twelve feet across, but all I met was the Day Watch and I greeted each man I passed. I knew many of them. I stopped to talk a few times. Then they were standing down as the Night Watch took their places. What the Watch could do against plague, I didn't know, or they either, but the Watch had been doubled.

Just past the Stone Gate was the stream of the Birsig Flow, pouring into the moat and into its canal to the city. I walked across the arch where it entered. There was a strong portcullis there, and barbican just after, because that would always be a weak place in a Wall.

Beyond the Walls were fields. Some were farms and some were only meadows. There were no cattle or sheep in them that night, but once a black horse came out into the open from some trees, and Daniel was its rider. He lit suddenly toward the gate, whipping his black, as if racing, yet with no other horse I could see. Then I did see a white horse, without a rider, nearly beside him. Then they were hidden behind the Wall. I turned and went on with my walk.

I saw Saint Leonhard's church spire and clock, and the Barefoot Church further in. As I passed them, the sun was just half-set and the sky an inferno. When I came to the Columned Gate the sun was gone. The moat below still was glowing red, like a candle wick's last spark. This was the city's largest gate, on the road from Alsace.

Then was the final long walk to Saint John's Gate, back to the river, and it was such a long and ever darker way that I only had the stars above and the points of light from the windows, and they both seemed as far away.

The Wall was complete and unbreached. I knew it for sure now.

As I stood at the gate, I saw another watcher was also on the Walls, confirming them.

"Good evening, sir," I said. Magistrate Faulkner recognized me in the dark.

"It's Leonhard? Yes, good evening."

"These Walls seem so strong."

"They are. Despite their age."

"They're kept well repaired."

I didn't know if he would answer. He was silent for more than a minute and I wondered if I should leave him. But then he said, "Leonhard, if you see Magistrate Caiaphas return to Basel, come tell me."

"Yes, sir. I will." And I nodded and left him.

༄

The return home on Saint John's Street led by Death Dance Street where I had to stop at Master Huldrych's house, and at the Dance that now he was partner in.

God gives all laws, as are found in books; no man may change them: hate lies, love truth. It was dark but of course I knew the Lawyer's words, and also Death's reply: *I accept no trick or flattery, give no postponement or appeal, I overrule man's laws and courts, both Prince and Church must yield.* No prince would ever have proclaimed a law that Death must obey him. The laws of God, of nature, of Mathematics, of death: man-made laws were weak compared to those. I looked across the street to Master Huldrych's house.

I wondered what would happen to his laboratory. It would be disturbed. Someone would sweep out that room and all the dust, carefully settled, would be dispersed. Dust to dust.

༄

I came in my front door and Grandmother was waiting. She had a stern look.

"Leonhard," she said. "You have a visitor."

"Me?"

"It's Master Daniel."

Daniel had found me in many places in Basel: in churches, on streets, in taverns, in his own house. But in the week he'd been home, he had never sought me in my own house. "Yes, Grandmother," I said.

Every house of any size in Basel had a sitting parlor, always with windows onto the street. My grandmother's sitting parlor was swept every day. The floor was bare. There were three straight wood chairs and two small tables against the walls. One held a candlestand and the other a Bible. This was where we would sit on Sunday afternoons when I read to her.

Beside such, they were rarely used rooms, but Basel was a city that wasted very little and the rooms had a purpose. They were the strong wall that kept the visitor who'd breeched the door from truly being in the house, and that was important.

Now Daniel was in a chair the farthest from the Bible, and his bright silk coat was a disconcerting shock of color in a somber place, though the room managed to dim it. "Look, Leonhard!" he said, springing from his seat. "I've come to see you!"

"I see that," I answered. Grandmother hadn't come with me. She was back to the kitchen. Daniel put his arm over my shoulder. "Is there another interruption you want me to be?" I asked.

It was Daniel without Nicolaus, Daniel not cocksure, Daniel in doubt. Daniel as drained of himself as his mother had been of herself that morning.

"Leonhard," he said, and then nothing, and I waited. "You'll say what you think, won't you? You always do."

"Not always," I said.

"But you think, whether you say what you think."

"I do."

"Then I want you to say what you think."

"Tell me what to think about."

"I will." But he didn't, and I waited again. "I've given my word on a matter, and I might want it back."

"What matter?"

There were many pauses in the conversation. "I won't say."

"You gave your word in good faith? And the other person, as well?"

"That could be yes or no. I thought I did, and that the other had, as well, but now that I've thought more I'm not sure."

"Well, Daniel," I said. "I can't say what I think if I don't know what to think. If a man gives his word, that's a binding to him. It's false witness to go back on it."

"I knew you'd say that, but this has a difference, and if you knew it you'd agree with me."

I had to laugh. "Then you know what I'd think, and I don't."

But Daniel was so forlorn. "Tell me, then, Leonhard, when would you go back on your word? When have you?"

"I don't think I have. I don't remember. Daniel, I'm no one whose word anyone would want!"

"Then when would you?"

"Give my word?"

"No, take it back. Break the bargain. When would you?"

"Well . . . if I'd been deceived. I think I could then."

"That's what might be. You'd say I'd been deceived, I think. I'm sure you would."

"Tell the man, then. Tell him how you think he's misled you, and you want the bargain off. Is there one of you who acts first?"

"He already has. Part of it. But a big part. Maybe he has. I don't know whether he has."

"What was it, Daniel?" I asked.

"I won't say."

The next pause was mine. "Was it anything evil?"

"Evil . . . ?"

"That you agreed to."

"Not that I agreed to, no. I wouldn't have. And that's a point, too, that I didn't. And it's done. Even whether he did it or not. It might not have been." He tried to laugh. "It wasn't anything a man would be thrown into the river for! Not what I agreed."

"What was it?" I asked again.

He was sober again, and finished. "Leonhard, it's best not said. There's much to think about and I will."

"I will, too."

"Don't. There's no use."

I think neither of us was much satisfied. Mistress Dorothea had asked me to watch for regret and remorse. I wasn't sure yet whether I'd seen any.

I sat late, through two candles, writing in silence about sound and waves. I'd been writing this thesis for very long now: two years. The scratch of my pen came to seem like thunder to me in the quiet night. With every sentence I also heard Huldrych's arguments against my ideas, and I wished I could answer him. Only when I could argue back did I know that there was some strength in my ideas. He was like the hammer that put force behind the chisel, forcing elegance out of my coarse and ill-formed proposals.

Finally I put the quill aside and closed the ink. I dressed for bed. I didn't know the time. Last, I looked across my bookshelf for which volume I'd have for my Saturday. It was hard. I was still diminished. It would take time to re-grow. I picked the *Ars Conjectandi* and extinguished the light.

My sleep was short but restorative and I woke to my Saturday morning more at peace. I was out to the well in good time, and I chose a different fountain than the Barefoot. At home again, I felt the Saturday morning buoyancy lifting me. It was like I had hold of some hourglass that didn't whip with the waves.

My grandmother found me more talkative, and she was, also. "What were you writing last night?" she asked, and that was a sign that she wanted to just hear me chatter. I was always writing and to her, one thing was mostly the same as another.

"I was disserting," I said. "It's still on sound and waves in the air."

"And what in particular?"

"On what a wave is."

And I said it eagerly enough that she had to ask, "And what is it, Leonhard?"

"I think it is a Mathematical equation."

"And how can it be?"

"I don't know if the wave is the equation or the equation is the wave. But this is what I've written, that the equation is the law that the wave must obey."

"Sound must obey laws? Like men must? And who gives laws to the air?"

"I think God does."

"And do they follow His laws?"

"Yes," I said, and firmly. "In every circumstance they do. They aren't unrighteous."

"Where do they learn the laws?" She was teasing my words, but I think they were interesting to her.

"They don't learn. They just follow. The laws are invisible."

"You see so many invisible things, Leonhard."

"It's only because there are so many," I said.

Then I was in my room and I read Uncle Jacob.

The subject was conjecture, chance, probabilities. To throw dice, what was expected? The cube would fall on one side of six, and any was as likely as any other, though only one would land upright. And throwing it again, there was still the same chance. Landing a three twice made the chance of another three no greater or less. But it was still unlikely to land threes thrice. What did chance mean? And how could chance be, when all the universe was ordered and clockwork? Did God choose which side would land?

I'd read the *Ars Conjectandi* a dozen times at least. I could have written out good stretches of it from memory. And now, though it's prideful of me to say, I could place it only in the middle of Mathematical writing. Leibniz, DesCartes, Newton, and others were still above it. But it had hints. The book couldn't have included all that Master Jacob thought, or even wrote. So I looked, as I read, for what had been written but not in these pages; I looked for the invisible writing.

Master Gottlieb had written the book from Master Jacob's notes. Perhaps he had them still. It would have been more likely that Master Johann had those notes, but that also seemed most unlikely. It would not have been Jacob's wish that his rival brother come into possession of them.

Instead, my thoughts turned in a spiral to another place the papers might have been. Most likely they had been gathering dust. Great amounts of dust, for many years. And then they were somewhere else.

And for a few moments, they may have been in Mistress Dorothea's kitchen.

At the dogmatic three thirty I put my knuckles to Master Johann's door, and it was opened by Mistress Dorothea. That sequence at least was as absolutely unchangeable as anything in Mathematics. There was no chance to it.

There was a change in me, though. I was not fearful, or

not as much. But there was one obstacle between myself and my proper place, and I couldn't overcome it. It was my hat.

I had no other hat! Gottlieb still had my humble student hat with the simple roll of the brim on either side, and I hadn't had the opportunity or purse to buy a new one. I had only this tricorne. Would it be monstrous of me to wear it into my Master's presence? But I couldn't have come without a hat, either. It had to be doffed in respect and set on the table. And there it would be! As I approached the dull door, I was in a sweat and un-confident. But not fearful. How could I fear anything when I was wearing a gentleman's hat?

What pure dilemma! And all my musings in Mathematics and Physics, Theology and Greek gave me no guidance at all for solving the problem. As the Mistress knocked on the final door, only Logic could help me. There were two choices, Hat or Not Hat, and Not Hat was impossible. So Hat had to be, so Hat was. The knock was answered, I opened the door, and not just a student but a gentleman went in.

I had a worry, as I came into the room and studied his face and mood, that our other meeting in that place on Thursday morning would not be forgotten. But I didn't see anything. Master Johann was seated at his table, as always, with his candle, his paper, pen and ink. His stare, as always, was just past my shoulder as if he still was in his previous thought. His wide face seemed at its least alert, which I'd learned meant just the opposite. I felt it would be a taut and grueling afternoon. He saw my hat. Surely it would only be a goad to him, to challenge me even more fiercely.

"Good afternoon," he said, and I answered the same. "Sit down," he said, and I did. This was the formula. I took my seat, and set my hat on the table. It was a little more between us than to the side where I would usually position it.

"Have you done your exercises?" He always asked this,

and even the turmoil of the last week didn't change what would be asked, or that I'd done the work. I handed him my papers and he looked at them critically. If there was ever an error, he would see it immediately and tell me with no attempt at gentleness. I would want no attempt; it was my fear of his rebuke that drove me to perfection. At least, that was one motive: I was driven by the rebukes I gave myself just as strongly.

"Yes, that is correct," he said after his study. "What have you been reading this week?" It was as if he knew. To tell him Uncle Jacob had been in my hands just an hour previous would have been effrontery.

"Boccaccio. Master Desiderius lent it to me."

"When?"

"Tuesday morning." Before the coach arrived, and before the Town Council meeting.

"It's satire. What did you learn from it?" He sometimes asked such questions, for him to learn about me.

"About death, sir. Black Death's not a subject for satire this week."

"It is not." That was the first acknowledgment he'd given of the events of the week. "At another time you might find that the book is much about life." He paused, and searched me. "You grieve for Master Huldrych, don't you?"

"Yes, sir. Very much."

"I do also," he said, and that was the completion of our beginning. But I knew him this well, that those three words were complete truth, and his grief was as deep as mine; but he was a deeper man than me. "We will begin a new discussion today."

Those were words that were even more wondrous than the offer of a book by Master Desiderius, or the prospect of a long, empty road begging to be run. To my great discredit, the thought of Master Huldrych stood back out of the light. But perhaps that was Master Johann's intent, to help me with my grief.

So I set my pen at the ready. How I loved to write! White paper was a heaven for me, and the beginning of a new Mathematic subject was like angels singing. I wasn't irreligious at all thinking this. God would be worshipped sublimely in sublime things.

"Consider a polynomial of the fifth degree."

"Yes, sir. A specific one?"

"That it was created from five known roots."

And we were off. He would ask questions and I would answer if I could. He would push until I could not. "In what way does it inflect? What is a description of its differential polynomial? How does Leibniz find the maximum values?" And here, already reeling and breathless, I had to also remember to use only Leibniz's words and none of Newton's.

"The maximum occurs where the ratio of infinitesimals is zero," I answered.

"What is the meaning of that ratio?"

"It is how the value of the polynomial changes as the independent varies. When the ratio is zero, the polynomial is neither increasing nor decreasing, and it has reached a point between those two. If it is increasing to the point, and decreasing after it, it must be a maximum."

"Must be? In every case?"

"It might also be a minimum."

"Every case is one or the other?" He was like a wolf with his jaws clenched on the neck of a sheep. I was the sheep.

"Yes. It must be a maximum or minimum." In that instant I knew I was wrong.

"What if the ratio of infinitesimals is itself at a minimum or maximum, even at zero?"

I was dizzy. "It would . . . the polynomial would increase to a point, come to level, but then increase again." I took a deep breath. "Or decrease, and decrease," I added hastily.

"Yes." He nodded, and also breathed. "And there are more cases where each following differential polynomial is itself such a leveling case."

❧

There was a book on my shelf, *Analyse des infiniment petits pour l'intelligence des lignes courbes*, by Monsieur de l'Hopital of Paris, written nearly thirty years ago. Some ten years before that, the great Master Leibniz had published in the *Acta Eruditorum* his article *Nova Methodus pro Maximis et Minimis, itemque Tangentibus*, on the Calculus, the first ever published. Monsieur de l'Hopital, certainly a great Mathematician himself, failed to comprehend it and hired for himself a tutor, a young man then, my Master Johann, who began a correspondence with Paris and instructed his elder. He was likely one of only three men in the world who could have: who had both the understanding of the material, teased from Master Leibniz's very obscure Latin, and also the ability to teach it. The other two were his brother, Master Jacob, and Mr. Newton in England.

Monsieur de l'Hopital then himself published Master Johann's notes, with just the barest attribution to their true author, as the first textbook in the world on the Calculus. I'd read *Analyse des infiniment petits* and I recognized it to be thoroughly Master Johann's own work. Only after de l'Hopital's death did Master Johann make his claim that the book was actually his. It was Daniel's opinion that de l'Hopital had paid Master Johann a princely sum for his silence. If that were true, Monsieur de l'Hopital at least for his own lifetime had purchased, and Master Johann sold, a very great renown. Now, though, all of that fame and prestige has returned. And Master Johann has only increased his, and all the world's, understanding of this vast new continent of Mathematics.

And this was the man who was before me now, teaching me the Calculus. His explanations of it over the last years had always been so lucid and straight. It has all seemed so simple to me, but I knew that it was only because I had been taught so well. When I would describe the mysteries to another student, they seem to understand nothing of it. They would only shake their heads at my gibberish. I was a very poor teacher.

On we went, and on and on, and as always I'd lost all track of time: of the clock and even of the calendar. Then there was always the sudden moment when he rubbed his hands and leaned back in his chair. This was when he would give me my assignment for the following week. I was already exhausted, but now had to pay the closest attention of all. But this time he didn't tap my papers and show me what from them I was to work on. Instead, he pulled out a paper of his own, but didn't show it to me.

"Let us address an issue of a series of infinite numbers."

This was quite different from what we'd been discussing. He nodded to me and I took up my pen and ink again.

"A sum," he said. "One half, one fourth, one eighth, one sixteenth, one thirty-second, one sixty-fourth, and on. An infinite series. What is the sum?"

$$\frac{1}{2} + \frac{1}{4} + \frac{1}{8} + \frac{1}{16} + \frac{1}{32} + \frac{1}{64} + \ldots$$

"Exactly one."

"And how is that? An infinite count of numbers, and they add to a finite sum?"

"Yes, sir. Because they grow infinitely small." This was very plain, and we had discussed it long ago. He was plotting something. He wouldn't have asked such a simple question unless he had a difficult plan.

"Then one half," he said, "one third, one fourth, one fifth, one sixth, one seventh, and on. An infinite series. What is the sum?"

$$\frac{1}{2} + \frac{1}{3} + \frac{1}{4} + \frac{1}{5} + \frac{1}{6} + \frac{1}{7} + \ldots$$

"The sum is infinite."

"But they also grow infinitely small?"

"But for this series, not as quickly. Not as quickly as the sum grows infinite."

"That is correct."

Oh, he had my interest piqued entirely. I thought he might really be a show-man, the way he drew out a puzzle and pulled his student into it.

"How do you know that the first series added to exactly one?"

"There is a method," I said. This was still all very simple. He knew the method, of course. "If the series is multiplied by two, it becomes one, one half, one fourth, one eighth, and on. If the two are subtracted, the infinity of terms is cancelled, and the remaining value is one. So, the series subtracted from twice the series is the value of the series, which is one."

"Does this method work for any infinite series?"

"No, sir. Only for this geometric type."

"Now write these numbers."

Then I knew, from his voice, that this was to be the challenge. The first questions had only been to set his stage, and now he was ready to play his drama. "One, one fourth, one ninth, one sixteenth, one twenty-fifth, one thirty-sixth, and on. What are these?"

$$\frac{1}{1} + \frac{1}{4} + \frac{1}{9} + \frac{1}{16} + \frac{1}{25} + \frac{1}{36} + \ldots$$

"They are one over the square of one, one over the square of two, one over the square of three, one over the square of four, and on. They are Reciprocal Squares."

"Yes, Reciprocal Squares." It was roast veal and wine, exquisite, the way he said it. "They are Reciprocal Squares. Is the sum infinite? Or finite?"

"Finite," I said, though I paused to think. "Yes. Finite. Besides the beginning one, the numbers are each smaller than the first series you listed. One fourth is smaller than one half, one ninth is smaller than one fourth, one sixteenth is smaller than one eighth, and on. So if the first sum was finite, this must be also."

"Yes. Finite. Very good, though that was simple." And he paused, and his pause was perfect in length and depth and width. "And what is that finite sum of the infinite Reciprocal Squares?" he asked.

"The sum . . ." I was bewildered. I stared at the numbers on my paper and tried to make sense. I looked at the pattern of them, at what they seemed to be adding to, at the other methods I knew, anything. They seemed very simple, as simple as the other sums we'd done. And finally I grasped that . . . "I don't know." I realized minutes had gone by. "What is the sum?"

"What is it?" He rubbed his hands. "No one knows. It is a number, somewhat larger than one and a half, and less than two. It has been calculated to a close value. But no one knows what it really is. Perhaps it's no particular number at all, just a number. But it should be something more important than that. A squared root, a cubed root, a ratio of important numbers. No one knows."

"It would be something . . . surprising," I said.

"Perhaps. Perhaps. And now, the Paris Academy has issued a challenge to anyone in Europe who might discover the true value of the Reciprocal Squares." He'd kept the paper in his hand closed from me; now he opened it. "Monsieur Fontenelle and Monsieur de Molieres of the Academy are very great Mathematicians. I have instructed them myself. Their challenge is to all Europe."

I was reading. The page was in Latin, of course, and it was just as he'd said. The two men were members and directors of the Royal French Academy, and their announcement was as weighty as a mountain: to explain the meaning of the Sum of the Infinite Reciprocal Squares.

Master Johann was a member of the Royal Academy; if he were not, the Academy would hardly have been worth anyone else's membership. Therefore, he had received the first copy of the challenge, and soon it would go out to all the rest of Europe. And whoever first solved it, or proved it unsolvable, would instantly leap to the highest rank of Mathematicians, if he wasn't already there. And I was being given this glimpse into their world.

"Will you try?" I asked. I had finally returned to the dim room in Master Johann's house. He was waiting for me.

"I have reason to believe it can be expressed in some other way than only as the sum. It has some special value as itself."

"Why?"

I saw in his eyes a look I'd seen sometimes before, which was like the Basel Walls when their gates were closed and a banner of plague or war was flying, to tell travelers that there was no entrance to the city, and they should keep a distance if they didn't want an arrow for warning. "I will leave you to explore that."

"A Reciprocal Square." Grandmother practiced the words. "Does it have use?"

"None practical."

"But men in Paris have challenged other men to learn the answer. A wise man doesn't answer idle dares."

"It isn't idle," I said. "It's not men in Paris who made the problem. The problem stands on it own. It's always been. It's men in Paris who've found it and asked for help."

"Asked for help." My grandmother understood that very well.

"No one's been able to."

"Would Master Daniel or Master Nicolaus know the answer? Or Master Gottlieb?"

"I don't know if Master Johann will tell them of the challenge." Then I thought about it longer. "Yes, he'll tell them, I'm sure. They'll have heard of it anyway. But Daniel studies the Mathematics of flows and pressures, and Nicolaus follows his father in the pure Calculus. Neither of them is expert in this Mathematics of infinite series. And Gottlieb studies the rules of proofs. So I think Master Johann will consider that none of his family would solve the problem, and therefore he would surely give it to them to try."

"He would give them a problem he is sure they couldn't solve?"

"I think that is the main reason he'd give it to them."

"Who might know the answer?"

"There is a Mathematician in Scotland, Mr. MacLaurin, who has the Chair of Mathematics at Aberdeen. He's a great genius in infinite series. I have his books. He should be the man to solve this problem."

"Would that please Master Johann?"

"No," I said. "Not at all. Master Johann has had disagreements with Mr. MacLaurin."

"Of course," she said, not surprised. "What kind of man is Mr. MacLaurin?"

"He is certainly a great Mathematician. I've read that he's eccentric and often neglects his lectures. He has had his Chair for eight years."

"How old is he?"

"Eight years older than I am."

⁂

The Boot and Thorn had more custom that evening. Fear of the plague and thirst for news of the plague battled, and the Common Room was half empty and half full. I knew Daniel would come, so I took a bench and waited. Charon the cat sat with me. The creature had nor wanted friends, but would sometimes be a companion.

Three men were at the table: Lithicus, Lieber, and a tailor named Scheer. These three, the stonecutter, the bookbinder, and the tailor, had a game of dice they played, and had for years. I watched them. It seemed all random to me, though they claimed there was both skill and luck to it. I watched the cup twist and the dice roll, as regular as a clock but always with different results. The three shouted and hooted and swore and all the faces of the flagons on the walls each watched his own favorite of the three. Even smoke from the fire seemed less willing to travel the chimney and stayed to watch.

⁂

There had always been two uses for dice.

Sortition was the act of chance, to choose and sort with no

obligation to the sorter. Gottlieb's *Ars Conjectandi* was the Mathematics of this method. There was great expectation of the accumulation of results, but no expectation for any single throw. The tradesmen's game was this use.

The second use, cleromancy, was the opposite, where some agent was thought able to control the dice. There would be few agencies that could be expected to have such a power, and cleromancy was used for fortune telling and divination. But it would also be the name for the casting of lots, the Urim and Thummim, and the choice of a new Apostle after Judas.

The selection of a new Chair, in the end, was the casting of lots. So it could have been just a choice by chance of one from three, or it could have been God's finger pointing to the man. It was worth thinking which of these it truly was.

Usually nothing could be seen of the outside through the windows, but I saw a black horse arrive and a stable boy coming to tend it. Then a loud laugh from the hall told everyone he'd come. He'd only been back for the week but already he had his universe aligned, and other ears and heads picked up and watched his entrance. Fewer may have seen his shadow Nicolaus follow him. Nicolaus hadn't been riding; he must have been waiting somewhere for the rider to arrive.

Daniel surveyed his duchy and chose my humble side by which to plant his flag. That meant that soon I was in the middle of everyone else, as the room coalesced around him. "Two days," he said, "and not a signal of plague. The Council's saying it's a hoax."

"Hoax?" the room said. "That old Huldrych died for a hoax?"

"No, he died for his own reasons and not for plague. It's a hoax to call it plague. Who's seen plague? Who's to tell that it was?"

The black bristling center of the smoke said, "I've seen

plague." We hadn't seen Gustavus but he was there, with us. "And so it was."

The room was deadened by that. Innkeepers had special responsibilities concerning Black Death, as listed in Basel's laws, so they were expert at recognizing it. They were responsible to send carts for corpses and collect clothing for burning.

"Jankovsky died of plague, didn't he?" That was another voice in the dark.

"Just a chill," another voice answered. "It's easy to die in a winter."

"If he did, then Desiderius has his Chair by honest death," Nicolaus said quietly, beside me.

"Desiderius?" I asked him. "How else would he have it?"

But Nicolaus only said to Daniel, "Then what were Huldrych's reasons for dying?"

"All the reasons that being ancient had for him. What were any reasons he had to keep living? That's the question."

"I'd keep living." That was Lieber, the bookbinder. "No matter if I was ancient."

"And you are ancient!" Daniel said. "But not as Huldrych. And you're not in a Chair. That's another reason Huldrych had, to be out of the way."

"Out of your way." That was Nicolaus. And Daniel, in his black humor, laughed at it.

⁂

They talked on, Daniel jesting and coarse, more than I thought him usually to be. It might have been that he was unsettled as the rest, or more, and that the doubt and confusion from his talk with me was still there. But he wasn't asking for my counsel anymore. I edged back from him and his throng, into a darker place, and somehow had Nicolaus beside me. He was quiet as always. I knew he had something to say, though.

"Was it plague?" I asked.

"It's a plague."

"But that he died of?"

"Not Knipper."

"What killed Knipper?" I'd never been told.

"A pan, I'd say."

The knot around Daniel laughed at something he'd said, and himself the loudest. I wasn't following either brother well. "A kitchen pan?"

"A heavy one brought down hard."

"He was killed in a kitchen, then?" I wasn't sure if he was leading me, either.

"You know that, Leonhard, and the kitchen, very well."

"Well, I do."

"And dust, too."

"Dust? Oh, Huldrych's laboratory?"

He just nodded. Smoke from the fire, like dust, swirled lightly around and suddenly I choked on it.

"Huldrych breathed the dust," I said.

"It's not often disturbed."

"I breathed it, also. And Gottlieb did. Or, no, we didn't. I tried not to. Was something in it?"

"It was dust."

"And I don't know which pan in Mistress Dorothea's kitchen, either," I said.

"You don't?"

"No," I said and I said it firmly. But Nicolaus was hard to read in broad light and it was narrow dark in the Boot and Thorn.

"But the imperative," Daniel said loudly across the room, "is that now there's a Chair open. Let the bidding begin!"

Returned to my bedroom, I chose Mr. MacLaurin's volume from my shelf. Finally, though, I put it aside.

I opened the Faustbook from Master Desiderius. The title was *The World of the Black Artist and Magician Doctor Johann Faust*. There might have been truth in the tale.

It had been two hundred years ago that Paracelsus held the chair of Medicine, and he held it only one year before he was thrown out for obnoxiety. He must have been exemplary in his ill-will and bad-temper. It was very rare for a man to be ejected from his Chair. I didn't know of any other besides him, and he was very famous for it. Theophrastus Bombastus must have been an apt name.

There might have been truth of history, that a man like Paracelsus would have had pride and blindness enough to think he might get the better of bargaining with a nemesis angel. Then there might be truth of Theology, that a Mephisto would take on the bargaining. If Paracelsus had made that bargain, though, he must also have come to Faust's end, as he lived no longer than any other man. What a terrible game it was to try, and what a fool to have tried it. I thought through all the possible outcomes, and all seemed that they would be tragic.

And finally I put my candle out.

8

The Eadem Medallion

Sunday morning I escorted my grandmother to Saint Leonhard's, and I had to do it as a gentleman and not as a humble grandchild; I still only had one hat. The service calmed and comforted us both greatly. Three days after the Inquiry there had been no other indications of plague, and the city was whispering what Daniel had announced, that Huldrych had died of a common cause. Yet there were those who still held with Gustavus. That morning on our benches we were reminded that the truth was that we were in God's hands. If there was judgment, we would not escape it; if there was mercy, we would receive it. That was an essence of the Reformation.

Two hundred years ago, in the years that Holbein's art came to Basel, and Paracelsus' darker art came to Basel, the Reformation also came to Basel. It came in a man. His name was Hausschein, which meant HouseLamp; for his scholarly name he took *Oecolampadius*, which was Greek for that same HouseLamp. And he was a very bright lamp in Basel. He came when he was thirty from Heidelburg, at the very moment that Luther was nailing his theses to the Wittenburg door, and that was the flame that lit Oecolampadius's wick.

He preached atonement at Saint Martin's Church and was the Reader of scripture at the University. He assisted Erasmus in that scholar's translation of the New Testament, and disputed that scholar's interpretation of it. Erasmus was finally bested; he admitted it himself, and Oecolampadius carried the city. Erasmus, near twenty years older, outlived him, though not for long. They're both buried in the Munster.

Zwingli was a student in Basel when Oecolampadius was in Heidelberg, and they became friends even as one had left Basel before the other arrived. They were partners in the disputations that ranged through Switzerland those years, arguing for Luther against Rome, arguing for Anabaptism against Luther, arguing for Luther against Anabaptism, arguing against anything, against each other if there was nothing else, and fracturing Catholicism in Switzerland forever, taking the land city by city and canton by canton into the Reformation.

Oecolampadius and Paracelsus were contemporaries. I could imagine the dispute those two would have had. And if Mephisto, on leaving the Alchemist's door, had, in the streets of Basel encountered the Reformer, that dispute would have been the greatest of all. And I'm sure who would have bested the other.

Within twelve years of Luther's nailing, the University in Catholic Basel was so engulfed in the Reformation's fire that the Pope suspended his charter of the school and took its scepter, its seal, its statutes, certificates, privileges, and its cash assets. Three years later, Protestant Basel reopened the school. Oecolampadius had died the year before. The University had lost its seal, but the Pope had lost his University. It had risen, the same University, but altogether changed.

⁂

My grandmother and I then walked back through Basel's same streets to our own home and were offered no disputes or bargains. I preferred disputes in Mathematics, where ultimately a correct statement was irrefutable and an incorrect statement was indefensible. A dispute of Theology must also have truth and error, just as in Mathematics, but it seemed every man still chose for himself which was which.

And this was why there were both judgment and mercy, and why sacrifice made it possible for there to be both.

We ate in humble righteousness, which was the only kind.

⁂

"Grandmother," I said. "I was speaking with Master Nicolaus last night."

"Were you?" she said, nodding. "Yes, I spoke with him yesterday, also."

"I thought you might have."

"He called on me. He's a very gentleman."

"You must have had a pleasant conversation," I said.

"He thought that you hadn't been able to answer a question that was put to you at the Inquiry."

"I hadn't been able," I said. "It was just then that Master Huldrych became ill."

"He asked me if I knew the answer to the question you'd been asked. I told him that in his mother's kitchen, you spoke with Knipper, and were sent to the inn for help with the black trunk."

"Thank you," I said. My grandmother was the wisest of women and always knew what was right and proper.

൬൭

On the next, rain-soaked Monday morning, I opened the kitchen door as I always did and wondered how I'd find Mistress Dorothea. She might have been as slow as she'd been on Friday or she might have been returned to her normal whirling state. But she was neither, nor in between. She was in her normal household attire, except that she had on a black housecoat, and she was standing in the center of the room, stiff, waiting. For me. "Leonhard."

"Yes, Ma'am," I said.

"Master Johann wishes to see you."

I looked down at my mud-splashed self. "But Mistress Dorothea," I started.

"He said as soon as you arrived."

"Then, please," I answered, and followed, all brown. We went to the hall, and to the stairs, but up only one floor. The door we came to was one I'd seen only once before, when my father brought me to Master Johann at my matriculation, to discuss my Saturday afternoons. Dorothea knocked and the voice answered, but it was different, as different as brown was from black and white, as different as Monday morning was from Saturday afternoon.

The room behind the door was as different and more. The Saturday room upstairs was sparse and dark hollow. Now I stood on the threshold of a chamber dense and bright. I'd never seen so bright a room in Basel. There was the usual curtained window, but the true light was from a dozen candles. And what they lit! A desk, a chair, a cabinet, a case of shelves; and papers. Thousands of pages. It was surely thousands! And all of them crossed like a market square with lines of text and diagrams and equations.

"Leonhard." He looked up and perceived me.

"Yes, Master Johann," I said. "I apologize for how I look . . . I wasn't expecting to see you."

He continued his stare. I stood in silence as the rain was still dripping from my hair, to my forehead, and one great drop splashed off my nose. Then he rubbed his hands and glanced back at his desk, and my apology had been accepted. "You said that you have been upset by Master Huldrych's death?"

"Yes. I have."

"As I said, I also. It was grievous and unfortunate. He wasn't always obsolete in his lectures. He was once advanced in his field. The University will choose a Chair who is more modern, but he is still a loss. Were you attending his lectures?"

"Yes, sir. His advanced class."

I was first fooled that the papers were in disorder, but I knew they couldn't have been. In an instant, I saw that there was an order, an order that I knew perfectly. To compare my own books and papers with this room would have been to match an acorn to an oak, but I was bold enough to call my desk an acorn at least. "I have a task for you."

"Yes, Master Johann."

He lifted a single sheet from all the papers. "It may help you in your grief. Do you know the stonecutter on the White street?"

"Lithicus? Yes, sir, I know him."

"Good. Go to him. I want a memorial made for Master Huldrych. Take this." He held out the paper, and I took it. "That is what it's to say." I looked at the page and read the words.

"How should the stone be made?" I asked.

"A wall piece. I want it a modest size and it will be placed in the Preacher's Church, which was his parish. Modest but well made. He was a modest man. Make it whatever shape is the current style. Let the stonecutter decide, or you. But bring me a drawing before he starts, and his price. Tell him I'll pay. He'll know what that means."

"Yes, sir."

"A new Chair of Physics will be chosen. And Leonhard, as for the coach driver. The Inquiry is closed."

I dared to ask. "Was any answer found?"

He looked at me, considering his answer. "Perhaps if I had completed my interview with Magistrate Caiaphas, there would have been an answer."

"Yes, sir."

That was all. I left the room both dimmed and dazzled. I was nearly desperate to see it again, to see in detail the books and papers I'd had only a few seconds to study.

But as my feet descended the stairs, another pair were ascending. As I passed Little Johann on his way up, I said, "The letters are still on his desk. Both from Paris and from Russia."

By a narrow passage between two houses I came to the stone yard. It was bare of grass or any green, part dirt and part stone flags, and dizzy of worked, unworked and part-worked stone. There were keystones, cornices and corners, and other architecture, but really the yard looked most like a churchyard for the monuments and figures and angels. And everywhere, there was dust. It was very fine and gray.

The man was there, too, his hammer hanging in his hand, staring very thoughtfully at a gray veined square. "Lithicus," I said. "who's that for?"

"Oh, is it you? It's not for you." In his yard he was a gray man. His hair was, his dust covered skin was, and his loose smudged shirt. But the veins in his arms were as stark as the veins in his marble, and I wondered what flowed in either.

"I hope not!"

"No, a fish merchant. He choked on a fishbone."

"It's a pretty piece. What will you put on it?"

"A long life and much to say about it. It won't fit on this. So this one's not for him. I'll want a bigger slab."

"Oh, I think I know who it was," I said. "Reinkarper?"

"That's him."

"He wasn't rich. It would be a big stone for a middle merchant."

"There's three kinds that take a big stone," Lithicus said. "The rich, the pious, and the sinful."

"The sinful? For atonement?"

"For their side of the argument."

"I have a job for you," I said. "It's a memorial, too, and not for any of your three kinds."

"What family of yours is dying? Or are they already?"

"He isn't and he is. It's Master Huldrych."

"Huldrych. Yes. That'll take a good stone. But what are you to him to be here?"

"I was sent."

"Sent." His eyes narrowed beneath his dusty brow. "Sent, are you? Who by?"

"Master Johann."

He dropped his hammer and the yard rang. "I would have known," he muttered. "And he's paying for it?"

"He said to tell you. Will you do it?"

"He knows all well that I will. What's it to say?"

I read the paper to him. "It lists when he died, and that he was Chair of Physics. It's for the church wall."

He stared at the words. "They'll balance right."

"What do you mean?"

"Can't have short lines then long lines. Those'll split." He pointed to spots on the paper between the words. "Plain words," he said.

"He wasn't a plain man."

"He is now, plain as any of them."

"It says what he was," I said, "not who he was."

"When a man dies he should die and be done with it. Not keep a hold on his place and people. Take a broom to his house and sweep it clean." It seemed an odd philosophy for a monumentalist. Lithicus's trade was memorializing in stone. A good portion of Basel's past would be remembered mostly by his chiseling. "Now, any border on this? Any decorations?"

"You're to make it whatever the current style is. And draw it first and send it to Master Johann with the cost."

"I'll do it. And when he says it's right, I'll carve it the same as it's drawn, to the scratch. I won't have any trouble with this one. Not like the other."

"Which one?"

"For his brother. Jacob. He didn't like what I did. If I'd seen what he wanted before, instead of after, I would have made what he wanted."

I didn't even say the word, *spiral*.

Master Vanitas lived on the Peter Square, which was wide and tree-filled, near Saint Peter's church. The Square was bounded on one side by the Grace Cloister, whose original monks were no longer present in Basel. Now the cloister was part of the city Armory. On the other side of the Square was a row of comfortable houses which, not content with the trees in front of them, also had large gardens behind.

Master Vanitas held the Chair of Theology. He seemed to be an old man, but was actually only aged beyond his years. He had a sprightly, devoted wife and a cherubic young child. In fact, he was surrounded by all the vanities of life. His best known lecture was on the certainty of death.

He hadn't many friends, and very few of his students admired him, but I did. His history was that he'd also come to Basel as a young man to study Mathematics, and he'd studied at the feet of Master Jacob.

No one else knew this. Daniel didn't, nor Nicolaus. Vanitas was a student in the years before they returned to Basel. I had even asked Gottlieb once if he'd known how Vanitas came to his Chair, and Gottlieb had told me a few normal details but not that there was Mathematics involved, and it seemed he would have told me if he'd known. I only came to know myself because of an odd moment in a Theology lecture.

It had been in just my first or second year as a student. I was listening very attentively, not realizing how stultifying it was. In the course of a discourse on the inviolability and invisibility of heavenly truths, he'd made a statement: "It is no more possible for man to see or feel God's law than to see a trigonometric identity." That, of course, had roused my interest, both that his point was so intriguing, and also that he was aware that trigonometry *had* identities.

We had talked a few times since. He had lost interest in Mathematics because of what he called its arrogance, that it brooked only one correct answer to a question, and within its own rules. He preferred questions that couldn't be answered, and answers that didn't satisfy. But I'd thought deeply myself about the similarities between Mathematics and Theology, how they were both invisible, unchangeable, and seemingly unfathomable. Both ruled us, and we could struggle and challenge them, but finally, we were bound by them.

He let me in and took me through his house to his garden. His wife was at play there with their daughter, who had only lately discovered walking and the possibilities of self-locomotion. We watched her explore. A soap bubble from some neighbor house settled lightly on a blade of grass beside her and a butterfly settled as lightly beside it. A clock inside sounded solemnly. The bubble popped, the butterfly soared from it into the sky, and the child, amused and bemused, turned away. These were reminders to me of ephemeral life.

"Master," I said. "I'd like you to tell me about Master Jacob."

"Master Jacob," he said. "Well, then, Leonhard, please sit and I will tell you."

Master Vanitas was a man who spoke carefully, slowly, and long. There had always been a tinge of sadness in his voice. Whenever he spoke, and whatever he spoke of, he seemed always aware of the weight and implication of humanity. This gave his lectures on Theology a meaning, a purpose, and a depth in which his students quickly drowned. Those who remained awake felt that they were hearing things that must be understood but were not understandable. I was always fascinated by his teaching, though I was careful to have a full night's sleep beforehand.

When he conversed on subjects more mundane, he wasn't abandoned by that weight of thought he always carried, and so if he was asking Lieber for a book or his wife for a plate of fish, or just considering the chance of rain, his listener felt that nothing was trivial, nothing was answerable, and nothing was even visible. It was so much like Mathematics!

Therefore, as Master Vanitas told me his thoughts and impressions of Master Jacob, it was as if that Master was an Old Testament Prophet translated via Latin from the original Hebrew. I interpreted the verses and imagined him.

Jacob had been like his brother Johann. He was brilliant, sullen, far-seeing, narrow, vengeful, could think like lightning . . . but there was a trait that the older brother didn't have which the younger did, the ability to control the men around him. And, he'd been very suspicious of Master Johann, especially because he'd known his younger brother had that great advantage and was honing it in Holland. In the ten years they were apart, they fought constantly and with only a little mercy. Their letters and publications were full of vitriol for each other, but they had respect.

And when Jacob had learned that Johann was returning, he fell into a thick, bitter, angry sadness. Vanitas had already stepped away from Mathematics toward Theology but he still called on his old teacher, and he'd seen that something final was occurring in his Master's thoughts.

"What do you mean by *final*?" I asked.

"Something that was an end and irretrievable."

"How did he die?"

"Of an illness. He was in poor health but I hadn't expected it. When I was young, death was still a surprise to me."

"Did he die before or after Master Johann arrived in Basel?"

"At just about the same time," Master Vanitas said. "There was a grievous elegance to it. That the Chair should pass from one brother to another. Death brought about change that in some ways was no change."

There was a growing risk that the entire Lecture on the Certainty of Death would proceed. I quickly asked a question on a different subject. "I was speaking with Master Desiderius. He said that it was you who nominated him to his Chair."

"Greek? Yes, I did. I'd not met him, but I'd known of him."

"Then you knew he'd be qualified for the Chair."

"Yes, I knew. But it was Master Johann who reminded me of him. I'm not sure who our committee might have nominated otherwise."

"Thank you very much, sir," I said.

Past seeing Lithicus and Master Vanitas, it seemed fit to walk to the Death Dance, which was nearby. That dance was certainly the most universal of all human gambols. No face in the mural was anyway joyful except for death's. While Death Dances dated from the years of the Black Death, the dance would be true even without a plague. In the most peaceful, healthful land, Death would still take every man and woman by hand. But when he did for any reason other than age, he was being more inevitable than he needed be. I wanted to look again at Master Jacob's epitaph.

Through Vanitas, I'd come from the stonecutter to the stone. I stood a long while in the Munster cloister, considering Uncle Jacob's memorial, considering the medallion, and thinking of what Lithicus the stonecutter had said.

To most people, a spiral was the Archimedean. It would begin at a center and circle out. Mathematically, it was a polar graph with the radius at every point equal to the angle from an axis. As the angle increased and reached the full circle and increased on, over and over, the arm of the spiral would increase outward. Every point of the arm was an equal distance from the circle inside and the circle outside. There was a satisfaction to it. It had its single beginning and continued growing forever. But it was the *spira mundanus*, the mundane spiral, and it had this failing: that as a viewer stood back from it, it would shrink as everything would with distance. The revolutions, always equidistant, would vanish into indistinction.

To Mathematicians, a spiral was the Logarithmic. This was a spiral like the other, but with a crucial difference: The space between the circles of the arm widened. It was the *spira mirabilis*, the marvelous spiral. Each repetition increased by a constant ratio. As a viewer would step back, the center might diminish, but the outer parts would just shrink down to exactly replace them. If the line were itself also to grow thicker, the spiral would appear the same from any distance, growing larger in its circling as it grew smaller from distance. And it had no beginning, either. Stepping closer would reveal an endless circling within.

The conch shell on my shelf was Logarithmic. I was so amazed when I first saw it, because I only had my own sketches before to imagine what the shape looked like. Then I'd seen that what I'd only known invisible existed visible, as well, at least a shadow of it. It may have been that everything invisible had such a shadow.

There were many other spirals: those of Phyllotaxis and of Fermat; the Golden Spiral of Fibonacci; the hyperbolic spiral, the lituus, the Theodorian Spiral which he received from Pythagorus. I've even imagined a reverse spiral which started in its center with no curvature, then tightened to a point like a fern. But none of these equaled the elegance of the Logarithmic. Perhaps someday the medallion could be replaced to fulfill Jacob's wishes.

But the rest of the epitaph was also worth study. I noticed again the shields that top the epitaph stone. One was a lion, which I knew by its paws. The other was Master Jacob's, and Master Johann's, family arms: three branches of seven leaves each. Master Johann's grandfather was a spice merchant in Bern, who left that city during a religious upheaval. The family brought its business to Basel and quickly took in the new city the place it had lost in the old. The son, Nicolaus, grew the business and had many relatives to pass it on to; these many cousins still operated it. But of Nicolaus' three sons and seven daughters, two sons, Jacob and Johann, went against their father's wishes into Mathematics, and now that was the business of their branch.

There was another also quietly deliberating leaves and spirals. "Why are you here?" I asked. It was Little Johann.

"I saw you."

"Have you looked at this before?"

"I shouldn't."

"No," I said. "You can. You should. Your father doesn't want mention of your uncle, but you can come see his place here."

"I do look at it some."

"Do you know what it means? You've been taught Latin."

"But I don't learn it."

"*Resurgo Eadem Mutata*. It means, 'I arise again the same though changed.'"

"Then it's the wrong spiral."

"Yes," I said. "You're right. The stonecutter made it wrong. It was meant it to be Logarithmic." Arisen changed, it would remain the same.

"What will Huldrych have for his memorial?"

"I saw the wording," I said. "There was no philosophy on it. Will you come with me? I'm going to the Watch Barracks."

"I'll come. Why?"

"To see the trunk again. It's there."

"Then I won't come."

"Do," I said. We turned from Jacob and the Latin and the Spiral. The cloister lawn was so filled with light that it was jewels and crystal, like the green glass in Saint Leonhard's windows with the sun full through them; there was growth and life. Little Johann followed beside.

"I saw Daniel's hourglass," he said.

"It's sure genius," I said. "So I think I know what the letter from Paris says."

"And Russia?"

"There's a new University. Tsar Peter has started it. He's calling for the great scholars of Europe to be part of it."

"What about Poppa, then?"

I laughed. "The *young* great scholars."

"What about you, then?"

I laughed harder. "The young *great* scholars. I'm only young. I'm no great and I'm barely a scholar."

"They only don't know you yet. Poppa would write a letter for you."

"He'd only dent his own reputation, he wouldn't make mine."

Little Johann was still following and I kept him listening. I talked about Russia and Paris and Italy. I'd never been beyond Basel and Riehen and the hills around them. I talked though about Italy, which was a ruin of Renaissance times built on a ruin of ancient times, where goatherds led flocks through emperor's palaces and the art of three centuries past was still more live and true than the superstitious villages the goatherds lived in; and I talked about Paris, which was the center of Europe and the world, all glittering and grand and rich and frightful to its neighbors, where the intellectual thought was richer and more glittering; and I talked about Russia, which was a new, exotic, mysterious land which might be barbarian but was rising and pulling and moving.

At least, these were my imaginations of those places. I didn't know.

And Little Johann listened. I don't know if he was as easily caught as I was, if he was with me in far-off lands, or if he only wanted someone to talk to him. He was still beside me as we came to the barracks.

"Simeon?"

He was there, snoring in a chair. He was Day Watch and it was Day.

"What?" he started gently. "What is it? Oh, Leonhard. It's not still an inquiry?"

"No," I said. "Except my own."

"What do you want?"

"Could I see Knipper's trunk?"

"That he was in? Why do you want that?"

"There was something written in it, and I wanted to see it again."

"What written?" Simeon's a friendly one, but he'll ask all the questions first. He'd want a reason to let me in.

"I'll show you." That was good enough. The hall we walked had no windows, just light from the doorways on each side. It was all as it had been with Gottlieb five days earlier. We stopped a moment by the rusted armors standing guard beside the weaponry store: swords, axes, maces, bows, and guns. The room across from it stored Watchmen, some sleeping and some at tables playing and talking. Another room stored grain, potatoes, dried meat, and more foodstuffs. The last had shelves loaded with closed boxes and barrels of less obvious meaning. But here there was a change from my last visit. The floor was empty.

"Has it been moved?" I asked.

"It hasn't been moved," Simeon said. "Where would it be moved?"

"But it isn't here."

"I'm not blind." He wasn't, even when his eyes were closed, and now they were open, narrow, and suspicious. But not of us.

"It's been taken. Would the Watch have taken it?"

"I'm the Watch for this room, and I haven't. It must have been Night." He stared at the space a moment, then at me, frowning. "Then do you know who might have taken it, young Master Leonhard?"

"I'd like much to know," I said.

"It was taken at night, I know that. Not on my Watch."

He left us then, suspicious and grumbling threats against the Night Watch.

"You won't see it now," I said to Little Johann.

"Leonhard, I have."

"When I looked in it before, I found something," I answered him. "A crumb of dough. Good bread dough. So I thought you'd seen it."

All he said was, "I won't tell you."

"I don't know what you'd tell me," I answered. "Did you know that Knipper came to your kitchen?"

"I only saw the trunk. It was dusty."

We walked slowly back to the Munster Square. "What was in the trunk?" I asked

"Not Knipper."

"No, he wasn't. He was still on the road from Bern. What was in it? Was it papers?"

"Notebooks of papers. It wasn't near full."

"Were they Jacob's?"

"They were. I don't like Latin and I didn't read them. But I knew they were. They were wrapped in bundles, in linen. I looked in one and saw them."

"Gottlieb wrote the *Ars Conjectandi* from them. He knew what they were. I heard what Gottlieb said to Huldrych and I saw the empty trunk. It had Jacob's spiral in it."

"Why was it in our kitchen?"

"I think it had been in your house for a few years. I don't know how it got there from Huldrych's. It had been in an attic, I think, or somewhere, and brought to the kitchen."

"Because Daniel was coming home," Little Johann said. "Poppa wanted it away so he wouldn't find it."

"Do you think?" I asked.

"I know Poppa would."

"Then he hired Knipper to take it somewhere away."

"There was a envelope in it, too."

"A letter?"

"From Poppa. It had his seal, but no name on it."

I walked with Little Johann. We turned into the alley, and through the gate I'd just mended into the back yard, and he held the door for me into the kitchen as if it was expected. So I went in with him.

It was about noon, as the clocks of Basel defined it. Lunch was past and the room was empty. Little Johann stopped in the middle of the floor, just before the spot the trunk had been. I stood with him.

"What pots are there?" I asked. "Any with a dent in them?"

He shrugged. "Heavy pots wouldn't take a dent."

"Did you look?" He nodded. "When did you realize that Knipper was here?" I said.

"When I heard how he came back."

"I know, and you know, and Nicolaus knows. Perhaps Gottlieb knows. Perhaps everyone in the family knows. And one person certainly knows."

"I don't care," Little Johann said. "Whoever hit him, I don't care." Which meant that he did, and was frightened.

I asked, "What came of the papers in the trunk?"

"I don't care." Which also meant he did.

"There was enough space in the trunk for Knipper and the papers?"

"I don't know." Which meant there was.

"Then it might be that the papers weren't taken out. They may still be here, or they may be somewhere else in Basel, or they went to Strasbourg."

I sat with my grandmother that night. I was always wanting to go to my books and papers. Sometimes, though, I reminded myself that she'd have companionship with me. So I'd sit in the kitchen, after we'd cleaned everything. Then we would talk and say slower and longer things.

"You say that Lithicus the stonemason seems anxious at every mention of Master Johann's name," she said after we'd talked about what I'd seen and heard that day.

"Always when I ask about the spiral on Master Jacob's epitaph. And when I said that Master Johann would pay for Huldrych's epitaph, he was very upset at that, also."

"What became of Master Jacob's papers?"

"They might still be in Master Johann's house. They might have been in the trunk when it was taken from the house to the inn. Maybe it was Knipper and Willi who carried the trunk back, and Knipper was killed after he was at the inn. Willi will be back on the coach tomorrow, if he's allowed out of Strasbourg. I'd care to know what he found in Mistress Dorothea's kitchen. And I'd care to see those papers. All of Master Jacob's papers, Grandmother."

"Would there be great things in them?"

"I don't know. Cousin Gottlieb used some of them for the *Ars Conjectandi*, and I've heard Master Johann's teaching for all these years, too, and he'd have known what was in them. They were at his house for him to read. There must be letters Master Jacob received. But most of his letters have been published. I don't know what else would be in his papers." Something from the day put another thought in my mind. "Or they might even be burned. Lithicus said a man's house should be swept clean when he dies. He said that of Master

Huldrych. If only he'd seen Master Huldrych's house! That would take a great deal of sweeping."

"Or maybe he did see it," Grandmother said. "If that was what he said of Huldrych."

"There would be no reason for him ever to have," I said. Unless he'd had reason. I remembered the gray dust mingled in Huldrych's golden dust.

"Tell me about Master Johann's room filled with papers," she said.

"It looks like mine," I said. "And it felt like mine. I think I could sit at his desk and know where every paper and book was. But it was much grander, fit for a Chair."

"Did he have Master Jacob's book?"

"No. Nor Daniel's. Nor Mr. Newton's, nor Monsieur L'Hopital's. But many others. Some that I didn't know. And ten times as many papers as I have." But that seemed an exaggeration. "No, I don't even have a tenth," I admitted.

"More papers than you?"

"He's a great Mathematician. Very great."

"Is that what you aspire to, Leonhard?"

"Is it right to aspire? It seems prideful."

"It can be done humbly."

"Humbly, I do, Grandmother. Someday I want to be a great Mathematician."

"For the pride of it?"

"No. I think I'd rather not be known at all. It would be for the Mathematics. I want to discover new Mathematics. Master Johann has already discovered so much, and all the other great men before him. I only hope there'll be some left! I know there would be, though it might be beyond me to understand it. But I want to sit in my study and read and think and write."

"And a wife, and children?"

"Yes," I blushed. "Of course, that. And students, too."

"You're eighteen now. When will you finish your school?"

"I think next year."

"What does a young man do who is a Mathematician?"

"Mathematics," I said. She shook her head.

"What are you thinking and writing now?"

I was embarrassed to say it. "I've tried to solve the Reciprocal Squares."

"Then tell me what you have discovered about the Reciprocal Squares."

It was very patient and generous of her to ask, and irresistible for me. "I have no start to a solution. There is nothing that this problem can be compared to. But I've been reading about other infinite series and infinite sums." And then, as she listened with her full attention, I described how each method I knew, and each method known at all, was full short of the problem. "But, I think the more difficult the problem is, the more elegant the solution must be."

"Elegant?" she said. "What is elegant in Mathematics?"

"Everything! But there is a special quality to some Mathematics that is specially known as *elegant*. The elegant solution to a problem is the solution that is clean, even pure, that cuts through obstacles like an arrow through paper. It solves the one problem but also a dozen others that hadn't even been proposed. It associates one world of Mathematics with another that had always been thought completely separate. It's the one invisible beneath the many visible."

"Leonhard," she said, "when you speak of your invisible things, they seem real."

9

The Triple Seven Leaves

On Tuesday at noon I went to Gottlieb's house to hear a lecture on Logic. I had been his student before and sat through his full course. I felt that now, as his one-time clerk, and wearing the tricorne he'd given me, I could claim a privilege of gentlemanly association and sit as guest.

He wasn't a poor lecturer, whatever Daniel had claimed. It was more that he was dry as dust. His lectures kicked up the dust to infiltrate and irritate his listeners' eyes and ears. What was this dust? Words and words and words. He would speak on Aristotle, and the air would be filled with the dust of ancient Athens. He would describe Pythagorus, and the dust would float in triangles. He would confess Euclid, and the dust would fill all the space in the room. He would attempt Descartes and Pascal and Newton and Leibniz and the dust would grows wings and claws and teeth and threaten the life and spirit of everyone in its cloud. Covered in dust, the students would stumble blinded and choking from the lecture room. Somehow, though, the dust would cling, and for months after the listeners would be surprised by logical thoughts sprouting in their brains like rare mushrooms in a dank forest, and paradigms sprinkling their conversations like momentary summer showers.

And Gottlieb's lectures were always absolutely straight, starting from the beginning and proceeding to the end in unbent linearity. When he was finished, there was no doubt of the truth of his original premise. Yet no one had doubted it at the beginning: the importance was in the proving. We, in black and white, heard it laid out in black and white. Truth was truth. False was false. It was, whether we knew it or accepted it, or did not. Deny that fish swim, but they still did; and fishing for a trout in a dry meadow would leave a man hungry. I liked logic. It showed that we must accommodate truth, and not the reverse. And in a way, that because *proof* exists, it was proof that God exists.

I thought also about the unproof of Gottlieb's Election, how it was only a chance motion that had made him, and not Daniel, Chair. I wondered whether Gottlieb, the beneficiary of the chance, had the same thoughts about it.

He didn't acknowledge my presence until the end of the lecture. Then he did, politely, befitting a gentleman scholar, and one who'd already attended his lectures, and was therefore an expert himself.

"I've been reading the *Ars Conjectandi*," I said, when the other students had left. "May I ask you about it?"

"Ask what?" he answered. It was appropriate for a student to ask questions of a Master, but Gottlieb showed no eagerness.

"Are there truly chances and randomness? Or is everything in fact ruled by laws of nature? Or does God own all actions?"

He had no interest in answering great questions, standing in his front hall. "Why are you asking such questions?" He scowled. "You, especially, who have already thought through those questions and answers more, you think, than anyone else?"

"I meant, when you were writing the book, did Master Jacob's notes show that he'd considered those questions about chance when he was writing about chance?"

This was only somewhat less onerous to him. "He had many notes, and on many subjects. Someday you may have the opportunity to read some of them." He didn't sound as if he hoped I would.

"I hope to very much. Where are they?"

He scowled. "You know well where they were, and that I'd like to know where they are now."

"Yes, sir," I said. I'd only wanted to be sure. "I stopped at the Watch barracks yesterday and the trunk was gone. Simeon didn't know who'd taken it, or where."

"There's no need for him to know. Nor you. Now, I'm in a hurry."

But into the already scalding pot, I poured another cup of boiling water. "One other thing. It's a small thing. It was one week ago that I was serving as your scribe, and you were very kind to allow me the use of this hat." I took it off my head and we both looked at it. "But I realized I should return it and retrieve my own."

"What? The hat? Keep it. I have no use for it." He seemed more surprised than angry.

"Thank you," I said, and very sincerely. That was very generous. It was a bit old, but it would have cost more than a few florins. "Thank you. I've been very proud to wear it but I was concerned as it was only borrowed."

"No, keep it." He was off guard and done with the discussion but I had one other small part.

"I hope it isn't poor of me to ask, though, for my old hat?"

"Why would you ask me?" Now he was suspicious and back on guard.

"I think you may still have it," I said. "When you put this on my head, you took the other that I'd had."

"Did I?" It seemed odd that he wouldn't remember. Gottlieb was very detailed and particular. But it was also a very inconsequential detail.

"Yes, sir."

"Then it's not here now. I'd know if it was. And I'm in a hurry. I have an appointment."

"Do you know where the hat might be? I'm sorry to annoy you with it."

"My appointment is to discuss the punishment of an annoying student."

"He is being punished for being annoying?"

"The student has shown disrespect to a Chair. I won't discuss it with you, Leonhard."

"Anyway, the hat," I said. "It was a hat given me by my father. I should have come sooner or spoken before."

"Your father. No, it's not here and I don't know where it is." And that was a very final statement and the end of all sympathy. "Good day."

His door closed. Above it, set in the timber, was a stone square with his family's emblem, the triple seven leaves. It might be odd that he had it made and set there, considering the many hostilities he and the other members of the family had with each other. Yet there were other bonds that held them together, nearly invisible, but which I sometimes could see.

❧

As I had a week before, I crossed the bridge to Small Basel out the Blaise Gate. It was like the other gates: a tall, thin tower directly over the opening in the Wall. It held a portcullis and also the gears and ropes to draw the bridge up from the moat. But as always, it was no impediment to me as I left the city.

To the left, just across a field, was the Rhine. The river was broad, strong, and usually peaceful. As a child I had walked often beside the Rhine, beside my father. When I would now stand beside the water, on a sunny grass or in knoll shade, I might still feel small, and his hand on my shoulder. And he still walked a path on its bank many days, though it's a distance from Riehen.

I went out from Small Basel at the Saint Blaise Gate as I'd done a week earlier, and I ran for a while along the road with its narrow field between me and the bank. Then I crossed the field to the water's edge and slowed because rivers were walked beside, not run past. But I didn't saunter. I kept a brisk pace.

It wasn't only that the riverside path was an old friend that I chose it over the main road. The main road had gawkers and I wanted to meet the coach before the rest of the city did. It took a mile to be the first and farthest. Then I went back onto the road, and after another mile to the edge of Basel Canton, where the tariff crossing to the Landgrave of Roteln and Saussenberg marked the end of Switzerland and the beginning of the Empire, and I waited there.

❧

It was uncertain who might be driving the coach. But when the coach was still just dust in the far distance, I knew it was Willi. There was a uniqueness to a driver who was coming home, and that driver was.

I saw him sure when he was closer. He was alone in his box, shoulders hunched forward. A lout was always a mess but this one looked to have been in prison for a week and all in the same clothes. He came to the customs booth and stopped to pay his toll and argue his way through. Knipper had been a match for any customs guard, but Willi was new to the job, unfamiliar to the official, and weary.

"No crossings," the guard said. "There's plague."

"I'm not wanting out!" Willi shouted. "I want in!"

"I'm from Basel," I said to the guard. "I'm come to see that the driver doesn't make trouble for you."

"You?" He looked at me closer. "I've seen you before?"

"Yes, sir. My father and I used to walk the riverbank together and we'd see you fishing."

"Your father? The pastor of Riehen?"

"Yes, sir."

He considered me, now much taller than in those years. "And you're here for the driver?"

"He's with the Inn in Basel. He's replaced the usual driver."

"Then let him pass! It's not for me whether they all want to die of plague. Just don't bring it back here."

That was enough. Willi moved the horses forward across the line. "Wait," I said. "Can I ride with you?" I asked, and he didn't stop me from climbing up beside him. Closer, he looked worn in his being with gaunt face and red sores on his wrists. "You'll be welcome in Basel," I said. "Strasbourg's hated for holding you."

"I'll hate the place, always," he said.

"What was it like?"

"Poor formed and evil." He spat. "And high ugly."

"Magistrate Caiaphas was a poor ambassador for it, too."

Willi jerked the reins, not to stop the horses but from surprise at what I said. But the horses halted anyway and the coach nearly toppled.

"You know his name?" Willi near shouted. "What's he to you?"

"He was here."

"What are you doing stopped?" he said to his horses. "Hi, get." He snapped the reins and the horses heaved and the coach started. "He's been here? To haunt Basel, too? When? I never saw him here. I'd never have gone to Strasbourg if I knew he was there, never."

"This last week."

"Liar! He wasn't! Why do you say he was?"

"Well, he was," I said. "What happened to you in Strasbourg?"

"I drove into that foul stinking city, and found that ash heap inn, The Broken Shield, and the keeper Dundrach, and told him Knipper was lost and I wanted a bed and food, and went to find them myself. And I had a bowl from the kitchen, and I had Knipper's bed and was asleep in it, and then the Guard was on me like on a thief! And dragged through streets! And to a filthy cell and thrown food like swill. The jailer's an ox, but the magistrate's a sheer fiend. He threatened me with red pokers and racks if I didn't answer his questions."

"Caiaphas?"

"Yes, him!"

"Did he do any of those?"

"No, I only saw him the one first day."

"He was here this week. He came in the coach. There was a boy, Abel, who drove the route, and Caiaphas came and a gendarme Foucault."

"For what?"

"For an Inquiry. For Knipper."

"Knipper, now when I get him I'll wring his neck. Where was he? I'll murder him."

We came about a curve, and far off the steeples of the Munster and Saint Martin's and the Preacher's Church and Saint Blaise and Saint John all stood up from the fields. And closer, gawkers by the road were pointing and waving. I thought furiously.

"What did Caiaphas ask you?" I asked him.

"There it is." Now, Willi had his eye on Basel. "Batwing, you mean?"

"He threatened you if you didn't answer?"

"Look out there at the people. What's the news? Is it the plague they're waving at me for?"

"What else did Caiaphas ask you?"

The closest knot, a half dozen children, were running to meet us.

"Well, he asked about that dust-eaten trunk, and why they'd sent it to him."

"Sent it?"

"It had Caiaphas's name on it! That's why I want Knipper, to wring his neck. And you! You're the one who told me to get it."

"Knipper sent me to get you."

"You say. I never saw him."

"He wasn't in Master Johann's kitchen?"

"No, he wasn't. And I had to lug that trunk myself onto the cart."

"But it was sent to Caiaphas? Who sent it? Was there a label on it?"

But I'd lost his attention to the crowd. "What are they saying?" The children were running beside the coach, and their elders were waving Willi to stop. I dropped myself from the box and wasn't noticed.

I was glad I had my grandmother to talk to at night. As we would eat dinner, she'd ask sharp questions, which seemed to cut through my thoughts and confusion.

"You didn't tell the coachman that Knipper was dead?" she asked.

"There wasn't an opportunity. I didn't realize that Willi didn't know until we were already with the crowds, and it seemed poor to kick him with the news and then jump off."

"So he heard it from the crowds instead."

"He must have," I said.

"What does it mean that the trunk was sent to Magistrate Caiaphas?"

"I don't know. There must have been a label."

"Does Willi read?"

"No. He must have had it read it him. Maybe in Freiburg."

"And are you done with this day, Leonhard? Are you getting your writing done?"

"I am, but not tonight. I'm back over to the Inn. I'd like to hear what Willi's saying."

The Inn was crowded. Willi was toward the back corner but not too close into it, so there was room all around him. His head was down and he looked to be displeased at the attention, but anyone knew he couldn't escape it. And maybe he didn't hate it so much anyway, because he looked up to answer the questions as they came, and he answered them full, or even overfull. Then I saw Gustavus at the counter, and I could see that he'd ordered Willi to keep the room full and occupied. Strife and gossip both put silver in Gustavus's pockets.

The men asked about the cell he was kept in: "Foul and evil, that we'd never put a man in Basel, vermin'ed straw and mealy bread that might crawl on its own." The town itself: "Rats in every street and every house, and stinking water for drinking, and more stinking air to breathe." And the inn: "The Broken Shield's a swine pen of mud and filth, close and narrow and tight and food no better than the pigs would eat." And in return, the throng told him over and over of Knipper, "what a stir that was, cursing, and rabble threatening. Opening the trunk and Knipper bundled in it like rags, and Caiaphas like a wolf at bay with the crowd like he'd blast them, then Faulkner arriving like lightning."

I had more that I'd have asked him, that I very dearly wanted to, but there would be no quiet moment with him that night. And it was common knowledge that he'd be away in the morning to Bern, as much as he was making it known that that would be his last drive and he'd never even look out the Blaise Gate toward Strasbourg.

And I noticed of course that Daniel wasn't in the room; he was as noticeable absent as present. It must have been that he knew he'd have no chance for anyone's attention on that night. Nicolaus was there for a while. I remained after he left, watching. There seemed to be many more than should have fit in the room, and more speaking, until the air itself, which was all smoke, seemed to be just faces and voices. The fire was the source of it. The smoke filled the room with mumbling. Something was burning in the fire more than plain logs. I edged close to it.

In the ashes of wood consumed and forever lost, I saw one small piece on the edge of the embers, charred but resistant to burning, at least to that fire. It wasn't rough timber but a finished flat surface, the remnant of a planed plank. And that one part that the fire couldn't chew had the Logarithmic spiral etched into it just as I'd seen it before in the Watch's barracks. I took that remnant from the hearth and left.

⁂

My grandmother was still in her kitchen when I came home. It was a smaller room than Mistress Dorothea's and was only used to cook for us two. I liked it better. Usually we had our meals at its table, where the larger kitchen in my Master's house was never used for that. The fireplace was just large enough for a nice fire and two pots. There was a niche in the stones for baking bread. Four good cupboards held all the pots and pans, and plates and cups, and knives and forks and spoons. The table was as sturdy as the trees it was made from, by my great grandfather who was pastor in Saint Leonhard's before my grandfather and father. That table would be used for generations more, for kneading, for chopping, for washing, for all the uses my grandmother put it to. It was also where my grandmother read her Bible, so it was sanctified and holy, and that was irrevocable.

When I set the charred spiral on the table to show her, my grandmother looked at it long and hard but didn't touch it.

"Why would the trunk have been burned?" she asked.

"It must have been better burned than not for someone."

"Who would have taken it from the barracks to the inn?"

"Only Gustavus would dare burn it in that hearth. Someone hired him to."

"Who would have?"

"Master Gottlieb says there's no need for me to know."

Then, in my room later, I put the spiral on my dresser beside the conch shell.

As I collected water the next morning, I watched the slipshod departure of the coach for Bern. Willi was groggy and staggering, the passengers complained at his slapdash treatment of their luggage, and the horses hadn't settled to the succession of new drivers. Rolling and reeling like a ship, the carriage heaved away from the inn and square. It would have been well served by Daniel's hourglass.

❧

When Daniel, later, on his black horse, rode me down in the street looking for me, he was also concerned with storms.

"It's the Election," he said. "The wind is rising! They're talking. They've begun deciding."

"Deciding what?"

"Who'll be on the committees, who the committees will nominate, which nominee will be chosen."

"I'll believe the first," I said. "Not the other two."

"I've been calling on Chairs today. I've called on Philosophy, on Law, on Botany, and on Greek." He clenched his fist. "Even on Logic," which required a pause. "And on the Dean. Brutus has them all in his hand. He means to steal the Election."

"It's meant that it can't be," I said.

"He means that it will be.

"What did the Chairs say?"

"Nothing."

"Of course! What would they say? There isn't anything to say."

"They know everything," Daniel said. "They won't say because they're told to not. They won't say who they want for candidates or when they'll have the Election, or anything else."

"Maybe they haven't decided yet."

"They haven't been told yet."

"But you said they already know everything! And why would they tell you, anyway, Daniel?"

"I'm the true candidate!"

"There might be other candidates. They need to have three, anyway," I said. "And you've spoken to Logic? I don't think Gottlieb will be told."

"He'll be told and he'll do as he's told."

"Or even more, Desiderius."

"Desiderius? Him?" Daniel laughed. "Poor little Leonhard. Desiderius even more than Gottlieb. Desiderius most of all. Jankovsky was cleared from the Greek Chair just for him."

"But Jankovsky died of a chill."

"Of the plague, just as Huldrych did."

"But you said Huldrych died of old age!"

Daniel shook his head. "I'll have the Common Room think that. But he was cleared from the Chair, just as Jankovsky was. It doesn't matter how he died, just that Desiderius had the Chair cleared for him."

"In that you're wrong."

"How is it that he was Brutus's candidate? And it's that candidate who always wins."

"But he was nominated by Vanitas."

"But he was told who to nominate," Daniel said. "Vanitas put the name to the committee, but only because he'd been given it. I saw the letter that came to my house, that had that name in it, and I saw that letter again in Brutus's hand as he went to call on Vanitas."

"You saw the letter?" I said. "What did it say?"

"I didn't read it. I only saw it in its envelope."

"Then you don't know what it said!"

"I know what it said."

"Without reading it? Where was the letter from? Who was it from?"

"Now, that's a nice one. It was a name I didn't know at the time, but I know it now, and you, also. It came from Strasbourg."

"From Caiaphas?"

"Magistrate Caiaphas."

"His name was on the envelope?"

"No, no, no! But I asked the coachman when he brought it."

"Knipper told you?"

"He didn't, but he was shaking in his boots when he came to the house to deliver it. Who else would it have been from?"

I finally laughed. It was all like an equation that cancelled to nothing. "So a letter came, but you don't know who it was from, what it said, or if it was anything to do with the Election. You don't know if your father ever talked with Vanitas about the Election. You don't know anything! Your logic's backward. And you stood for the Logic Chair? It's well you didn't get it."

"And should have had it. And I know better what was in that letter than if I'd been told."

"Well, I'll tell you this: Your father did suggest Master Desiderius to Master Vanitas as a candidate."

"What? You knew?"

"I know it because I asked Vanitas. It's a better method than your guessing and wrong-way logic. And Daniel, I still haven't found a man or woman in Basel who'll say how Master Jacob died, or just when. Only that it was the same day your family arrived."

He shrugged. "Leave it covered, Leonhard. Leave it."

"Daniel! You're maddening!"

"I don't care. There's another Chair now, Physics, and I don't care about Mathematics now."

"And what did Jacob have to do with you getting either?"

"Leave it covered. Bury it deeper. Let the whole Rhine flow over it." He was not to be brought back to the subject. "And when the Rhine does, I'll tell you the rate and the force and the pressure of it. Mathematics is nothing, Leonhard. It's Physics that has greatness in it, that has fame to be grasped. Hydraulics, and optics, and your sound waves. There's a world to it."

"It is Mathematics."

"Mathematics is only a tool."

"But that's the miracle, Daniel! Why does Mathematics tell how a river runs or light bends? Does a stream study its equations so it knows how to flow?" I was too overcome by it all.

"Be at peace, Leonhard," he said, very amused. "Think on your mysteries and miracles, and not on Jacob. Let the river flow. I'll take the Physics Chair. That's the one for me."

"Then it's a pity that your father will steal the Election from you." I said it as a joke but Daniel heard it as a warning.

"He'll try to, I said. He'll try. I didn't say he will, only that he'll try."

"Then you'll have the same chance as the other candidates. That is, if you're one of them yourself."

"I will be. And there'll be no chance to it."

"Oh," I said. "So you mean to steal it yourself."

"No, I'll have Brutus steal it for me."

"Daniel! But you said—"

"What I want from you, Leonhard, is to keep an eye on him. Let's be sure he doesn't outwit us. That's all."

"That's all. Only to be sure that Master Johann doesn't outwit you and me. That's all."

"That's all!" Daniel laughed.

"I've no wit to be outwitted."

"Ha! Keep your eyes on him and tell me what you see. I'll find you when I need you."

With which he left. He'd be pure frustration if he wasn't a mix of that and absurdity. I could only laugh. Gottlieb, Johann, and Daniel: Each was a seven-leaved branch of the same family.

A century after the Plague, the Pope of the time, Martin, called a Council in Basel to consider some matters current and important at the time. This was of course before the

Reformation, and Basel was a significant Catholic city. While they were in Basel, one pledge the Council received from Rome was the promise of a University for the city.

Wars with the Turks intervened; Constantinople fell and the Byzantine Empire ended; the French recaptured Bordeaux and closed their Hundred Years war with the English; the first Bible was printed by Master Gutenberg. But finally, twenty years after the promise was made, it was kept, and a deed of foundation was issued by Pope Pius. The opening ceremony was held on a spring day in April, and the University of Basel commenced.

Even now, most German universities will have no main building. The lectures were given in the Professors' houses, and many lectures in Basel would be delivered this way.

But the Guildmaster of Basel of that time, named Siebold, had married the Mayor's daughter and built an impressive home overlooking the Rhine, beside the bridge. Yet he and his son both died, leaving his widow alone in the largest residence of the city. So she sold her great white house to the new University

This University Building had been completely renovated, at that time, and times since. It had foyers and an office for the Bursar and the Registrar, and a salon for the Provost. It had several small lecture rooms, used by lower lecturers who had no room or house of their own large enough to give their lectures. But primarily, the building housed the University Lecture Hall, in which hundreds could gather on benches to listen to Chairs.

So, on that Wednesday afternoon I attended to the University in that Grand Lecture Hall. Master Johann was giving a public lecture.

Every Chair must give lectures to the public. It was as traditional as black robes and wigs, and anyone might attend, except women of course. These public lectures were given through the year, with every Chair speaking at least twice between September and May. This was in fact the main use of the Lecture Hall, although even some of the public lectures were given in the homes of the lecturers.

Master Johann, though, was unique that he only lectured in the Lecture Hall, even for his normal classes. No student ever was allowed into his house for mere teaching; no student but me. Besides that it was beneath his dignity to have his home used for public events such as lectures, even when they were only his paying students, it would also be impractical for the size of his audience, as every student attempted to attend his class.

He accepted this. It was not beneath his dignity to accept their tuition, and he alone charged a higher rate than that which the University set for all the other Chairs. He would accept the money but not the attendant responsibility to educate his students. He would only lecture in Latin, which the newer students were not fluent in. He would not allow questions, as some of the younger Chairs would; instead, he demanded absolute quiet. Then, he would choose only the most obscure and obtuse subjects within the Calculus to describe. And this was only when he did lecture, which was only every other scheduled meeting. For the alternate classes, he would send a proctor to grade the students' homework. The solutions to these assignments, being the same every year, were easily obtained from every boardinghouse in Basel.

Why, then, did anyone, let alone high-spirited University students, endure this regimen? Certainly it was not for the purpose of learning the Calculus, which none would understand, or want to understand, any more at the end of the term than at the beginning. There was even a risk in that a student who annoyed the Master, even inadvertently, would be marked for a dunce through his entire career in Basel, and might even be hounded out completely.

No, the reason was that Master Johann's prestige was so great that the mere right to say, "I have attended his lectures!" was worth all the pain and suffering. Indeed, it was a rite of passage in Basel. I myself made something of a profit, as well, off his students, as this was my main source of Latin tutoring.

His public lectures were better. Here, with the citizens of the city and eminent guests, he burnished his reputation with chamois rather than with sandpaper.

The lecture that day was on a very basic principle of Calculus, the statement that if a function has a certain value, then increases or decreases in any way while staying continuous, and at a later time returns to that same first value, then there is at least one point in between where the function must have been level. Monsieur Rolle of Paris, and who was a member of the Academy there, first stated this principle.

Of course, Master Johann's description was far more clear and more easily understood than I could have attempted. He smiled, gestured, was even humorous. He gave examples, that there must always be a top to a hill and a bottom to a valley, to make his audience understand.

The lecture hall was filled with Basel's gentility. The Chairs' lectures were a powerful bond between the City and the University, allowing each to be acquainted and improved by the other.

And not only the City attended, but several students, also. There were a few new to the University taking the opportunity to first see the famed Master Johann; there were a few who had a sincere interest in the Calculus, though this was a very few; and there was an occasional unfortunate who had fallen under the cloud of Master Johann's disapproval and was trying to regain favor. I remembered Gottlieb's appointment concerning a student who'd shown disrespect to a Master; and I saw a student I knew, named Gluck, in the second row, who was usually proud and joyful but was now desperate, eager, and ignored.

That night Grandmother asked about Master Johann's Theology and Philosophy. "Leonhard, you've said that Master Johann was accused of being a Cartesian. Tell me how it was heresy."

"The Mathematician Descartes a hundred years ago said that only what was sensed or touched was real. So he determined to reason, from only his own senses, what he believed."

"Then does he say that God is not real?"

"No, the Monsieur claimed that he was able to reason that God was real."

"Is it heresy?"

"Some people say it is, because they say God's word makes a thing real, not a man's reason. But Descartes said he didn't know God's thoughts, that he only knew his own thoughts, and he would have to decide for himself what was true."

"What does Master Johann say?"

"I think he is very thoroughly a Calvinist. But for him, there's a world of Theology, and a separate world of Mathematics."

"For you?"

"They aren't separate. One is the rain and one is the river."

10

The Remembered Meteor

Thursday morning Nicolaus tapped my shoulder as I was carrying a sack of flour into Mistress Dorothea's kitchen from her cellar. "I think we'll talk today," he said.

Then later when I, in black and white and beneath my tricorne, left my house for a lecture with Master Desiderius, Nicolaus was beside me in the street. I knew better than to wait for Nicolaus to start a conversation. "I tried to talk with Daniel about Master Jacob," I said. "And he doesn't want to hear a word."

"He's done with that."

"I'm not."

There was never any menace to Nicolaus. He was only quiet and intent. I could wait silently, too. "Why?" he asked, finally.

"It's worth some looking." Usually I walked a brisk pace

to lectures, or anywhere, or I just ran. But I was in my tricorne and talking with a man in his. We walked deliberately. I waited again.

"What did you see of Knipper in my mother's kitchen?" Nicolaus asked.

"I saw him there," I said. "I'll never deny that. He only asked me to fetch Willi from the inn, to carry that black trunk."

"It might have been made known to the Inquisitor."

"I thought you wouldn't want him to know," I said. "Did you want the Inquiry to come into your own house?"

"The Inquiry would have found its own Inquisitor there and he could decide himself what to make of it. That might have been why he was made Inquisitor. I think it more likely that you didn't want the Inquiry to find you in my own house."

"I wasn't asked anyway."

"Answers needn't have questions."

"Questions needn't have answers, either," I said, but only as it seemed a properly ambiguous remark to make.

"Does the Reciprocal Squares have an answer?"

"Not that I know. But it must, I think. Have you tried to solve it, Nicolaus?"

"I have." And he smiled. "Everyone in the family has for years."

"But the challenge only came from Paris this month!"

"The problem is older than Monsieur de Molieres' challenge. It's older than the Monsieur himself."

"Has Daniel also played at it?"

"Dearly."

I knew enough about my Master's family and their Mathematics to make a guess. "Nicolaus," I said. "Would it be that Daniel wrote to the Paris Academy and pressed them to make the challenge?"

"Why would you think that?" So of course I was right.

"Because Daniel couldn't solve it, and was afraid his father might. Now all Europe will try. Daniel would rather anyone else solved the problem than his father."

"You know the lion by his paw."

"But Daniel wouldn't have solved it anyway," I said. "It's not the kind of Mathematics he's genius at. It's too . . . invisible."

"Nor I," Nicolaus said. "It's too invisible for me, as well."

We'd reached the house of Desiderius. "Master Desiderius came from Strasbourg."

"Many of us have come through Strasbourg. The trunk has now, also."

"What do you know about the black trunk?" I asked.

"Everything."

"It was Master Jacob's. It had been in Huldrych's laboratory and then in your father's house. And Jacob's papers were in it."

"And then Knipper was. This is what I want of you, Leonhard. Come with me tonight to ask Willi what he found in the kitchen."

So now, I was Nicolaus' clerk. "I was wanting to. Nicolaus, should I tell Gottlieb that Knipper was in the kitchen? Should I tell the Council, or Magistrate Faulkner?"

"Whether only a few know that, or everyone does, it will still mean the same thing." And he tipped his hat. I did the same.

⁂

After his Greek lecture, I asked Master Desiderius about the Faustbook. "If a bargain is made with mere men instead of Mephistopheles, what is at stake? Can a man wager his soul?"

"I hope he can't," Desiderius said.

"What else would he wager?"

"In truth, all a man has is his soul."

"So there isn't any wager, then," I said.

"I hope there isn't. In your Mathematics, are there problems without a solution?"

"There are some. And there are some that might, but the solution hasn't been found yet. Last Saturday Master Johann gave me a problem just like that. Either there is no solution, or it will be very elegant."

"An elegant solution." He was wistful. "Yes, that's what's needed." He smiled. "Leonhard, I have a bargain for you."

"You'll give me fame and knowledge?" I asked and we laughed.

"No, you'll do something very small for me, and get nothing out of it in return."

"I'd want nothing anyway. What may I do?"

"You'll know soon."

On that Thursday it had been one week from Huldrych's death, and there had been no other deaths. The Council ordered that the black flags be taken down, and commerce be resumed. Commerce hadn't been embargoed, as it would have been in earlier years, but it had slowed. In just the course of the day it quickly revived. The piers were busy with boats coming and going, the gates were thick with carts, and the Market and Barefoot Squares were bustling to make up what had been missed.

In the Market Square I saw all the people of Basel. Wives with their baskets, kitchen girls on errands from their mistresses, booths of leather, cloth, ironmongery, and pottery and the craftsmen who'd made them, fish and fishermen, bread and bakers, farmers and all that their fields made, butchers and meat, and passing through the Square was a pastor one moment and a lawyer the next, a scholar of the University herding a flock of flapping black and white students, then a troop of the Watch.

All the Death Dance was there, but Death himself. Or, he was invisible.

❧

Thursday evening came, and among all the men affected by Knipper's death, finally one of them had reason for real joy. Beside Willi in the box was planted a booted and weathered man of goodly girth and mirthful visage, though Willi's smile was wider by far. This was Knipper's replacement, a man from Bern who'd been recruited by the innkeeper of the Roaring Lion. And Gustavus seemed to be expecting him and went in with him to the stables once he'd unloaded the passengers and luggage.

"That one's a coach driver for any road," Willi said as the horses disappeared into the tunnel. "See that smile? Oh, and do you think he's just fat and pleased? There was a highwayman blocking the road on the pass over Solothurn, and his partner on a horse right out from the trees behind us, and fat old Rupert shot them both dead, one pistol shot each. And he never slowed down, and he never stopped smiling."

"And he left them?"

"He never slowed down. He just told sheriff in Solothurn they were there." Willi shook his head. "Knipper would at least have been put in bad humor by it. This new driver, Rupert, never stopped smiling."

❧

There was evening and morning in each day of Genesis, and Master Desiderius read the Hebrew this way: a twilight of turning and twisting, to a dark night of dark things, then a breakthrough dawn to the age of day. The earth turned from the sun as I walked Basel's streets, and though Basel was not too tightly a part of the earth it rested on, it turned from the sun, as well. I passed a Night Watch on his way to his post and he greeted me. Basel had watchers in the night, some visible. Charon the cat was watching, also. I didn't see Nicolaus.

Daniel was in the Common Room, and I stayed away from him and his dice and cards. He was too boisterous, and still off balance. His voice rose and swayed like a pass through the Alps, and he sounded in danger of falling off its edge. And he laughed, and no one else was yet. But his rough humor served us when he chided Willi too hard for his failings as a coach driver and drove Willi to leave the Common for his own room.

And as I stepped back into the hall outside the Common Room a shadow came beside me. Nicolaus had been watching for me.

I took Nicolaus to the hall, and up the stairs toward the living, moist smell of horses. Below us we heard neighs and shuffles, and Knipper's niche was in an invisible corner. The door was poorly fit and glow of a candle leaked through and around it. I held up my own candle and knocked. "Be away, and if it's food leave it."

"It's not food," I said. "It's just Leonhard."

"Then just be away."

"No, Willi, I won't bother you." I pushed on the door, which had no latch, and Willi was hunched sitting on the straw pallet. The room might have been any size, a closet or a cathedral, beyond the meager part that the candle lit. Likely Knipper had never seen it except at night. "And it's Master Nicolaus, too." As little light as Willi's candle gave, nearly as much seemed reflected from his face. Or maybe it was his own glowing anger that we saw in his eyes and cheeks and chin.

"I'm weary," he said.

"Weary of talk," I answered. "I know you are. But you won't drive the coach anymore, will you? That Rupert has it now."

"No, I won't drive it. I won't ever drive it. I'll throw myself into the River rather than drive."

"Will Rupert have this room?"

"He'll have to find it first, and get me out of it when he does."

"He won't find it if he hasn't already," I said. "Can I ask your help, Willi? I want to know who killed Knipper."

"I don't know. I didn't."

"I know that. Nobody knows but one man, the man who killed him, and I want to know who it was. That's the one who'll be thrown into the River. So I just want to ask you a few questions and they're not hard."

"I don't know anything."

"You know if Knipper was there in Master Johann's house in the kitchen when you fetched the trunk."

"Oh, you! You sent me after that trunk! That's what started it!"

"I did," I said. "Knipper sent me for you. He said it'd been brought from the coach by mistake."

"I didn't take it there. It was never on the coach."

"Was Knipper there in the kitchen with the trunk?"

"I already said he wasn't! I had to lift that myself."

"Was it heavy?" Nicolaus asked. It was always startling when he spoke and Willi shrank back from the question. "About the weight of a man. Was Knipper in it, do you think?"

"Aye, yes, he was." All the light in Willi's face faded. It was as if the candle had been blown out, though it burned unchanged. "He rolled around in it, and I could feel it. I thought it was poor packed, and whatever it held would be bad broken by Strasbourg."

"How did you know it was going all the way to Strasbourg?"

"The label on it said so."

"How much can you read?" Nicolaus asked. It was a surprise that he could any.

"I know that word, Strasbourg."

"What else did the label say?"

"That's all I knew. It wasn't till Freiburg that the innkeeper read it to me. The trunk was for Magistrate Caiaphas in Strasbourg."

"For him?" I asked. "Then it was being sent to him! When was the label put on it?"

"I never saw it put on. When I got to the kitchen where I picked it up, the label was on."

"How long did it take you to get to Master Johann's house from the Inn?"

"I was pounding horseshoes that were bent; Gustavus had told me to do it. I wasn't going to go help Knipper before I finished what my own Master had told me to do. I won't cross Gustavus."

"Then ten minutes or more." I asked Nicolaus, "How long was the family together? Who would have left or gone to the kitchen?"

"We were together long enough."

I didn't ask more. Willi wasn't understanding what I was asking Nicolaus, but he might start if I asked anything else. So I asked Willi, "Do you think anyone could have opened the trunk that night after you'd put it on the coach?"

"They'd have had to tie it up again just as I had, and I tied it fast."

"Did you take the trunk to Caiaphas?" Nicolaus asked.

"No, that was for Dundrach to do. That evil—that evil, evil bat came to me. From Hades he came."

"What did Caiaphas want?"

"He wanted to know how I came by the trunk, and what had happened to Knipper. He threatened me with torture if I didn't answer him."

"He didn't tell you that Knipper was in the trunk?"

"Never! He never did."

"Did they say you'd been arrested for bringing a corpse into the city?" I asked.

"They said that, and I called them evil liars for it. They didn't say it was Knipper."

"Did Caiaphas ever ask you anything else?"

"Only about the trunk. I told them I'd just been told to put it on the carriage, and I never knew who tagged it. And I told him where I'd got it, from the Master's kitchen, and I told him it was you who came for me to get it." And he pointed at me.

"You told him by name?" Nicolaus asked.

"I said, The student, young Master Leonhard, who's servant to Master Johann's house. And he screamed at that, that you'd be a Master or a servant, but you couldn't be both."

"I am both," I said. "You were right. And Magistrate Caiaphas remembered my name. Willi, tell me about Strasbourg."

"That city's all evil. All the people, down to the dirt in the streets."

"They'd have good people there, too," I said.

"They've like been cast out. The city's evil."

"I don't remember it that way," Nicolaus said. "We stopped there for some time, a month, when we were coming to Basel." Nicolaus would have been ten years old then. And his impression, even from twenty years ago, might have been more accurate than Willi's. But Willi's impression was as black and evil as a place could be. It made me think of the courtyard outside Caiaphas's window at the inn. "And Gottlieb went on to Basel before we did." He nodded to Willi. "Then that's enough. You've been a help."

"I'll want to know who killed the old man," Willi said. "I'll throw him in the river myself, for the trouble he's caused me."

Nicolaus and I stood outside in the dark Square, at first saying nothing. But he had something to say and I waited.

"A hand brought that pan down on his head," he said, finally. "A hand in my father's house."

"And a hand put Knipper in the trunk," I said. "And took out Master Jacob's papers that had been in it."

"There could have been space for Knipper and the papers both. They could have gone to Strasbourg together. Or the papers might have been taken out years ago. You'd want those papers, wouldn't you, Leonhard?"

"I would. And they were in the trunk."

"You know they were?"

"I do, though I didn't see them. Had you ever seen them?"

"No. Gottlieb had."

"Nicolaus," I said, "who killed Knipper? Who came into the kitchen?"

"You came into the kitchen," Nicolaus said.

"I did no harm to Knipper." And at that we parted.

Sometimes I doubted my own memory.

Once I saw a meteor. I had been walking back to Basel from an evening with my parents in Riehen. The sky was clear, with no moon and many stars, and it was very quiet.

It was in the winter. I'd been thinking of how, if some action occurred, it would be by sight that we knew where; but it was more often by hearing that we would know that it had occurred at all. I considered the Cartesian implication that only by sensing did we know what was true. But something noteworthy could have been happening just behind me, and if it made no sound, I might never have known of it.

This had startled my imagination and I'd turned abruptly and looked back. At that instant, that very, elegant, instant, a meteor had cut the sky. It wasn't just a thin line of white, what we often called "shooting stars." It was a true sphere and engulfed in flame, and I saw it fragment, and all its splinters keep their line through the night. It was so quick that I couldn't even spin my head fast enough to follow it, and by the time I did, it was gone. And it was silent; if I hadn't turned, I would never have known that it was there above me. And it was very noteworthy.

But it *was* gone. I didn't know what meteors were, and where that one ended, or if it endured at all. The only truth I had of it was my memory. And as I'd returned to my trudge to Basel that night, I'd begun to doubt. I had only turned in reflex, at my own imagination, so that it might have been only more imagination that saw the meteor. And always later, I still wondered. What was real, what was visible, what was true about a memory? If Monsieur Descartes only believed to be true what he sensed himself, was my meteor true once I no longer saw it? Was memory a sense?

So, after my talk with Nicolaus, I walked the short path home, saw no meteors, and I tried to remember, in truth, what I had seen and done that evening in Mistress Dorothea's kitchen. I had entered; I had talked with Knipper; I had seen the trunk; I had left. Did I do anything else? Did I really do what I thought I had?

And had there been a label on the trunk? Yes. It was in my memory that there had been, pasted on a side, too plain to be noticed. And it had not been still there when the trunk had returned to Basel.

⁂

Even early as I was to fetch water Friday morning, there was life and motion in the Barefoot Square. The sun was up, though newly, and most houses were awake and awork, as this was Basel. I greeted Old Gustavus at the door to his Inn, watching the Square as a general his battlefield. And as I put my buckets under the water stream I heard a bell toll. It was sharp and very clean, to split the air as lightning splits the sky. I was impelled to look for the source. I'd never heard that bell before. Then it rang again. But it wasn't a ring, it was so pure and pointed. It was a cry, a sigh, an exultation, and a song. Something very great and mysterious was speaking.

I found it. The bell was the stone gate in the Wall, and the hammer was a chisel. It was Lithicus, high on his scaffold.

The Wall was rooted deep into the city, in time, and in understanding of what the city even was. It was the city, this inner Wall. So the bell was Basel and that was why its ringing pierced so deep to anyone who heard it.

"What is it you're doing there, anyway?" I asked.

Lithicus put down his hammer and decided to answer. "The Wall's old and gate's old, and the stone they're made of is old, too."

"As old as all stone," I said.

"But there's stones loose in the arch, and that's new."

"It was just the shield on the capstone that was broken."

"The cracks go deeper. Deep into the gate. You can't see from down there, but the whole arch is breaking."

And perhaps the cracks in Basel were deeper, too. "What do you do for that?"

"Mortar them back in."

"It's taking you weeks to do."

"Well, it's not done quick, it isn't."

"I guess you're doing it well, then, instead."

He liked that. "Take any stone from an arch and the whole of it fails. And I need to take them all out."

"How do you?"

"Match a brace to each stone, pull it out and put the brace in, then fix the stonework behind it, put new mortar in, and push the stone back in. And I'm carving in it. They want the lettering on the stones."

"What's the lettering to say?"

"What's it to say? I don't know. I only know the letters for each stone. I haven't read them all out."

"Tell me the letters."

"E, G, O," he said. "N, U, M, Q, U, A, M—"

"C, A, D, O," I finished for him.

"You already knew!"

"No, I guessed. *Ego numquam cado*. It means, *I never fall.*"

"It won't. Not when I'm done with it. And tell your Master Johann I'll have his stone done, too."

"I will."

"Come tomorrow to my yard. I'll have his drawing."

"I will come. Lithicus? Did you know Master Huldrych?"

"I knew him."

"Did you know him well?"

"I only knew him quick, and now dead."

"You're carving his epitaph. Did you ever even speak with him?"

"Why is it," he asked, angry again, "that you keep asking about that spiral? I'll not speak more of it!"

"I wasn't either. What did Huldrych have to do with the spiral?"

"I'll not speak of it, I said. I'll not speak of infernal spirals, I'll not speak of spirals on stone, I'll not speak of spirals on paper, I'll not speak of lot stones." And his hammer landed on his chisel and all Basel shook.

I watched him for a few moments. It was impressive to see a master at his craft, but even more to hear Basel ring. But then he sent me off. "I'll have the drawing tomorrow night. Come for it then. Now leave me alone."

I did leave him, but not alone. The Square was filling as it would in the morning, Rupert the new driver was climbing onto the coach, and Gustavus still watched. I turned back to watch. I saw Lithicus raise his hammer and with all his might bring it to his chisel. The air split, the Square shook, the inn trembled, and the church sang.

My studies with my father long ago were not allowed to remain abstract. My Botany he taught in the garden, my Latin in the Bible, my History in the ruins, and my Theology in life. For Geometry, as I studied triangles and rectangles and the theories of congruence, my father put me to practical work learning carpentry. If an angle was not defined properly as a right angle, the cabinet door would not close; and just as there were many different quadrilaterals which could have sides of the same length, there were many shapes other than square that a box would form if it wasn't properly braced.

I'd had more practice under Mistress Dorothea, who was not interested in geometric theorems but was very interested in the sturdiness and level of cupboards and tables. So that Friday morning I was forcing a table to be parallel to the floor beneath. Both lengths and angles needed correcting. "It's this leg," I said. "It was cut crooked, and pulling it straight has made it too long. But I don't want to push it back crooked again."

"Do what's proper," she said. *Proper* meant that it must not be done easily, or quickly, or unconventionally. Instead, *proper* meant that it must be done carefully, and laboriously, and frugally. To add complication, Daniel was watching me, and he found my task amusing.

"Cut it until it's long enough, hey?"

"Subtraction by a positive always results in a lesser value," I said.

"But can you prove it Mathematically?"

"I can prove it with a table leg, but I won't."

"Is that Cartesian?" he laughed. "A proof by senses?"

"It's proof either way," I said. "But Daniel, if you accuse me of Cartesian thoughts, tell me this: Was Master Johann really accused of being a Cartesian?"

He laughed louder. "You want to see? Here, come on, I'll show you." He jumped to his feet. "Come on!"

I went with him to the stairs, and up, three flights, to a hall I hadn't seen since I'd been there with him before years ago, and to a door, and through to his bedroom.

There were memories for me there. As a thirteen- or fourteen-year-old it had been a refuge when he took me there to escape. There were no chores, no frowns, no confusion in that room, just Daniel's attention and friendship. It still held that feeling, as a pie rack holds its smells. The room was the proper size for a Basel gentleman's younger son, with more space than it needed for a bed and desk and dresser, but only just. He'd always had a good shelf of books, though not as mine, and I saw that now they were less on strict Mathematics and more on the new topics of Physics, mostly Hydraulics and gases. There weren't many books on those subjects, and he had more than I knew had been written.

His desk was fairly clear, but that was because he was actually very orderly. There was another shelf of fileboxes, and I knew what those were filled with. He had a vast correspondence all over Europe, as he was as quick with his pen as he was with his tongue.

"Are they useful?" I asked, meaning his books. He had to see where I was looking to know how to answer.

"Those? No. Vacuums, all of them. Pure emptiness."

"You'll write one, then?"

"It's started, Leonhard, be sure of it! I don't use all my time riding the countryside."

I would have asked him all about it, but I knew he'd be impenetrable until he wanted to tell me, and then he'd be uncontainable. "But what did you want to show me?"

He had a filebox already open and was riffling papers. "I'll find it," he said, and then, "Ah, yes! So Leonhard, you've heard the legend, how Brutus was accused of heresy in Holland."

"Of being a Cartesian?"

"The very. What would he do now, if someone made that accusation?"

"No one would accuse."

"Because he isn't a heretic?"

"Well . . . he isn't, but I also don't think anyone would even dare."

"Yes, that's it. They'd end up accused of heresy themselves, or thievery, or murder. And if a student tried? Do you think he'd even get an answer?"

"No. He'd be out of the University instead."

"But in Holland he wasn't the emperor he is in Basel. Here. It was a student who accused him in Groningen. And old Brutus did answer him. See this."

It was a printed pamphlet of just a single sheet folded to make four pages, titled on the first as a *Dire Warning to the Rector of the University of Groningen* by the student Petrus Venhuysen. I read the first page.

"The Latin is so poor, I can hardly understand it. It says Master Johann opposes the Calvinist faith?" I turned it over. "He follows the teachings of Descartes, and so he deprives all believers of their comfort in Christ?"

"The Brute's the last to give anyone comfort and the first to deprive them of it. But he doesn't bother with anyone's Theology. So what do you think he did about the charge?"

"Would he answer it?"

"Sure he would! And in twelve long pages, too! Look at this!"

He gave me another pamphlet, thicker and more expensively printed. My eyes caught a few lines:

> . . . all my life I have professed my Reformed Christian belief, which I still do . . . he would have me pass for an unorthodox believer, a very heretic; indeed very wickedly he seeks to make me an abomination to the world, and to expose me to the vengeance of both the powers that be and the common people . . .

"It's a terrible charge," I said.

"Keep reading!"

> . . . I would not have minded so much if Venhuysen had not been one of the worst students, an utter ignoramus, not known, respected, or believed by any man of learning, and he is certainly not in a position to blacken an honest man's name, let alone a professor known throughout the learned world . . .

"Oh! Poor Venhuysen!" I said.

"And see?" Daniel laughed. "Known throughout the learned world! He says it himself."

"He is," I said. "And he was then, too." Then I had to laugh, too. "But it seems low of a great professor to call a student an ignoramus."

"I'll take that back before you read more. I can't take the risk of you ever admitting I showed it to you, even by inadvertence."

I handed it to him. "I won't."

"This little epistle has a fame of its own, and I'm not the only one with a copy. And you can see how he's aged. The spirit's the same, and more, but he's doesn't waste words or swat flies in public where he's seen doing it. He saves his vitriol for worthy opponents."

I had to shake my head. "I know that what you say has truth in it, Daniel. But I still think he's better than that."

"Do you know the student Gluck, from Zurich?"

"I saw him in your father's lecture."

"He won't last the month. Not even the week."

"What did he do?"

"He was disrespectful to a Chair."

"How was he? Gottlieb said the same of him."

"That's all that's been said." Daniel leaned close to me, though the room was empty besides us, and smirked. "But I'll tell you. He called on the Dean and demanded his tuition be returned. He said he was dissatisfied with his Master's lecture."

"That would be poor to say of any Master," I said, "and poorer to say to the Dean. But which Master?"

"The very wrong Master to slight in any way. The Master, in fact, who lives in this house."

"I feared so. But I've heard nothing of it but from you and Gottlieb."

"You'll hear nothing else but cautionary whispers. The Brute won't let his own name be dragged into it. But I still have it in my head to take that pamphlet to Lieber the printer and have him make me a hundred copies. Everyone knows the Brute's a tyrant, but then they'd see how petty he is, too."

"You won't. And Lieber wouldn't print it anyway."

"You're right, Leonhard, he wouldn't. He'd be run out of town. Or worse. Far worse."

I strayed past the Boot and Thorn midafternoon. A half dozen students were at a table and I joined them. Gluck was among them, very glum.

"We're toasting Gluck, on his departure!" I was told.

"What's he departing for?" I asked.

"Master Cassini's told him that his studies aren't satisfactory, and he'll not have him any more in his lectures."

"And Master Paleologus has said the same."

"And his room at Frau Minn's is needed for another boarder, so he's to be out of it."

He himself turned to me from the end of the table. "It's good riddance, too," he said. He took off his student's brimmed hat. "And I just bought it. Who would buy it from me?"

A student at the table, who was also new to Basel and who'd been friendly with me, said, "Sell it to Leonhard. He needs one."

But another student, who was my elder, answered, "No. He's a gentleman now. He won't wear a low student's hat." I was in brown, the only one at the table so.

"But look at him!" They took to jesting with me, which I didn't mind. "In brown? He's no gentleman!" "But you've seen his tricorne!" "Is he below us or above us?" "Is he buoyant or sinking?"

"I lost my hat," I said. "And I'd dear like it back."

"Then I'll sell you this," Gluck said, and named a price.

"I'll find mine own instead."

"Too expensive?" the elder student said to me. "Ask Gustavus. He has old robes and hats and rags."

"Plague-ridden rags, you mean!" he was answered.

"He'd have burned anything from a plague house." Besides the clothes of plague victims, innkeepers would gather clothing from any sickbed, usually to burn, though sometimes to sell to travelers.

So then, the talk turned to Huldrych and plague. I said to Gluck, "No, I'd like my old hat. My father gave it to me."

"Afraid he'll roast you for losing it? My father'll chop me to pieces when he hears I've been sent down."

"You should keep your hat," I said. "You may find yourself at another University."

"I will," he said, the hat in his hand. "And no Master Johann at it."

⁂

Friday evening I took early to my room. My grandmother would have questioned me about my day but I had my door closed before she had all the kitchen cleaned.

The thoughts in my brain were like a billow of starlings, too many to count and too whirling to hold. I did what I only could, then. I took paper, and pen, and ink, and lit my candle. I knew when I did that I would just blink and hours would go by.

I thought of squares, and circles. I put my quill on the pages and took it around a circle. The ink drained from the feather to the paper. But instead of putting it back to the well, I kept it travelling the path it had made. Around it went, and again, and again around. There was no end to its infinity.

I felt something in my coat pocket and I pulled it out, and it was Desiderius's Faustbook. This Faust was a man who sold his soul for knowledge. And renown? The man in Basel who held the greatest renown was Master Johann; and there was renown for any man who won a Chair in Basel.

The circle continued to return to its beginning, though it had no beginning.

Why had Desiderius pressed this book onto me?

Knipper had been in Master Johann's kitchen.

From the edge of the paper, the quill would only seem to go up and down. And from the top of the paper, the quill would only seem to go back and forth. But as I looked down, from above and outside the page, I could see the whole circle.

Huldrych had choked on the dust. And the trunk had been in his house. And Jacob, who had owned the trunk, had died . . . of the plague also?

The circle was an infinity contained on a single sheet of paper.

Daniel had stood at one side, seeking everything about his Uncle Jacob. Then he'd been on the other side, claiming he didn't care at all.

Master Johann was the center, never moving, but with everything orbiting him. Caiaphas was a meteor from some far end of the cosmos appearing in flame.

What was a Chair worth? What would anyone give for it? Or do for it?

And then I understood. I knew. I was Saul with my face toward Damascus. I didn't deduce it myself, but instead I was told. It was given to me. I just knew. I took my paper and ink and began writing. It was so elegant.

11

The Reciprocal Squares

I awoke Saturday morning, first doubting, then sure, then doubting. But no, I was sure. The whole of the story was laid out in my mind unchanged from the night before.

I worked my chores, but said nothing to my grandmother. It would need to be said first to Master Johann. At that thought, I trembled again. He would confront me, attack every point, doubt, accuse. I knew it all. I loved my Master and all his family, and I knew it would be a strike against them all. But it was all so plain and simple and elegant.

No other assignments or errands were waiting. I set out to read. I cleared my mind of the whole chain of logic, for I knew it would drive me mad to concentrate on it more. I read MacLaurin, then Taylor, but when two o'clock tolled I put them down. It was impossible to keep my mind closed to what was stored in it. I opened that treasure chest and there it all was, like the mountains outside a window that were there whether the window was open or not. Every line of the story sprang back into its place, more sure than ever.

So I just sat at my desk and waited and waited for the longest hour to pass, and finally I dressed and presented myself to Grandmother and then walked the short blocks to my Master's door.

I arrived at three thirty, as usual. And all the forms were as usual: the solemn door opening and the silent stair climbing and the grave single knocking and the summoning. Even the candle on the table attended to its proper place. But beyond the visible, behind it, beneath it, was a difference.

"Good afternoon, sir," I said.

"Yes, good afternoon." He examined me very closely. "And what have you studied this week? What exercises have you done? Have you had any time for studies?"

I answered with always perfect respect. But my heart raced as it never had before. I'd rehearsed the words in every way, experimenting between candor, circumspection, and innocence. "Yes, Master Johann," I said. "I have had time." And now I chose to be forthright. It was no longer possible to hold back and ignore what I'd discovered. I knew his reaction would be swift and merciless, and the risk to myself was great. Yet my knowledge was so sure and undeniable, I spoke the fateful words anyway:

"Master Johann," I said. "Sir."

"Yes, Leonhard?"

"I have solved the Reciprocal Squares problem."

"You have . . . what?"

He gaped, open mouthed at me. It was the first I'd ever seen him confounded! Then he frowned, and frowned deeper, and I saw the storm gather, and strike. "I will see a proof, then." He was outraged. Alexander had besieged Tyre over a milder insult; Tamerlane threw down Isfahan for less an affront.

Augustus couldn't have been more stern, and Nebuchadnezzar couldn't have been more menacing. But I saw it, too, in his eyes, that the chance of a solution was irresistible to him.

"Yes, sir. I have a proof."

"Tell me first, what is the value?"

No one else knew the proof besides me, among all Mathematicians, among all ages, and now I would give away my secret knowledge. I might have seen jealousy in Master Johann's stare, and maybe greed, and maybe even scheming and betrayal. But I decided I knew him better than that, that he was better than that. And I decided that I could presume to read the thoughts of a much greater man.

"The value *pi*, which is the ratio of the circumference of a circle to its diameter—"

"Yes?"

"The infinite sum of Reciprocal Squares is equal to that value of pi, squared, and divided by six."

He leaned forward, closer, I think, than I've ever been to him, and his mouth open and his eyes wide open.

"It is . . . *what*?!"

And even now I faltered and nearly failed under his extreme intensity. I was so unsure. But then I remembered the vision. I was sure. "I've conjectured . . ."

He was still leaning toward me. "Yes? Yes? What?"

"I imagine a polynomial and its roots, and it continues and continues, always crossing its axis."

"How many times?"

"Many, many. An infinity of times."

"An infinity of roots? Then it would have an infinity of terms, and an infinity of order."

"Yes, sir. A polynomial of infinite order, and whose roots are every integer multiple of pi, positive and negative and zero."

He sat back. "Indeed."

I proceeded. I described the steps, from one statement to the next. I was building a castle, or a palace, or a mountain. It seemed like each of them. Every part was just a breath of air and a few sounds that touched the room, then were gone. The castle was the thinnest unsubstantial thing ever built, yet it was as hard as obsidian and adamant. Nothing in creation could break it. And when I reached the end it was irrefutable and impervious.

"There are errors," Master Johann refuted. He began stating them.

The errors he claimed were complex, where the foundations of the walls rested on untested rocks, and I'd known just where he'd mount his attack. But they weren't errors. They were proofs yet to be found, but they were truths and I knew the proofs would eventually yield.

"An infinite product," he said, "and you claim to still know the individual finite terms. That is unproven."

"But they must be," I said. "It can be proven that they're nothing else. There would be no other part to them."

He circled, he probed, he thrust and I parried. He challenged every line. But he was hesitating and pausing, and then he began answering his own attacks. Then finally he shook his head.

"This will take more study," he said. "It is intriguing, Leonhard."

"Yes, sir."

"But it is far from convincing."

But I was convinced.

"Have you shown this to anyone else?" he asked.

"No, Master. It only came to me yesterday."

"Do not discuss it with anyone. I will continue to study it."

It was very unusual for him to not give me work for the

coming week. But it was plain that nothing so mundane would be taken up in the rest of our session. Indeed, the session was over. I heard the bell in the Munster tower.

"Yes, go on, Leonhard," he said as I stood. "It will take a great deal of study."

"Thank you, sir."

But instead of dismissing me, he paused. I waited. He had some other subject that had come to him. "Leonhard."

"Yes, Master?"

"You'll be finishing your studies soon?"

"I hope to present my dissertation by next year."

"Yes. I have expectations for it. Leonhard."

"Yes, Master?"

"You said that this proof came to you."

"Just last night."

"Not that you solved it, but that it came to you."

"It did, sir. I don't believe I could have solved it myself."

"I see. Then who would you say did solve it?"

"I . . . don't know. Do you understand what I mean, Master?"

"Yes. Very much." And he looked into me in a deep, searching way, seeing something in me he recognized. "Yes, I understand." And he seemed to see something else in me. "If the proof is true," he said, "it will be an elegant solution."

"Thank you, sir."

"To many things. But only *if*."

"What does it mean," my grandmother asked, "that you've proven your answer but Master Johann doesn't believe your proof?"

"There are things that I believe are true, and he doesn't."

"Are they true, then? You've said that in Mathematics a thing is true or not, whether it is believed or not."

"There are some parts of Mathematics that aren't understood well enough to be sure what is true."

"As with God," she said.

"The two are very close. Sometimes I think Mathematics is the thing God made that is most like him."

"What will become of your proof?"

"I want to write to Paris."

"You? Is it acceptable for you to send letters to this Academy?"

"I think not, Grandmother. I'll need to ask Master Johann to send a recommendation."

After that afternoon I felt as if my thoughts had been swept clean. Everything had ebbed away that had occupied my brain and it was like a hunting dog asleep and twitching on its rug. I was exhausted but nervous and edgy. I needed something to fill my empty head again and so I thought of dust, and I went to see Lithicus.

His yard was mostly as before, but somehow dustier. The stonecutter was mostly as before, as well. "And it's you?" he greeted me. "Here to question me?"

"You told me to come. And to ask for my Master if there's progress for him."

"Progress, there's progress. Does he think I'm idle?"

There'd been little rain or wind in the last few days, though I thought that yard would always be filled with dust. Of dust was man made and to dust man returned. Here the carving of epitaphs and memorials left dust which was surely a part of a man's return.

"I don't know what he thinks," I said.

"Nor anyone does. And there's progress. It's this." From his leather apron he'd found a folded page of paper, and unfolded it was a sketch of scroll bordered with the folds of a robe and headed with insignia of the University. "That's what I'll do, meeting the Master's approval." The sketch was drawn with skill and art by a charcoal stick. The words were centered, and all the lines balanced. Master Johann's text had seemed short, but laid out in lines and capitals it filled the scroll. "And the slab is this one." He pointed his hammer to a rough flat oblong of clean gray with one bright vein branched across it, like a lightning on an empty twilight sky.

"I think it's fitting," I said. "I'll show him the paper."

"But no other symbols or dabbles. That's all."

"I'll tell him."

"No, don't tell him! He'll have me wrung. You—" and he aimed his hammer at me, "—you keep him from asking."

"I will," I said.

"And thirty florins."

"I'll tell him that's the price."

"Aye, thirty pieces of silver. Tell him that."

Gustavus had taken note that I had become a regular patron of his Common Room, where I'd been now more times in three weeks than in three months before. Also, my status had changed with him: Now I was always a Master.

The talk in the room was of the Physics Election. There was speculation of when it would begin, whether in two weeks or two months or two years. It was an eager conversation. In black and white there were students and a few lecturers, for whom the Election might have a real effect, and a merchant and guildsman or two, but the larger number were in brown. Craftsmen, laborers, peddlers and farmers, all were far removed from the inner parts of the University and would never set foot in a lecture or understand a word of Latin. But in Basel, the University was owned by all, in that it was a part of the city, and all of the city was one. And there were many questions about how the Election was conducted, and many answers.

There were three stages to an Election. The first was the selection of the three committees of six members each; the second was the announcement of each committee's candidate; and last, after each candidate was allowed an opportunity to give a guest lecture, one of the three names was drawn at random. Of course it was the second, and even more the third, of these which caused the greatest excitement; but it was the first, which was accomplished through a Convening of the University, that had the greatest pageantry.

The lengths of time between the three were also variable, as it might take weeks or months for the committees, meeting in secret, to choose their nominees, and then, if any of these men were distant, it might be months more before each of them would have arrived and lectured, and it was traditional that at least one candidate not be from Basel. If the drawing was later still, the men were unlikely to have remained in Basel for it.

A small, iron casket was kept by the Provost for the drawing. It had a lock to which he kept the only key. Within the casket were ten small carved stones, all about an inch square and a half inch deep, so that any two could be put together as a one inch cube. The stones were smooth and plain on all their sides but for a specific exception, that seven, each on a square side, had a symbol carved into them, so that there were seven different symbols. The other three stones were all plain.

As the names were announced, each new candidate, or his committee, would choose a symbol stone. This stone would become that candidate's lot. A clerk would take the stone, make note of which symbol would now stand for that candidate, and then seal the lot.

The sealing was done by dripping wax onto the symbol itself, filling it and more, then fixing one of the three plain stones to that side. Once the wax had dried, the lot would be a simple cube with no outward sign, the symbol hidden inside. When all three candidates had been named, the three sealed lots would be kept in the casket. The unused stones would be set out. The casket was locked and set on the lectern, where it would reside until the final choice.

It was an odd ritual, part tradition, part compromise, like Basel itself laid out on older patterns of purposes no longer remembered.

The three candidates were then invited to give their lectures. A very poor lecture might disqualify a candidate; otherwise, the lectures were an opportunity for the University to hear these eminent scholars. Some men from distant cities and universities would decline the offer, as a one-third chance of a Chair wasn't worth the journey. Occasionally the University would accept a written lecture, to be read by a member of the nominating committee, but more often would take the refusal of the lecture as pertaining to the entire candidature, and nominate a replacement who was more appreciative of the honor.

Once the lectures had been given, the University would meet a third and last time. The casket would be unlocked and the Provost, humbly submitting his high position to the ignominy of a blindfold, would choose a single sealed lot from the three. The seal would be broken and the symbol revealed, and the new Chair congratulated and presented to the city.

In the Common Room, all the details of the ritual were discussed.

The casket is left out on the lectern, without guard? Could it be pried open and the stones exchanged?

Gustavus, as blacksmith, had made the casket. "That casket will never open unless the lock is turned," he said.

Could a pick-lock turn the lock?

"Keppel the locksmith made the lock. I told him to make it safe against picks." And if Gustavus had told him, then it would have been done.

But where were the keys?

"There is only one, and the Provost has it."

Before the casket was made, what had been used then? A previous casket?

"The old one was lost in the river, twenty years ago."

But the stones? Where had they come from?

"Lithicus carved them when the new casket was made."

And the Election itself? When will it be held?

To that, Gustavus had no answer, and Daniel's was morose: "The Election will begin when Brutus says it will," he said. "He's doing all the choosing now, and when he's told everyone their parts, he'll let it start."

No one had a reply. Basel had great faith in the integrity of the University's Election, and there might have been a protest. But Master Johann also had a place in the city's beliefs. No one would claim surety of what that man might do.

And what of the unopened stones?

The Senior Chair of the College owning the Chair would take the casket and verify the stones, then return it to the Provost. That had been Huldrych; now it would be Johann.

I walked early Sunday morning by the Rhine.

There was a moment, as a child, when I realized numbers were infinite. I didn't then yet know the names of Thousand and Million. I may not have known even Hundred. I was watching the raindrops falling on the river. It was even before my father moved us to Riehen to take the pastorate of that village's church. I could have only been four or five years old. My thought, walking with my father on the riverbank, where we were caught in a shower, was that the river was made of all the drops of water, all the rain. I'd looked at the wide surface, which was vast to me then, and considered how very, very many drops of water there were: innumerable, then no, they could be counted. It would only take a very long time. Perhaps all day! in my childish calculation.

But I watched more drops fall. We were under a tree, father and I. We'd had to run to it. I remember that well, laughing and running, how we both loved to run. The rain decreased and the raindrops lessened, but I was fascinated at those small beads crashing into the river and being absorbed by it, and my father let me just be and watch. One branch over us tilted steeply down, so I could see its last leaf just inches from the surface, and finally after minutes of staring, the drips from that leaf had slowed to only one, by one, by one, each falling across the last space to their sum. And then I knew, that whatever their sum was, it could always be one more, and if always more, then never to end. For any number, there was one more beyond. Always.

I had only one way to comprehend that. The Mathematics of infinity was still beyond me. But my father's preaching was already deep in everything I would know about my world. From him, I knew a word for something that was beyond everything else: *heaven*; a place where "one more beyond, always" did reach its end. So I had always understood the infinite end of all numbers as God showing himself in his creation. Everything he made had his image, and part of his image in Mathematics, was infinity. It was invisible because it was far past the end of sight. It was the greatest elegance.

Then later that morning at Saint Leonhard's, with my

grandmother, all my thoughts were on infinity and the infinite sum of infinite things. We were instructed in the sermon that the gulf between ourselves and God was vast and unbridgeable, which Mathematically would be infinite. Yet, we were reminded, it was bridged, by sacrifice.

We had our Sunday dinner.

"Grandmother," I said, "I think highly of Master Desiderius."

"He seems a pious man."

"He has a Chair at the University, yet he doesn't seem proud. I believe he's humble about it."

She looked at me shrewdly. "Yes, Leonhard. It is possible to have an eminent position and not be brought down by pride. But it's rare. Pride may be slow to increase but it always does."

"I've never seen any arrogance in Master Desiderius. Am I mistaken?"

"I'll speak no evil of him."

"Daniel is hoping to win Master Huldrych's Chair."

"You know Daniel well enough."

"I do. I think he's very full of pride. And I am, too. I try not to be."

"At least you try, Leonhard. Does Daniel expect to be nominated to the Chair?"

"Oh, of course he does. He's very sure he will be. And he should be nominated. He's already famous."

"We'll know soon."

"Everyone says it'll be weeks before the Election starts."

"It will be sooner than that," she said. "Much sooner." I didn't question her. I've always been surprised at how she knows much more of the University than I'd think she would.

I believed that, as I would see the invisible, she would hear the inaudible.

❧

I was prepared on Monday. I came to Mistress Dorothea's kitchen in brown but as neat and respectably as I could. Mistress Dorothea was solemn and severe and took me upstairs to the door. In a shadow in the hall I saw a darker, paler shadow, and that was Little Johann watching me as I knocked.

"Come," and I opened the door. "Good morning," he said, and I could see immediately what hadn't moved and what had. Two books that had not been on his shelf before were set about on his desk: MacLaurin's *Geometrica Organica* and Taylor's *Methodus incrementorum directa et inversa*. The papers on the desk were mostly changed. Some few were only moved, but most were new.

"Good morning, sir," I said. The books on his desk were set atop the papers, I thought, to obscure them. But I could still see a few edges.

"Do you have a drawing from the stonecutter?" On the exposed edges of the papers were equations, and I recognized parts. They were his own experiments with infinite polynomials.

"Yes, sir, I do." And also, another letter had been moved. It was the formal statement from Paris, of the Reciprocal Square challenge. It was also open on his desk. I held out, from my pocket, the sheet that Lithicus had given me.

"Thank you," he said, and unfolded it. He studied it briefly. "And a price?"

"He says thirty florins."

"Reply to him that he'll be paid a hundred."

"One hundred?" It was a huge sum.

"And tell him I want an additional line added."

"Yes, Master?"

He took ink and a quill and wrote on the back, *INLUSTRIS MORBO CHRONICO MENTE AD EXTREMUM INTEGRA.*

"That."

"Yes, sir." I left him there with my mind reeling. It was an extreme surprise to me that my Master Johann should have been reading MacLaurin, and especially Taylor. It was prideful of me to think it, but it seemed the only reason was that he was comparing them to my proof.

⁂

I was surprised that Master Johann would have been reading MacLaurin, because the Scotsman was an ardent supporter of Mr. Newton. But this Scotsman had also written on infinite series. I'd read all his books and eagerly awaited the others I expected him to publish. Only four years ago he was awarded a prize by the Paris Academy.

But the spectacle of the Master of Basel with a book by Taylor on his desk would have wagged tongues from Paris to London. They were terrible enemies. When Master Johann answered a challenge raised by Mr. Taylor some ten years ago to integrate a peculiar differential, the Englishman disputed my Master's solution. The dispute has continued unresolved, even to the point of threats and hostile wagers against each other in their various publications. But the *Methodus incrementorum* greatly extended the theory of writing differentials as infinite series. It was precisely the book in which to seek an answer to questions that my Reciprocal Squares proof raised.

⁂

I felt that I should hurry to find Lithicus, but I was also hesitant. Every mention of Master Johann seemed more fretful to him. Though the new and higher payment might hearten him, I'd want caution and mildness speaking with him.

"You!" a voice spoke from behind me. I turned and it was Daniel, of course. It was another chance encounter in Basel's streets.

"Me?"

"To the Boot. I'm getting my horse. But you'll do for now."

"I'll do?"

"Though you're a poor substitute for my Coal."

"I'll try my best."

"You always do, Leonhard, and it's credit to you. But now, this is why I found you. I've a use for you that even a horse can't match."

"What is it?" I asked.

"There's fire and fury back under my Brutus's roof."

"I don't have my water buckets."

"This fire won't be put out with water, and I don't want it out anyway. Have you heard of the Reciprocal Squares?"

"Yes . . . just recently. I've heard of the challenge from Paris."

"Well, Brutus has a proof for the Reciprocal Squares."

We'd just come to the Barefoot Square and I tripped on the first paving stone. "He has?"

"He has, and it's stunner."

"Is it his own proof?"

"Someone's sent it to him, I think. I don't think he's come up with it himself."

"Have you seen it?"

"I have and it's written in his own hand. But it's just that he copied it."

"But is it valid?"

"That's what I want you for. I want you to look at it. There's some of it I can follow and some I can't."

"Why did your father show it to you?"

Daniel laughed. "He's under torture. He'd die rather than allow that someone else solved it before him. And that's worth it being valid just by itself."

"Daniel!"

"He's desperate to know if it's valid, and he's not sure himself! He just had to show it to me, and Nicolaus, and Gottlieb, too. It's Mathematics, Leonhard! He wants so much to find a flaw in it he'll even show it to us! Oh, it's delicious, it is. And if there's something to be found in that proof that Brutus can't find, I'll ask anyone. Anyone. And I'd give about anything."

"It's not worth that much."

"I'd trade anything I had for it." He wrinkled his nose, suddenly thinking. "Maybe that's what Brutus has done. What do you think? What's nefarious? He's got a proof he's always wanted, just out of air."

"You make it sound like Faust," I said, and Daniel pulled back.

"Don't say that." He said it vehemently.

"I won't, then."

"It's not a joke."

"I won't say it again."

He breathed deep. "You look at the proof, Leonhard. You see things we don't, we all know that."

"I . . . I won't help you humiliate your father."

"Oh, that's the small part of it. The real part is whether it's valid. That's what we most want to know."

"Well, then bring it to the Inn tonight."

"I will."

"And are you really all working together on it, Daniel? You and your father together?"

"It's Mathematics, Leonhard. Of course we are." We'd

come to the Inn and I followed Daniel through the tunnel to the stables. "Where's my black?" he asked Willi.

"Shoeing. Gustavus has him in the smithy."

൭

When the Olympic gods had been overthrown by the true Church, it was Gustavus who took Hephaestus' forsaken anvil and hammer for his own. Only Gustavus could ever move those weights of iron, and the sparks they made were Zeus thrown lightnings.

The smith shop of the Boot and Thorn was in another far corner of that many-cornered building, near but beyond the stables. As with all the corners, there was fire. This flame was in a kiln-like oven, charcoal fed and white hot, the hottest fire in Basel.

We watched Gustavus form a horse's shoe. No metal could withstand, between that continent of an anvil and that mighty hammer wielded as the earth wields mountains. It was a place to wonder about nefarious purposes. Gustavus in his black apron struck the shoe with his sledge, and I thought the sparks flew into it instead of out, to add fire to the horse's speed.

The smithy was more a cave than a room. The walls were rock and the oven was in the rock, with a chimney bored straight up to the air above. There was water in a pit carved into the floor. When the shoe, still glowing, was dropped into that pool, the water was barely able to cool it. Water was always unwelcome by the fires that ruled that inn.

When Gustavus nailed the shoe on, the black horse suffered him gladly to do it.

"He's ready, there?" Daniel asked.

"He'll take you well, now," Gustavus said.

"I'll let him!"

The room was so dark compared with the white fire that everything in it was invisible.

❧

Outside the inn, I was quick to find Lithicus on his scaffolding using the bright light of day to reach the shadow high and deep in the arch of the Coal Gate.

"What does he say?" he asked, indignant as sharp gravel and anxious, when I told him what Master Johann had said. "More lines? Show me the words."

He didn't climb down, so I put my foot on the first cross piece of the wood frame, then the second, to hand it up to him. He squinted in the poor light. "I know that line," he said. "I've used it before. Most with University men."

I said, "It means, *Despite his illness, his distinguished mind kept its integrity until the last.*"

"His mind? What's that to anyone? The merchant, he's proud to keep his money to the end, and the churchman his piety and the wife her family to the end. But the end comes and they all lose all. And tell him, I'll need a new slab. The other one's not big enough."

"What will you do with the other one?"

"It'll be for someone else who kept nothing to the end and doesn't need the extra space."

"There'll be an Election soon to replace Master Huldrych," I said.

"I've no part of that."

"But you are part, Lithicus! You made the stones they use to cast lots."

"I made them. And that was all I made."

"I've only seen them from across a large room. What are the symbols on them?"

"Why are you asking that? What would it matter to you?"

He got hold of his anger, but kept it ready in hand. "What would you do with it if I told you?"

"I only want to know. I was curious."

"I won't tell you." He'd come calm, but was all suspicion. "There's no good you'd do from knowing."

"Then I wouldn't want to know. I didn't know they were secret."

"They are or aren't. I don't speak of them."

"Gustavus said it was twenty years ago. You wouldn't need to have even remembered."

"I remember."

"And you'll never need carve them again."

I'd meant to be agreeable and calming to him, and he had been more at ease, but he suddenly was angry again.

"I'll never carve them! That I'll never do again!"

"Of course you wouldn't."

"What do you mean by that! What do you mean?" He was nearly yelling at me. "Who'd say they needed to be done more than once? Who said it?"

"No one!" I dropped back to the paving stones. His hammer was waving too wild to be close to him. "I don't know why they would be."

"Tell that man he'll have his stone, and fast as it can be done. I'll need a new slab. That will cost more"

"And he'll pay you more," I said. "He said he'd pay you one hundred florins!"

But his reaction was only worse and worse. "I don't want any! Tell him I won't take any payment! I'll just be done with the stone and never any more!"

"No payment? But he's willing to pay."

"What do you mean at that? Willing? You don't know how willing. No more. He'll have it and nothing else. Thirty was enough for Judas, and he thinks I'll take more?" In a quick motion, he put his hand against an arch stone above his head. "Don't slip out, you!" It wasn't me he was talking to, but the stone. "You've bothered me," he said, and that was to me, "and now I'm addled! I'll drop a stone and lose the day's work."

I couldn't think of anything else to say, as everything I did say seemed to make him more angry and alarmed. There were even a few others in the Square who were turning to look. Gustavus had finished his shoeing and was standing with the horse and with Daniel at the stable tunnel. I backed away to them.

"What's afflicting the stoneman?" Daniel asked.

"He's just touchy," I said.

"Touchy and with a chisel and hammer, that's bad! What is it about?"

"I was asking him about the lot stones. They'll be used in the Physics Election."

"And soon, so I've heard. The University's convening Wednesday."

"For the Election?"

"In two days. The Chair's to be filled."

"The Chair's only empty ten days," I said.

"Brutus commands, the plebs obey. Tomorrow the committees will be chosen. It's the first step. And Leonhard, I want you here at the Inn tonight. I want to show you this proof."

"I'll be there to see it."

⁂

"Is it gossip or trouble you're pursuing tonight?"

I was glad to answer as we finished supper. "Neither, Grandmother. It's Mathematics."

Then I was out in the last dusk light. My heart was full of both joy and caution. The prospect of Daniel and Nicolaus and good round dispute over a proof, whatever proof it was, was tonic. Even more, that it would be the Reciprocal Squares! But which proof? Mine, or another . . . that was worth caution. And though it was likely impossible, I wanted to be no cause of strife.

The stars were vast, but their infinite sum still was only a finite portion of the sky. They were vastly far away, and who would know their bright essence? I knew I was very small on the great planet, beneath the greater heavens, but it was within me to comprehend them and know how they were governed. What could it mean that God had put in finite man the chance to study the infinite?

And so I came to the door of the Boot and Thorn, and stroked Charon for passage, and looked in at the smoke and dice and flagons and fire and thought how this intersection of minute man and immense man was all in God's image.

I paused and knew that Daniel and Nicolaus were waiting for me. And I was met by someone else.

"Leonhard."

It was Gottlieb. I thought a moment that I was meant to bring my paper and pen to another questioning, but for this time it was I who was to be questioned.

"Have you heard?" he asked. "The proof?"

"Yes. Daniel found me earlier."

He nodded to the windows. "He's in there?"

"I think so, and Nicolaus."

"What do they want of you?"

"They just want to show me. It's generous of them."

"None of that," Gottlieb said. "There's no generosity there, not likely in this whole pile of a building. All right, then, go in and we'll see what they really are after."

Together we went in. Daniel was indeed there, at a table near the fire where the light was best, and Nicolaus with him.

"What! Cousin?" he said as he saw us. "You're here again? Is there another Inquiry?" Daniel teased as he always did, but he also seemed somehow welcoming.

"Yes, there is," Gottlieb answered. "Into that." And of course *that* was the set of papers on the table between them.

"Then let's get to it," Daniel said. "Sit down, Cousin, sit down, Leonhard, sit and tell me what you see here."

"We're not all here." That was Nicolaus.

"What? Who?" his brother asked, and Nicolaus crooked a finger to beckon to the door. Pale even in the dark and red, we were joined by the one other: Little Johann. "Come, come!" Daniel said. "Welcome and plant yourself; you're right, Nicolaus, we need the full measure. We're not all unless we have our best."

"I thought you'd be here," the newcomer said.

"I'm glad you're here, too," I said. "Not your father, also?"

"Full measure," Daniel answered. "Not running over."

"Come on, look at the pages," Gottlieb said. "That's what we're here for."

And so we were.

⁂

I quickly saw that it was indeed my proof. The words were mine, the equations just as I'd written them. I'd known it would be. I hardly knew what to say. My first concern was to not betray Master Johann's confidence. He'd chosen to keep the proof anonymous.

"Pi squared, and divided by six?" Gottlieb said to start. "And the reciprocal squares? Are they even nearly the same value?"

"They are," Nicolaus answered. "I've calculated them both to the fifth decimal." I was amazed. That was an entire day's work!

"That proves nothing," Gottlieb replied. "It could be in the sixth place they diverge. Or the tenth."

"It doesn't prove," Daniel said, "but it does convince. Now look at this." He was on the third page of the proof. "This is at least obscure. What's the reason for the sine? It comes out of pure air."

"It's to make the polynomial," Nicolaus said.

"But the polynomial could stand on its own. Anyone could write it."

"Would they, though?" Gottlieb said. "An infinite polynomial? That's what's of pure air."

"No, I'll take the polynomial," Daniel said. "But the factoring of it. Now that's the worst of all."

"The sine's for knowing the factors. That's what it's for."

"But how could it be infinite? An infinite angle?"

I could hardly breathe, listening to them.

"Draw me that triangle, then. It's absurd."

"But it's not meant to be a triangle."

"A sine without a triangle?"

Oh, it was torture to hear them argue, with each other and with the papers!

"But see what it means. The hypotenuse becomes the radius of a circle."

"Then the polynomial derives from a point on the circle as the radius rotates."

"And the roots are periodic. I see . . ."

"But the infinite factoring?"

"An infinite polynomial for an infinite series. It's clever, that I'll say. Very clever. Elegant."

"What do you say, Leonhard?" It was Nicolaus who asked.

Despite that I'd known I'd be asked, I was still lost for an answer. "How do you think your father came on to this?"

"I'll say MacLaurin," Gottlieb said. "See how the Taylor Series is used? He'd be first to try an infinite series for a sum."

"Never," Daniel said. "First, it's nothing like his series. And second, the trigonometry. He'd have to have that idea from someone else. And more than those, he'd never send it to Basel."

"He might for malice. I've heard he's vindictive as any of us."

"That's not possible. And he'd have to know it would be stolen, too. Whoever'd show this to the Brute without publishing it in their own name first is a knave."

"It might be already published in England."

"Then it wouldn't have been mailed here." This was Nicolaus. "No, it's someone who wants it validated before it's published."

Daniel said, "I claim it's Newton."

"No!" Even Little Johann joined in the denials. And that young man added, "Not after fifty years of him trying. Nicolaus is right. It's someone new at it who wants to know that it's true."

"An unknown? A novice? The Brute wouldn't waste opening his letter."

"He might," Gottlieb said. "Or it's someone he knows."

If before had been torture, this was torment beyond it.

"Who would he know?" Nicolaus asked. And it had perhaps been inevitable.

"Leonhard," Little Johann said.

They all four rounded on me like hounds on a deer. "What, is it?" Daniel asked, and right away he answered, "Yes, it is! I see it in your face. Of course it is!"

"No," Nicolaus disagreed. "He's clever, we all know, but—"

"He's genius," Daniel said.

"But this is past genius." Nicolaus cocked his head. "It's

greatness. It's pure elegance. Isn't it? Who's the greatest Mathematician in Europe? Newton?"

"The Brute, I'd say," Daniel said. "And this isn't his."

"I'll still say it's MacLaurin," Gottlieb said. "He's young. He's a novel thinker."

"I think it's Leonhard," Little Johann said. "Ask him and let him answer."

"All right then," Daniel said. "Here it is, Leonhard. Is it yours?" He pointed to the papers. "Answer us. If you don't, Nicolaus will ask your grandmother and she'll tell us."

There was no escape. Why wouldn't I want to claim it? But I was overwhelmingly reluctant. It wasn't for fear of betraying Master Johann. It seemed instead that I was at a gate, an Ash Gate, that could only be entered once; it was ten times the weight of being given a tricorne, or a hundred times!

"Yes," I said. "It's mine."

"I knew it was!" Daniel crowed it like a rooster.

"I'm not convinced," Nicolaus said.

"He'd lie?" Gottlieb asked. "He had it from someone else?"

"Let him explain it," Little Johann said.

"All right," Nicolaus said. He pushed the papers toward me. "Show us this proof."

I pushed the papers back to him.

"I'll explain it," I said. "Where's paper and ink? Blank paper. And more light."

❧

We brought candles and paper, and swept the table of crumbs, and I readied myself.

"Here's the start, with the meaning of sine. It's as you said, to make a circle. It's not a mere ratio as it's used in triangles. It's a true function. I understood it more when I wanted equations for waves."

And so I passed the gate. We went for hours, I think. I took them through the infinite polynomial made by a radius that circles endlessly, and what the roots of it would be.

"Though what is an infinite polynomial?" Nicolaus asked. "How do you write it?"

"Think of the wave on water," I said. "But every rise and fall is a root."

And then, how the polynomial would appear on a plain of Descartes, and then how its infinite factors were derived from its infinite roots. And then, how the pairs of roots could be combined. And then, what the coefficients must be when all the pairs were multiplied together.

"But there are infinite other terms! And each term is an infinite sum."

"But each term, on its own, must have a particular value," I said. I showed them the expansion of the sine function, which Mr. Taylor in England had proposed. "And this sum must equal six, which is the factorial of three. And if the equation is divided by the cube of x, and multiplied by Pi, then the proof is complete."

And they, as their father also, considered the proof was far from complete. They disputed and fought every step, with me, with each other. It was as Saturday with Master Johann had been, but in four directions and fiercer questioning, and Little Johann as sharp as any of them.

But in the end they were convinced. "A new lion," Daniel said at last.

"And what does it mean that there is?" Gottlieb said. "A new rival."

"We could end him here!" Daniel said. "The four of us. And we'd have the proof for our own!"

"Father knows where it came from," Nicolaus said.

"Cut him in on the spoils, then. We'll publish under the

whole family's name. Or do away with the Brute, too! Then we'd have the Chair open, too."

"Only one can have it," Gottlieb said.

"Then watch your own throat."

"Those are poor jokes," I said, but I laughed. I felt lightheaded from the long debate.

"He's not joking," Nicolaus said. "It's Mathematics."

I answered,"I don't have fear of any of your family."

Daniel said, "But on to other matters. There's a propriety to answering a public challenge from the Paris Academy. It's meant for men of reputation and position. You'll need someone to write a letter for you."

"I mean to ask your father."

"And he'll sneer, won't he? That will be a lesson in derision. Even to you, dear Leonhard."

"He won't sneer at Leonhard," Nicolaus said. "He'll be civil. But he'll still turn him down."

"And if he doesn't," Daniel said, "Then that will be near as interesting as the proof itself."

"What do you mean?" Gottleib asked him.

Daniel only shook his head. "Cheers to you, Leonhard. Remember this night, when the Reciprocal Square was solved and proven. We'll leave the intrigues for tomorrow. This night is yours."

I let it be. So we went on to talk of other things. I asked about Italy, where the three of them all had lived and had Chairs. The conversation was affable and the only jabs were good natured. Little Johann asked more questions than I did. We talked about other Universities without sarcasm or bitterness. If the night was mine, their gift to me for it was conviviality. We talked of Paris and Holland and Heidelberg. We talked of kings and princes, the courts of Prussia, Austria, France, Hanover, Saxony, and even England, and which would be more advantageous in which to gain a position, which would be more cultured, which would be more lucrative. Then we talked of Empires and Kingdoms, the present wars and recent wars and Basel's place among them all. It was well that Louis the Sun King of France had died when he did, for Basel would have been his next cherry to pick.

Then at the end we parted, all close friends. The forces that pulled together were stronger than the forces that pushed apart.

12

The Physics Election

On Monday, Daniel had said the University would convene on Wednesday. On Tuesday, everyone in Basel had heard. But the true Announcement was yet to come, and once Basel knew that the University would Convene, Basel knew that it would be Announced.

After the recent fearful days of the plague, the news was like fresh water. The announcing and convening of the University was a ritual as old as the University, and in austere Basel, where any feather of pageantry was suspect, only the academic and ancient in alliance justified a display. And as long as it was justified, the citizens would gladly spectate a spectacle.

It had been two years since the last convention, for the Election to Logic, and the elevation of Gottlieb and the departure of Daniel. I knew the ritual fairly well from watching it then. It was all pompous pomp on the outside, Basel's gaudiest rite, as ritual as a coronation; as ponderous as a planet's orbit, and as full of robes and regalia as a cathedral choir and dressmaker's shop together. To Italians or French, it would seem just as black and white as everything else in a Protestant city. Yet color was measured by contrast, and in Basel, bright colors were kept in their proper place.

But there was what was seen, and there was what had substance. It was the invisible part of the convention that had the most meaning: the quiet conversations before the loud gathering, the two heads leaned close across a table in a dim room, the sparse written note then thrown in the fire. Daniel claimed that when finally the University sat to deliberate, its deliberations had already been done.

Master Johann was now the senior Chair of the college and had a critical role in the first meeting. What would happen in the conclave, and what had been agreed beforehand between the most influential members, would never be known outside.

❧

The carriage returned that evening from Strasbourg and Freiburg. I was in the Barefoot Square at the time, just coming out from the Barefoot Church. All day the rumors and gossip had been pouring out the Inn and every other door about the coming Convention and Election. When the coach arrived, it seemed a part of the disturbance. It was surrounded by hounds, and wolves, and hunting dogs, and then I saw Jehu in the seat next to Abel. That King of Israel looked up to the windows of the Inn, and there, Jezebel looked down at him. He shook his fist at her and she jeered back at him, and all the dogs bayed and howled back at the face in the window.

❧

When I came home that night, my grandmother met me with a note that had been sent from the Dean of the College of Arts. It instructed me to report to his own home the next morning at nine o'clock. I knew what this meant. "It's part of summoning the Faculty," I said.

"You'll call on Master Johann?" Grandmother asked.

"I think it will be Master Desiderius. He told me I'd be asked to do something for him."

⁂

Wednesday morning I was up early and quickly done with chores. I dressed in my immaculate black and white, and my grandmother sent me out the door to the Dean's house. The Convening of the University was to begin.

The first spark always would come from the Provost. Four students in their brightest black would issue from his front door. They would be mature and responsible young gentlemen but still sprightly, to prance to the homes of the four Colleges' deans. There, they would rap smartly on the doors. A great part of the ritual was this knocking. Neighbors would step out of their homes to watch it. Through the morning, as the summons would unfold, great men would be answering their own doors to receive the news: the University is Convening.

Then the sparks would spread into flame. The deans would acknowledge the call and send out their own. They must step back from their door, apparently to summon their own messengers, but in truth to not be knocked over. From their doors would burst a flock of students sent to summon their professors, and as the most respectable students were already serving the Provost, and there were more professors and lecturers than mature students anyway, this herd of flapping, flying black robes would be worth seeing and worth being out of their way.

I was to be one of them. Master Johann as Senior Chair of his College would have to be summoned by the same messenger sent from the Provost to the Dean. I was meant for Desiderius.

I ran! The young men chosen were favorites of their teachers, and high spirited though they were, they were counted on to play no pranks on a serious occasion. We raced through the streets, crossing paths between deans' and professors' houses. In all, there were some fifty. Most went for the lecturers and officials of the University, but fifteen or so who could make a good bow and had the nicest wigs were sent to the Chairs.

These several would carry tokens of authority. The Dean of Theology sent hourglasses to the Chairs of his college, that life was measured and would end. The Dean of Law sent quills, that words were the structure of authority. The Dean of Medicine sent pestles, that man was mixture of soul and body. And the Dean of Arts, who had the largest college, sent candles, because knowledge was light. The tokens signified an important notion. The Deans were between master and servant of the Chairs. They were a higher position, but not a higher rank. They were often former professors of whom it was thought best that they no longer profess, the moon moved aside to make way for the sun. They had an important role and were usually men of substance, but not always of eminence. So the tokens were a command and a plea to the Chairs, who were Great Men not to be called as if they were Less.

But of course they would come. Their doors were knocked upon and they opened them and stared out into the street. There were many houses in Basel on many streets, but not so many of either that provided such high residence: the Chairs furnished only certain areas. They received the token and the summons and they stepped out their doors into the light. As if it was their daily habit, they were in their finest robes. Often more than one would be in sight at a time.

The people were watching. Basel was proud of its University and viewed the great men with satisfaction. They appeared in the streets, rounding the corners, enrobed in black and scarlet, black and emerald, black and azure, black and sienna, black and maroon, black and canary. The striping was in corvettes, diagonals, diamonds, and arcs. Their vast wigs curved, curled, and coiled like rioting ivy and wide mountain waterfalls. Atop the wigs were triangular, square, rectangular, trapezoidal, and pentagonal velvet caps, and each color and shape imbued by tradition with centuries of meaning.

As streams to the Rhine, the Professors would flow into the University. They would come from all directions, though none across the bridge, for no professor lived in Small Basel. They would come on foot, slowing as they approached the portal, gathering like an army and then entering their Fortress, the University Building itself.

୭ଽ୦

As part of the flood, I arrived at the House of Desiderius and knocked on the door. All the children of the street were out to watch, and even a few of the wives had their curtains drawn aside. The door opened and the Master himself, brow furled at my completely unexpected appearance, leaned out into the street.

"What, Leonhard?" he said. "How is it you're here?"

"I'm sent by the Dean," I said. "I'm to bring you to the University."

"To the University? Why, what is it? I'm being summoned?"

"The University is convening, Master. And I've a token for you of the seriousness of the matter." And I held up the candle.

Master Desiderius took it carefully and examined it thoroughly. "Then I'll come," he said. And of course it was no signal at all that I was expected, that he happened to have on his University robe and cap!

So we set off. Master Desiderius was not too senior a Chair to keep his own lively pace through the Basel streets. And when we turned one way or the other in our path that wasn't the straightest route, I thought it was that he even wanted to be seen by some acquaintances. While Master Johann would surely be stepping his slow, stately beat, only hurrying at all because it would be tiresome to be a spectacle for the common people, Master Desiderius knew that he was on display and made well of it. His robe flowed behind him like an exultation of larks.

His appearance in the Barefoot Square was especially meant to be jubilant. We came to the Coal Gate and saw the Square beyond, over full as people had planned their marketing to coincide with the Convening. We even paused a moment in the shadow of the gate in anticipation of our entrance. And as we stood in that dark spot I had a sudden sense of something, motion or sound, but really of rending. I took hold of Master Desiderius's arm, and in the instant felt him also gripping mine, and then I lunged, pulling and being pulled. Above me, and then as I fell headlong forward, behind me, there was weight, and force, and a terrible plunging, and collapse. All the stones of the arch came crashing into the space they'd stood over, with roaring and tumbling clamor, piling in an instant into a mountain of rock, a blockade, and a destruction. I was on my face on the paving of the Square, and Desiderius beside me, and we turned to see the tons of gate where we'd stood three seconds before, while still more stones were falling, and finally the last did.

And a great cloud of dust rose from the pile.

In a few seconds more we were being helped to our feet. Master Desiderius was unscathed; I think I'd tripped and he'd been pulled more gently down by his hold on me. But I was battered and scraped and felt unsteady from unexpected pains as I stood. Small, bright red lines appeared from the brown dirt on my hands. And I was covered with dust. I stared at the great wind of dust that wrapped the pile of stones.

"Are you well?" Desiderius asked me, very anxious, and I nodded. And other people around me were asking, also, and holding me as I swayed.

"Yes," I said. "I'm only bruised." I looked at myself and saw torn sleeves and breeches. I could feel that my face was as bad as the rest. Beside the black and brown dust of the Wall, there was fine gray dust, among it but separate.

"You'll need help," Desiderius said.

"No. But you'll need a new guide." I grabbed the shoulder of a child I knew from Saint Leonhard's, one I'd tutored and who I thought might achieve the University himself someday. "Friedrich, here, you take Master Desiderius, and get him to the University! I need you to!" And I pushed them off, encouraging them both as they looked back in reluctance at leaving me. "Go, go! The University's convening! They need the Master!" And finally they did turn, and go on, and the crowd parted for them. Then I turned, back to the stones and the dust.

Already a few men were stooping down to see the pile, and I thrust myself in with them. "Pull," I said. "Move the stones!" And with my bleeding hands I tore at the stones, and my urgency flooded the other men, and they pulled, too. The dust was still high and we stirred it and added to it. And it wasn't long, or many stones, before there was a cry of dismay, and a carved block was lifted from a hand, white with dust but dark veined, and still in death gripping a hammer.

I fell back. Others untombed the stonemason.

And even as I reeled and sat, and the dust swirled, and the stones were pushed away from their heap, and shingle and rubble were thrown out from the un-pilers, one handful of the debris landed close to me, and one piece of the ruin fell nearly in my hand. It was soft and wadded and black beneath thick dust. I was stunned by it. Then I thrust it into my pocket.

⁂

I didn't wait there longer. I stepped back, brushed off my dust, and smoothed my rumpling. The door of the University would be closing soon as the black starlings flocked to their nesting. There was no use following them. Instead I went into the church.

The Barefoot Church was made all of stone. It was old and plain stone, not patterned, not chiseled. I put my hand on it, close to the door. It was cool. And it seemed weightless as if the essence of it was flown away; or, as if the stone had flown from its weight.

All my little cleverness, my Mathematics and papers, my deep thoughts as deep as a scratch, in all of them there was no warmth or comfort.

I pulled out the wad from my pocket, black and coated in dust. I could do nothing for Lithicus, so I put all my care and gentleness into smoothing out that creased, smashed thing, and slowly shaped it from its shapelessness into what it had once been. I pushed out the center to a bowl and curled the wide brim on each side, and the material seemed to remember its old form and was desperate glad to return to it. As desperate, I wanted to set it on my head and be just a child again, running from class to class and learning subjects which were only visible; it was my dear old hat.

But that was past.

So I forced the hat back into my pocket and turned my eyes toward the door of the church, and to the Square and world beyond. The hat on my head was tricorne.

❧

It might have showed, as I entered the Common Room, though my stride was more stagger. But I thought it showed that I was tall and stern and weighted. Few of the many gathered noticed me, but the tankards did. They stared at me warily, suspiciously, and challenged me. It was daunting. Then Gustavus saw them all looking at me from their shelves and turned to notice me himself. He knew I was changed.

And Daniel was there and didn't notice. And Nicolaus was there, and did.

"What do you require?" Gustavus asked me.

"What you can't supply," I answered. He nodded and stepped away to another customer. But he kept a watch on me. I kept a watch on the rest of the room. The discussion was fast and free, the large part on Lithicus, but still some on the University and its Convention. Daniel was of that part.

"All peacocks, all of them," Daniel answered. "It's all parade. It's gaudy."

"They should wear your Italian silk instead," Nicolaus said.

"I'll have a scarlet robe made, not black."

"And what of you?" Nicolaus asked me. I never knew what he meant.

"I'm shaken," I said.

"Oh, the gate?" Daniel said. "And the mason? Nearly you, too, they said!"

"And Desiderius?" Nicolaus said. I nodded.

"Nearly him."

"And why any of you?" Daniel said. "The stonecutter's

no slipshod, I'd have thought." He hardly seemed to care that the man was dead. "But maybe he was blinded by the peacocks and lost his hold."

"He had the keystone out of the arch," Nicolaus said.

"He's no slipshod," I said. I didn't want to listen more to them. I moved to a different table and just watched. But even there I could still hear.

"Then it's an odd instant for the gate to fall, with Desiderius in it," Daniel said. "That's worth thinking on." He turned round to find me. "You should have been watching him better, Leonhard!"

"He was watching me. He pulled me out in bare time."

"And they said the mason was crushed by the stones," Daniel said.

"And you sent Desiderius on his way without him knowing that?" Nicolaus asked me. I nodded.

"Wasn't that better for him?" Daniel said. "They'll deliberate better without the tragedy weighing on them. But it's still worth thinking on. What would be gained if Desiderius had been out of the deliberations?"

"And out of his Chair?" Nicolaus said.

"I don't want Greek," Daniel answered. "What would it do to Physics, though? I'd say nothing. It's all decided and all the bargains are made. Nothing but death can change it."

"Then you've nothing to fear, have you?" Nicolaus said.

"And it's only the committees being decided," someone else said. "They'll still each have to name their candidates."

"They'll be each told who to name," Daniel answered.

"They won't be told," someone said. "They're most all proud men."

"Those who won't be told," Daniel said, "will be outwitted."

"Would Master Desiderius?" I asked, from my own table, finally able to speak again.

"That's why you think he had a wall dropped on him? To keep him out of the committees? If that's why, then it wasn't Brutus who did it. Desiderius will do as he's told most of anyone."

"And you will, too, when you're Chair?" Nicolaus asked.

That was enough to close Daniel's mouth. He dropped his chin onto his hands in a pout. Nicolaus watched him a few minutes then came to join me.

"I think he's right, that the deliberation's already set," he said to me. "And you're shaken by a third death."

"Yes, I am."

"And you've been close by all three, very close. Knipper, and Huldrych, and Lithicus."

"Nicolaus!" I said. "What do you mean by saying that?"

"You're not such as a child as you've seemed, and maybe you've never been."

⁂

Some time went by, about an hour. The talk was still mixed between the University and the stonemason. I would have left but I was too grieved to stand.

I was sitting by the door. Nicolaus was nearby watching me, and Daniel was in the thick, talking spurts, and I couldn't hear for the din. I saw that Daniel was having no pleasure in all the rumors that he was hearing and repeating. He was agitated and soon turned to the wall and shrugged away questions. Then we all were waiting.

Until there was a tug on my sleeve, and then a soft torrent of words. And when Little Johann was finished, he said, "Don't tell anyone that I told you."

And then he was gone.

I'd had nearly a score of names thrust into my ear. I'd only barely kept up with them. It meant the University door must have been opened and the announcements made, for they were all the assignments to the committees, though no one else in the room seemed to have heard them. The minutes passed and I began to wonder that no messengers were plunging in from the streets outside. And I also began thinking through the assignments and what they might mean.

But finally Pheippides arrived: a student, Stottfeld, I'd tutored in Latin some year in the past. He came breathless into the Common Room and instantly was bread to the ducks.

"They're out, just now," he proclaimed, though instead of collapse he only gasped.

"And who are they? What are the committees?" was asked.

"It hasn't been said yet. They'll give an announcement tonight."

"Oh!" Daniel said. "That's murder! Tell us now!"

So I waited for the waiting to resume, and then I came close to him, and leaned closer, and whispered into his ear what had been whispered into mine.

"The first committee's led by Master Johann himself," I said, and I told him the others that made up his six, all fine Chairs and Lecturers.

"Melchior? Bost? They're his own fish. They'll be leaping to do what he says. Hoppenfeld? Cassini? Van der Veld? A little stiffness there in those three, but they won't stand up to him, not in the same room. Oh, there's no doubt of that committee."

"The second committee's led by Master Desiderius," I said, and the list of those five, the Dean of Law, the Chair of Law, Chair of Anatomy, the Chair of Botany, and Vanitas of Theology.

"Paleologus? Tertullus? That's Desiderius held in check. He'll dance the jig played for him, and Paleologus will make sure he does. They're as like to Brutus as if they're himself.

So there's the first committee that's all his, and Desiderius has the second committee and he's the perfect finger on the Brute's paw."

"Paws don't have fingers," I said.

"Leonhard, he's Brutus's Cassius. That I know. And Vanitas to be sure of him."

"Anyway, the third committee is Gottlieb's."

"Oh, that's the pudding, that one. Oh! That dear cousin! Only two years a Chair himself, and he's to decide who'll take the next."

"And he has Suvius of Latin, three lecturers, and the Bursar."

"Gottlieb's no one, but there's less than no one to gainsay him." Daniel boiled in his seat. "The Brute's done it, in every way. He has it all in his hand. It's all under his thumb. It's under his foot. He's picked every name, the very ones he wants."

"Who else is there?" I asked. "They're the Deans and Chairs and Lecturers. It's near half the University, and I'll even say the most distinguished half."

"And that's the rub. They're best of the University and he has them all in his pocket. And if he has them, who doesn't he have?"

"I think the University convened, and chose proper committees, and they'll do what they're meant to do. They'll nominate a man from Basel, a man from another University, and one other. You can rave, Daniel, but you're only seeing shadows."

"Seeing things that aren't there?" We were both startled by Nicolaus, always beside us. "So how do you know what the committees are, Leonhard? They're not announced yet."

"Well, I was told."

"Then maybe you're seeing the same invisible things that

Daniel is. And if they're shadows, then they're shadows of real things."

"Who will they nominate, then?" I asked. "That's more important."

"And will it be the best men?" Daniel answered. "The greatest? The most esteemed, or skilled, or brilliant? No, no, and no. It'll be only those who'll dance to his pipe. It's the whole University that Brutus wants."

"He doesn't want the whole University, anyway," Nicolaus said.

"All right, if that's true," Daniel said. "It's one part that he cares for. To thwart me."

"Or two parts," Nicolaus said. "There's both of us."

But then, Gustavus, always nearby, it seemed, seemed to be nearer even. Like a hound catching a scent, Daniel lifted his head and his eyes opened wider. "Who will they nominate?" he asked, it seemed, but not as a question. "How'd Brutus get his own Chair?" Gustavus didn't answer, of course, but he waited in the case that he would be asked a service he could perform. "If Brutus is sure to get his man, then the need is to be his man. That's all."

"When the committees were posted," I told Grandmother, "they were all the names Little Johann had said they'd be."

"How did he have the names before anyone else?" my grandmother asked. "He was telling you while the door to the University had hardly been opened."

"Before it was opened," I said. "I think he saw them on his father's desk." We'd talked of the committees, and Daniel, and the Convening, and all that had been said at the Inn, and most we'd talked of Lithicus. "But it's well known that the Chairs discuss their business before they convene. They'd have already made their decisions of who would be on the committees. And . . ." I looked down at myself, still dusty, "I've torn my breeches."

"I'll have them mended. How nearly did the stones fall on you, Leonhard?"

"Not near at all," I said. I hadn't told her I'd been close. She must have heard that from another.

When I finally sat at my desk, with only my candle awake with me, I took the crushed and torn black lump from my pocket again. I un-wadded it again and smoothed it again. It was surely my hat. I knew it full well. What I'd worn for all my years in Basel, that had been taken from me in the Inquiry, and that had now been finally torn by falling stones.

Then I shook off the mortal dust that coated it. I turned to my dresser, to the wooden head and wig, and moved off the tricorne that had taken residence there. With respect I put my old student hat in its old student place. It was as battered and torn as I was, and it was mine. Ten times as much punishment would not have marred it enough that I would have disowned it, or failed to recognize it. It still bore the marks of having been crushed between two stones. I felt much the same as it did. It was as if we'd been assaulted together.

On that place that had always been its home, it still had some stiffness, and some of its shape, though it would never again be what it had been. I would never throw it out, or any gift from my father. Yet I would never wear it again. For five years it had adorned my two heads, the wooden on my dresser and the live on my shoulders. I wouldn't be a minor student anymore, and a gentleman would never wear brown. It was all over; though, for a few more days, even as a gentleman, the brown would be useful.

Habits and routine were refuge in turbulent times.

I did my chores and fetched water the next morning without needing to think about anything more than the tasks at hand. But I'd been slow and I was a little late that morning, with the dawn already advanced as far as gray and pink. The water flowed in the fountain in the Barefoot Square as always, and the church's glow was more like daylight. The Boot and Thorn was still deep in night, though not at rest. A giant stood at its door watching and towering until the giant became Gustavus, only watching. Of course, no coach was there: it was Thursday, not Wednesday or Friday. And in the opposite door, an angel also watched, with Bare Feet, though only I saw him.

Willi came out of the stable tunnel leading the black stallion, so I knew who Gustavus was watching for. And soon he came. In some cities, a gentleman may leave the early morning to the servants, yet neither Basel nor Daniel conformed to that rule. But before he mounted he stepped into the dark doorway with Gustavus.

I could have taken my buckets and left but I waited. The angel also had a horse, white and cool as the other was black and hot. I didn't know who would come for it, but I had a mind to wait and see.

Daniel and Gustavus had left the Square entirely into the inn. They were together as the minutes passed, and it was time for me to return with my grandmother's water. Then finally just Daniel came out the door and took his horse. He was jaunty and as assured as he'd ever been. He took a deep, satisfied breath and swung himself into his saddle and made a quick and easy gait across the Sqaure. The collapsed gate had been cleared enough to let him by.

I looked to the Barefoot Church. The angel was still there, but the horse was not. Then I saw it passing the ruined gate after Daniel, following.

Mistress Dorothea's speech that morning was a wall, endless with no opening, which I'd learned meant that her mind was not on her words. She was the only of the family that I saw. Her only mention of the day before's affairs was as I was leaving, and she said to me, "And Leonhard. Do you remember what I've asked you?"

There were always many things that she had. But I answered, "I haven't seen the remorse that you asked of. Not yet."

When I was finished there, I went to see Lieber the bookbinder. His games and quarrels at the Boot and Thorn with Lithicus had been as much a part of the Common Room as the hearth.

I watched him at his book press. He'd allowed me before to pull its lever and press the inked type into the paper. I'd rather have set the type. It must have been like writing: it would be much slower, yet the letters were beautifully shaped and the whole set page was such perfection: considered, ordered, arranged, squared, and final. But lives were lived by the quill and inkbottle, instead of carefully chosen from drawer cases and laid straight.

"Young Master Leonhard," he said when he came to me. "You're not torn."

"No, though I nearly was yesterday. Just scratched."

"And Lithicus is rent. Who'll carve a stone for him, I wonder?"

"Someone new will," I said. "And there are no books to remember him by."

"Not him. It's not many who've written books. But I'll remember him."

"Lieber, do you remember when Master Gottlieb brought you the *Ars Conjectandi* to be printed?"

"Well enough," he said. "That one I'll always remember."

"What did he give you? Was it his finished manuscript? Did you see anything of Master Jacob's papers he wrote from?"

"Only Master Gottlieb's own written papers," Lieber said. "Very neat he is, though he angles his lines to the bottom of the page. But the drawings were from old Master Jacob."

"Who carved them into the printing plates?"

"I did that."

"I didn't know you were an etcher."

"I apprenticed under Meynenden in Frankfurt, and he was a hard Master. He had me learn every skill of making a book."

"They're excellent figures. Did Lithicus ever see them? He'd have appreciated good etching."

He lowered his forehead and looked at me through narrowed eyes. "And why are you asking, young Master Leonhard? Yes, I showed him the figures. I wanted him to see what could be done with the printing press."

"Surely you would," I said.

"And he didn't like what he saw. He would have torn the pages out if I'd let him."

I nodded. "It was the spiral, wasn't it?"

"Aye, it was the spiral."

"He carved a spiral for Master Jacob's epitaph stone. But it wasn't the kind he'd been meant to carve. I think Master Johann wasn't pleased with it."

"Lithicus wasn't much pleased, either. And he wanted to know where I'd got the drawing that I made that etching from. He said he'd been looking years for that figure."

"You had them from Master Gottlieb," I said.

"Oh, I told him that, but I told him if he wanted to see it himself, he'd just need to visit Master Huldrych."

"Master Huldrych!" I said. "Why him?"

"Master Gottlieb didn't keep all those papers of Master Jacob's. Master Huldrych kept them."

"Why did he?"

"I don't know the affairs of University men. That's not my place!"

"But how did you know that he had them?"

"Master Huldrych came and stood just where you're standing, to tell me to take care of the papers that Master Gottlieb had given me. He said he had them in his charge and he wanted them held safe. And I told him they would be."

I was a gentleman now, and of substance, and from speaking with Lieber, I took it upon myself to call on Cousin Gottlieb. I chose ten thirty in the morning as a respectable time to knock on his door. I was in complete black and white. All traces of anxiety and grief were cleared from my face. He answered the door himself. He saw me and understood that I was presenting myself as respectable, and accepted me as such, although it was a thin claim; he'd been the one to place the tricorne on my head. But we'd spoken as equals over Mathematics, and that alone was sufficient.

"Good morning," I said.

"Yes, good morning," he answered. "What might I do for you?" It was abrupt, to let me know that my claim was accepted, but thin enough to not to be relied upon heavily.

"It's a very small thing, and I'm sorry to bother you."

"Well, go ahead." That meant he was also sorry that I was bothering him.

"I asked last week about the hat that I had? I remember of course you said it was lost."

There might have been a difference in his annoyed glance. "What of it? Yes, it was lost. I have an appointment, Leonhard, and no time. What do you want of me?"

I hoped it was not another disrespectful student! "I still have a desire to find my hat."

"Then find it. Elsewhere. It isn't here."

"But might you be able to tell me what became of it from here?"

"It must have been thrown out. I don't allow rags to be left about in my house."

"I really must insist," I said, "to find what became of it."

"And why is that?" He was saying plainly that he wouldn't answer.

I paused a moment to prepare myself. "On the night that Daniel and Nicolaus returned from Italy, I saw Master Jacob's trunk in the kitchen at their house. I think my hat will assist me in learning how that trunk came from Master Huldrych's house to Master Jacob's."

He raised an eyebrow and pursed his lips. "And I suppose Knipper the coachman was in the kitchen with it?"

"He was. I spoke with him."

"I don't see that your hat will be any assistance."

I might have piqued his interest, but he still seemed in a hurry.

"I considered telling you before the Inquiry—"

"It's plain why you didn't." And Gottlieb's tone made it plain that it was plain. "You're tantamount to accusing one of us in the house of murder."

"I was afraid I might be misunderstood to be, so I said nothing."

"It might well not have been a misunderstanding. But I'm

not any Inquisitor now, so I won't ask you any more of it. And it's still nothing to do with the hat."

"And I realize," I said, proceeding, "that it had been you who had the trunk taken to Master Huldrych's in the first place when you arrived in Basel twenty years ago."

"Who else would have? Jacob asked me to keep it away from Johann. This still isn't worth bothering me over a hat."

"And you had Knipper carry it there for you. Then he would have recognized it later when he saw it. He was very anxious at it being in Master Johann's house. I'd never seen him so distraught."

"I'm sure he was so. He should have been. When I first sent him with it to Huldrych's, I instructed him very strongly to never tell Uncle Johann he knew anything of it."

"And later, some few years ago," I said, "Lithicus the mason carried it to Master Johann's."

"The mason? Who was killed just yesterday? Why do you say it was him?"

"He was told where Master Jacob's papers were. It was just by chance. And he knew Master Johann wanted to find them."

"The papers were still in the trunk?"

"Yes."

"All of them?"

"I don't know how many there ever were."

"How many did you see?"

"I didn't see them myself. I only saw the trunk."

"Who did see them?" he said, and he was still as impatient, but only that I wasn't answering quick enough.

"I have a witness . . . but I won't say who it is."

"There aren't many who it could be. What else does this witness claim?"

"Only that there were papers in the trunk, and they were Jacob's."

"Tell me who this witness is. Would he know also who killed Knipper."

"I pledged that I wouldn't tell." But after a moment, I said, "I still wonder what has become of my hat."

"Why do you want it? What does it have to do with any of this?"

"I do think it would be of help to me."

"Then tell me," he bargained, "who is your witness? What papers did he see? And I will consider the hat."

"Little Johann. But I told him that I'd not tell anyone that he'd looked in the trunk, or even seen it."

He frowned at that. "And that was who came here to take your hat, and I made the same pledge to him."

We stared at each other for a moment, considering.

"What was the danger you spoke of at the Inquiry?" I asked. "You said there was a danger to Basel."

He wasn't angry at my question, and that seemed to show he was accepting me. "If it comes, Leonhard, you'll know. If it doesn't, then you needn't know."

"Is it the plague?"

"I think it is not. It will be from outside, not within. Though plague might be part of it."

"I have a few other questions," I said, "though I doubt you would answer them."

Gottlieb had put his hand back on the doorknob to close it, but he paused, with almost the same look for me that he'd had for Daniel at the inn during their questioning and jousting.

"What are they?"

"I wonder what Magistrate Caiaphas has to do with this danger. I wonder why he demanded the Inquiry, but then tried to prevent it. And I wonder what you meant to ask Caiaphas. I believe that you pressed the Inquiry because you had questions of him that you wanted answered, which had nothing to do with Knipper."

"You are correct, Leonhard," Gottlieb said. "I won't answer those. And you are impertinent. I hope you find your hat." The dismissal was polite. He pushed the door to close it.

"Thank you," I said. And just before the door was shut, "Actually I did find it. I have it."

⁂

My Friday began dark and full of storms. I didn't need to go out for water; a great deal of water was coming directly to us. Our barrel beneath the eaves was flowing over. I knew it was without looking. As I lay in bed, dark before the sun, I listened to the rain and I could hear the pattering of the drops on the surface. It brought me to thinking also about Grandmother's warning that a pot will overflow and I wondered how full any pots were, and what sounds would change when they were full. I also thought how a tricorne had more purpose than to make a gentleman, because its practical use was to shed rain.

The hat would be first manufactured round and very wide brimmed. Then the three curl folds would be done to make it an equilateral triangle, the two sides angled toward the front to make the high prow, and the back as a wide, low stern. When the storm would rage and the sea flood over it, the water would empty from the stern's port and starboard corners. Thus, the gentleman's back was spared the spouts, which spewed to the sides.

The hat of a student would begin with the same wide round shape, but would be rolled on just its two parallel sides, and the flood would then pour directly down his robe. This would certainly be an impetus to the young scholar to finish his studies and be graduated, so that his back would stay dry.

But it was a noteworthy point to consider that the two hats began the same. This might also have been a reminder to both the student and the professor that in the shaping, a man would be made one thing or another. We were only earthen vessels, and all made of the same dust.

As I prepared to leave my room for the morning, I took both hats in my hands: my secondhand tricorne and my torn and rumpled student widebrim. They were both as clean and brushed as I could make them. The one was from my father, precious to me but never again to be worn. The other was from Gottlieb, from the University, from the wide world, from Basel, and I would wear it until a new one came.

I would take neither though, for that day. I was in brown and neither the child nor the man.

When the sun had taken hold of the sky and cleared it, I went to the Barefoot Square, not to collect water from the fountain, but to watch it. I'd filled my buckets there so often; again, I wondered on the water's source. I wondered again on the ancient-ness of Basel's fountains. The Romans had had fountains in the city.

Beyond, the Birsig Flow's deep path beneath the city was unknown; it came to the Rhine somewhere between the Munster and the Bridge. I walked to the Outer Wall. The Stone Gate was a high, narrow tower over the road from the Birsig's valley, and the Birsig entered its tunnel in a culvert beside the gate. I walked out the gate and followed the stream.

Outside the city, before its cloacal length, it was a good, pure stream, ten or more miles long and as wide as three houses where it came to the Walls. I'd walked its length, before and it always reminded me of walking with my father beside the Rhine. I set out to walk it again.

It passed its first mile well ordered, with quiet banks by farms and pastures on the left and a nice hill on the right. After two miles and the villages of Therwil and Oberwil, it turned right through a wide valley with low peaks on either side. The hamlets came every mile: Benken, Leymen, Rodersdorf, Biederthal, Wolschwiller, each smaller and less changed from its far past. There was a road directly from church to church, but I followed the path beside the stream, under trees with new unfurled leaves and by wildflowers needing to be seen.

The companionable stream became narrower and more talkative as I stayed with it. I just listened, as it had many interesting things to say. There were men in the fields and women in gardens. The air was a very tolerable and drowsy warm. Near the end, the water was pure garrulity, and childish, and I didn't pay close attention. I counted cattle in meadows, then steeples. On one hill I could see seven.

At the very end the water was just rivulets that hadn't even learned to speak. The whole of the stream's life had passed by me, from old and hard working in the city to this infancy. For my own life, I could not walk back and forth the length of it. I could only be in one moment and move in one slow tread, in one direction and pace. What if I could skip forward and back beside and see all my life, and know what was to come?

There were horses plowing, led by farmers on their hard journey back and forth through the fields. There were horse-drawn carts on the road. And once, a white horse free in a field watched me a moment and then with an easy gallop was gone behind a hill. I watched a moment. Then I ran. Not after it, but on my own path by the river. If the horse could run, I could, too!

So all the way back, I ran, and what a run! Up and down, but more down, faster than the water, faster than the breeze, breathing the breeze, being the breeze. Once I was started I couldn't stop.

I didn't tire the whole length of the stream. But finally, when I knew Basel's Walls would soon confront me, I paused. I came to the top of a crest, which the water cut through. Behind me, I could see the stream's valley and the high hills containing it, and the road, empty of living things; before me was Basel full within its Walls. All the sky was blue and blue, empty of any bit of cloud. I rambled down, in view of my home city but reluctant to finish my journey. I paused again.

A sudden thunder of hooves was all that warned me. I jumped aside and a black mount flew over the crest, Daniel on its back. He saw me and waved but wouldn't and couldn't slow his flight. And he hadn't passed me even when the white charger I'd seen far back in the fields was after him.

Like lightning they went. I'd seen one race before from the Walls. Now they were faster. Half across the open field the white was even with the black, still pulling ahead. As the Wall approached, it pulled back. Daniel's horse, the winner by default, slowed. Daniel finally took charge of his reins, laughing loud. I was there. I'd run behind them. I was no match with two legs for four, but once they'd slowed I caught them fast. And already the white horse was gone, back out the road and over the hill.

"What's that?" Daniel cried to me. "I'd say you frightened my Coal, but he doesn't frighten."

"He's a good racer," I said. "They both were."

"Both?"

"The white horse. I've seen you race him before."

"What white horse?"

So I laughed. "If you couldn't see him, your Coal could."

Inside the Walls, among Basel, I went to return Master Desiderius's book.

"Was there any lesson in it?" he asked me.

"The well-known one," I said. "But it's no danger to learn it again."

"Learning is hard, and un-learning is often too easy."

"Master Desiderius, how is it to be on a nominating committee?"

It was a strange, weak smile he gave me. "You mean, how does it feel to be the offerer? To be Mephistopheles?"

"Oh no! It wasn't what I meant—"

"It's not an enviable place."

"I didn't mean that. But," I said, "there are Fausts I've read that have an unwilling Mephistopheles. He's not eager to make the bargain. He warns against it."

"Then should I warn a candidate against taking the Chair, or even be reluctant to nominate?"

"What do you gain from the candidate winning the Chair? Not his soul."

"Though for winning the Chair, he may lose it."

"What do you mean?" I asked.

"Oh, Leonhard, I have a fear of the Election. It unburies things."

"Master Desiderius. Do you have regrets over your own Election?"

"I didn't know this city five years ago. I do now."

"I don't understand you," I said.

"I might have chosen differently. Thank you for returning this; I will read it again myself. Have you noticed the weather, Leonhard?"

"It's rained."

"Yes, but I think that was the last. It will be very dry. I feel it."

"What have you written this week?" Grandmother asked as we sat at supper.

"Several pages. I've thought more about waves and that they can go on without stopping. It was Master Johann's puzzle of the Reciprocal Squares that led me to these ideas."

"What does he think now of your solution?" She knew this wouldn't be a simple answer.

"I believe it troubles him. He's very intrigued by it. But doubtful, too, of course."

"Are you still sure your solution is correct?"

"I'm sure."

"If it is true, can it be proved false?"

"No. Mathematics doesn't allow such a thing. All the principles of Mathematics are true once they're proven, and Mathematicians accept proofs if they're according to the principles. That's part of the elegance of Mathematics. It is only made of proofs, and nothing else. There are a very few simple truths that are accepted as themselves, and all the rest is proved from them. I think there's no end to it."

"And will Master Johann be persuaded, then?"

"He will, I think."

"Then Mathematics is very different from most other things," she said, "if it can overcome a stubborn man's beliefs. What troubles him with this proof?"

"It might be that it's unlikely that a young, poor, unnoteworthy student would solve it correctly."

"But if it is true, it couldn't matter who first proved it."

"It couldn't. It may be that he is just jealous. But he's too great a man to be resentful." I tried to be sincere, but she knew he was very capable of resentment. "And Daniel accepts it. And Nicolaus and Gottlieb have doubts but still accept that it might be true. But also . . ." I was afraid to say it. It was such a boast on my part.

"What?"

"I don't think any of them truly understand it. Even Master Johann. When I explain it, they just touch it but they don't grasp it. So I wonder if I'm so poor at even explaining."

"How did you first conceive this proof, Leonhard? How did you invent a proof that exceeds great men's understanding?"

"I don't know. It was just there. It was given."

"There might be a purpose," she said.

And last, before sleep, I chose to read Leibniz in the morning. I would be put into the right mind for my lesson with Master Johann, and I would have opportunity to think on the question of how Mathematicians become great.

13

The Logarithmic Spiral

It had been three years before, when I was fifteen, that I wrote my thesis on Descartes. It was precocious of a child who knew so little to attempt so much. I blushed now to think of my gray-haired Masters, steeped in decades of long thought, regarding my chubby cheeks and naïve, earnest eyes as I, the dwarf, described my opinions of giants. And even more, that I compared Newton with Descartes, to the faculty of Basel, the Mathematical hotbed of anti-Newtonism, and the theological nemesis of Cartesians. It was a miracle that I even still existed! But those generous and patient professors allowed me past, and Master Johann, who could have sunk the whole battleship with one raised eyebrow or finger tap of annoyance, instead allowed me passage across his cannon, and himself signed the parchment of my Master's degree. For a while afterward a few people called me Master, but I'd never wanted that. Even with a tricorne, I still felt I was no Master.

Between those two, Newton and Descartes, I believed

Mr. Newton to be more correct; and three years later, I was more convinced. Many criticisms of Mr. Newton complained that his theories were too precise: they applied such a severe Mathematical exactitude to the beauty and gentle motions of nature. This was, besides, the completely invisible Gravity that he proposed, and others rejected as absurd. But the comparison was to Monsieur Descartes, who believed that the only truth was what we experienced, and could know with our own senses. If the universe was to be measured by Mathematic rules, or else by man's experience, then I knew that Mathematics was superior. I believed that the universe would exist and follow its Mathematic orbits even if no man ever lived to see it. I even believed that if there was no universe, the laws of Mathematics would still exist. And I thought Mathematics was beautiful itself, and added to the exquisite harmony of creation rather than degrading it. And for Gravity, well, I very greatly believed in invisible things.

It was still early on Saturday, though already the day was warm, when I sat at my desk to read Herr Leibniz. I'd read *Nova methodus pro maximis et minimis* many, many times, but it still put me in the best frame for my meeting with Master Johann. The two had been correspondents and friends. I thought this was one real reason that Master Johann sided so passionately with Herr Leibniz over Mr. Newton on the discovery of the Calculus. His passion had carried all the Mathematicians in the continent with him, turning the whole continent of Europe against England, and England against Europe.

It was strange that a subject as perfect and rational as Mathematics could stir disagreements and conflict. Yet it did in two ways: first, in discovery, where a man's pride would lead him to grasp a new theorem as a dog did a bone, and yield to no other that it was his original; and second, in proof, where claims might be shaky or unfounded, and the rigorous deduction to prove or disprove was beyond knowledge. So, the Newton camp and the Leibniz camp had warred over which champion first discovered the Calculus. Then, there was a civil war within each camp over what had actually been truly proven and what had not but would be, and what was actually false.

Then, there was a third hostility that arose from Mathematics, founded in the first two conflicts, and that was outright, which was the pursuit of Publications, of Eminence and Esteem, and most of all, of Chairs. So reading Leibniz, I thought much more about these qualities of humanity, and not as much about the qualities of polynomials.

On my dresser, beside my friend the wood head, and my marvel, the conch shell, and the small charred slat with the Logarithmic spiral, I had two other items, my bowls. They were pottery and seemed very normal. Each was only eight inches from rim to rim and somewhat shallow, just a few inches deep, with the sides becoming steep at their outer edge. They might even have seemed identically shaped, though they weren't. In color they were plain but had interiors which were very polished. However, each had its own unique and amazing property: one was brachistochronic, the other was tautochronic.

The tautochrone was the easier to demonstrate. Set a small flat pebble that would slide on the smooth surface, or a very round pebble that would roll, near the rim and it would accelerate down and quickly travel the long distance to the center. Place it farther from the rim, closer to the center, where the slope was less, and it would accelerate more slowly, but would still reach the center quickly because it was closer. Indeed, place the stone anywhere in the bowl, and the combination of the steepness and distance from the center at any point would contribute to the stone's reaching the center in the exact same time. *Tautochrone* meant *identical time*. Set two stones, or three, or as many as would fit and could be held, anywhere in the bowl from rim to nearly the center, and after they were all let go at the same time, they would all reach the center simultaneously.

That the second bowl was a brachistochrone was more difficult to demonstrate. In this bowl, the pebble set anywhere would reach the center faster than it would in a bowl of any other shape. If the side were steeper, the stone could accelerate more quickly but have a greater distance to travel; if it were more shallow, the reverse applied. *Brachistochrone* meant the *fastest time*.

These bowls showed another reason why Master Johann was so hostile to Mr. Newton.

The shape of either bowl could only be derived with a special set of the Calculus. The shapes were first sought by Galileo nearly a hundred years ago, but were beyond the Mathematics of the time. Only after Herr Leibniz published his *Nova Methodus* were the necessary theorems available. The equation of the tautochrone was fairly easy. But Master Johann, thirty years ago, and only a little older than I was now, published the first solution to the brachistrochrone, which was much more difficult. Yet only his solution was correct.

His proof was not. Often in Mathematics this would happen. It would be the same as stating that the source of the Barefoot Square fountain was the Birsig, which I believed was true but was not certain; and having given as my proof that it was water in the fountain, and it was water in the stream, so the one must feed the other. This would not be a valid proof, and neither were Master Johann's calculations of the brachistochrone.

This soon came to light, and Master Johann's proof was invalidated. A challenge was sent out to the Mathematicians of Europe in the journal *Acta Eruditorum* to find the correct proof, and also presented several variations to the problem. The challenge was actually posted by Master Johann himself, but anonymously, as he had a scheme to remove the stain on his reputation.

Only five men among all then living could have solved the problem, and they each did. Herr Leibniz solved it, of course. Monsieur L'Hospital also sent in a solution, though it was apparent that he'd corresponded with Herr Leibniz and had mainly repeated that Master's answer.

Two others able were the brothers Jacob and Johann. Master Jacob solved it in an original way, and as the two brothers were then still cordial, he showed his proof to Master Johann. Master Johann, expecting this, took his brother's proof and attempted to pass it as his own.

All of these proofs were published in the *Acta*, anonymously as always, though each of the men quickly recognized the others' work. Accusations flew and the brothers were permanently sundered. They'd all spent days and weeks at their calculations, each sure of his own unique genius.

There was, though, a fifth proof published in that same edition, superior actually to all the others. Mr. Newton in England, it was said, had solved the problem in a few moments the very night he received the journal, after a tiring day of work. Though the attribution was anonymous, the notations made it obvious that they'd all been bested by the Englishman.

As Master Johann said when he read it, "I recognize the lion by his paw." The saying had persisted in his family. The feelings between them had also persisted.

⁂

After Leibniz, I read Newton. The *Principia* was a book that would stand forever: it bested all his peers, just as his proof had bested them. Whether Mr. Newton or Herr Leibniz first understood the Calculus, I did not know. I did know that Mr. Newton's work reached farther, and his principal that Mathematics ruled, and also explained, the motions of both planets and pebbles, of both raindrops and rainbows, was a new beginning of history. He would be famous forever. Whenever he died, and he was now very old, his fame would only keep growing.

My Master Johann would also hold a place in history. Again whether Mr. Newton or Herr Leibniz first discovered the Calculus, it was without doubt that everyone who now knew the subject learned it through Master Johann's explanation. His books were not on the same pinnacle as the *Principia*, but they would always be known. He had the renown that Master Faust sought.

Daniel and Nicolaus and Gottlieb would also be remembered. In Mathematics, their family had been a constellation. Daniel wanted to outshine his father and would have paid a dear price to do it, and Nicolaus had more ambitions than he showed. And, in some obscure journal, an author might even be remembered for the first proof of the Reciprocal Squares.

⁂

It seemed to be the warmest day yet of the spring, and the sky was cloudless. All sound was deadened.

When I was admitted into Master Johann's house, there was a thickness to the silence. I could hardly hear my own footsteps in the stairs, and Mistress Dorothea's knock on the inner door was like a leaf fall. The call from within sounded as from a grave.

"What have you been reading this week?" he asked, and he seemed much older and worn.

I was able truthfully to give an answer pleasing to him. "Herr Leibniz."

Though less, he was still omniscient and omnipotent in his dark room. He'd known. "I have been, also," he said. "Even now."

"The *Nova Methodus*?" I didn't see a book on the table, only some papers. But these were what he set his hand on as he answered.

"Our correspondence."

"From himself?" I asked, awed. I knew, of course, that there had been many letters between them, but these were those letters themselves.

"I was younger then. Leonhard, why do you pursue Mathematics?"

"I can't not."

"How does Mr. Newton describe the study of Mathematics?"

This was disturbing. It may have been the first time I'd ever heard that name from my Master's lips. It was dangerous, as well. To deny my respect would be foolish, as he certainly remembered my thesis of three years before. But to show too much admiration would also be unwise. "The *Principia* states that Mathematics explains the revolving of earth and the motion of water and the colors of light," I said.

"How can Mathematics do this?"

"I believe there are deep laws that govern motion and substance."

"So is that Mathematics?" he asked, and I sensed his dissatisfaction with my answer. "It is just a principal of natural philosophy?"

"No. It is more."

"Then what?"

"I think that natural philosophy, and Physics, and all of such things are built on Mathematics like a castle is built on a mountain. There is more to the mountain than just the portion that holds the castle."

"There is more of Mathematics," he said, and now he was satisfied, "than is used in the earth and heavens."

"I believe so. Master, what do you understand that Mathematics is?"

"It is an invisible world," he answered. "Greater and deeper than anything we see."

"I do see invisible things," I admitted. "Sometimes."

"Then you see that world," he said, "also."

"Where did it come from?"

"Where?" He hadn't thought that question before. "It would always have been. The world we see is created on it."

"But could it have always been? Even the invisible world must have been created, also."

"The created world is as it was chosen to be," he said. "Mountains and rivers are where they are, but they could have been otherwise. Mathematics can only be as it is. There is no other possibility. So, was it created?"

I tried to think of a Mathematics different from the one I knew. Could one and two add to something other than three? Or did they only because that was how they were created to be?

"That would mean they are beyond the Creator."

"We will keep our discussion on Mathematics and Mathematicians."

"Yes, Master. But then I have another question. What makes a Mathematician great?"

"If he discovers great things. Then he is known." He looked at me a moment. "Is that what you mean?"

"No, sir. What would make him able to discover great things?"

"What are his qualities? Is that what you mean?"

"Yes, sir."

He sat back into the silence of the room. "He sees."

"Into the invisible."

"Yes." Then Master Johann laughed. "But then he must also publish and he must become known. A great Mathematician who is unknown is not great."

So I plunged forward. "Then I wish to send my proof to Paris."

"To Paris? Monsieur Fontenelle will deride and dismiss the work of a young student. Monsieur Molieres would glance through it and find every fault that I do."

"It would be treated respectfully if you wrote a letter of recommendation for it."

"Yes, it would." He did not deride me. He even seemed unsurprised that I had asked. "But should I? I am not fully convinced of it myself." The one word though, *fully*, showed that he might soon be. He considered me, his young supplicant, in the same way he had the last Saturday, and it seemed that he was seeing something new.

❧

My mother's father was pastor of Saint Leonhard's for three decades. He died before I was born. My grandmother didn't speak often of him, as she was not given to reminiscing. Mostly she used him as an example to me of a sound, pious, dedicated, and competent man. Everyone else who remembered him spoke more highly even than she did.

This pastor's daughter, my mother, married a pastor. He was a young man of good family and humble means, unshakable in his faith and in every part of his life. Beneath his calm demeanor, though, his heart burned with a slow, steady fire so hot that all the flames of the Boot and Thorn would be just a sputtering candle beside it.

For several years he had the pulpit at Saint Leonhard's. It was even now still warm from him. When his son was born, the child was named for his father's parish. Then, instead of taking a higher perch at the Munster or beyond, this man took his wife and child out of Basel to pastor a village in the hills north of the city and settled into its smallness. Whether the cottages of Riehen ever knew what great spirit they had, I would not be certain. He was certain of the choice he was making. He was my father. I learned from him that God was not served by our greatness but by our humbleness.

On Sunday morning I took my grandmother to church, and in the preaching we were instructed on the very greatness of God: his righteousness, his love, and his sacrifice. I would never tire of that lesson.

⁂

Monday morning, Mistress Dorothea poured words as a fountain pours water. Basel's fountains provided a greater flow than the citizens need, so that a great deal simply flowed over the basin and into the streets; and Mistress Dorothea had more to say than there were ears to hear.

But as I was finishing, the fountain stopped. "Leonhard."

"Yes, Mistress Dorothea?" I said.

"Master Johann has instructed me that you are no longer to be obliged to perform chores in this house."

"Not obliged?" I was dumbfounded.

"From this moment on."

"But . . . Mistress Dorothea . . . why not?"

"I don't question the Master's reasons."

I was trying to understand, and reeling, though I also did notice that she'd let me put in my full morning's labor before she'd said this. "Then . . . am I no longer to come on Saturdays?"

"You'll need to discuss this with Master Johann. He is expecting you upstairs."

"Come." This was the third Monday Master Johann had answered my knock on his door.

It seemed more difficult each time to concentrate on speaking. The room was too marvelous. "Mistress Dorothea said I was no longer obliged to do chores for her in the mornings."

"That is true." From where I stood and how he was seated, I couldn't see his desk well. There were just a few papers visible at the edge.

"Then I'll no longer come on Saturdays?"

"You will still come."

"But, Master, how will I pay you for the time?"

"I've written a letter to your father. From the present, your lessons will be at my pleasure. They will not be in exchange for tuition or service."

"Thank you, sir . . . but I can't. It would be unearned. An imposition."

He shook his head. "It is my decision."

"Yes, sir. Master Johann?"

"Yes?"

"May I still be allowed to do chores here nonetheless?"

I saw no reaction. He just said, "You may request that of Mistress Dorothea."

"Yes, yes, Leonhard," was Mistress Dorothea's answer to that request. "I'll keep you for my kitchen, for the present. But there's a time coming when it won't be fitting."

"At least a little longer," I said.

And when she was out of the room, Little Johann came in to ask, "You'll keep coming?"

"As long as I can."

"Why?"

"It's right to do. I shouldn't take lessons without paying."

"That's all?"

"It would be an exile to not come." Of all the family, I was least sure of Little Johann's thoughts, and all the family was an opaque set. I didn't know if he was glad or thought me a fool. He took a covered basket from beside the hearth, opened it, and took out a plump, risen ball of dough. "I'm not gentleman enough yet to be above work." I sighed a wistful sigh. "But I'm not sure I'll ever wear my old hat again, even if I did have it. It might be only tricornes for me now."

As he began working his dough, Little Johann seemed grieved as I was. He squeezed the dough. He had such strong hands.

Then I said, "What became of my hat, Johann? Did you lose it?"

He stared at the dough, kneading and pressing it so hard. Then he nodded.

"It's all right," I said. "I have it back."

"You do?"

"Yes. I just wonder how it came to be where I found it."

"Where did you find it?"

"Where did you lose it?" I asked.

"I had it from Cousin Gottlieb. I took it to the Barefoot Square to find you in the inn or the church."

"What happened?"

"A gust blew it out of my hand. It was away too quick. I didn't see where."

"I found it in the Square," I said. "So it's all right. And

Johann, on your father's desk. There's only one letter for Daniel. The letter from Paris. The other, from Russia, is gone."

I stayed home that afternoon and evening. Sometimes I was driven so strongly to write that everything else fled aside, as if an angry bull were let loose in the market square. That evening my thoughts had piled so high from Saturday morning that they were riotous as the bull and the scrambling market-goers together. The quill in my hand flew tempest and my pages drifted into deep snowbanks against my books. It was a blizzard! Once I noticed a plate of supper had alit at my side, and another time I noticed it was empty, and some other moment I saw that I'd lit a candle. Or it might have spontaneously lit itself.

And finally I dimly perceived that I was in bed and the candle was out. Saint Leonhard's bell sounded three times. But all of that was only the visible world. In the invisible, I was still writing and every word was exact and clear.

As I was in Mistress Dorothea's kitchen Tueday morning, scrubbing an iron skillet, I was called upon. It was a student, Heidelmann, who clerked for the Provost, and he watched me work my elbow.

"Your grandmother said you'd be here. That's nothing for a student or even any man to be doing," he said, but in friendship.

"It's rusted. It needs a hard hand."

"I have man's work for you. I have a task from my Master, and you know who he is."

"I know."

"He wants you for an errand."

"Me? Why's that?"

"I don't know that. So make yourself look like a young gentleman, if you can, and get over to Master Provost, and he'll tell you what to do."

⁂

I could make myself look like a young gentleman, though looks were deceiving, and I could do it fast. Grandmother was curious over my summons but there was little I could tell her.

"What would the Master Provost want with a student?" she asked.

"To learn his lessons, pay his tuitions, and comport himself decently."

"Oh, Leonhard! What does he want of you?"

"I pay my tuitions," I said, "so it must be I'm lacking the others."

⁂

But I did know a few reasons the Provost might have to call a single student, and one was to be a messenger. When just the Senior members of the University met for a routine matter, they were simply sent a message the day before. It was much less picturesque a gathering than the Convention, and a single student was given the task. He was given a day for it: some score of Chairs and Deans and Officials took a few hours at least.

So I called on the Provost at his home as soon as I was presentable. He lived not far from Magistrate Faulkner and in a similar house, though Faulkner's had more pleasant trees and gardens. I was shown in to the front parlor and soon greeted by the Provost himself.

He was a bit of a jovial man, once a Chair of Law, comfortable in his office, unafraid of it, and placid in its exercise. It was the Deans who saw to the affairs of their Colleges, and the Chairs who *were* the affairs of the Colleges. A Provost held a high position that depended on his wisdom and light touch. But there was a weight on his shoulders and duties to be performed. So he wanted me for a messenger.

"You know the names, Leonhard," he said. "Tell them, the faculty will come together tomorrow morning at ten."

"Yes, sir. For what, should I tell them?"

"The reports of the committees. The nominations."

"I'll tell them all, sir."

I started my door-to-door. But I couldn't run, which was a pity, as young gentlemen didn't, at least not when they were seen, and there were only a few streets and alleys that were empty. And I came to each door, and knocked, and said I must speak to the Master himself, and when the Master was produced, gave him the message. It wouldn't usually be proper to demand the sight of the mighty men, but they knew that the day would have been coming soon and were expecting it. A few weren't home so I asked when they would be, and rounded on them again. The people of Basel were in their homes much more than anywhere else, and the Masters of the houses really had little reason to leave besides church.

The only door that worried me was my own Master's. I could have easily come in the back and sent Little Johann up for his father, but the University had to be served in its own way. So I knocked, and Little Johann answered, and I told him I had an important message for Master Johann. Then I was let in. A gentleman wasn't kept waiting outside, even if it was me.

I took a seat in the front parlor, where more often I was cleaning or tending the fireplace. As always the room was in twilight. Then with no warning the door opened. I was up on my feet like a rabbit.

Master Johann regarded me. "Sit down," he said. His near-round face was caught somehow in a shaft of light; I hadn't seen the light before he came in. His wig was bright white in it. "You have a message for me?"

"Yes, sir." I jerked up again. "The Provost requests that the faculty attend to important business at the University tomorrow morning at ten o'clock."

"Sit down." He stood watching me. I sat down. Then he sat down. When I came on Saturday afternoons we both sat, but the table was between us, and he was already sitting. That was very different. Here, he was sitting to converse, with me. "Leonhard," he said. "I have written a letter to Paris. It is to Monsieur Frontenelle of the Academy, to tell him that I have seen a solution of the Reciprocal Squares problem by my student, and that he should await a letter from Master Leonhard."

"Master Johann . . . thank you . . . thank you! I don't how to thank you!"

He dismissed my amazement. "The Monsieur is also an editor of the *Acta Eruditorum*, and I have suggested that the proof should be published."

I nearly fell from my seat. The *Acta* was the journal to which Master Johann submitted his own most important papers! It was incredible that he would consider promoting me this way.

"I . . . but Master Johann . . ."

"I believe your proof is worthwhile. Leonhard, you have great potential. It is time to consider plans for your future."

This was all beyond my greatest hopes. I'd had so many small evidences that Master Johann was favorable toward me, but many others that contradicted those. And I knew well how little he was given to selfless generosity. Yet here we sat, almost as equals, and he, the truly famed Master Johann of Basel, was advising me for my future.

"I've thought of the future," I said, "but not of plans."

"Then listen to this counsel." Oh, of course I would! "Should the Academy accept your proof," and of course, with his recommendation they would! "or the *Acta Eruditorum* publish it," and with his suggestion, how could they not? "then you will find many opportunities open to you." Many? All! Any door would open! "I would advise you," he said, "to choose carefully."

"Yes, sir," I said. "Of course I would want to."

"There are numerous positions that seem significant but great men aren't found in them."

I nodded.

"And there are other positions," he said, "which are fewer, which great men do hold."

"I wouldn't know which was which," I said.

"And the men in these positions recognize each other."

"I'm sure you must," I said.

"Even great ability will only raise a man to a certain level. Occupying one of these highest Chairs, holding office in one of these exceptional Academies, or attending one of these erudite Courts, is just as necessary."

"I'd aspire to such a position," I said.

"These positions are never simply given."

"They must be achieved?" I asked.

"They must be negotiated."

"But . . . with whom?"

He had leaned forward, slowly, as he talked. Now he leaned back and his manner changed from conspiratorial to magnanimous. "An introduction to the Royal Academy in Paris will be a step forward, and I have every hope the Secretary will receive it graciously. Now, Leonhard, the Provost and I both thank you for your service today."

All the bells of Basel tolled three o'clock as I walked back to my grandmother's house. They were a cacophony but pleasant and grand and noble. I felt them calling me to noble and grand places. Then they fell silent, and their echoes circling the city dwindled. From far off, I heard the single bell of Riehen answer two o'clock, quietly.

Later, I made a visit to the Boot and Thorn in the chance of finding Daniel, which I did. Nicolaus was there, of course. I don't think he enjoyed the smoky dungeon any more than I did.

"It's all for tomorrow," Daniel said. "Just hours."

"It's a Chair," I said, "but only a Chair. Daniel, you're nervous as a sheep that smells a wolf."

"As a wolf that smells a sheep," Nicolaus said.

"You'll be nominated," I said. "I'm certain you will. And you're certain. Be at peace."

"It's a certainty that doesn't bring peace," Nicolaus said.

Daniel snarled at him. "What's that?" His anger flared, but Nicolaus was still as always. "You'd take a nomination if you could! You'd give as much as I."

"How much have you given?"

Daniel shrugged him off. "He's just jealous," he said to me.

"There are three nominations," I said.

"And two are worthless."

"Worthless after the stone's drawn, or before?" Nicolaus said.

"After," I said. "They're each worth the same while they're each still in the box."

"Don't under-guess Mighty Brutus," Daniel said. "He'll squeeze just what he wants out of that box. There's no telling what he might do."

"I don't understand you," I said. "You seem so sure that you'll be nominated and chosen, and you're sure your father will be sure that you aren't. What does it mean? And your father isn't so vengeful as you think, anyway."

"What do you mean by that?"

"He's conceded my proof. He's said he accepts it and even admires it."

"Brutus? He said that?"

"To me, this morning."

"That's easy enough, I suppose, when there's no one to hear him."

"He says he's sending a recommendation to Paris that I've solved the challenge."

Daniel leaned close, and even Nicolaus did, too. "But has he sent it?"

"It'll be on the Post to Belfort tomorrow. It will be in Paris in a week." I couldn't help myself, boastful as it was to say it. "And he's recommending it to the *Acta Eruditorum*, as well."

"What? Never. It's not the same man! You've been captivated by a conjurer, Leonhard. It wasn't any member of my family who said that."

"Or father's been captivated," Nicolaus said, thoughtfully.

"If he's been," Daniel said, "it's worth guessing by whom. No, Leonhard's the one captivated, and by Brutus."

"Would you want a nomination, Nicolaus?" I asked.

"I have my Chair already in Bern, and I'm wise enough," he said with a nod to his brother, "to not give up my own until I have something better."

"The nothing I have now is better than that Chair was. And you've neglected your Chair this past month."

"It will stand a rest when I have more urgent business here."

I asked Daniel a question. "Which part is Gottlieb of the schemes? Is he of yours or your father's?"

"That's a question," Nicolaus said. "Which is he, Daniel?"

"We're fire and stone," Daniel answered. "Enemies that can't help or hinder."

"And cousins, too," I said, "who've been friends before."

"And aren't now. Brutus won that match. But he can't win this one. Watch, Leonhard. The committees he's put together so carefully, he can only use to nominate me. He's forced into it."

"Then when you're nominated, you'll be sure it's your scheming. Oh, Daniel. I think the only man caught in your nets is yourself."

He laughed. "Then you'll believe it when the lot is cast."

"If you win the Chair, will you take it?" Nicolaus asked.

"What? Why wouldn't I?"

"Something better might come."

Daniel laughed again. "That would be a trick. What card might Brutus pull from his sleeve? I'll accept he's clever enough at the game that he might."

At that I left.

❧

I crossed the Barefoot Square, to the Barefoot Church, and sat in the back corner I preferred. I even took off my shoes; it seemed right to do so. At times the light through the windows was straight as taut string, which reminded me of the weight of the whole city which the church held up. Where the light struck was lit, and where it did not, was not.

But other times, and this was one, the light was diffuse. It reflected and spread, seeping and merging until every spot was some mixture of glow and shadow. When I would see this, I wondered whether there was light and dark, or only lighter and darker.

Shod, and in the Square, I stopped at the Coal Arch. The rubble was cleared all away, and the good, formed stones of the old arch were piled to be repaired and replaced. I lifted one. They were all the same, the same size and the same shape, a proper trapezoid front to back, and square on the sides where the stones rested against each other. The stone in my hands was almost as much as I could lift. A good arch would stand by just friction. There'd been mortar between these stones, but not enough to hold the arch from falling. I wondered who'd finish the stonework. Then I wondered who would make a stone for Lithicus.

⁂

Tuesday evening I felt an odd chill in my room where I was writing. It was penetrating enough that I set down my quill, and once I had, my line of thought was broken.

To find it I stepped out of my house. It was twilight. As I seemed to always do in these recent weeks, I walked toward the Barefoot Square, and there, took a place in the door of the church. But the chill just wrapped me more and I shivered. I heard horses and wheels. The clatter seemed more real than the actual appearance of the coach from Freiberg. Rupert the driver, always grinning, brought the carriage to a hard stop at the door of the inn, almost against it, blocking it from my view. But I was hearing, not seeing, and I heard the coach door open and I heard black robes and black boots pass through the brief air into the inn.

Faint as it was, I even heard the fires' greetings inside.

⁂

From the Barefoot Square I went on further. The chill was gone, replaced by a heat in the air like a fever. I followed through evening streets beneath the stars and past closed windows with lights like stars. In a while it led me to a garden beneath trees and a door that was closed but hospitable anyway. I knocked. It was soon answered.

"I'm sorry for the late call," I said. "Might I speak with Magistrate Faulkner?"

"Come in," I was requested, and I did. I didn't wait long. I'd been in the room a few other times. Even in a great man's house, in Basel the rooms are quiet and simple. But there were portraits on the wall and upholstered chairs and flowers.

"Leonhard?" Faulkner smiled and greeted me. He was in his black coat and breeches, as I was. But his black was the purest in Basel.

"Good evening, sir. When we met on the Wall, some days ago, you had asked me to come."

"It's Tuesday night, isn't it." His voice was like black ink on white paper. "Did you speak to him?"

"I only heard him get off the coach. I knew it was him. I didn't see him."

"I don't doubt you."

"Do you know why he is here, sir?" I asked.

"Yes, I do. Were you born in Basel, Leonhard?"

"Yes, sir. Though my father took me to Riehen soon after."

"I remember when your father left the city. I hope someday he would return."

"I don't know if he ever will. He visits, of course."

"Yes, he's close. But outside. Basel is separate from Riehen and from everywhere else." He was musing, and I'd never before known him to be indirect or to wander. "But the outside is very close. Riehen is close, and the Empire is close, and France is close."

"Yes, sir," I said, and stood. He opened the door for me.

"Thank you, Leonhard. He may leave on the morning coach, but he will soon return. Tell me what you see of him."

"I will, sir." So, then I understood the danger to Basel. At least, I understood what Magistrate Faulkner and Master Gottlieb believed was the danger to Basel. I'd already known the true danger, which they didn't know.

୨୧

Grandmother met me at my door and I knew at once I had a visitor. Her palms were pressed together as they had been when Daniel had come, but her expression was very different. Instead of that knot of disapproval, the cord was more a tangle of impropriety and aversion and surprise, all of them mild and polite as befitting her.

I entered the parlor and found a rotund guest, hat not on bald head but clenched in hand, a hand that usually clenched reins. Rupert the coach driver stood in the middle of the room, nodded his head, aware and unbothered that he was in a house above his own station. "Master Leonhard," he said, "good evening," and I nodded, too.

"Good evening, Rupert," I said. "Welcome."

"Thank you, sir. I do feel so. I'll only take a short minute of your time, if you don't mind."

"Not at all. Go ahead."

"I've only just taken the coach," he said. "I'm not accustomed to your city yet, and its ways. I hope you'll forgive my familiarity." He didn't seem at all uncertain.

"Of course."

"Yes, sir. And as I've taken the coach, I've looked through it to know it, and what I've found I'm not sure what's to be done with."

"What have you found?"

"This, sir. It was in the post box."

He handed me a letter which I had seen before. Daniel's name was in the most beautiful script, covering much of the front, and the wax seal covering much of the back of the envelope had the Tsar's own double Eagle. "And I'm not sure how long it's been there." I knew it couldn't have been long, as I'd last seen it in Master Johann's office only a week before.

"It was in the postbox?" I asked.

"There's an edge to the box, you see, and a bit of a place a letter could be caught and hid."

I handed it back to him. "Why did you bring it to me?"

"I asked Gustavus, the keeper at the inn, if the man was known in the city here, and he said he was."

"He's at the Inn under Gustavus's own nose near every day."

"Yes, sir, he has been shown to me. But there's a saying, I'm told, to treat all that family with great care, and it might even go ill with the one who brings him a letter that's been delayed such. It seems an important letter."

"I think it is," I said.

"And there's another saying, that you're a friend to most, sir, and you might hand it to him on my behalf and with my regrets." And he held the letter back to me.

I stared at it. The story was implausible in every detail, but most of all in this last statement. If Rupert were to walk direct back to the Inn, Daniel would surely be there even at that moment, and Gustavus could hand the letter to him without any fear.

"All right," I said. I took the letter. He bowed and smiled and I let him out.

I went to the kitchen where my grandmother was waiting. "He's gone away," I said.

"Was there anything he wanted?"

"He had a question for Daniel, but was told to be cautious of all Master Johann's family, so he wanted some counsel first."

"It's not well to speak of a man behind his back to a stranger."

"I only told him he had nothing to fear." I thought that to tell her about the letter would only be a confusion should Nicolaus stop in again with questions. "And Grandmother. Master Johann said he'd write a letter to Paris for me. He's accepted my proof. And now, I must write a letter to the Academy myself, to explain the proof."

She was astonished as I'd been. I told her everything about it, and even Mistress Dorothea couldn't have spoken as much in an hour.

൭൭

I sat at my desk and took my pen and ink and poised myself for the words to come. For the moment, though, they did not. This would happen, though rarely, and I'd never found a solution for it but to wait.

So I stood and went to my dresser. I felt the curve of my bowls, and ran my finger through the conch's spiral, and finally took my hat and tried a little to soothe it again into better shape, and to smooth out the marks of its crushing.

It seemed evident that the hat had been lodged in the arch after escaping Little Johann's hand. The peculiarity of its return to me was remarkable, greatly.

I looked more closely at the marks on it. They made most of a square. The square was just the size of the stone I'd held that day in the Barefoot Square.

I held it to different angles, and close to my candle light. Then I saw that my hat's journey had been even more astonishing than I'd realized.

It had been crushed between two arch stones, and not

just in the falling of the arch. It had been placed between the stones.

And if it had only been the hat between the stone, and not any mortar, then the arch would have been weakened. When Lithicus had loosened some other stone close by, there would have been no friction where this hat had been.

The arch would have fallen because my hat had been set in it.

I still believed Little Johann's word of how the hat had been accidentally lost. So the peculiarity remained, but it was not only remarkable. It was wicked. And it was a challenge. And there was an enemy.

I was staggered by it.

⁂

Though a restless sleep on my bed intervened, the next morning found me again in the door of the Barefoot Church. Willi didn't know I was watching as he led the horses and carriage out into the Square and put piled baggage that had two black trunks into the rack, and neither did Rupert even know me at all as he came out of the inn with his face bright with firelight and conspired with Gustavus, who also knew nothing of my observing.

But Caiaphas knew I was there as the coach door was held for him and he climbed in, pausing and knowing and staring straight into the shadow that hid me. He seemed satisfied that I was there.

The carriage crossed the Square to the Coal Gate and I felt pulled after it. When it was gone I was somehow out in the middle of the Square. I crossed on to the Boot and Thorn and looked in. There was a yellow light from a lantern down the hall and from the Common Room the red fire glare was both intense and dim. I stood looking in. It was empty, I thought, but then on a near table was a bundle, the size of a footstool. I looked at it closely. It was rectangular like a small trunk, wrapped in heavy cloth, and tied with string.

"That is for you," Gustavus said. Of course he was there, also.

"What is it?"

"Take it."

"Is it to be returned?"

"Tomorrow evening it is to be returned."

⁂

The parcel was heavy as wood for its size but not solid. Its shape shifted in my hands as I struggled home with it. So I knew what it was, and I feared what it might be. I left it on my desk as I did my grandmother's chores, then Mistress Dorothea's chores.

I finished in Mistress Dorothea's kitchen, under the eye of Little Johann with his bread dough. "This is a big house," I said. "How well do you know it?"

"I know it," he said.

"Do you know its hiding places?"

"I know them."

"There's one I want to see, if I can. It would hold a good-sized box, so big." I measured for him with my hands, that size of a footstool.

"I only know where they are. I don't know what's in them or how big they are."

"Could you see if any are empty?"

"I never look in them. I only know where they are."

"I think one has been newly emptied," I said.

"I'll find which one," he said.

And back in my room, the package was still there as I dressed, and when I left at nine thirty for the University.

Several hundreds could sit in the University lecture hall. It was filled, and more. The Professors and Deans and Officials I'd called on the day before were seated uncrowded in the front, attending each other as peers and familiars. Upward and back the lesser in rank grew greater in density. It was all very black, with wigs and collars of white, and the scarlet, azure, and other brilliant stripes on the robes of the chief birds were brighter for their contrast.

And the room was mighty. It wasn't somber and accusatory, as the Town Council Chamber was; Master Holbein never set foot here. It wasn't similar to any church, lofty and plain like the Barefoot Church, or grand and heavy like the Munster, or beautiful like close-by Saint Martins; no friars or almsgivers had ordained it. It was secular to itself and holy to itself, not of the Boot and Thorny earth or the Barefoot heaven. It was something in between.

Beside me was Daniel, and beside him was Nicolaus, and even Little Johann was crowded in. But not Mistress Dorothea, of course, for no woman has ever passed the portal of learning into that room. Daniel was in a froth, gibbering, then stony, then mopping sweat. It seemed hardly a reasonable time to mention to him the letter for him I now had.

"I know the nomination will come," he said. "It's certain. Certain, at least."

"You're certain?" Nicolaus asked. It might have meant that Daniel was certain of the conclusion, or that the conclusion was certain for Daniel.

"I'm certain," Daniel said.

The Provost was seated at the front, between Deans, talking with Theology and Law. He noticed me, in the midreaches, and nodded. It was my payment for being his courier. The three committees were also represented by their leaders. Master Johann alone wasn't leaning to his neighbor and whispering, and nodding. The bell in the Munster rang and it was time to begin.

Some things were ritual and some were not. The convening of the University was. The announcement of its candidates was not. The dignity of so many Chairs in one room made the occasion momentous, but the moment was brief. "Gentlemen!" the Provost said and the room quickly was silent. "The report of the committees appointed to nominate candidates for the vacant Chair of Physics. Master Gottlieb?"

Daniel went rigid. But I heard words escaping from his clenched teeth.

"The Brute's outdone this time. He'll have a taste of what it's like. There's no chance he's got around me now. If only I could see his face . . ."

Gottlieb said, "We nominate Master Staehelin."

Daniel shuddered. "What? No. Not him!" A quiet storm of murmurings rose immediately, approving and unexcited. Master Staehelin had been the lecturer in Physics for a decade and was a very competent scientist. He seemed an obvious candidate. Daniel's reaction was mixed of contempt and suspicion. "That's no surprise. He's a plain choice."

"He's a good choice," I said. "I've heard him lecture. He's able and he's diligent."

"He's a distraction, a trick. Brutus has higher plans for Physics than a plain, diligent lecturer." Daniel was speaking to himself. "He needs two other nominees besides the man he's picked for the Chair. That's all Staehelin is."

Staehelin himself had turned white. He was across the room from us in about the same row. He was a plain man, as Daniel said, about forty and probably not with the ambition to expect a Chair. But he'd take it, of course. His white turned to red and his dropped open mouth turned to a grin, and hands near him reached, discretely, to shake his. Daniel might have been right, that his candidature was only a ploy, but seeing his surprise and gratitude, I hoped for him that he'd be successful.

He made his way to the front of the room, and it was a slow journey across his row to the aisle and down the steps. He was obviously still surprised, even to stumbling as he reached the front. Then he waited, for the Provost was unlocking the casket.

Around his neck, on a long and thin but sturdy chain, the Provost had the key. The casket, resting quietly on the lectern, was a foot long, and less wide and tall, and pure black. The keyhole was the only mark on it; even the hinges were inside and unseen. The key was small, about an inch, and solid. I could tell from its weight on the chain, and how the Provost held it, that it was heavy for being small. It went into the hole and turned with effort. The lid was opened.

From the casket, the Provost lifted a wood tray.

"Master Staehelin?" the Provost said. "Please choose a stone."

He looked at the offered tray. On it were the seven stones, each with its emblem. It didn't seem that there was anything important to him in his choice, which the *Ars Conjectandi*, of course, said there was not. Each would be equal. He took the center.

"This one," he said, hoarsely.

"Master Staehelin has chosen the Tree," the Provost said. Also on the tray were three blank stones of the same sizes. He took one of these in one hand and the chosen stone from Staehelin in his other hand. Heidelmann, the Provost's student clerk, had a bar of sealing wax and a candle, and he held them over the two stones, dripping wax on them both.

The Provost pushed them together and they became a sealed cube. The wax was held entirely within the carving of the emblem and none extruded to the outside, so the cube was perfect and without blemish.

The Provost set the cube into the black casket. Staehelin clambered back to his seat. The Provost waited. Then he said, "Master Desiderius?"

"Maybe it's Desiderius you're waiting for," Nicolaus said.

"No," Daniel said. "It must be the Brute himself! Oh, that'll be everything!"

We only saw Master Desiderius's back. Master Johann's face was also forward and unseen to us. Desiderius stood and just said, in a voice that was dry and carved in stone, "We have nominated Master Daniel."

Too much happened at that for me to see it all. Of course Daniel popped like a squeezed melon. I felt him beside me. But I also tried to see any expression from his father, any motion from his shoulders or back. He did react, with a slight but sudden lean and twist of his head, like he was having trouble hearing. Or maybe it was something else. But he didn't turn.

"So that's what? That's what!" Daniel said.

Then Desiderius did turn to look up at us. There was something in his expression as he looked to Daniel that seemed resignation, or worse. I don't think Daniel even noticed, as his eyes at that moment were fixed on his father. Nicolaus stared quietly at his brother for a few seconds, then looked away. And Little Johann seemed pleased and proud.

The rest of the room reacted far more wildly than it had for Staehelin. Daniel was spice to any dish he was mixed with. Especially the older students who knew him better knew that. I shook his hand. "I know you deserve it," I said. "You'd be an honor to the Chair." I meant it strongly. Despite his machinations and cunning, he would be. "Go on, go choose your lot."

He almost couldn't stand. All his anticipation and anxiety had finally met their goal, and it was as if he had nothing left. But he did stand, and as he descended the steps his spirit ascended until he was at the front, toe to toe with his father.

Master Johann's back was still to me. Daniel looked down on his father, and the most unfathomable expression crossed his face, between triumph and longing, and joy and grief. For an instant Johann looked back, also impenetrably, but there was at least no defeat or regret that I could see.

"If you please, Master Daniel," the Provost said peaceably.

Daniel glanced over the stones, then delicately lifted one and handed it to the Provost. He seemed to have considered the meaning of the emblem.

"Master Daniel has chosen the Throne."

For the second time Heidelmann performed his duty. Daniel was transfixed watching his chosen stone merge into the indiscernible cube. After one more glance at his father, and this glance also had suspicion in it, and doubt, he returned to his place beside me.

"It's there," Daniel said.

"And it was there for Logic two years ago," Nicolaus said.

"But there's a difference," Daniel answered.

"Master Johann," the Provost said.

"Thank you." He stood. This was really his first motion since he'd sat, and his first words.

"This is the clever part, now," Daniel said. "So Brutus isn't worried? We'll see him play his hand now. This will be the foreign candidate. What's the trick going to be?"

And Master Johann said, gravely, "The committee nominates Master Leonhard."

I didn't know who it was. I'd have thought I would have heard of the man.

"It's you," Nicolaus said. I felt something at my hand, and I saw he was shaking it.

I looked down at the stage at Master Johann, and saw that he was also intent on me, and also the Provost and Deans. And then I knew it.

❧

It seemed someone else, not me, who walked the steps down to the lectern. That person was greeted by the esteemed men there and returned their nods and handshakes. It was even that man who graciously and sincerely thanked Master Johann. But then, when the tray of five stones was offered, then, it was me. My question of Lithicus was answered as I saw the emblems he'd carved. The five that remained were a sun, a candle, a lamb, a raindrop, and a fish. It was my hand and no one else's that chose the symbol and handed it to the Provost.

"Master Leonhard has chosen the Candle." He accepted my choice pleasantly, and the wax was melted and the stone was placed into the casket with the other two.

Then the casket was locked and set on the lectern, where it was to remain until it was opened again.

14

The Sealed Stones

I was hauled off to the Boot and Thorn. I'd meant to leave quiet and get home but the forces were too great. The mass of my fellows, students I knew and had lectures with, manhandled me through the streets and into the Common Room. I'd have sooner settled in at the other side of the Square. Staehelin was brought, too. He wasn't pulled as hard by the students but he was a bachelor with no family at home, so he didn't resist, either. And Daniel took no pulling or hauling at all; he was the motive force.

The room was uncommon raucous. I was toasted and celebrated, though Daniel was given far more acclaim. And I was a leaf in the wind, in a narrow street of hard walls. I couldn't tell if I or anyone was surprised. Only the tankards on the shelves seemed to be thoughtful at it, staring in every direction to see what it might all mean. And the oddest was that Charon the cat settled into my lap and purred. His weight alone was too great for me to stand or leave.

All things must end, though. All things human, at least. The room thinned and the smoke thickened. It was after two o'clock, hours since the casket had been closed with my stone in it. But Charon still held me prisoner.

Then Daniel was with me. The melee of the celebration had swept him past several times but we hadn't talked. Now he was ready to speak. He sat across the table, deliberately, and I saw that, for all the jubilance in his laughs and grins, there was a calculation in his stare that contradicted all his jollity. He took a breath and his firm set jaw and bright eyes were like a duelist examining his opponent.

"Then Leonhard," he said. "I should have known. That's all right. We'll have the best man win, then?"

"The best lot chosen," I said. "I hope it's yours."

"I'll see that it is. The best man will win."

"Of us two, you're the best. That won't help with choice of the stone."

"I don't mean the best between us," he said. "It's the best between Brutus and me. That's the game."

"What do you mean, Daniel? You've said this over and over. What is it, really? Explain this plot that your father has, and how you'll beat it, and what the game even is."

He had a cup of dice in his hand, still there from some other table. "What's your reason for asking?" he asked. He rolled the cup around and around and the dice tumbled inside it.

"I'd like to know. All this you have been saying for days!"

He shook his head. "No, that's not the right answer. There are two reasons you might ask, and that's what you'd say either way."

"What reason would I have beside that you're maddening with all your hints and threats?"

"What other reason? I'll tell you. That you're in the game, too, and wanting to know my next play."

"What game, Daniel?"

"Take care, friend. Be a piece on the board, and defeat is only a disappointment. Make yourself a player, though, and the stakes are higher."

"The stakes are to have the Chair, or to not," I said firmly, not driven quite to anger. "The game is just chance, one chance in three. That's all."

"I'll let you think that, if you really do. But I'll give you this, Leonhard. If Brutus is under force to give the Chair to one particular man, and he doesn't want to, what's his move? He puts up another who might put the first out of the way. But how could that be done? That's the question."

"What force, anyway?" I said. "That's my question."

He only shook his head. "And," he said, "to make that other glitter, he sends letters extolling him to Paris! He says he will, anyway. That's all he needs to do to get you past his committee. I wonder if he'll waste the paper and ink. He's even stingier with his reputation, to spend it on recommendations."

"Daniel." They were harsh words. "The day has overwhelmed you." Indeed, it had. His color was pale and his breath short.

"Your proof, though, that's the nut of it. That's elegant. Where did it come from, Leonhard?"

"Not from anyone."

"It came at an opportune time. Almost as if it was for the moment of the Election. It certainly put you in the thick, didn't it."

"Daniel, I forgive you for what you've said about your father, and about me, and everyone else. You're conquered by the day and your nerves. Go home, have some food that's more wholesome than what you've had here, then sleep, and find your senses."

"You're a good man," he said and laughed. "I'll do that. I'm raving and you're gracious in return."

It was well into the afternoon. We left together and parted in the Square. I still had the letter from Russia in my pocket, but it still didn't seem a right time to give it to him.

Grandmother was in the kitchen, sitting at the table, which I saw was set for lunch. Soup was in a pot hung near the fire, and bread with butter was on the sideboard; they were covered with a white cloth, but I knew what they were.

"I'm sorry to be late," I said. "I didn't mean to be taken to the inn."

"Be taken?" she asked.

I corrected myself. "I didn't mean to go to the inn. But they wanted me and I went."

"You had reason to be with friends." That meant she knew, though of course she would have known. I expected that.

"I wanted to come here first," I said, and though she knew, I still had to say it. "I've been nominated, Grandmother. For the Chair in Physics."

"That's well done, Leonhard. I'm very pleased for you."

"Thank you. And Master Johann nominated me."

"He would only nominate a candidate he thought highly of."

"And Daniel's also a candidate. It's he who should win."

"It's in God's hands."

"I hope so much that it is."

We talked awhile more. She said nothing condemning or accusatory; I felt those myself and wasn't sure why. But as I was there in her kitchen and she served the soup and bread, the smoke of the Common Room dwindled. I finally began to feel a good joy and a decent pleasure. I'd been nominated for a prestigious Chair by a committee of intelligent and accomplished men. Knowing that I didn't deserve the honor let me more freely accept their knowledge that I did.

"Are you able enough for this Chair?" she asked.

"It would be prideful to say yes."

"Would it be pride or truth?"

This was the difficult question. "I would learn, and work very hard, and I would become able."

"Do you want this Chair?"

This was the more difficult question. "It would be a wondrous life, I think. To devote my time and effort to writing, and reading, and thinking, and teaching."

"That would be a noble life."

"And devoted to God, too," I said. "All devotion is to God. I think it would be a way to serve." She'd always had a keen sense of my heart, more than I did. She must have known whether I was truthful in my humility. I didn't know.

"And all three candidates were from Basel?"

"It was Daniel who was the foreign candidate. They decided he was coming from Padua."

"Which symbol did you choose?" she asked.

"The symbols were the seven days of creation. A candle for light, a raindrop for the separation of waters, a tree for living plants, a sun for the lights of heaven, a fish for creatures of the sea and air, a lamb for the beasts of the field, and a throne for God at rest. At the first of creation God created the laws to govern the rest. So I chose the light."

"That was a wise choice," she said.

"I'll need greater wisdom than that," I said. "I'll go to my room now and think. I need to think."

Was anything still in the storm? When waves were taller than mountains and ships in them were leaves and splinters? My thoughts were raindrops in a gale. And on my desk was the package Gustavus had given me. It was a rocky island that might be a haven or might shipwreck me.

I opened the wrapping and it was just as I'd known, Master Jacob's papers. I'd never seen the handwriting but I knew the words, even from the first sentence. There were a dozen sheaves, each tied with ribbon, each a hundred or so sheets. I untied one and sifted through it. Near the top was a careful sketch of a Logarithmic spiral.

I studied it awhile. I felt drawn to it, as if this was the first step I was to take into those many pages. Then I saw a description beneath it, in the same Latin that filled all the sheets.

> "The Logarithmic Spiral may be used as a symbol, either of fortitude and constancy in adversity, or of the human body, which after all its changes, even after death, will be restored to its exact and perfect self."

When I'd accepted that as the premise of all the writing, I began to read.

It would have been impossible to read every word in one afternoon and evening. It wasn't necessary. Many pages I immediately knew from the *Ars Conjectandi*. Others I knew from Master Johann's lectures, though the comparison of what in my room I was reading and what in lectures I'd heard seemed to draw an edge between what the two brothers each knew himself and what each had learned from the other.

There were other pages that I recognized from a score of

books, most by men I knew had corresponded with Jacob. There were his solutions to the brachistochrone and tautochrone, and even his attempt of the Reciprocal Squares. As I read, more and faster, there were only a few pages I'd never seen before.

Then also, there were the letters he'd received. The pages were without envelopes, all smoothed flat like the other papers. On many, only the signature showed who'd written them. These I would have studied carefully, but I saw that many were questions and comments on his own work. Few of his correspondents had had greater understanding than Jacob himself.

Finally I heard Saint Leonhard's bell strike six and I realized I was hungry for supper. I stretched and went down to the kitchen but the room was empty, the table clear, and the fire nearly spent. Then I saw there was no light in the window, and then I saw the sky was gray, but in the east.

So, it was time not for evening meal but for morning chores. And when I reached the Barefoot Square to draw water, the fountain was low and slow filling. The dry days had taken a hard toll on the Birsig.

⁂

I was weary as I approached my Master's house. But that was no excuse. I had work to do.

Mistress Dorothea's most amazing quality of her speech, even more than its quantity, was that she never spoke ill of anyone. She spoke truth, which was a close neighbor, but never spite. And there was wisdom in what she said, if a listener was willing to pick through the wide field for the single blade among the grass.

Her words were spilling out the kitchen door when I reached it. She was discoursing to her girl about the morning's eggs and the dry weather and cabbages in the market and her cousin's gout. It took effort to open the door against the stream. But when she saw me she paused a long pause. And then she just said, "You'll still do kitchen work, Leonhard?"

"I will," I said. "And I hope to always." It wasn't only kitchen work, though, that I had to do.

"I've no allowance to spare for a man who's a Chair," she answered. "There's one already in this house." But she said it graciously.

"I want no allowance, and I'm not yet a Chair. It's twice as like as not that I'll still be a poor student a week from now."

She approved. "You're a credit to your father and mother, and to your grandmother." And that was more praise than I deserved.

I set to work as hard as I could and kept my jaw as firm as I could against yawning. And when I finished, as I'd known he would be, Little Johann was waiting.

"You're near to be a Chair," he said.

"*Near*'s not *in*," I said. "And I'd rather Daniel had it. I have a question."

He knew, and he nodded. "Come and I'll show you," he said. But reluctantly.

❧

He led me out the back door, which seemed strange; but then he went immediately to the cellar door, and I understood. The top of this door was set against the back of the house, and its base, though angled up and out, was still beneath the level of the ground. Two steps led down to it. It was kept locked, and the key was in on Mistress Dorothea's key ring, but Little Johann had already asked for it and had it in his hand. So, like mice, down we went into the foundation of the house.

It was dark and cool and moist, which was its purpose. We took no candle, as the morning light came plenty in the door. It wasn't a large room, only the space beneath the kitchen. I'd been there many times. There were old tools and kitchen ware, useless enough that they wouldn't be missed, but useful enough to not yet discard. Some meat was kept, though not much. Mostly the room was piled with root vegetables in wood bins. And even in the dark, I could see what Little Johann had to show me: one of the bins had been pulled out and pushed back in place. The tracks in the earth floor were obvious.

"I'll pull it out," I said. Little Johann said nothing.

I moved the bin forward. It wasn't heavy. Behind it was the foundation wall. It was easy enough to find that one large stone was loose, and was only a thin flagstone fit in place. It would have been hard to find if I hadn't been led to it.

"Have you ever looked in it?" I asked. He shook his head, no.

I lifted the stone away and behind it was a niche, about sixteen inches high and deep, by twenty-four wide. I put the stone back in place. It was shaped perfectly and showed no sign of the space behind it.

It was skilled stonemasonry that had made that hiding place.

Back in the kitchen, just us two, Little Johann was still anxious.

"Are you bothered that you've shown a secret?" I asked, and he nodded. "I'm sorry. But I think I know what was in that place. I'll never tell anyone what I've seen, ever."

I was still weary but there was no use to sleep. The mountain on my desk was not nearly climbed.

What I'd read, hundreds of pages and scores of letters, had all been of Mathematics. Most I knew. Most I recognized, and of most I knew how they had travelled from those pages to others' book and articles. A few pages were new, though not profound.

Before I started again, I tried a different sieve. On a page of my own, I began a catalog of my own Master's writing that was not just a reflection of his brother's. It was a long list. Master Johann's discoveries were at least as great and numerous as Master Jacob's. Oh, what would their sum have been if they had partnered, not just in Johann's early years, but on, into his tenure in Holland! Yet they'd been enemies by then. And if Jacob had lived longer; if he'd still held the Chair of Mathematics while Johann had been Greek. That would have taken a humble man, but the two together in Basel, cooperating, sharpening, consorting . . .

But Jacob, already estranged from Johann, had died before they laid eyes. Or within a day after: Which had it been?

One package was left of all Jacob's papers, and I turned to it.

It was the first I'd seen, topped by the spiral, and by other indications appeared to be the last. The other reams had been in order by subject, more or less, but this was from just one period, the final year of his life. So I steadied myself and started reading.

The Mathematics of the later pages was mostly the same. There was less new and more repetition of the earlier work, though purer. That one ream of paper might almost have replaced all the others. It was the elegant restatement of the rest.

But there were notes and whole pages that went beyond the Mathematics, and these arrested my quick reading. In his last months, Jacob had bared his soul.

He'd written of his disputes with Newton and the English.

He listed his enemies, which was a long list, and his friends, which was short.

He'd written of his weakness and age. There were several pages of his plans to confront his brother when they met. And he feared the meeting. He knew that Johann was a stronger, more forceful opponent.

The last pages were in a hand that was still his but crabbed and shaken. He knew he was dying. He'd written that Gottlieb was with him, and he'd given him instruction to keep his papers from Johann.

Finally I came to the last page, which was the first sheet I'd seen, with the spiral, and *Resurgo Eadem Mutata*. On its back were his last notes, nearly illegible. I read them, then again as their importance struck me, then again and again. This last sheet I took out from the others and set on my dresser to keep.

൭൬

Thursday afternoon, very weary, I greeted Charon the cat and asked him to find his Master. And when Gustavus came to me in the Common Room, I only had enough strength to hand him the wrapped bundle of pages and stumble back toward the door to the Square.

But he stopped me.

"There is payment due for these."

"Who wants it?" I said.

"You'll be called for it."

"Why were these pages given to me? Who told you to put them in my hands?"

"You must know, Master."

I nodded. "Yes, I know."

൭൬

The Barefoot Church was at peace that evening, as it most often was, whatever raged outside it. It was as separate from

Basel as Basel was from its own outside. But Basel was Basel only with the church. I sat long enough on the bench to see the cast light move across the floor from side to front, and sanctify the altar, and rise. The air was moist. Even the world's drought seemed stopped at the church door.

Fortified, I entered the Barefoot Square which seemed, more than it most often was, to be a bridge between two sides. I felt the invisible chasm that it crossed and heard roaring depths beneath me. Part way across I saw both Daniel and Nicolaus enter the Boot and Thorn. As I came to the door of the inn, the coach from Bern arrived.

Rupert brought the horses to their stop at the door, and one passenger, from the look of him perhaps a new student, emerged with shudders and relief and backward glances. A medium trunk was lowered to the ground for him but two other trunks, heavy and black, were left in the rack. Willi had come out, but Rupert kept the reins and led the horses and coach, all still harnessed, into the stables tunnel and out of the Square.

I looked into the Common Room, but neither Daniel nor Nicolaus was there.

As I had before, I called on Magistrate Faulkner later than was polite. He answered the door himself and took me into the parlor and had me sit beside him.

"I can only tell you that he was in the coach from Bern," I said.

"I knew he would be."

"Then I shouldn't take more of your time."

"I will take your time, Leonhard."

I suddenly thought of Jacob's papers and wondered if I was to be asked for my payment. "Yes, sir?"

But not. "You are a candidate now for the Physics Chair." A lion would regard its cub with mercy but its prey with none, and each knew which it was. But I wasn't sure.

"I am, sir, yes."

"The University is a power in Basel. You may attain an authority you aren't expecting."

"If I am chosen—"

"Or, if you are not. I will not yield my own prerogatives in either case."

"And I would ever yield to you! Magistrate Faulkner, it's a terrible thought to me that I would consider a challenge to anyone of your position, or at all to you. I—"

"You may have no choice." He sighed. "But, nor may I. What will come, will come."

I paused, thinking very hard, and he waited.

"Sir," I said.

"Yes, Leonhard?"

"I understand what Master Gottllieb meant was the danger to Basel."

"Then you also understand why Magistrate Caiaphas is here and why this Election is important to him."

"Yes, sir. But . . ." And I wasn't sure how I was regarding him. "I will do what I must do. Because it is more than just Basel."

He didn't understand. He frowned, and I didn't know if he was disturbed or disappointed. He nodded and we stood, and I left.

❧

At home Grandmother had supper for me. I hadn't seen her in the morning, or the evening before. We didn't speak much, but I saw that neither had she slept the night before.

❧

I was so, so tired! Yet I still had more to do. I took my black cloak from its hook in the closet and wrapped it on.

"Is the night cold?" Grandmother asked. She knew it wasn't.

"No, but I'll wear it."

I went out. It was nights like this one when I saw so many things in the streets. Slow, heavy, unshod footsteps were behind every corner. The shadows of strange beasts were ahead of every turn. I wondered, when I was invisible, would invisible things more easily see me? But I didn't have far to go. I came to my Master's house, in the back alley. I chose the very darkest place. Then I stood and waited.

I didn't know how long I'd wait.

I didn't know how long I did wait.

Finally the back door of the house opened and Master Johann came out with a small, dim candle. He went to the cellar door and opened it, and set the candle on the steps. Then he went back up into the house.

Just a moment later he came out again, with a heavy bag in both hands. I couldn't see just what size it was. He went down the steps into the cellar and another moment later took the candle in with him and shut the door.

I waited, not long.

The cellar door opened and he came out with just the candle. He closed and locked the door and went back into his house. I heard the bolt on that door turn.

And then, I could finally be done with the day. I went home and to my room and threw myself into the bed.

Water, water. It had not been long since the last rain, but all Basel seemed to be drying out. The fountains were all pinched. The streets were lethargic and filled with dust.

Yet the fountains still brought out their stream, reduced but valiant. I filled my buckets, and as always on Fridays the coach's preparation for departure was a performance for me to watch. I did watch and I saw no black, cloaked passengers.

I would always hurry through my chores. Time was far too valuable to waste. Yet I paused there in the Barefoot Square for twice or three times the minutes it would usually take to get my water and leave. And finally, with the gray dawn light just at its last edge with morning, I saw a tall young man, black cloaked and crowned with wig and tricorne, slip quietly into the inn.

I lifted my buckets but only carried them as far as the inn's Common Room window. Then I stood still again. It was dark looking in and I didn't try. I didn't want to be seen through the window anyway.

A property of the morning air was that it would often be very still. The Riehen church bell would sound as close as Saint Leonhard's. The Rhine's murmuring was like the streets speaking. I waited and finally I heard the voices I knew I would.

"Why will you not come to my room?" which was Magistrate Caiaphas. "This is a poor place to talk."

"Negotiations must be neutral," which was Nicolaus. "Not in father's room, and not in yours."

"It's no negotiation. It's only a message. What is the message?"

"That it's been done."

"That's what I want."

"Do you have a reply?" Nicolaus asked.

"There's no reply."

"There is a second message."

"What message?" Caiaphas's voice was suspicious.

"That there be a different choice."

"What use would that be to me?" He was speaking quietly, but there was no difficulty hearing him. Something was torn with every word. "My reply is, I'll have the choice I've made and the bargain I've made, and it's no matter to me that he detests it. Give him that reply." It was a challenge, not a refusal.

"There is a third message, then."

"Then tell me the third message." Caiaphas was intrigued, and even pleased, as if he'd expected it.

"That it will be to your profit."

"That's the message?"

"That's all of it. There are no other messages."

"My profit? That's no matter to him! He'd care more for a gnat than he'd care that I'd profit."

"But he says, that it will be to your profit."

"Then take this reply. I'll account to myself what's to my own profit and what isn't."

Nicolaus was silent, then, as he always was when he had more to hear. And Caiaphas finally said, "I will account which is to my profit. Make that the reply. And I'll tell him if I account any difference."

"I'll tell him." But Nicolaus stayed, and still waited. He would wait when he knew there was something else to be said, and he waited, and it became impossible for it not to be said.

"I know the choice he wants," Caiaphas said, "and I have already begun that accounting."

"Good day, then," Nicolaus said, and stood.

I was gone out from the Square before anyone else came out into it.

෴

I hurried through every chore my grandmother had for me, and then all that Mistress Dorothea had. But as I finished there, I was thinking all the more of the papers I'd read of Master Jacob, and I said to her, "Mistress."

"Yes, Leonhard?"

"I want to tell you that I have seen repentance."

She stopped to give me close attention. Then she said, "Thank you."

Then I heard Daniel's laugh in the hall as he was coming toward the kitchen. I didn't want to talk with him. As I had already done once that morning, I left before I was seen.

⁂

That Friday ran long and hard. I had my lecture to write but I held myself away from it. I had my letter to Paris to write, but I restrained from that, also.

Instead I gave time to thought. I sat in the Barefoot Church from before noon to long after sunset.

At home, at night, no book on my shelf seemed fit for reading. I put myself in my bed and eventually slept.

⁂

The quality of early light was thin, clean, sinless, and Adam-like innocent. I'd seen many dawns. The gray and the quiet were one mixed thing and I walked the morning like an ash mote floating from a fire; we were only ashes. Or like a raindrop in the river, traveler on the road and part of it. I came in solitude through air like water to the Barefoot Square and filled my pails with water clear as air. Then I set them by the door and went in to the Boot and Thorn.

The Common Room was empty but for Charon the cat half sleeping on a shelf of tankards, who were all half sleeping, as well. I sat at a table to think and wait. A very thin pall from the near dormant hearth and even from the last night's candles just turned the air from pure to impure, though the difference was so fine. I knew I wasn't undetected though I'd been silent. A few of the tankards were alert enough to call their Master. And in only a minute there was a tread in the hall and shadow in the door. Old Gustavus looked in on me. The only light was from the windows, and it was absorbed in vacant space before it reached the far wall. Gustavus watched in silence. Then he came closer.

"How can I serve you, young Master?" I was in black and white, as fine as I could make them without my grandmother's touch. And they were fine enough. The ambivalence I'd kept was lost and I would only wear brown a few more times. It was strange that it was with Gustavus that the change seemed most significant.

"May I ask about a day twenty years ago?"

"Twenty years. Yes."

"The day that my Master Johann returned to Basel. Do you remember?"

"Yes. I remember." His arms were folded and he waited for me. I'd never seen him impatient. I thought his servants were too afraid to have ever kept him waiting. And for all his strength and fearsomeness, he was always greatly respectful to his customers. But this was a different waiting, as if he were in a place he knew I would come to, and he had been waiting for me to arrive.

"Was it Knipper driving?"

"There was no driver but Knipper."

"Do you remember," I asked, "the day ten years before that, when Master Johann left Basel for Holland?"

"Yes. I remember."

"Was that also Knipper?"

"There was no driver but Knipper."

I didn't doubt that he remembered, but I wanted assurance. "What time of year was it?"

"It was an April day. The coach left in a thunderstorm."

"And the day they returned?"

"In August, and also in a storm."

"It was near the day that Master Jacob died."

"It was that day," Gustavus said.

"The day itself?"

"It was that day."

"Gustavus," I said, "do you know how Master Jacob died?"

"I know all of how he died."

"I guess that he was ill."

"He was."

"And he died of his illness."

"He did."

"Was Black Death his illness?"

For every question I'd asked, he'd only paused a moment to answer. Again, with his dark eyes intent on me, he answered immediately. "His family has held that as secret."

"It was Black Death," I said. "I know it was. And he died before Master Johann arrived? By hours? By minutes?"

Gustavas didn't answer. He was just still and intent on me, as if he was measuring.

"Why did you come here, Master?" he asked me.

"Master Johann took the Chair of Mathematics after Jacob died," I said.

"He did."

"Daniel wants the Chair of Physics."

"He does." It was unusual for an innkeeper to admit to knowledge of University affairs or a gentleman's desires.

"Master Johann stayed four weeks in Strasbourg on his travel to Basel. Did he send any messages while he was stopped there?"

"He sent messages."

"Did Magistrate Caiaphas send any messages?"

"Why did you come here, Master?" he asked me again.

"Master Gottlieb was also in Strasbourg with Master Johann, though he didn't stay as long. He came back a week earlier. And Master Desiderius came here from Strasbourg."

"There has been coming and going between the cities for many years. The coach has been well used."

"I'd like to speak with Magistrate Caiaphas," I said. "I'll come back tonight."

"And you are welcome to come any time, Master."

"Please tell him it will be the same conversation he had with those other gentlemen."

"I will tell him you wish to speak with him."

The light was still clean and innocent, and, it seemed, pure, though that was always hard to tell.

⁂

"Leonhard," Grandmother said, even as I came in the door. "Where have you been?"

"Just walking," I said. "It's very dry. There hasn't been rain."

"You're dressed fine."

"It seemed proper for the early morning. The morning light was very clear."

"Stay in it," she said. "Stay out of the shadow."

"But I'll change now for my chores."

⁂

I did my chores, though perhaps not well. Then I had a hard time reading, like pouring water into an overfull barrel. It seemed that three o'clock would never come.

⁂

Mistress Dorothea's speech was so continuous that her silence was inscrutable. In its shadow I followed up her stairs. I saw her looking at me with eyes very narrow.

"Why did he do it?" I said, and it was like thunderbolts thrown.

"Just ask him, Leonhard."

That was all I could muster and that was the only answer she could have made, and the worst. She knocked on his door. The "Enter" following was deeper and from deeper. The room was larger and darker and the candle on the table was far, far away and the journey to it was eternal.

Before I'd even sat, he began our lesson, and it was as if nothing had happened in all the last weeks. "Consider a simple quadratic," Master Johann said. "But one having no intersection with the horizontal axis."

"Yes, Master."

"Does it have roots?"

We have discussed this before. "I believe that it does."

"Even with no intersection?"

"They aren't seen." Then I knew that perhaps he was answering.

"An unseen number? Describe it to me."

"The principle," I said, "is that negative numbers might have square roots. If a positive number is multiplied by itself, the result is positive. If a negative number is multiplied by itself, the result is also positive. So, the root of a negative is neither positive or negative. It is something else. So it is unseen. I've read about these numbers since we talked about them before."

"What did Monsieur Descartes say about such numbers?"

"He derided them and called them *imaginary*. He considered them foolish. But he did concede they might exist."

"Why foolish?"

"Real numbers can be seen and counted with real objects. He said that imaginary numbers can't be counted. There was no use for them."

"Does that make something foolish, if it can't be seen?"

"No, Master," I said. "There are many things that can't be seen, and they are more real than what can be seen. Numbers don't need usefulness to exist. They exist on their own whether anything seen ever reaches their count or not."

***

We talked longer, not about theorems or proofs, not solving problems. We didn't write, we only talked. He questioned me, and I him, on meanings and reasons.

And at the end, after a Saturday afternoon unlike any I'd ever had, I paused and gathered my thoughts. "Master Johann, thank you for your nomination."

"It was the committee's nomination. Each of the members approved."

"I don't believe that I could be qualified."

"You don't believe that?"

I had to pause again. "I believe that I will become so. But Master Daniel and Master Staehelin both are, already."

"The Chair is both for now and for the time to come."

He gave me no exercises for the next week. When I came home, I could only tell my grandmother that we'd talked, and I wanted very much to study Mathematics for my whole life.

15

The Tree, Throne, and Candle

After dinner I went to my room to rest. I lay on my bed some while, delaying my visit back to the Boot and Thorn. I nearly fell asleep, but finally I put my wig and hat back on my head and went out. It was dark night by then.

The Square was empty, as far as I could tell, it was so dark. There was only one light to be seen anywhere, if it could be called light. The windows of the Boot and Thorn seemed to pulse red. Somehow I didn't see anything of the Barefoot Church.

As I came close to the Inn, I felt its heat. I stepped across the threshold and all outside vanished. I didn't think I could have gone back out. The streets I'd left had been empty, but now the Common Room was full and bubbling. The smell was sharper, too, earthy and hot and damp. I couldn't make out any one person at the tables, but every bench was full and nothing was still, every hand and shoulder and head were moving. The sound was like the smell, sudden and overwhelming and of too many parts to distinguish any one. Only the light was low and undersaturated. It was just the fire in the hearth. There were no candles and no lamps. It was just red, and orange, and throbbing. Chthonic Charon nodded to me and his eyes were red as the fire.

I stood in the doorway and then in the room, unseen. I might have been seeing what was invisible any other time, and I would be invisible to it. But there were crossings between two different worlds, and nephilim who straddled both. All along the walls the tankards and steins were jostling and striving against each other for space on their shelves. They shoved with their thin legs and arms, and I could hear them grunting. Their fat eyes, though, slowly fixed on me, one by one, and they went still. Then Old Gustavus saw them watching me, and they watched him come to me in the door. "Welcome, Master," he said, and he seemed curious to find me in this dark half of the world.

"Gustavus. I said I'd return."

"Come."

He led me. I followed. Down that hall that twisted and amazed, ignoring the stairs and doors and side passages that grew from it, we stayed in the taproot, down and into. The heat and pressure increased, yet I shivered; and we finally came to a door framed in bedrock. There was no latch or lock. He pushed and it opened.

It was a cellar, a cave, a meat cooler, a larder, a pantry. Hooks held sides of cattle and shelves great barrels of ale, a close, crowded place, with walls not of stone but living rock, and floor and ceiling, also, and it wasn't carved by human hand. Part of one wall was only a void and a bottomless roar. Anyone in Basel would have known it was the Birsig Flow that rushed by in that black hole, the stream buried in ancient times beneath the city, and this room was some eddy of its old course, worn into the rock by its constant force. I could have put my hand into its cold water. Beside the foodstuffs, there were other things stored here: a few very old wooden chests with locks on them, fitted into the rock as if it had grown around them.

The room was cool and mossy damp, yet even here there was fire. An oil lantern was mounted on a shelf and it danced and flickered in the whirling air that was no more still than the water that troubled it. In the center of the small open floor were three chairs, and Gustavus gestured to one, and I sat. He sat facing me. I'd advanced from commoner, to Master, and now to equal. "Yes, Master Leonhard," he said, as respectful as always but now, not as a servant, "what do you want to say?"

"I've been nominated for the Chair of Physics."

"I have heard so."

Then we waited. I listened to the constrained waters. Finally I heard what he may have heard before, or had been waiting for, the sound of quick steps in the corridor outside. The door opened and the light dimmed before black capes and robes.

"What is he saying?" we were asked, and I answered.

"I've come to pay," I said. "For use of Master Jacob's papers."

He was pleased. "What payment have you brought?"

"What payment are you asking for them?"

Magistrate Caiaphas answered, "That you tell me what they mean."

"The Mathematics? To explain it?" That was not what I'd expected.

And it wasn't what he'd meant. "Not that! Tell me their meaning!"

Then I did understand. "They don't have great value. Everything in them is known and published. They're twenty years old."

"Then why were they sent to me?" He was angry.

"Why did you bring them to me?" I asked. "Why not to a great Mathematician?"

"I was told you were to be great."

It had been a test. But it was beyond him to comprehend if I'd passed. And he would never have understood the one page I'd kept for myself.

"I've been nominated for the Physics Chair," I said.

"I know you have." He nodded, less angry. So he was satisfied enough with me.

"I want the Physics Chair, Magistrate Caiaphas."

"Yes," Gustavus said, a deep rumble to Caiaphas's crackle and tearing. "It is what I told you."

"I already knew it," the Magistrate said. "Why have you come to me? What are you asking me?"

"Why have I come?" I said. "Because Master Johann came to you, and Master Gottlieb, and Master Desiderius, and now Master Daniel. All of them came. I have, too."

"Why would you say they came?"

"They believed you had it in your power to give them their Chairs."

"And you also believe that?"

"I also do."

"Then you must also believe that Master Daniel has already been given the Chair of Physics."

"I am more able than he is," I said. "And he's ruing the gift. He'd give it up if he could. He's asked me how to renege on a bargain even when he's given his word on it."

"What is that to me?" His voice was still cracked and cracking, but like parched ground that was eager for water.

"I will offer you more than he does."

"And what has he offered me?"

"He doesn't know," I said. "Only to repay you whatever you say."

"And you would take a blind bargain?"

"I wouldn't be blind. I know what you want. And I know I can offer more than he can."

Magistrate Caiaphas stood, and I was in his shadow. "What can you offer?"

I looked up into his knifelike face. "All the renown and all the fame of the greatest Mathematician who will ever live."

"That is what you believe of yourself?" he asked.

"I could be," I said. "I need the chance of this Chair to make my start."

He was still standing over me and he seemed to grow as a covering. "And what use is that to me? You're offering me your fame?"

"I am."

"Then who do you take me for? What would your fame be for me?"

"It's what you want."

"Why would I want it?"

"To give Basel to France."

He backed away, or receded, and he was sitting again. "Basel to France?"

"You plan for Basel to leave its independence and come into France. You want the University to lead and pull and force the city. The University has that power in Basel."

"Why do you believe this?"

"That was how Strasbourg was brought into France."

He waited a long time before answering. He was still and

I waited with him. "So, for the Physics Chair," he said, "you would do this. Betray your city?"

"It wouldn't be a betrayal."

"And the promise already made to Master Daniel?"

"He regrets having made the bargain."

"You say he does."

"And he doesn't want the Chair. He only wants to offend Master Johann. He'll give it up once he has it."

"You speak for him? I won't believe you."

"I would still be more valuable to you than he would as the Chair."

"Daniel is a persuasive man in this City. But you would be greater?"

"Yes. Before many years, I would be."

"And you mean me to choose between you?" He was silent again, and for a very long time. I couldn't see his face at all. "Then this is how I will decide. I will let you decide."

"Me? How?"

"Daniel has this Chair. It is his. But it will be yours if he doesn't take it."

"That would be his decision," I said, "not mine."

"Then he will win the Chair."

Then I understood. "I must keep him from taking it."

"If he doesn't take it, it will be yours."

I thought through all that his words implied. "Did Master Johann cause the Mathematics Chair to be open? Did he cause Master Jacob to not be in it? And Gottlieb caused Master Grimm to leave the Logic Chair? And Daniel the Physics Chair, now? They caused those Chairs to be empty?"

"If a man is worthwhile to me to have a Chair, I will give him the Chair. But the Chair must first be open."

"And Desiderius, also?"

"Daniel has this Chair," Caiaphas said. "If the Physics

Chair becomes open, you will have it." He put his palms together, as if he was praying. "Do you accept the bargain?"

"If you give me the Chair, that I will serve your purposes. That is the bargain?"

"Yes, that is what I offer."

"Then I accept," I said. An image came to me, from a week earlier. "I saw a chase," I said. "A white horse in pursuit of a black."

"What do you mean?" This confused him. "What chase? What horse?"

"The white horse was swifter. And Daniel was too heavy a burden. I did see it."

"You see what doesn't exist," he said, perplexed by my words, but very sure of his.

"It does," I said. "I know what exists. Please help me find my way out of this cellar, Gustavus. I'm not sure I can."

"Come with me."

I did come with him. I only seemed to find myself farther in and more deeply lost. We passed corners and traversed passages, all so dimly lit as if the lanterns and torches were only part in these halls and a greater part in the halls of some other inn. That other inn might have been the one I knew. I didn't know this one. All I could do was follow Gustavus.

The walls and rafters ended and I was out in the Square. I must have been. The sky and stars were above me and I saw the front of the Inn, but I didn't see the Barefoot Church across the paving stones. In the dark I started toward home.

But it was so dark that I could hardly find my way through the Square. It seemed endless. Finally I stopped to gain my bearings. While I stood, in the pitch black, there was an abrupt galloping, from nowhere. I couldn't find its source but it was coming onto me. I would have run but it was in every direction.

In an instant I threw myself to the stones and an iron hoof clove the air just over me. The horse reared and I threw myself again away from it and the shoes came down just where I'd been.

"Stop!" I cried and I scrambled back.

"What? Who's that?" Daniel's laugh rang over me. "Leonhard?"

"It is Leonhard," I said.

"In the dark!" It sounded at least like Daniel. I couldn't see him "Well, get out of the Square if you don't want to be run over!"

"I am. It was dark."

"The more reason to not wander! Home with you!"

"Yes," I said. "I will. I am." Even still on both hands and feet I fled the horse and voice until I finally reached the end of the Square, and found a street.

Then I was at my grandmother's door and I went into a dark hall, though I seemed to smell the stables and see the red torches of the inn. I found stairs to my room.

And finally, I was in my bed, without memory of getting into it, still dressed. My candle was low on my desk and its gentle yellow glow told me I was fully home again, almost as if I'd never left.

I stayed close by my grandmother all of Sunday, as we two together were stronger than either apart. I kept away from the inn as I always did on the holy day. We didn't talk much, only necessary words.

The sermon at Saint Leonhard's had been concise and thorough, on God's perfection: His own, and that of all He has created. Because of our imperfection, he provided a sacrifice to restore us.

I would deliver that message of perfection to the University. All Physics and all Mathematics were His creation. Mathematics was His command to the Universe. It was an important message and it was necessary that I should give it. It was important that I have a position whereby I could speak these truths, and that the academic universe would be attentive.

That night I wrote out my lecture. Writing was work, which wasn't meant for the Sabbath, but it was contemplation of Deity, which was proper.

I wrote late into the night, which I often did, though never before on a Sunday.

There were many things to consider. I had to remember the opinions of the men who would sit under my lecture. It would be the first public statement of my own beliefs, and every word I spoke would be examined in the light of the controversies and disagreements of the day.

To lecture to this University, I must know to frown at mention of Descartes and harrumph at even the thought of Newton, who in Basel was a usurper and cad. All the while, though, I knew that their Mathematics and Physics were pure as light and water.

Basel's University and Church still believed that God motivated His Creation, and rejected the notion that all the universe was just a machine operating on its own. My own thoughts were muddled. I didn't believe that man abode in a clockwork. The Creator touched and moved every life, most certainly. But a great deal of nature did operate on a set path and by laws as rigid as Mathematics, and the laws were

Mathematics. A dreidel given a spin would continue on its own without my further touch.

So I wrote, and wrote, and walked a perfect narrow path between cliff and abyss, juggling Leibniz with my right hand and Newton and Descartes behind my back.

And as I carefully trod that path, I ignored that the whole mountain it was on was shaking harder and harder to see if I was loose or fast on it.

❧

Monday morning was very dry. The fountains were slack. Waiting to fill my buckets was my only delay as I rushed through the morning. Both my grandmother and Mistress Dorothea left me to myself as I did their chores; they seemed unsure of me.

As soon as I was able, I went out, black and white. Staehelin's lecture would be at two o'clock in the afternoon and I had an errand I wanted to complete before that. That errand meant finding Daniel. I'd never had difficulty in doing that, but search Basel as I did that morning, I didn't see him.

Instead, as I finally stood on the Rhine bridge, thinking where I hadn't yet searched, I found a different candidate.

"Master Staehelin!" I said. "Well met. There's an excellent lecture this afternoon I'm anxious to hear."

"Master Leonhard," he answered, and bowed, as I'd done. That was surely polite of him, to address as Master a child half his age. His hair was short and gray and rough, and his face square and blunt. He looked as much a stolid farmer as a University lecturer. "The lecture will be a plain one, not excellent, not poor. It's on buoyancy, and one I've given often."

We talked a few moments more. The River flowed beneath us, and boats on it were examples of Staehelin's subject. I was about to bow again and resume my search when a startled cry captured both our attention.

We turned toward the Small Basel end of the bridge. In the same instant, I heard, and saw, and most of all felt, the pounding hooves and flying weight of a black horse without a rider.

In the next instant I saw that it was flying and pounding toward us. Its eyes were wild and its ears flat and vicious.

I had a sudden memory of the Barefoot Square on Saturday night, all dark, and the unseen horse riding me down. But that had been invisible. This horse was fully seen.

In the next, final instant all its force and fury were upon us.

The blow that struck us was from our side. We were smashed against the bridge's railing, not by iron shoes but by a human shoulder. The horse went by.

But I sensed another motion. We were both leaned over the railing, and Staehelin was unbalanced and falling into the river. I grabbed hold of his black justaucorps coat and pulled down, and I was pulled by him up, until another hand grabbed my own coat.

And then there were three of us in a heap on the bridge.

We were all a jumble, then. I didn't at first realize the oddity that one of us three was Desiderius. But then I did, and that it had been he who had thrown himself at us to knock us out of the horse's way.

"Master Desiderius!" I gasped.

"And you, Leonhard," he said, as out of breath.

"And Master Staehelin, too," I said. That Master was not yet speaking, but seemed near to it.

"Whom we nearly lost into the river," Desiderius said. "Oh, Leonhard, that was close! The horse would have ridden you down!"

"Both of us," Staehelin said.

"And that would have been two Physics candidates with one crack!" Desiderius said. "Are you both well?"

"I am," I said, and Staehelin nodded. But the mention of two candidates made me look to the rest of the bridge, for what had become of the horse, and who else might be close: for I had recognized the black horse.

And there, hurrying toward us, and his face a perfect fright of shock, was Daniel.

"Most intense apologies!" he cried. "Oh, Leonhard, Staehelin! What a crime I've done to you both! Fiercest apologies!"

Then it was all confusion. All the more we talked and described and explained, less was heard and understood. Staehelin gave up on it quick and went running to brush himself off for his Lecture. But finally Daniel and Desiderius and I had all exhausted our excitement.

"And Master Desiderius," I said. "How was it that you were here on the bridge to rescue us?"

"By chance," he said. When he saw the look in my eye, he added, reluctantly, "And just to see that no accidents might overtake anyone of the Election."

He took his leave then, to also make himself presentable for the coming lecture. I needed to, as well, but I had another task first.

So I had found Daniel, which I'd meant to do. I walked with him as he led his horse toward the Boot and Thorn. "I don't know what took him," Daniel said, and many variations of that, but the panic and worry were faded. "I was in from my ride and Coal was serene as could be. Then just at the bridge, off he went! I can't say what he saw. But he seems all right now."

"I'm right enough," I said. "I think Staehelin was the most dusty of us."

"A dunking in the river would have cleaned him off."

"Daniel! He'll be pressed to make his lecture now."

"He'll make it. Or not, but it'll be the same either way." We'd reached the Inn, and Willi saw us and took Daniel's horse. That left us at the front door, a few steps from the Common Room, which was as good a place as any to finish my errand.

"I'll come in with you," I said.

"You know me all too well," he answered, and led the way.

Charon's milky eyes were on me, and the steins on the wall seemed to be expecting us. The rolling of dice and murmuring voices made the room just as it always was, just common. We sat, and Daniel was as serene as his horse. The calamity on the bridge was already far forgotten.

"Look, Daniel," I said as we were settled. "I need to give you something."

"Then I'll take it."

"I was given it," I said. "Rupert, the new coach driver came to me. Have you seen him?"

"I think I have. Jolly and round, isn't he?"

"That's him. But he'd met me and he hasn't gotten to know many others in Basel. That was why he brought this to me, which he'd found in the post box of the coach. So it might have been there for weeks or months."

As I was saying this, Daniel's serenity was replaced by alert attention, then by narrow eyes and furrowed brow. "What?" he said. "A letter? Is it a letter? Leonhard! From Paris?"

It's not often I have a higher roll of my dice then he of his. I was tempted some to tease him with it, but that was poor behavior for anyone, and most for a gentleman. So I took the letter right from my pocket and handed it to him. "Not from Paris. From Russia."

"Russia!"

He was amazed at it, its beauty and its importance. "In the post box of the coach?"

"Rupert didn't know how long it had been there."

"But do you know what this is?! It's from the University! In Saint Petersburg! It's my invitation!"

"Open it first," I laughed, amused at his amazement, "and see if it is."

"But it's been lost? For months, even. Oh that coachman! It's worth his being murdered, if he can't find a letter in his own post box!"

"Just open it," I said, without amusement.

He broke the seal and took out the folded sheets, of the same ivory linen as the envelope. "Yes, yes it is! Ha! Leonhard, I'm invited to be Chair of Mathematics!" He showed it to me: half the first page was a gilded printing of a two-headed eagle beneath three crowns, with a scepter and orb in its two claws. "The Tsar's own arms! How's that, Leonhard? And look, it's dated just two months ago, even less, so it's not so late."

We both stared at least a minute at the perfect French script and the final signature, of the Chancellor of the new University. And finally, I asked, "What will you do with it?"

"Do with it? With the letter?"

"No! With the invitation."

"Take it, you mean? Or leave it? Which?" He started to laugh from joy of the opportunity. Then the laugh died in his throat as he looked at me, and the letter, and at me again. "Do with it?" he said. "What should I do with it? Take it, and throw Basel aside, is that what you mean?" He continued to stare at me, harder and harder. "And step out of your way, you mean? That's what you mean?"

"Daniel! No!"

"And just found, is it? The letter was lost in the post box? And it comes at just this moment? To your hand! How is it, Leonhard? How is it?"

"Daniel," I said. "You're mad. What are you saying, that the letter's forged? It's from Saint Petersburg. Look at it! You think I called on the Tsar and asked him to take you out of Basel, as a notion to my favor? What are you saying?"

He took a deep breath. "Yes, then, it is from Russia. It's no forgery. And it's Rupert that gave it to you?"

"Ask him. He'll come tomorrow night from Freiburg."

"I'm sorry, then. Forgive me Leonhard. A base accusation and I apologize. But it's two days until the Election and the Brute will do anything to keep me out of the Chair. Even to put you up against me, and that's not your fault."

"I forgive you, Daniel. Of course."

"I'll trust you. I always will. But if any other hand than yours had handed me this, I'd have known it was a plot from Brutus. And it's he who should ask your forgiveness, to raise your hopes for nothing."

I swallowed my first answer and said, "I'll be better for the lesson of it."

"It's a good lesson, I've had it myself. And hey, there's a gathering at the University, I hear. A minor Physics lecturer who'll give a mediocre lecture. Shall we go to hear him?"

"I'll go."

"And dusty, too. A minor and dusty man. Why, he'd be perfect to replace Huldrych!"

We'd stood and I followed him out. But I made sure, before I was in the sunlight, to catch the eye of Gustavus, who'd heard the whole of our conversation from his shadow.

⁂

There was no trace of dust on Staehelin. The University hall was full and listless. The warm, dry air had come in with the audience, and everything inside was dreary as the streets outside. The lecture was just as the lecturer had said it would be, not excellent, not poor. The subject was buoyancy, the principle that an object will float or sink in a fluid based upon the relative densities of the two. He spoke specifically on wood and stone in water. He didn't describe the Mathematics of buoyancy, that the force propelling the object up is equal to the weight of the fluid it displaces, while the force down is equal to the weight of the object itself. And my mind wandered, or floated. I considered that air was like water, gas instead of liquid but still a fluid, and that we sat on the surface of the earth because we sank through the air, while a cloud, or smoke, was buoyant and would float. Huldrych had always disagreed with my opinions on this, though we had good discussions, while Staehelin considered the idea useless. And I thought further, how the lesser could supersede the greater, how oil could make its way above water, and what strategies could be learned from Staehelin's lesson.

Then the lecture ended and all the black robes floated up and out of the lecture hall.

⁂

"That was Physics?" Daniel said beside me as we came out to the street. "That was? A mutter, a splot, a twitch. And that makes a lecture?"

"It was adequate," I said. "And more than."

"Not an equation in it! Not even a number. Nothing that Huldrych himself wouldn't have said."

"Daniel, you're like vitriol. You need more grace."

"Oh, it's all feathers. All floating and away with the breeze."

We walked a while without speaking, both of us in thought. Then I felt a breeze, a chill draught. We'd reached the Barefoot Square. It was midafternoon and the sun was still high, but there were shadows. The place seemed full of them like cobwebs clinging to the buildings.

In the Common Room, where shadows were spun, Daniel finished his hoisting of Staehelin. "Can you defend him, Leonhard? What can you say?"

"I said it was adequate."

"And that's all. And that's generous. You'll hear my lecture tomorrow and call it adequate?"

"Yours will be magnificent, Daniel. It will be worth the Chair."

"Oh, it will be."

"It will even be worth the Tsar's Chair."

"That. Yes." He took the letter from his pocket. "Would I take a Chair in Russia? If you didn't get Basel's, would you take the Tsar's?"

"I would. It would be history," I said. "The first man to hold the Mathematics Chair at the University of Saint Petersburg."

He nodded in sympathy with me. "It would be. And I'd take it. I'd even take it gladly. But it wouldn't be spite enough against Brutus, so I'll keep Basel instead."

"That's the only reason?"

"It's enough."

"Then give me Russia!" I joked.

He held the paper out for me to take, then grabbed it away. "No. I'll hold this. Maybe I'll win Basel, then throw it off for the Tsar. How's that? I might. Spite Brutus, spite them all."

"You sound as if you don't even want the Chair in Basel."

"I want to win it. But keep it? That's more a question, now."

"You'd be obliged, wouldn't you?"

He frowned at that. "Maybe. Maybe I would, maybe not. That's to think about."

"You're the same as you've always been," I said. "And you always will be."

"Constant in my inconstancy. Now, where's that keeper? I think I want my horse."

"I'll bring your horse." Daniel started at the deep voice, nearly at his elbow. He hadn't seen Gustavus in the shadows, but I'd seen him. Him, and more.

"He was nervy this morning. He nearly ran down poor Leonhard."

"He's been rested now," Gustavus said.

"I'll wait in the Square," Daniel said. He wanted out of the dark. But I stayed in the room. The fire was drowsy but watchful, and the hundreds of eyes looking out from the shelves all seemed satisfied.

"Do you see?" I asked.

Caiaphas came out of the shadows where he'd been with Gustavus.

"I heard you," he said.

"He won't stay. He's not here for the Chair or for Basel. He's only wanting to tweak his father. Once he has the Chair he'll leave it for something else. He's already resigned his Chair in Padua."

He studied me. "And you would stay?"

"This is my home. This is all I want."

"This city is Daniel's home, also."

"If he wins the Chair," I said, "I'll convince him to leave it. The father and son are already set against each other. I'd know how to drive them so hard apart to break the University in halves."

"You would ruin your own University?"

"You'll lose everything you have here. Give me the Chair."

I was searched. Like a wolf tears a fence to get the rabbits inside, I was torn and opened.

"Then I will give it to you," he said. "But be careful with your treachery." He still stared at me. "I think it more likely you'll be thrown to the river than hold a Chair."

⁂

I went out that night as I'd done four nights before. I waited in the alley behind Master Johann's kitchen. It was a longer wait but the time came, and the door opened, and Master Johann came out with his candle. This time he didn't leave it and return to the house. He descended into the cellar and closed its door behind him.

He was there for some ten minutes. I might have heard the box pulled out from the wall and the wall itself opened; or I might only have heard the noises of any night in Basel's streets. Through slits in the door, the light from the candle moved, then was still, then moved again, back and around, and was held up and lowered.

Then the door was opened and the candle extinguished. He came out through the yard to the gate, and passed through it, just feet from me. He might have felt someone was there; or he might have felt the presences of any night in Basel's streets.

Then he was silent and gone. His direction was toward the river, away from the Barefoot Square. I stayed.

The night was mainly timeless. Clocks sounded eleven but I had no measure of when he'd passed the gate. I'd left my house before ten.

But finally, in the quieter and quieter dark, I heard him returning, though only when he was already near. He opened and closed the gate, then his own door. Through the window I saw a candle lit in the kitchen and then taken on to the hall.

And then I went home.

A jitter vibrated the streets that Tuesday morning as I left my house toward Master Johann's. Something unsettled, something jubilant, something uncontrolled was walking with me. Something anticipatory. I reached the back fence and gate at the usual time and found the usual activity inside: Mistress Dorothea pouring words, and her maid barely keeping her head above the tide of them, and still adding her own to the flood. And if one or two of the streams might have been pots or chickens or sheets, the majority was people. Then, given that they only used pronouns, the sentences become like a stew: "They told her mother to wash it himself, but he had his hat on her head and they boiled it, and *she* wanted them both, but *she* didn't want either . . ." she was saying as I opened the door. I would rather have calculated a determinant of seven rows than calculate the meaning of those sentences! But when she saw me, she acknowledged me.

"You're diligent, Leonhard. Diligent for a young man who might be made a Chair on the morrow." It should have been a simple compliment or simpler statement. I couldn't tell if there was some other meaning, perhaps suspicion.

"Yes, Ma'am."

"Please do all you have time for. You've other duties today that are more important." And that was certainly the first she'd ever said such.

"I'll finish everything."

"Thank you."

Then later, when she was upstairs, Little Johann had more to say. "Daniel has the Russia letter, and you gave it to him."

"I did."

"He said the coach driver had found it?"

"The coach driver said that."

Little Johann doubted. "What did you do? How did you get it? Did you take it from Poppa's desk?"

"No. Rupert truly brought it to me and told me he'd found it."

"You must have done it somehow, Leonhard."

"I didn't." I hoped that was also true.

"And Mama's not pleased that he has it."

"Because he might leave?"

"I think so. I don't know."

"What about your father? Is he pleased?"

"Yes. I can tell. He even told Daniel, *That was well done*. Except it didn't seem he was talking about Daniel being invited to Russia."

"It was that I'd given him the letter," I said.

"What do you mean?"

"Nothing."

"What about the other letter, from Paris?"

"He'll have that soon, too."

"He'll be a Chair tomorrow. Or you will."

"Or Staehelin," I said.

"No. Poppa's decided."

"It's by chance. No one can decide or know."

"It was to be Daniel. It's the way they'd look at each other. Daniel smirking, and Poppa angry. But it's changed. Daniel can't tell, but I can. He was always angry that it would be Daniel."

"How could your father force the Provost's hand to pick a stone?"

"I think Poppa is stronger than chance."

"I think, this time, chance will be stronger."

"But Leonhard," he said. "We don't want it to be, if he's chosen you."

"But it can't be by his choice." I looked at him closely. "It has to be that God moves the Provost's hand."

I had never seen my grandmother as unsettled as that morning. It might have been the disorder in Basel's air; it might have been the anxiety she felt for me as I prepared for my lecture. My blacks and whites were clean and pressed and my wig smelled of new powder. I didn't touch my shoes and their buckles: I slid in my toes and heels, and my smudging fingers never came near the polished exterior.

In the kitchen she inspected me as always, but not at all as always. If I'd been in a burlap bag I don't think she would have noticed. She was unsettled.

"What will you say in your lecture?" she asked.

"Just what I've practiced. Physics is only understood by Mathematics. The first is nearly a branch of the second."

"Will they understand you? Will they disagree?"

"They will consider it respectfully," I said. "I'll be upright and serious, though they'll think I'm too young to be a Chair. And it won't matter because the choice is in the chance when the name's picked tomorrow. All I need for this lecture is to not be challenged and disqualified."

"Then God be with you, Leonhard."

"He is, Grandmother. With you, also."

"He is." Then she was at peace.

I'd been in the Lecture Hall so many times, but it seemed I never had; or that I had but only in imagination; or this was the imagination. All the professors and officials, the students, the gentlemen of the city, all were entering and being seated as if . . . as if a real lecture were being given.

The division between whether this room and time were imaginary, or real, ran deepest through my own thoughts. For all my doubts and feeling of pretense, I also knew that the time and purpose of the lecture were very real. In my hands were notes that described great truths. I would profess them with all assurance that my words were worth being heard.

I was standing in the front, in a corner, waiting. I stepped to the lectern. The iron casket was there, and below, on a shelf, the wooden tray of unused stones.

Every seat was taken. I tried to comprehend the faces. There were many I knew. Daniel, Nicolaus, Gottlieb, Little Johann, Great Johann of course. Desiderius, Vanitas, all the men I'd sat under in five years. The Provost, the Deans, the Mayor had all come, and Magistrate Faulkner. A hundred of my fellow students. There were so many I couldn't name them to myself as fast as I saw them.

I heard clocks strike the hour. I set my papers on the lectern.

Even a man was there that I was sure I knew, but whose face seemed shrouded. When I looked closer, I didn't see him.

Instead, I began.

"Gentleman, my subject today is the importance of Mathematics in the study of natural philosophy, that philosophy to which we have given the name of Physics. It is my belief that the Creation in which we abide has been established by its Creator, established with a regulation by Mathematical principles, and these principles unfold with delightful intricacy and profound elegance."

I'd opened my lecture with the strongest statement I could. I'd unfolded myself as a thorough Newtonian in a room sharply divided on his philosophy, but willing, even eager, to consider grounded arguments and valid assertions if they were presented clearly. As best I could, I did that.

I was not a man of gravity. I wasn't imposing, as Master Johann was. I wasn't formidable, nor solid. I didn't have years of wisdom written on me. I was only somewhat tall and gangling, with a voice pitched like an old cat, and eyes too large and close about my angular nose.

But what I spoke to those men was full, great truth.

ꕥ

At the end I stood down. I was congratulated and my hand shaken. I'd shown that I was able to hold the Chair. I'd shown to myself that I was able.

Then in the sunlight, I recovered to my own self, but only nearly. I was surely different, and more than just the three corners of a hat could make me. Greatly learned men had listened to me and sat under my instruction.

Daniel and Nicolaus were jovial beside me. I breathed in the plain air and was relieved to be plain again. I was exhilarated but exhausted and I had a great yearning to be on a hillside, wearing brown, and running.

ꕥ

Only a half hour was to pass before the next lecture, hardly time for the listeners to return home, but a long wait in the hall. Daniel soon abandoned me and went back in. I took the time to walk the streets close by. Although I'd been often on each of those roads, I noticed small things I hadn't before: gates and arches into yards and gardens. These houses, and even more their foundations, were very old, but there were still spaces between them, small pockets with rows of herbs and flowers and vines.

But then it was time to return. I was back just in time. I went up and shook Daniel's hand and gave him some encouragement, and by the time I was looking for a seat, there were none. So I stood in the back with those too late to get chairs, and those to lowly to keep theirs.

Far in front of me were the others of the family. Nicolaus and Gottlieb were together, and in the second row was Master Johann. Little Johann was close beside him. Daniel at the podium was confident and sure; the only betrayal of his anxiety was his occasional glances at the iron casket placid on the shelf beneath him.

All eyes were on him as he began as I had. "Gentlemen, my subject today is the Mathematics of Hydraulics." Which was the last word I heard as the door closed quietly behind me.

16

The Lost Hour

The streets weren't less filled than any other late morning. They were only empty of black robes and black gowns. For all the importance of what was happening inside the University, outside of it was still unaffected.

I returned home. My grandmother was at the market square. I knew she wouldn't be very long, so I was hasty in changing from my scholarly self to my humble. It was only minutes and I was back out in the dry sunlight.

Then I ran; I loved to run. I came to the familiar alley, and then into the more familiar yard.

Now came the first chance: I looked, and Mistress Dorothea was not in her kitchen.

I went in as quiet as still air and passed through as silent as sunlight. It was a large house and the high attics could be in a frenzy with hardly a notice down where I was, but I heard nothing and felt nothing.

As light as sunlit air I climbed the steps and came to the

hall where my Master's office was. I crossed the hall. Another chance was that the door might be locked, but I thought it wouldn't be. The command of its Master was stronger than any lock. No one, not even Daniel, would have dared to open that door. No one but me. I put my hand on the knob. Then, another chance, a very great chance: I opened the door, onto an empty room. Then I closed it behind me, and I was in my Master's office.

This was a place of wonders. The short moments I'd seen it before had impressed themselves on me completely. I knew the room as if I'd always been there, as if it were my own. If I sat in the chair, I would know where every paper was and every book. I did sit.

Immediately I felt, ten times as much, the thoughts and weight of being a Master and a Chair. I felt the center of Europe. Letters from every corner were here, from all the great minds: from Paris, from Lyon, from Potsdam and Berlin, from Padua and Bologna, from Master Leibniz himself—and even, even alone from the others, a letter from Newton.

And also alone, away from all the correspondence, just where I'd seen it before, was one letter to Daniel from Paris.

The room was just as my room would be if I were Master Johann. My own room was part study and part bedroom, and my collection of books was small in comparison, and my papers were trivial in number and content. But I knew the room, just how it was settled and ordered. Master Johann and I, we were very close, closer than he and his own children, close in our thoughts and visions.

I returned my stare to the books. They were all the ones I knew, of course. Then, in a closed cabinet that I opened, I found, to no real surprise, Newton, Daniel's *Exercitations*, and Jacob's *Ars Conjectandi*. And also MacLaurin, and Taylor, and all the other Mathematicians that Master Johann of Basel had publicly reviled and fought, and whose books would never be found in any corner of his house; except that now they had been. I closed the cabinet.

Then I looked at the papers on the desk. A new set of scrawled pages covered it, but few people would see that they were any different from the others I'd seen at my last visit there. I saw that they had to do with the integration of Logarithms. I would have studied them closely but I would never have stopped.

But I did see papers looking out from beneath those others, and I saw that they were calculations of Reciprocal Squares. I saw his considerations on my proof, and a specific error he'd made. I resisted the desire to correct it. Then I saw there was a correction, from the notes I'd written for Daniel and Nicolaus at the inn.

But all of this had been without touching anything but the cabinet door. Now it was time to break that rule, and I was reluctant. I sat waiting another moment.

Master Johann's black robe was hanging on the wall behind the door. I couldn't handle these things in my simple brown clothes. I looked at the robe and imagined wearing it. It was a simple black, not the scarlet trimmed most formal robe he wore to gatherings such as today's. This was the robe he would wear to reprimand an undergraduate or meet with a committee. I stood and put my hand on it. Then I removed it from its hook and held it, and then I slid my own arm into its arm, and then my other arm, and then I stood, enrobed, as if I was a true Chair. I felt the heavy hood hanging across my back. It was the first I'd ever worn such a robe. The folds didn't come to the floor as they should have, and I thought of having the tailor cut me a new, longer one.

What the tricorne had begun, I now felt was finished. I sat again in the chair, necessarily bold.

I took down the letter for Daniel. It was not so grand as from the Court of the Russian Tsar in Saint Petersburg, but it seemed more refined, simpler, and more beautiful. I set it back in its place.

Then I sat still. Time was crucial, but I waited, and thought what I would do in this room, with these books and papers. What would I do? Where would I set any particular thing? I would have this room, one like it. I waited, letting myself know what I would do here. Where I would keep any particular thing.

I leaned back down to the cabinet and opened it again. At its end, which needed the farthest reach, I felt beyond Newton and MacLaurin. There was another book behind them that I hadn't seen. I pulled it out. It had no marking on its cover so I turned to the title page and read, *Magia Naturalis et Innaturalis,* printed in Passau and dated over a hundred years ago. It was a Faustbook. It would have intrigued me that it would have a place in that room, but I knew immediately why it was there, and that I'd found the single place I'd wanted. I leaned even more and felt behind where it had been, and felt what I knew would be there. I closed my fingers on it.

In that moment, a voice from the Square screamed, "Thief! Thief! A thief in Master Johann's house!" I knew the voice, rasping and shrill, like crows and like wolves. Then another voice took the cry, a voice like smoldering fire and red, hot iron.

In immediate answer, I heard a clatter on the stairs, and a screeching I recognized that was Mistress Dorothea's servant girl. "Mistress!" she wailed, "there's a thief in the house! Oh, Mistress Dorothea!" And beyond all the cries and racket, I heard the Mistress's step on the floor above.

The robe had a hood. I pulled it over my head, pushed the Faustbook back into its place, closed the office door behind me, and ran.

❧

I shoved my way to the hall and flew down the stairs, but with care, so the girl wouldn't be hurt, and passed her before she knew. I landed in the hall. The girl was quick, too, snatching at the robe, and I had a hasty choice: through the passage, through the kitchen, and to the alley behind, or straight ahead to the front and the Munster Square. The alley would lead to winding paths and hidden places, but it was longer and the kitchen might have obstacles. Out the front I went. And there, in the broad Munster Square, was the Munster itself, and at the far end of the Square a troop of the Day Watch. There were already cries from a dozen voices now, of "Thief!" Everyone in the Square turned to me.

I loved to run.

The first cries from the Munster Square had raised a wild alarm, all confused and cross-countered like waves in a high storm. I flew from the door into the open and became a magnet, and every motion was suddenly centered toward me. It was only that I was quick that I was not taken in the first moment. I already knew the way to run, straight ahead to the Cathedral with my wake of flapping black robe. And just before I reached the Munster door I dodged right, into the cloister.

This quiet place was just then undisturbed and empty.

I thought that I hadn't been recognized and there was a chance that I could throw off the black robe and pretend to join the chase. Yet before I could, the Watch was after me. But I knew a way.

From the Cloister a path led, by a small alley behind the

church, to the Augustine Street, close by the River. If the Watch had been quick, they'd have blocked it, but I was quicker. Only by a few steps, though, and they were just behind me.

Everyone was behind me. Beside the Watch, there was now a mob of men and boys out for the adventure of the chase. So far I was ahead of their shouts and the road ahead was clear.

The Augustine Street narrowed to become the Rhine Leap, the road passing the University and coming to the Bridge. As it did, the Martin Street turned left from it, away from the River, up toward Saint Martin's Church. I took the turn.

I'd been on this street only an hour earlier, wandering between my lecture and Daniel's. I remembered fenced, hidden gardens.

The road turned again in just a few steps and I was out of sight of the pursuit. This was a very narrow street with tall, quiet houses and a few thin gates into private yards. I pushed a gate open and closed it, and I was hidden in a small, empty courtyard. Immediately the street outside was filled and noisy, but I had an instant to think.

There was a crack between planks in the fence. I looked out and saw a Watch with a sword and a pistol, and two tradesmen with clubs, pass the entrance. It seemed that now would be the time to throw off the robe and become myself. The gate would surely open very soon. I looked away from it to see where I might hide or escape through.

There facing me, five feet away or less, was a man. He was in black as I was, but his was terribly black: a cloak, boots, a mask.

I often see invisible things.

All of his body that was not covered was his two hands holding an axe, and his eyes. He lifted his axe and he stepped toward me.

He had been waiting there for me. He moved quickly, the blade raised higher.

Some hands had torn my hat from Little Johann; and some hands had guided my hat into the stones of the arch to weaken them; and some hands had flung my hat back at me from the ruin of Lithicus's death; some invisible hands whose malice was concentrated against me; and now I saw them.

Before I could move he let the axe fall.

The invisible was still real. More real than the visible.

The axe would have cloven me except an angel stayed his arm. The white and gold hand grasped the black wrist. I had seen that angel in the Barefoot Church, and I knew that hand as well. That hand had brought one paper, and the words on it, from years of dust to my dresser-top.

The black arm was very strong and broke the angel's grip that had only held for seconds. Yet that was enough. I threw myself out of the axe's arc.

The angel was tall as the assassin, which was very tall, and strong as, which was very, very strong.

I broke back out the gate into the street. And then I ran but I felt flame behind me, just as fast. And the street was empty. I didn't know what angel was still with me but I knew my nemesis was on my heels.

"He's here, thief!" I shouted. "He's here!"

And like a match struck and thrown into straw, the street filled as the men returned from where they'd run past me. They were quick behind me, but they were all. No one else was with them.

So the chase was on again and I ran.

I could only think of one direction to run, to leave Basel. And all the gates would be warned that the chase was on. Or only in Large Basel. The word may not have yet been sent to Small Basel. So I ran toward the bridge.

Around a corner, and the bridge was before me. The Bridge Gate guarded Large Basel against attacks from across the bridge, but also the bridge itself against escapees from Large Basel. I'd have to get through it. Strange as it was, though, no Watch stopped me as I sprinted through the gate. I was out on the bridge.

The wood planks bounced under my slamming feet. I dodged a cart and a few walkers. Shouts from behind me told the people on the bridge to hold me, but I was too fast. I saw the far end: and the Watch there had already seen me. They were pulling their barricade closed, and two came onto the bridge toward me.

Then I saw why I'd been let through the gate so easily. That barricade was also closing. I was trapped.

I'd reached the Yoke Chapel and stopped. I was caught between the two ends. Watch from both were approaching.

I stood and the moment stood, also, still. I was the center, the zero of numbers, and the bridge like stopped time on either side from beginning to end. But the Watch and the distance to them were finite and their advance like time compressed from future and past to now, like numbers descending toward their origin.

The Yoke Chapel was beside me. It was no refuge. It had never saved any of those who'd prayed their last prayers in it, and now I was in their place. The thought of the condemned somehow led me to follow them. The Watch were walking on, pikes held forward. I put my foot on the rail and they saw at once what I was going to do and broke the walk into a run. But I had time, if I would use it. I hoisted myself onto the narrow rail, holding to the chapel to steady my balance, but only for the instant. And now I was standing where the criminals had stood. I looked down and saw the Rhine. The flow of water pulled my thoughts down and in. All my years

I'd been beside it. But I'd never been in the river. There was nothing else left to do for the chase; it was finished.

Then I leapt.

My moments in the air were endless. My arms flailed. I thought of birds' wings and gravity. I accelerated down. Then there were noise and splash and wetness as I plunged beneath the surface. I had no idea what to do; I had never swum. My arms were still flapping and I had no idea which direction was up or down. I thought of density and buoyancy. I knew my density was less than that of water. But I was still under, and I also realized I should have taken a breath while I was still in the air. I could not now! But I didn't think to *not* breathe. A cold, choking fluid filled my mouth; it was water.

I spewed the water out of my mouth, and I realized my head was in air. Coughing and spluttering took my attention, and blinking, and shaking like a dog to get water out of my eyes, and when I had enough sense I looked at where I was. I was in the Rhine.

I found the bridge. It was already far off, and receding. I could see the guards on it, converging to the chapel. They were waving and pointing and shouting. I could still barely hear them. A musket was pointed. I couldn't tell if it was fired.

Then the men ran, to both ends of the bridge. I could see what they meant, to reach the banks and run the streets to the gates, but they'd have a long way of it. And the water was running swifter. I slowed my splashing and could hold my head out of the river with calmer motions. I worked my way more to the center. The water was chill. The robe was tangled around me. I fought it and pulled myself free. It floated beside me, then was pulled by the current away.

A landing at the end of the bridge was just then boatless. A boat was nearby in the water, and a Watch waved and shouted for it.

Only a small part of me was above the water, with which fortunately I could breathe. I stopped my limbs from moving and let myself hang in the water and be still. And just float.

For a while I did just float. I was facing forward. The Wall of Small Basel and the Blaise Gate passed me on the right, and Huldrych's house on my left, and the bridge was too far to see. Then the last Walls of Large Basel on my right were passing, and the Saint John Gate, and then were left behind. When a man left Basel and Basel Time, he was given back his hour that he'd lost at his entry. So I regained mine. I pushed myself toward the right bank. It wasn't difficult to move across, though it was slow.

I saw that the boat had been commandeered; the strong pull of two Watch on its oars was bringing it closer to me. Then it came even with me, but nearer the far bank, and then passed me, and I was never seen. I must have been a small thing, just my head, in the wide rippled river. Then I passed the boat, and the men on it were pulling the black robe from the water. They still never saw me. Then they were behind and I went on. All the city was behind me and gone. I felt beyond all the living.

It seemed strange to be standing on water, not walking but still making a good pace. I moved forward, or the bank moved backward. Which was really still and which in motion? The cold was numbing me but still I didn't feel like leaving it.

Perhaps two miles passed, and at least a half hour. I was becoming very cold, submerged as I was all but my head. I waited for a great fish to come swallow me. Three days in its belly would take me long past the final Election. I began to imagine the last bit of me sinking and all floating down into the deep water. It seemed for a moment a pleasant thought.

In all the dry, rainless world, only the Rhine still had abundance of water.

Then I began pulling my arms through the water, and pushing myself out of the flow. It was harder than I'd have thought and my arms were sluggish from cold. But the closer bank became closer and my feet touched mud and stones.

I wriggled onto and up the bank, to a warm, dry set of grass, and stopped. Now I felt how very cold I'd been and I was shivering in the peaceful sun; shivering from the cold, and in the pause from the chase. I thought a moment about how the chase had happened. But I was interrupted in that by falling asleep. It was a long sleep.

I was not alone when I woke. Two black shoes rested in the grass near me, and black parson's stockings from them, and all the rest of a man, all in black, a generous and gentle black. I only needed the shoes to know their Master, and mine. I said, "Father!" and he considered me. His eyes, which always saw so much, were now on me and I was all that was in them. He was sitting on the top lip of the bank, his arms crossed about his knees.

"What are you doing here, Leonhard?" he asked.

"I was in the river."

"Oh. You were in the river."

"Yes, Father."

"Why?"

"I jumped in."

"You jumped. From the bridge?"

"At the Yoke Chapel."

"You weren't thrown in?"

"I threw myself in."

"The river is cold," he said.

"I'm cold from it." I shivered.

"And why did you jump in the cold river?"

"The Watch was chasing me."

"The Watch chases lawbreakers and criminals. And criminals are given to the river at the Yoke Chapel."

"I did a crime, Father."

"A crime. What was the crime?"

"I was in Master Johann's house without his permission."

"Why?"

"To take this." It was still in my pocket from when I'd taken it from the cabinet. I handed it to him.

"A key."

"Yes, Father."

"Then you've done well, son." He handed the key back to me.

"Thank you."

"Use this properly."

"I will. Are you walking today, Father?"

"I'm walking back to Riehen, from Basel."

"You were in Basel?"

"I was there this morning."

"I gave my lecture this morning."

"I watched your lecture."

"I didn't see you."

"Some things even you can't see, Leonhard."

I smiled. "I did. Just at the beginning. I didn't recognize you."

"I'm always close," he said.

"In the chase," I said, "there was a man in a cloak and hood. He was my enemy."

"He was." My father's eyes hadn't left me in our whole time.

"How would he be defeated?"

"Not by strength. Be on your way now, the path back is long."

"Yes, Father, I'll be on my way."

"I'm always close." He watched me as I started back to Basel. When I turned, later, I couldn't tell if I still saw him or not.

It was long into the afternoon when I saw the city Wall over the riverside meadows. In my pocket was the extra hour any man receives when he leaves Basel, and it was now time to give it back.

With the river, the Blaise Gate faced north. I came to it just as the sun, red as dye, was coming to rest on the hills west. Its path across the planet's far side was certain, but mine was less so. I watched it descend into the earth, redder and bloodier, firing the sky, leaving void in its wake, and the east horizon was already black. The last hot spark extinguished and the sun was gone to me. I began my own descent.

I entered the Blaise Gate. The Day Watch and the Night Watch were changing, one into the other. I wasn't noticed; I didn't really know if, to them, I was a fugitive or only myself. But the two men at the gate, whom I knew though not by name, didn't even nod to me as I came in; and they were the only men I saw.

This was a first assurance that in all the chase I'd never been recognized.

The streets of Basel were always darker than their sky. I walked the main passage of Small Basel, the houses darker than the streets, and all empty. When I came to the bridge, finally there was another man besides myself, and then a second, both Watch. Beside the Night Watch just arrived, the Day Watch was still there and I heard him telling a story.

"And I saw him," the Day man said.

"What did you see?" the Night man asked. "They say he was a monster."

"Not him. He was only his shadow to be seen, and fast as wind."

"All the city's filled with stories." I still didn't see anyone, besides these two, and they hardly saw me. "And he vanished into the river?"

"I saw him leap. And then, nothing left of him."

"He drowned, then. I hear they found his robe. But why would he jump? That's better than the Watch taking him?"

"That's the real story," the Day man said. "It wasn't the Watch he was fleeing."

"Then who?"

"I saw a man in the shadow, by the Bridge Gate. A huge man, hooded, and with an axe."

"You saw that?"

"I did. He was after the thief. I wouldn't want an enemy as terrible as that after me."

"Then that's the one the storytellers were saying about," the Night man said. "They said a monster. But what monster is in Basel? There are none."

"Simeon saw him, too, and he doesn't imagine."

"And an axe? Who could it have been?"

"Not anyone of Basel. Nor the thief, and he's dead and drowned."

"Too bad for him."

Too bad for him! I left them talking and walked out on the bridge. At the Yoke Chapel I stopped. Too bad for him. He was dead and drowned. But not that only. He was also raised, the same though changed, *Resurgo Eadem Mutata*. So on and into the city I went.

⁂

In the rapid dusk, my shadow was only made by the light of thin cracks in the shutters of shuttered windows.

I climbed the hill from the bridge, not on the main street, but in lanes and alleys. I didn't expect to be noticed, or that anyone knew I was someone to notice; I just wanted to be in those narrower places. I passed the University and behind Saint Martin's Church, and then by ways where I could hold my arms and touch the houses and fences on either side. I touched the fence behind Master Johann's house, and the gate that I'd opened many, many times. I didn't open it. I went on.

Through the wide streets, all still empty; and then the Barefoot Church was high above me. It was all dark, and I couldn't remember when I'd ever seen it with no candles, no lamps, no lanterns, in any of its windows.

I waited.

Someone must have been in the church. Through one high window I saw a lantern descending, though I didn't know of any high stairs against the front. A small candle was lit in that window. Then the lantern came to another window, nearer the ground, and set another candle. Then I saw candles, one by one, come to all the windows, with pinpoint flames, but the flames grew. The walls themselves began to glow, as I've often seen them.

I went in the door and the whole lofty room was bright with dozens or hundreds of candles. The air was warm and scented. No one was in the whole room but me. I sat to wait.

And then I went back to the door. The Square outside was dim from the evening but men and women strolled in it, and walked through it, entering and leaving the Inn and the houses. A few of the day's booths were just finally being removed. A student I knew nodded to me as he passed. The clocks began chiming, eight o'clock as the coach from Freiburg rattled in from the bridge. I'd returned the hour given to me. I was finally wholly back from the river.

Standing in the door, I felt a tug on my sleeve and turned to see Little Johann, eyes intent on me. "Come here, Leonhard," and he pulled me back into the church. His brow was set and determined. I wouldn't have dared contradict him.

The candles were gone but for the few that were always there.

We took a seat in a corner. "Listen close to me," he said.

"What do you mean?" I asked.

"I'll tell you Daniel's lecture."

"His lecture?"

"I'll tell you the whole thing, and if anyone asks where you were, you can tell them what Daniel said."

"But—"

But not. He was like a horse tensed to run, and he started at a spurred gallop. All that I could do was listen. And as I did, my own runaway thoughts came to a canter, and a walk, and a halt. And how could I think on anything else? Little Johann's account fascinated me too greatly, for Daniel had lectured on the problem of Hydraulics.

As I listened I began to realize that Daniel must be the greatest authority in Europe on the subject. I hadn't realized what thought and genius he'd brought to this study of water and its strange ways. The greatest part of the lecture, both in importance and in portion, was his reduction of flows and pressures to simple Mathematics. It was as elegant as it was convincing.

As I listened, my own experience of the day merged with what I heard. I knew the force of water, its buoyancy that had held my head in the air and its flow that had carried me a mile and more. Daniel showed how gravity had become the river's strong current, and how it could push me like a hand against my back, yet could also flow around a tree anchored in its bank. Somehow I'd felt an invisible grip that had carried me straight and true to my specific moment of appointment. Here was another invisible hand.

And as I was watching and feeling these invisible forces, I was hearing Daniel's words in Little Johann's voice. He wasn't merely repeating from memory. At times he used words and descriptions that weren't usual in Daniel's speech, but that Little Johann used commonly. It was plain that the boy in front of me understood completely the Mathematics and Physics his older brother had lectured on. I didn't know whether it was Daniel or Master Johann who'd been tutoring him, but he was speaking as their equal.

It wasn't his goal, though, to show off his intellect. It didn't seem that he knew he was. He only had one intent, to quickly and fully as possible give me the whole gist of Daniel's lecture so I could recount it as proof that I'd heard it with my own ears, if that was ever necessary. He was being my protector, which also meant that he knew, or guessed, why I hadn't attended the lecture myself.

"Did he say that?" I asked. Little Johann had just finished an explanation of the law that governed the force that a fluid exerts on a wall while passing parallel to it.

"No. But he should have," Little Johann said.

Daniel would have spoken for an hour, and Little Johann's summary took only fifteen minutes. When it ended I'd lost my own thoughts completely. "You've got that all, now, haven't you?" he asked.

"Yes. It was well done, Johann. Very, very well done."

"Oh." And then I saw, of course, that he was showing off some, and I was even more touched that my admiration was worthwhile to him. But he still had another purpose and wasn't distracted from it. "And Daniel will get the last letter, won't he?"

"Yes. It's certain now. Within a day."

"That's good." He was relieved, but still cautious. He wouldn't be free of this concern until both letters were in Daniel's hand. And meanwhile, I didn't know that I'd need the details of Daniel's lecture. But I had them, from Little Johann's mouth, and I'd never forget. "And I told Poppa that you explained the lecture to me."

"But you explained it to me! Do you mean, to make him believe that I was there?"

"He'll think that. He won't have noticed that you weren't. Nor Daniel. Nicolaus might have."

"Thank you," I said. "If anyone asks what Daniel said, I'll know all of it."

I walked home. It was well dark. In the short distance from the Square to my grandmother's house, I found myself glancing to my right, to my left, over my shoulder. The shadows seemed full of quiet murmurs, the rustle of swords, furtive footsteps. I reached the front door in a sweat.

Grandmother was waiting in the sitting room, in her black dress and white apron, patient and still.

I sat next to her and she stayed quiet. "I'm home from this long day," I said.

"Not home for the first time today."

"No."

"Are you afraid?" she asked.

"I am afraid," I said.

"In this Parish of Saint Leonhard," she said, of the church that her husband and her daughter's husband, my father, had been pastor, and in which she, who was blameless and righteous, could say it, "you'll be held safe."

"Thank you," I said.

So I went up to my room. I quickly was in my night clothes, and in my bed and I hesitated to extinguish my candle, which was the last light between me and the darkness. But it was only the last light that I could see, not the true last. So I put it out.

Through the night, as I slept, I faintly heard and saw battle outside my window, but none of it came in.

17

The Iron Casket

On the day that I knew would bring great changes, the rise and fall of many, I rose so early that even my grandmother wasn't out of her room yet. It may have been that I hadn't even ended the evening and night before, but was just continuing them. I dressed quickly, in brown for the last time.

I went out into the early morning night, through the short alleys, to Master Johann's back gate and opened it. Only one obstacle, the locked cellar door, was between me and my first object. But I knew that door very well: I'd repaired it a half dozen times. I quickly had its hinges off.

Then, in the cellar, I pulled the potato bin away from the wall, and the stone out from the wall. Behind it was a wooden box a foot long and six inches square at its ends. It was very heavy for its size. I took it, closed the space and repaired the door, and left.

There should have been a beginning of light by then, but Basel was dark. The shadows of houses and churches covered the streets like the Flood, and the air was so dry! There was dust in it. I paced the cobblestones to the white University. It glowed like lightning behind clouds. The door opened to my touch, and no one was there. I hadn't seen anyone in any street.

The lecture hall was empty, not just of men but of time, of everything that made a place that place. But it had one black, iron casket on the lectern in its center. I went to it and set my wooden box, which was the same size, beside it. I put my hand on the cold black iron and felt the lid and sides, the corners, the keyhole. At that I drew back my hand to my pocket, and felt another iron, but this was warm from the heat of my own blood. I took that key and held it steady to the hole it was meant for, and inserted it, and turned it, and heard and felt, more than anything else I had that dark morning, the tumblers rise and fall, and the clasp give way. My hand left the key, still turned, in the lock, and lifted the casket lid. Inside were three stones.

I opened the wooden box. It seemed at first to hold a single carved square stone. But I ran my fingers over that, and the single stone was in truth many smaller stones all perfectly fit together. I set some of them out onto the lectern to see what they all were.

In all, there were thirty-six pieces. Thirty were half cubes, fifteen in the bottom of the box, carved with symbols, and fifteen set blank on top of those. The other six were sealed cubes. The symbols were three each of raindrop, tree, sun, fish, and lamb. Three of the sealed cubes were at the left of the box, replacing the candles, and three were at the right, replacing the thrones. Those three I took and put back into the casket. The three I'd taken from the casket I put into the box.

The transaction was made. I closed the iron lid and turned the key back.

It had been easy in opening but was reluctant now, and required effort. I mastered it and withdrew the key. Then I set it in the wooden box and closed its lid, and turned to leave. Light escaped in around the edges of the closed door. When I opened it the street was in brilliant morning, though for a moment I was still in the shadow. When I was finally seen, by Simeon of the Day Watch, I was enough away that no proximity could be guessed. He greeted me, and I answered. He didn't remark on the wooden box under my arm.

It was only a few steps from the University to the bridge. I walked out to the middle, to the Yoke Chapel. I could still see, in the dust on the railing, the mark of my hands and shoe.

The bridge was high above the water. I leaned out to see it below. And I hardly heard the splash as the wooden box broke the surface of the Rhine and sank below it.

Then everyone I saw walking home gave me the cheery good morning a Chair would expect in Basel.

But I was no Chair. Instead my first task was water, as always, and I went to a fountain in a street away from the Barefoot Square. When I came home my grandmother was in the kitchen, but I only set the buckets on the back step and went on. She heard me. I heard her open the door and take them in.

The door I did open was to my Master's kitchen. Mistress Dorothea, like my grandmother, was well started on her kitchen chores. But she acknowledged that a day of changes would begin with changes. "I thought you might or might not come," she said, and I told her that I would have said so if I would not have. I worked hard and very quick, as fast as I could, and also in this Mistress Dorothea accepted me. She and her servant girl talked all the time about the thief of the day before but I closed my ears to it.

I carried and stoked and burnished, and I finished nearly in half the time. She didn't load me with extra work.

"Good morning and good day," I said, and the Mistress stopped her own scrubbing.

"Good to you, as well," she said. "Leonhard."

"Yes?"

"I don't know what will pass today."

"It will be in God's hand and in his will."

"That is where it should be," she answered. "May it be."

⁂

The sky was thorough blue without spot or blemish, and the sun already high and lifted up. It was hot, too. Heat like a close fire made the stones warm. The sun and heat and drought of this last week were reaching a pinnacle.

I reached my own kitchen.

"Leonhard!" Grandmother was very intent on me. "What have you been doing?"

"What I've needed to be," I answered. "I've done everything."

"What have you needed to be?" Her look wasn't distress, or disquiet, or belief, or assurance. It was just intent.

"I've needed to be obedient."

"You've always been. Your clothes are clean and ready."

"I'll be done quick." I left for my room and my blacks and whites. They were set out for me on the bed, washed, ironed, and perfect. The brass would have reflected starlight. I pulled them all on with the most deliberate hurry, or the most hurried deliberation. But then I paused. My wood block head, always patient, was waiting, perched on my dresser, for my attention. I gave it that. Without eyes or ears or mouth, it was watching and listening and ready to speak. I waited. I knew it must be important.

The wooden block did nothing. That was its counsel and it was very wise. Now it was my time to just wait and allow. I studied the conch and its Logarithmic spiral and the meaning of it. I traced the curve of the brachistochrone bowl and the tautochrone bowl. I left my room and my house.

❧

The black and white gathered in the University Assembly Hall was blinding in my eyes, that while the two colors were stark and more dominating than ever, they seemed more to blur and blend and make gray. I'd never seen them do that before. When I let my attention sit on this gray cloud, my own thoughts were the same gray, and indistinct.

But as had been earlier, one point was focused sharp, the casket. I saw it easily.

The three candidates were given special seating at the front of the hall. I sat in the middle, with Daniel on my right, and Staehelin on my left. In the row to our sides, and in the row behind us, were the committees who had chosen us. At the front wall the deans and provost sat facing us. I set my attention on Daniel.

He was like the Birsig. His intentions and plans were sometimes babbling and clear, sometimes deep and obscure. I couldn't fathom anything from his face, which was, for the first time I ever thought so, very much like his father's. And beside him was his father, and his face showed more care and even fear than also I'd ever seen. It seemed very little like Master Johann.

Many others were in the room: of course Nicolaus, and Gottlieb, and Little Johann. Magistrate Faulkner was at the end of the front row. Next to him, but not easily seen, was a magistrate of a different city.

The Provost spoke and I listened, but heard very little. Daniel beside me was a taut coil.

The key was suspended on its chain which still circled the Provost's neck. The whole weight of the room seemed to be in it. The Provost finished his words and there was light applause, and I had no memory of what he'd said, any single word even. I clapped. I was only watching the key; its moment had finally come. I thought of the life a Chair would have: it could be everything noble.

The Provost took the key in his hand, and leaned forward, and put it into the lock. I could feel with my fingers' memory the twist and pull. He removed the key.

Then the Dean of Arts, standing beside him, placed a kerchief of black silk over the Provost's eyes and tied it behind his head. The Provost spoke to the Dean, and both laughed, and many in the room smiled. I felt them. I was now only watching the black iron casket.

The Dean opened the casket, and held it out to us to see the three stones inside. Then he offered it to the Provost, and guided that man's right hand to the open top. The Provost felt inside.

This was the moment that Master Jacob had written about, whose result the *Ars Conjectandi* said could only be described as three equal chances. But the results weren't equal. With one result I would be Chair, and with two others I would not. The Chance of the Election was meant to put the result in God's hand. This was the moment that His hand would move the Provost's hand.

It was over before I could comprehend it. The Provost had a stone, one of three. Now there was no chance. There was just one result, and it was only left to make the choice known.

With the stone tight in his right hand, the Provost waited

as the blindfold was removed. Then, seeing, he grasped the stone also with his left hand and with a twist broke the seal. He looked at it, frowned, puzzled, showed it to the Dean, who pursed his lips, perplexed, then turned to us with a gentle smile. "It is the tree. Master Staehelin. You are now our Chair of Physics."

I had an impression at that moment that a man was behind me, who I would have recognized, and who loved me, but as I turned, he was gone.

❧

There were many other impressions I had. The sound was first, of clapping and a hard burst of many people talking. Then motion. People standing and moving, some a stream forward and some back toward the doors. The room seemed to deflate of a sudden. Then, close by, Master Johann's face, his stare fixed on the stone broken open, and thoughtful.

Then I perceived Staehelin beside me, and Daniel beside him, and both were astounded.

Staehelin was simply immobile. His mouth was gaping open, his eyes the same. But Daniel was the full comprehension of astonishment, disappointment, and fury. He stood and moved toward his father, but then away, and into the black and white throng.

I shook Staehelin's hand, most to shake him from his catatonia. I nodded to the Provost and the other men at the front, and they nodded sympathetically back to me. Then Master Johann turned to me and studied me.

But I couldn't bring myself to speak. I nodded to him as I had to the others, and I turned, and returned to the plain crowd.

❧

The Election was done. Finally I could grieve alone.

I left the University for the dry streets. Basel's wide, busiest roads were paved with black, gray, and white stones, but all the rest, the alleys and byways, were brown soil, and it was all hard and dry. Every motion, every footstep, raised dust. The city was full of dust. I walked slowly and found that I came to Master Huldrych's house and the Death Dance. I met another wanderer there.

"Master Desiderius," I said.

"Leonhard." He was anxious, or bewildered.

"So, Staehelin wins the Chair."

He shook his head. "It is a mystery to me. Of the three, how was it that he was chosen?"

"Just by the chance of the stones," I said.

"No. Of all the answers, I know that is not the answer."

"But I know it is, surely."

"Then you know more than me."

I shrugged. "But what will it mean?" I said. "I don't know that."

"And I don't. It will not be well, though. I'm very sure Staehelin was not meant to win the Chair, and there will be consequences."

"For whom?"

"For Master Johann."

"What would threaten Master Johann? All Basel is with him."

"If a tree is rooted deep in a field, then to uproot the tree, the whole field must be torn out. Oh, Leonhard, I fear for your Master, I fear for the University, and for Basel. And I fear for myself and for you. Basel has been its own and separate, but the world outside its Walls isn't dormant. And cities have been brought to ruin from within."

We were only feet from the Death Dance. "It's been four weeks since Master Huldrych died of plague," I said.

"That's only dormant, too, Leonhard."

"Staehelin won by chance, as the Election was meant to be."

"I believe you, that he did."

"But chance . . . I don't know what that is. I've read Master Jacob's book, and I know what the Mathematics of chance is. But I know there are laws that are even greater than Mathematics."

"I've never known how it was done, but other elections have been ruled by someone stronger than chance."

"This Election was, also."

"I mean," he said, "by man's hand."

"I know. And this Election was in God's hand."

"He took it?"

"I put it there."

"That's a bold statement, Leonhard. And it might be arrogant. How could you give this Election to God?"

"Because it had been given to me. That was why I could give it to Him."

He frowned, and slowly understood. "It was yours?"

"Yes."

"And you gave it up."

"Yes."

He was troubled by that. "I was given an Election five years ago, and I kept it for myself."

"I think you were meant to have it."

"That's kind. I'll think on it." He smiled a moment. "But Magistrate Caiaphas considers all the elections to be his own, not to be given without his permission."

"There are laws that are greater than him," I said.

I crossed the city to the southwest, to the Barefoot Square, but through it without stopping or looking, through the old Wall and then by the Birsig Flow where it flowed in its canal between houses and under bridges, to the Stone Gate. I climbed the steps there up the Wall and took a place looking out, over the Birsig and the fields, the trees and hills in the distance. Very far I could see mountains still cutting the sky. The sky was enormous, limitless and immeasurable, featureless but for the sun. Then I waited.

The sun was to my right, but looking out I still had to shield my eyes with the brim of my hand. Nothing freckled that sky, as nothing had in the week since the candidates had been announced. I waited. Minutes passed, and more. An hour passed and the sun far past its height; three o'clock outside and four o'clock inside the Wall I waited more.

Watching the sky, I began to see horses crossing it, passing the sun and pulling it. I saw ships sailing in the high winds. I saw strongholds high in the blueness, which were castles and towers with pennants. I saw armies marching. They had cavalry in ranks, and phalanxes of soldiers. And as I held my arm out at length, and my fist clenched, I saw one small cloud.

I ran, as fast as I could then, down into the city toward the Barefoot Square and the Boot and Thorn.

18

The Value Pi, Squared, and Divided by Six

I reached the Square. The sky above was still empty but I felt a wisp of breeze.

The Common Room of the Boot and Thorn was thronged thick and boisterous. I stood in its entrance. The tree trunk pillars and branching beams were a forest, but red not green. The only faces I could see were the hundreds of steins on the walls glaring in firelight. All the men were too shrouded in smoke and dim to be seen. There was a wind blowing in the forest, of contention, argument, dispute, and anger.

Only part of the wind was from the men at the tables quarrelling over the Election. Daniel had partisans in every layer of the city, and his second rejection in two years had stirred a frenzy of resentment in the Boot and Thorn. Charon brushed against my ankles to warn me against entry, but I entered.

I pushed through to the hearth. The brightest light was

there and to the side of the fireplace was the darkest shadow. Daniel was at the edge between them, and at the center of fury. His brothers and cousin were with him.

I listened to him rail, yet I could tell he was on the tail of it. The hours I'd been on the Wall had worn him down. He'd blasted the foolishness of Election by chance, and reviled the committee that had put up such a poor candidate as Staehelin. His listeners had thinned; bitterness was unpleasant on the ears as it was on the tongue. He'd tiraded against the University in whole as unworthy of him anyway, and that drove more of his supporters away. And he'd delved even darker in his accusations of corruption and foul play. And now, after that, he was alone. But not completely: Nicolaus, and Gottlieb, and Little Johann remained. In the end, it was their ties to him that didn't break.

"Oh, finally, it's you," he said to me. "And how do you grieve? How do you plot revenge?"

"I don't do that," I said.

"We'll do it together. You're as cheated as I am! Oh, oh, oh, there's payment due now. What's the exaction, Leonhard?"

"We're not cheated."

"You're cheated that you've lost to Staehelin, and I'm cheated that I lost to you. No, double cheated, that I lost to both."

"Then Daniel," I said, "I'll say it. Yes. I cut you out of the Chair."

"But who changed the stones?" Nicolaus said before Daniel could answer.

"I changed them," I said. "It's no great trick."

"It was," Gottlieb said. "I never knew how it was done. But how'd Staehelin's stone get picked?"

"By chance. True chance."

"Then you put the first stones back?"

"That was my object," I said.

"That's lunatic!" Daniel said, his canvas filled again. "You swayed Caiaphas, and once you did, then you changed the stones yourself anyway? Then why even breathe with Caiaphas? For the pleasure of betraying me?"

"There's no pleasure in any of it. I did as I needed. Daniel, you're free."

"Free? What freedom do I want? The Chair."

"You came to my house and asked how a word given could be taken back."

"Then that's the word I want taken back. Is that why you've done this?"

I shook my head. "The Election is done and the man meant for the Chair has it."

"Then blast the Chair, and the University, and all Basel. And blast you most of them."

And that hurt me most of them, and I knew it had to be.

"What will become of Basel?" Nicolaus asked Gottlieb.

"You'd know, Cousin," Daniel answered, but only as an attack on him. "Didn't you warn us all at the Inquiry? Tell us."

"Do you know?" I asked Daniel. "Or you?" I asked Nicolaus.

"I thought he meant the plague," Little Johann answered, the first he'd said.

"There might be plague, now," Gottlieb said. "Now that Leonhard has thrown every other plan askew." Then, to Daniel, "For the Chair. What you were to do for return?"

"You know. France. Lunatic France! What would France do with Basel? There'd be no difference here. One flag for another, and petty price for the Chair. Gottlieb's already paid for his Chair."

"I've paid nothing!"

"Your stone was chosen. You have your Chair. You agreed. You'd agreed to France."

Gottlieb answered with as much anger, "I agreed to nothing! I made no bargain."

"You did, though," Nicolaus said. "Twenty years ago, in Strasbourg."

"I asked. But I was refused. I never asked again, and I shouldn't have then."

"You weren't refused, only delayed."

"I made no bargain," Gottlieb said.

"He said you did," Daniel answered.

"He lied."

"You're so sure? Why did you ask him, then? You pressed him at the Inquiry. Old Knipper was no matter to you. Your Inquiry was to Caiaphas, and whether he'd given you your Chair. Because he did."

"I made no bargain."

"Caiaphas wants you to think there was," I said. "But there wasn't. There isn't. None of it is any matter now, anyway. All of it is over."

"Oh, no, Leonhard," Nicolaus said. "You've torn your bargain, but that's nothing to the others."

"But it is," I said.

Little Johann spoke again. "That was the danger? France?"

I answered. "The city was to fall to France. And the University was to lead. But that's ended now, though not done."

"It will fall to the plague, now," Nicolaus said.

"That, not either," I said.

"What do you know, Leonhard?" he asked.

"I know there are laws that govern this creation."

"Oh, lunacy!" Daniel said. "You're Caligula? Nero? Evil and lunatic both."

"You were lunatic to want the Chair," Nicolaus said to him, "and lunatic to treat with Caiaphas." He said it with greater heat than I'd ever heard him use, and he stood over his brother in real anger. "You should thank Leonhard and beg forgiveness that you're free of it all."

Daniel's answer was a deep breath and long silence. Finally he said, "I'm done for this place. I'll go home."

"What place?" Nicolaus said. "And what's home?"

"Basel," Daniel answered. "And Russia."

❧

We all left the Inn and never had seen Gustavus. The Square was dark. It was later afternoon and should have been still light. Above, though, the sky that had been empty so long was piled with clouds. Beneath those mountains the Barefoot Church was luminous white.

❧

It was a short, silent, and sharp-edged walk to Master Johann's house.

I bowed in with them through the front door, and we were awaited. Mistress Dorothea was in the front hall. She stood silent as we five came into the severe dim and stopped. Then she only said, "He's waiting." And she nodded to the closed door of the parlor.

I bowed and stepped back, to leave, but she halted me. "Leonhard. You also."

That was all that was said. Nicolaus opened the door, and his mother a force behind us, we entered.

Master Johann was seated, of course, and we all sat. I would not have, but his look told me I was to. Mistress Dorothea stood sentry at the door. Then we waited.

Master Johann only frowned. He was seated with his legs somewhat apart, as he always sat, and with his hands resting on his breeches. He wore his daily black and white and the same wig he wore on Saturdays. In that room, where the small part of outside light that ever penetrated was a fraction of very little outside light at all, he was bright in comparison to all of us. And when we'd seen that he was the center, and that we were all in his thrall to wait as long as he chose, he did speak.

"I wish to congratulate you, Daniel," he said.

"Me?" Daniel replied. "On what? Receiving the Physics Chair? Do you know, sir, that I did not? But you would have known. Long before I would."

"Perhaps, instead," Gottlieb said, "the congratulation is for something you deserved."

Daniel would have answered, or anyone might have, but the pause to compose a reply was long enough that the silence settled again and then couldn't be broken. Master Johann waited until the words had faded, and their echoes had, and then longer until any impression that was not of himself had faded.

"You have won the prize of the Paris Competition."

No one could answer, for as he spoke, he lifted his hand to his waistcoat and transfixed their attention, and from his inner pocket he withdrew the Paris letter. He stood and crossed the room halfway toward Daniel and stopped.

It was not too large a room, but the letter was beyond Daniels' reach. He stood and crossed his half, the bridges of Great Basel and Small Basel meeting in the Rhine's center, and took the letter from his father. And as he did, Master Johann said, "Well done."

"Thank you."

These statements both were formal, partly hostile, partly wary. But I saw that Daniel was thrown back by surprise and elation, and as his father had known he would be. And as he was off balance and off guard, Master Johann said, "It will serve you well in Saint Petersburg."

Daniel from his greater height answered, "I know it will. I have already sent my acceptance, yesterday."

"Then would you have taken the Chair here if you'd won it?" Gottlieb asked.

"He wanted it in order to resign it," Nicolaus answered.

"Then that's what he's angry at? All his rants at the Inn?"

"When will you leave?" This was Mistress Dorothea, and all her sons and nephew respected her with silence, and Daniel with a respectful answer.

"In two weeks, Mother."

"I'll be glad for two weeks, then," she said.

"And I'll leave with him," Nicolaus said.

"You'll what?" Daniel was surprised at this.

"I'll see Russia. Send them a letter, brother, that you'll arrive doubled."

"I will! You'll come? To stay?"

"To stay as long I will."

"I'll be glad for two weeks with you both," Mistress Dorothea said. "And for you to have chosen a wise path."

"You'll both be gone, then," Gottlieb said, thoughtfully. "So that's done."

"You'll both be gone," Little Johann said.

"Come after us," Daniel said to him. "In a few years we'll be ready for you."

"I will be pleased," the final voice said, which was Master Johann, "that you both have a position in Saint Petersburg. And now I wish to speak with Mistress Dorothea, so please leave us."

We all stood and moved to the door. I let the others ahead, and as I was about to follow them, Master Johann said, "Stay, Leonhard."

The door closed, and just the parents and I were in the room. The Mistress sat, beside her husband. "Leonhard," she said.

"Yes, ma'am."

"We wish to discuss what you've done." She was as stern as her husband.

"I'm not very sure what I've done."

"Magistrate Caiaphas," Master Johann said, "has worked toward a purpose for many years and this is a setback to him."

"I know that," I said.

"I've worked with him."

"Yes, sir," I said, with a swallow. "I've known that, also."

"Then, was it your object to thwart his purpose? Our purpose?"

"Yes. It was, sir."

His only reaction was a slight tightening of his mouth, and an even slighter rise of his brow.

I waited as he stared at me, or through me to somewhere else. Then Mistress Dorothea said, "We considered that you might choose to do that."

"I felt it was my only choice."

"Describe your actions of the last two days," Master Johann said.

Now, the examination began. I knew the answers to the questions he'd ask, but I doubted they would be accepted.

I frankly told them of entering their house and taking the key, and of then taking the stones from their cellar, and of choosing three stones to replace in the casket. I was brief. The chase through the city and river seemed irrelevant and I didn't mention it, nor Little Johann's help. But I did finish by telling of my last act on the bridge, and that the stones and key were lost to the Rhine.

He accepted that. "Did you examine the stones before you chose the three?" he asked.

"No, sir. I feared that if I did, it would be too difficult for me to not change the chances in my favor. And I was reluctant to break the seals. So I only chose those three, which I hoped were the original three. And they were the originals, or at least the same combination."

"Tell us," Mistress Dorothea said, "about giving Daniel the letter from Russia."

I told them. I described handing it him, but also the conversation we then had, with Caiaphas as witness, and the result of that.

"And tell us," Master Johann said, "of your other conversations with Magistrate Caiaphas."

So I did that, as well. I gave the summary of my Saturday night meeting, and also the hints from my other conversations that he had an interest in me.

"Now, tell us what you know of Magistrate Caiaphas's designs."

"I believe that he was trying to accomplish the annexation by France of Basel."

"Yes, that has been his plan. He is a Magistrate of France and is among those who have that assignment. Do you believe that you've halted him?"

"No, sir. But . . . that wasn't my objective."

"You said before that it was."

I paused and took a breath to order my thoughts. "It was my objective to thwart Magistrate Caiaphas. And though I would dread annexation of Basel by an outside power, that was not why. I had a profound reason for my opposition to him."

Master Johann frowned, and I saw that for the first time in our conversation he'd received a truly unexpected answer. "What reason?"

I knew the next few words I would speak would the hardest of all I ever had with him. I hesitated and drew all my strength together.

"Master Johann," I said. "And Mistress Dorothea. Magistrate Caiaphas's purpose was for France, but his method was to have control of the University, and his tool was to use divisions and jealousies to force ambitious men to seek his own help to achieve their positions."

"Speak more plainly," Mistress Dorothea said.

"Master Daniel turned to Magistrate Caiaphas for the Chair when he knew he could not ask your help." I said this to Master Johann. "The Magistrate has worked to increase the hostility in your family so that he could exploit it. That seemed to me the greater danger. That was why I was opposed to him, more than any other reason."

Master Johann only frowned, and Mistress Dorothea said nothing. I waited for them and couldn't imagine what either would say. So, perhaps, there was nothing to say.

Then he said, "I understand what you mean, Leonhard, and it will be seen what comes of it. But Caiaphas will still accomplish his purpose. And if he is thwarted in using the University, he will use other means to weaken the city. You may have released a calamity on Basel."

"I hope I have not," I said.

"Leonhard," Mistress Dorothea said, "what part of this was Knipper?"

"He was charged by Master Jacob to take the trunk of papers to Master Huldrych for safekeeping. When Master Johann hired him to take the trunk from this house to the coach to be sent to Magistrate Caiaphas, Knipper recognized it. I went to the Inn to fetch Willi to help him, but I told Gustavus, also. And Gustavus came here to your kitchen. I don't know what was said. I think Knipper tried to stay true to Master Jacob's charge to return the trunk to Huldrych, and Gustavus killed him for it. I knew and believed that it was no person in your family, Mistress, who did that crime. Only Gustavus knew he was here."

"I wanted the trunk away from Basel," Master Johann said. "I sent it to Magistrate Caiaphas because he would not have understood the papers' meanings."

"What part was Huldrych?" Mistress Dorothea asked.

"He'd been keeper of the papers. But I think he was killed only because his open Chair was necessary for Caiaphas. I don't know how. I know that plague rags have an enduring potency and Gustavus kept them. I don't know why the plague didn't spread from Master Huldrych, but that he was very old and couldn't withstand the illness and the others close to him could."

"And what part was Lithicus?"

"He had made the counterfeit stones. Gustavus weakened the arch to kill Lithicus when he seemed close to confessing. But Lithicus made the stones at Master Johann's command, and for his payment and he was afraid for twenty years since, of what would come of it."

"Yes." Master Johann spoke. "I had him make the stones." He, and Mistress Dorothea, had listened to my statements with quiet reserve, though I couldn't guess what grief they each felt. And there may have been much more that I didn't know, but what I did know was laid out plain between us and was hard and stark and scorched. I stood and walked close to him, and knelt, even as I had with Huldrych in his last moment.

"Master Johann," I said. "All of this is ending now."

"It is not ending." His grief was deep, but had not overcome him. "What you have done is no end."

"Master, I believe that there are laws of Mathematics that prescribe the actions of the planets and the river and every object. And I believe there are greater laws that govern the Creation in deeper ways."

"And what do you believe these laws will prescribe?"

"That sacrifice will be stronger than Magistrate Caiaphas. Thank you for nominating me as a candidate, sir. I believe it was necessary to accomplish this solution."

Mistress Dorothea said, "Then, that is why you were nominated, Leonhard."

Master Johann said, "But this is not what I had expected. I am not sure your solution is valid."

"I'll test the proof of it now."

൭൬൭

Through the streets, now dim beneath huge clouds and setting sun, I returned to the Stone Gate, from where I'd watched the afternoon. I did think, as I walked, what it would have been to walk as a Chair and a man of position. But I found it was difficult to intrigue my imagination with thoughts of prestige. I was at peace. I climbed the stairs onto the Wall and looked to the west. And there, the storm was approaching.

Basel was still calm, but beyond, the valley was gone behind a gray sheet of rain. The disquiet Birsig, usually so placid, churned and the sky piled cloud on cloud, all writhing with wind and water but still held away, for a little while, by Basel's Walls. The city was dry and the air mostly still, and all heavy. Only the Birsig pierced the boundary and I stood by the Stone Gate and watched it break into the moat, and fall into its cave beneath the Wall. The water rose, objecting to its path; I watched it rise fast. All the storm beyond the city was pouring into it. The stream reached the top of the tunnel and exceeded it. I retreated from the pool that began to grow; I turned away, came down from the Wall, and ran again, as fast as I could, as I possibly could, like the wind, to the Barefoot Square.

The windows of the Boot and Thorn were their most fiery red against the shadows of the Sqaure. The Barefoot Church was luminous white, receiving the light that reached all Basel just to itself. I stood in the Square between them, where somewhere beneath the Birsig flowed. I felt the paving stones groan beneath me.

What was to come next, I feared. But it was necessary. Whatever the sacrifice was to be, it must be complete. I wanted to be obedient to the laws that were ruling the night, though they were mostly invisible to me.

I went into the inn. Charon, ten feet long, and my own height as he reclined, bared his merciless teeth and swept the hall with his tail. Gustavus was beside him waiting for me.

⁂

We followed the same path, inward and down, though it was longer this time, by innumerable closed doors, past niches filled with dust and jars, beneath an ever lowering ceiling, between narrowing walls hung with ancient pictures so smoke-blackened that all their first meanings were irrecoverable, and their present meanings were drawn by the smoke itself. Every length was singly lantern lit, and each turning was dark with just a glimmer of the next flame beyond. We went always down, sometimes by one step, sometimes by two or three, gradually but only descending.

We came finally to the same rough door. He pushed it open and followed me in. There'd been a lantern before but that now was a half dozen bare flame torches bracketed on the stone wall that still gave no light at all. Everything was black except those flames. I could hear and feel the rushing water in the cave near, but I couldn't see it. I felt for the barrel I'd sat on before. It had a different feel and I stayed standing. The roof touched my hat.

The light expanded, on its own, and by it I saw Magistrate Caiaphas. He was seated. First I saw his face. Then I saw his whole form just in outline, as if it had its own source of light behind. Gustavus glowed red like ember.

"Then what shall I do now?" Caiaphas said, speaking to himself. We seemed to have interrupted his musing. But, I was the object of this thoughts. "What shall I do with you?"

"Leave Basel," I said.

"Not that. Not yet." His voice was cutting as a saw but quiet. "But you will."

"This city will never be part of France. There is nothing for you to do here."

"You say that?" His anger broke, like water that had been rising and building behind a dam. "What are you to say anything?"

"You've lost the Chair."

"One Chair is nothing! I own enough Chairs in Basel. And what I don't own I will wipe away. I have rags enough from plague deathbeds for that. But what shall I do now with you?"

"You can't do anything. I don't you owe you for anything. I don't have the Physics Chair."

"That was your own madness." In the dark, I could still see him perfectly by his voice. "You have accomplished nothing, and yet you will pay heavily."

"You won't be allowed," I said.

"France will take Basel. I will twist this University between my fingers, and I will put an end to you."

"You won't be allowed. Not any of those."

"Not allowed?" He screeched it, between hatred and fury and laughter. "Nothing disallows me."

"There are laws," I said. "Laws stronger than we can oppose."

"I am every law here. Whose laws are stronger?"

I told him. "You meant to gain to Basel for France, which is your right to attempt. But you've sown division and hatred within the families here. You've torn down men who were intended to be noble. And you've murdered."

"And I will more," he answered. "Much more."

"That, you will not be allowed. That was not your right. There are laws stronger than you can oppose."

"There are no laws!"

"There are only laws," I said.

"What do your laws command now? When Gustavus strangles you, what will they command?"

"I don't know," I said. "I only know they will be obeyed. God will be obeyed." I sighed, "That is why I'm here."

Gustavus put out his hand toward me. Then I saw, what I'd known to be, that behind him and about him was an even stronger and greater giant, in black but plain and visible.

"Even you," I said to him, "are under God's law."

He, as Gustavus, loomed above me and the torches dimmed to sparks.

"Those who are with me," I said, "are more than those who are with you."

He set his hand on my shoulder.

At that, the Birsig Flow burst.

The water filled the room in an instant.

I was thrown against a wall. There was no time to think, no time to respond, no time to even try to move my arms or legs. Barrels and everything else heavy were lifted and caught in the sudden havoc.

But I was pushed out of the room, and for me that turmoil was over.

I was on the floor of the hall. Yet water was pouring up from the door, flooding the hallway. I staggered up in it and looked for an escape.

The passage was different than it had been before. It was well-lit and short with a flight of steps at its end close by. It must have been that I was seeing the visible inn. Floating beside me was my tricorne! I grabbed it and slogged through the water, now at my knees, and up the steps.

At the top, I saw the front door and the Common Room thirty feet away. I stopped. The water was still rising below me. I ran to the door, and outside.

19

The Deluge

I stepped into pouring rain. My tricorne spewed like a house gutter. My soaked shoes and stockings were soaked now more. It was a long way across the Square and took me a long time to cross.

The downpour in the Barefoot Square seemed so heavy! The church floated in the falling sheets, and Noah steered it. Jonah hung to the upper window, to throw himself out. Peter stood ready at the corner to walk out on the waves. Still the waters came, and the Spirit moved on the face of them, to divide them. But as I came closer to the church's warmth and glow, I felt the rain less.

I reached its porch. I looked in the door and saw the quiet, unmovable place, with its column-mounted candles making more light than candles could anywhere else. The stone floor was dry and cool and smooth, and the air was warm. I felt the soak lifting off of me. I stood for minutes, then turned to watch the river falling from the sky.

Back from where I'd come, I saw the embrous windows of the Boot and Thorn, flame within flood, fire in the waters, all the rain flying futile off the steep roofs. I had the feeling of standing on a river bank watching unmoored boats moving. The whole roof of the inn seemed to be pitching like a ship. I and the church were Daniel's hourglass in a heaving world.

Through the pounding rain and wind I heard something else, too, the roaring of moving water. I knelt down at the edge of the dry church floor and put my ear to the stones. I heard it more: a river flowing beneath, somewhere. I even recognized the specific stream sound: it was the Birsig Flow, in its hidden channel beneath the city. I stood and looked out again.

What I'd seen before of the inn's roof might have been my own sight of invisible motion, but now it wasn't invisible. The center of the roof, four stories above the Square, had moved. It had settled lower and inward.

But the fires inside were furious. The Common Room windows were red and bright as a setting sun. Through the rain, through the whole width of the Barefoot Square, I could feel them. The hearth must have been like a smelter.

Then the roof settled in again, and I could hear it. I was in wonder at it. At first I thought the fires had finally broken loose from their stone places and were consuming the pillars, but the place was in essence earth; it couldn't have burned. And I still felt the rumbling beneath.

All the servants of the place, the cooks and maids and laborers, and the patrons of the Common Room, all emptied the building into the Square, scattering to cover under eaves of houses, and off to their own houses.

The front of the inn split. Its plaster suddenly had a hundred cracks, and it was the wall cracking behind. Smoke poured out of the windows, denser and blacker. Then it was smoke and steam.

The Birsig, flooding from its tunnel, had filled the cellars of the Boot and Thorn and now was consuming the foundations.

The flames returned the attack, violently. Great pools of water were boiled out the windows. The fire had grown enormously and struck at the incoming flood. And it was of no use. The disquiet, unleashed Birsig was a fountain in the Common Room. All the floors above were being pulled down into it.

A mad rush issued from the tunnel as the panicked horses, and a panicked Willi and Fritz, escaped the stables. They fled out to the Square, and then into the streets. Fritz ran on but Willi reached the middle of the Square and turned in the rain to watch, as I was. There seemed to be no one else.

The windows went dark, one by one, each with a violent billow of steam. Then with a shaking I think the whole city must have felt, the fire of the Boot and Thorn was submerged, and quenched. All of the Birsig was flowing into the Common Room, opening a void to take the inn. The roof sank lower; the walls collapsed inward and the swelling water spewed from every open part.

Then it was gone, swallowed and extinguished, and there was only a wide, deep hole of water.

The rain decreased. There was a beginning of light in the west.

I was still in the door of the Barefoot Church, and there was a feeling, like a motion, though I couldn't see movement. But the feeling was as if a weight had been cut from a spring, a heavy weight, and a very strong, slow spring; a slow up-and-down oscillation, like a wave. All of Basel was part of it. And the church rode peacefully on the motion.

The streets were rivers, all flowing into the Rhine, cleansing the city of its dry dust. The sky to the west had opened of clouds. I walked home through the lessening rain. Light shown from my grandmother's front window.

She was in the front parlor with the curtains open. I sat beside her. She took my hand and held it, which she had never done.

"Daniel is going to Russia," I said. "Nicolaus with him."

I saw what she was watching, a rainbow.

"When will you go, Leonhard?"

"Next year." The sunlight diffracted through the rain was bright as jewels. "I believe I'm finished with Basel."

"What you did was very dangerous."

"When I read Master Jacob's papers," I said, "I knew what had to be done. On his last day he repented of his disputes and his break with his brother. His last wisdom was that malice and dispute and betrayal were the greatest danger to a family, and by that to everything else. And he proposed a solution."

"A Mathematic solution?"

"It is. A law of creation. That evil is defeated through sacrifice."

"And all of this," she said, of the storm, and of all the past, "was the defeat."

"It was slow, and terrible, and grievous," I said. "But the end is sure. It's the greatest law of any."

Paul Robertson is the acclaimed author of five novels including *Dark in the City of Light* and *The Heir*. He lives with his family in Blacksburg, Virginia.